A THOUSAND ORANGE TREES

Kathryn Harrison is a graduate of Stanford University and of the Iowa Writers' Workshop. Her first novel, *Thicker than Water* was a New York Times Notable Book, as was her second, *Exposure*. She lives in New York City with her husband, the writer Colin Harrison, and their children.

A THOUSAND
ORANGE TREES

Kathryn Harrison

Fourth Estate • *London*

This paperback edition first published 1996
First published in Great Britain in 1995 by
Fourth Estate Limited
6 Salem Road
London
W2 4BU

A catalogue record for this book is available from the
British Library

ISBN 1–85702–407–9

3 5 7 9 8 6 4 2

Printed in Great Britain by
Clays Ltd, St Ives plc

In memory of my grandmother,
who told me tales

I die because I do not die.
—SAINT JOHN OF THE CROSS

A THOUSAND
ORANGE TREES

N A YEAR OF AMPLE RAIN, ONE HECTARE, carefully tended, would sustain enough mulberry trees to feed about one hundred and forty-four thousand silkworms. The trees' first buds appeared just after Palm Sunday. They unfurled by Whitsun and were in full summer leaf by the time we celebrated the feast of Our Lady. In autumn we pruned the bare branches and with the wood we collected we made more bonfires for Saint John the Baptizer than any other family in Quintanapalla.

Our lives followed those of our trees and our worms. Each year we carried almost seven thousand pounds of leaves to the silk house. Leaves bundled in baskets and bags and yoked to tired shoulders or pushed in the old barrow. Leaves wrapped in a linen and balanced on an upright head, or dragged in a sack along the dry ground so that they got dusty and had to be washed.

I was a child of five years, smaller than other girls my age, small enough that I could walk under my grandfather's table without ducking my head, but I was not so small that I could not carry my share of the mulberry leaves; and, like my father and mother, my grandfather and my sister, I carried leaves from our trees to our worms, bearing them on my head in a basket that was broad and flat like my mother's, except that it was half the size.

The silkworms ate without cease. Day into night into day, we forced them to feed; they paused only to split their skins. After the fourth and final molt, each worm as long and as thick as my grandfather's thumb, they were ready to spin. One hundred and forty-four thousand worms of good quality, vigorous and industrious, could spin almost ninety pounds of silk cocoons, that total including the weight of the worms inside, which we killed by steaming the trays of sleeping cocoons over stones heated by fire and doused with water, smothering the worms in rising clouds of hot vapor. We had to kill them. If we did not, they would turn into silk moths; they would escape by chewing through the silk they had spun.

Each year, just before All Souls' Day, we took our ninety pounds, more or less, of raw silk cocoons from our one hectare to market. There we sold them; and from the market they were carried with the harvests of other silk farmers on a great tumbrel pulled by oxen to the cisterns in Soria, where they were soaked and soaked and soaked again, and then unraveled. The unraveling required the labor of comb girls, who clawed the silk apart with the nails of their middle fingers notched in one, two, three places—notched to the detriment of their lovers' backs, or the flesh of anyone else they might care to touch, themselves included.

After the labor of the worms was thus undone, the silk was ready to be twisted into thread at the throwing mills, also in the city of Soria. In the mill yards the crated unraveled silk was unloaded by the men who worked there, the shining work of our worms thus passing from the hands of maidens to those of swains: from one to the other, like a secret, like a greeting, like a whispered promise of more and better gifts to come. Or so I liked to dream as I fed the worms, for, though I had never seen a twisting mill myself, I knew that its clacking, groaning machines were tended by young men who labored long days for little money, not even a hundred maravedis, a scant handful of coins—barely enough to buy them their suppers and an occasional trinket for a sweetheart, my papa said.

Twisted into hanks of fine, strong thread, the silk was crated again and carried from the mill to the wash works nearby, where it was tied in bags and boiled in soapy water, then rinsed and dried and bleached in fumes of burning sulfur.

From the wash works, the silk was crated one last time and then carried to the dye artists in Epila, whose hands were permanently stained black from endless immersion in pigments; their ears and noses, too, if they were like me and in the habit of absentmindedly scratching an itch. The dye artists made our silk purple, perhaps, or red or green, dropping each white hank into a cauldron of color. I could picture the nearly naked vat boys as they slowly stirred the strands with a pole, sweat running down their thin chests and into their loincloths. For in the dye works with its boiling cauldrons they could wear nothing more, and naked they carried the dripping hanks out to the factory yard's great racks and hung them there to dry.

Woven, then, by the weavers in that same city: each lustrous colored thread held tight by a loom's jumping heddle until it was battened fast to another, made to lie forever between its neighbors—one slender stroke of color after another, placed so as to create a pattern, a shining, dreamlike scene of ever-leaping deer and wheeling birds, of imagined animals following one another, caught in the fabric for all eternity. Or an endless, meditative weave of repeating geometric symmetries: squares inside squares, stripes and circles and crescents, trapezoids and triangles and pyramids of silk.

A year of ample rain. In truth, I cannot remember a year of ample rain, other than the one in which it all arrived between one Sabbath and the next and coursed down the mountain and through our house. But by the end of a tolerably wet season, our worms produced silk sufficient for about forty pairs of hose—a modest accomplishment given the work it took, the efforts of our whole family, though one that grew in my imagination, and in my dreams. Grew until it was enough silk to clothe the grandest assembly the land had ever seen.

Enough silk for a state wedding, or funeral. Hundreds of dresses, thousands of doublets. Collars and cloaks and cuffs and ruffs of silk.

Enough silk for tapestries to drape every inch of cold stone wall in the king's palace in Madrid. Enough to carpet each stone stair and to lay a shining path for the king to tread to his queen's bedchamber.

Enough for his forces, too, his armies and his navies. Enough to rig an entire armada—sails, shrouds, and yards of silk: red and green, white, blue, gold, all shimmering on the surface of the ocean, like light broken by the water into every conceivable color.

Enough for a thousand silk dancing slippers.

Picture it like this. Picture it as I have countless times: unfurled, one endless, slender, shining strand. Once I took a cocoon and soaked it and unraveled it myself, and though I broke the silk repeatedly, still the one cocoon, undone, unspun, took me around and around and around our house more times than I could count. Mama went in and out of the door; her skirts tore through the strand I'd stretched across the threshold. When I went to catch it from the breeze it eluded my fingers. But away from the perils of clumsy hands and busy skirts, in the care of comb girls and mill boys, our silk would not break.

Even without the magnification of my desire, our worms—our ninety pounds of cocoons—would yield about fourteen thousand leagues of spun silk. I asked Papa to do the arithmetic for me, and as he figured, squinting, I squinted, too, and saw a filament so fine that in the wrong light it might be invisible, and yet so magically strong that it could withstand the wind of any maritime storm.

Enough to take me back and forth to the New World seven times.

If I were to follow the route of Cortés, embarking from La Coruña, as he did one hundred and seventy-one years ago, in 1518—that is to say, if I were to sail more or less straight into the sunset, west, that same compass point which the poets employ to evoke death, Helios' burning chariot sinking into the waves with a hiss of steam—the length of raw silk required for the manufacture of, say, a dozen dancing slippers would take me far past the Azores and past the dreadful glass-flat calm of the Sargasso Sea, past Hispaniola and Cuba and over the Nares Deep (into which ships sank as far down, they say, as Mount Ararat was high) and on past the tip of that distant land of flowers, La Florida, where Ponce de Léon died seeking a cure for death.

Another few slippers' worth and I would be across the warm gulf and into the Bay of Campeche, docking in the port of that city named for the true cross of Christ, Vera Cruz, the city that is the entry to the new, unspoiled world: the land of another chance, the land of hope. And what better name for hope than

that of the cross? For isn't hope what flowed from Christ's side?
From his heart and hands and feet? Isn't it hope that makes one
don slippers and dance? Either that or despair. Yes, despair does
quite as well for dancing.

As if those silk-slippered feet, like some mischievous crusade
transported into the air, would trip and skip and pirouette
across oceans and past islands. Gliding and dancing over waves
and past storms and on to the gold and silver of New Spain.

Seven times across the oceans.

Seven. A magic number. And an odd one, which would not
bring me home but leave me on the green shore of a land of
savages who wore no clothes at all, silk or otherwise.

I was a dreamer. Of course I was. Spending so much time in the
company of silkworms, watching the worms, I learned to be a
worm. From leaves the worms spun silk, and I apprenticed myself to them. I found a way to transform the life I was given into
another life, one that was fantastic, unexpected.

It was a family failing, imagination. Each night after dinner
we sat before the fire, Papa in his chair, Mama and Dolores and
I on our bench, and the mathematics of greed and desire, of our
rich future, kept us awake until we stumbled at our chores the
next morning. It was a family failing, but I was the worst afflicted. Even after I finally lay down to sleep in the bed I shared
with my sister, I dreamed of silk. Of all the silk in the kingdom
of Spain. To me it seemed as if this bounty were truly ours, as if
it were we who wore such dresses and cloaks as those perhaps
spun from the work of our worms. And if my poor linen shift
did not keep out the cold, my dreams of silk were very warm,
almost as warm as the cloth itself would be, and all people know
that there is nothing both so warm and so light as silk. Or
dreams.

I dreamed that when Papa and Mama became sufficiently rich
they would hire enough workers to relieve them of their chores,
and then Mama could sit in a chair with a footrest and wear a
beautiful dress of purple silk damask. We could wear silk then,
when we were rich. Mama could be a lady of leisure, a señora
who lived with her family and her servants in a big house and

had nothing to do all day but sit by the fire and change her clothes and think of what it would be that she would have to eat that night; and whatever it was would taste very good when the rest of the people were mostly hungry. But Mama would not be idle, no, she would use her time wisely and learn to read, holding a book in hands now soft and always clean. She owned several books already, little devotional texts that Papa had brought home from market, all of whose letters and words were nothing more to us then than pattern on paper, inscrutable and frustrating. I opened the books and I stared at the pages too hard, trying to make sense of the words inside, and the little marks wriggled and twisted before my straining eyes like the worms on their feeding trays. But not forever would they so defeat me, for when we were rich and Mama had learned to read, she would teach the words to me. Spanish, and Latin, too.

When we were rich, Papa would sleep. I knew sleep was a pleasure he had not gotten nearly enough of so far in his life; and so for my father I imagined a remarkable and astounding bed: a bed like a boat with high sides, a bed like a horse with tall legs, a bed like a fortress that no one could storm. Under his covers (made of silk, of course) he would sleep for as long as he pleased, which would probably be months or even years, and then, when he was truly rested, he could decide what to do with his money. When I told him about the dream bed I had built for him, Papa would shut his tired eyes and tip his face up toward the ceiling, toward heaven, and laugh at the luxury of endless and uninterrupted sleep in a man-sized cocoon of silk. Of course, even as a child I knew that this was unlikely. My father could not rest, not when there was money to be made; he would never consider himself prosperous enough to sit still.

I told my big sister, Dolores, that with the huge dowry she would have when our fortunes were made, she could marry Luis Robredo. She was not even sufficiently old that she had received her first communion, but already her thoughts had turned to weddings and matchmaking and I picked out this husband for her, a man of some twenty years and the son of a local estate owner. Her usually pinched face grew almost pretty when I spoke of her dowry and dress. "You'll be wed on Ascension Day," I said, and she nodded eagerly, no doubt picturing herself rising into heaven just like Christ himself. My dreams made her that buoyant. She would be rich enough that the sacrament of marriage would be performed by the archbishop of Burgos, I told her, and not by a backward Pyrenees priest who wore crude leather sandals through the winter snows. No, the archbishop's feet, which touched only the floors of cathedrals and palaces, would be shod in our silk, and Dolores and Luis would live in a house such as only grandees have, and it would be not in Quintanapalla but in some place where it never snowed, far to the south, in Andalusia perhaps, or in Valencia where orange blossoms drop from the cliffs into the Mediterranean Sea.

"What about you, Francisca?" she would ask, her hands clasped together earnestly. "Where will you live when you are a lady?"

"I will stay at home with Mama," I said. For even then I knew that I had what I wanted. Though I dreamed endlessly of what might be—though I conspired with our worms and their creation and made up all manner of fantastic fates for the silk we raised—I never wanted to move from my place at my mama's hearth, where I had her skirts near enough to touch and where I breathed her very smell from the air around me.

"But there must be something you want, Francisca. Something your papa can buy for you," my father would say, pulling my braid to get my attention. I said that I wanted a lamp like the one that hung over the church's altar, a lamp of silver with red glass around a flame that never burned low. I would give it to Mama to read by, I told him. I pictured how its light would touch the pages of her book, touch her hands and face as well, making everything as red as flowers.

Nights, awake in my bed as my sister slept beside me, I went over and over my father's calculations. "Fourteen thousand leagues," I whispered again and again to myself like a spell, until, tired and dizzy, I was left clinging to the end of a strand of silk, poised between the fishes in the sea and the wild men on the coast of New Spain.

. . .

Once, when a messenger of souls passed through our town, one of those old men who charge a maravedi for a minute of their time—they pocket your money and close their eyes and tell you that they see your departed—one of the messengers took my chin in his hand.

"This one," he said to my mother, "this one will stray." He looked in his sack. "Take this," he said. He pressed a charm into her hand. "And see that you drive some nails into her bed." For it was believed by some that iron would keep witches away.

He shook his head. "Tell me, child, do you know your Paternoster yet?" he asked, and with his hand still on my chin he turned my head this way and that, looking carefully.

"I do," I answered, insulted. "And the Ave and Credo and the Commandments as well."

"You say them, then, and do as your mama tells you." With that he moved on to our neighbor waiting her turn after us, the hand that had held my chin collecting another coin.

He was right, of course, I did go far afield. But that was after my mama was gone, after my father's greed had conspired with fate to take our worms, then our mother, and then all the rest. Not that I had no part in the ruin of my family. For dreamers are reckless people, after all; and when I found I had fallen from the safety of my place by my mother's side, I set about looking for solace elsewhere, without any thought of sin, or of danger.

The journey I made, however, was not the kind of which a child might dream, not one of vast geographies, not one requiring ships or dancing slippers. I went only as far as Madrid, a mere two days' travel from Burgos, whose cathedral I could see from the house where I was born. We had three windows in our house, two of greased parchment, which, in the warm months when the shutters were unnailed, admitted light but no view, and one window of glass. Bubbled and so wavy that to look through it was like gazing through heat rising from a flame, the glass pane showed us a distant southern vista where the river Arlanzon cut through Burgos and around the great cathedral there, its distant spire like a thick finger pointing up to God.

Either that or a monument to passions more base than those that might project a body heavenward.

Two days' ride south from that spire would bring a traveler to Madrid. Madrid, whose palace rises square and white at the end of the grand Calle de Arenal, and whose prisons, underground and vast, extend beneath that same palace's foundations. Above Madrid's streets, the palace took my mother's life. Below them, the prison of the Inquisition is taking mine.

My father believed he had everything figured out. He reworked the arithmetic each night, not to be sure it was correct, for he had an exceptional talent with sums and could do almost any mathematical contortion in his head, but for the pleasure such calculations gave him. "Francisca," he would say, "give me some numbers." I would make up some puzzle like this: "If we planted thirty-eight more mulberry trees, and each produced seventeen bushels of leaves in a year, and silk cocoons were selling for twenty-nine maravedis per pound, then how much more rich would the addition of thirty-eight trees make us?"

Papa looked into the fire as he figured, his eyes narrowed, his cheek twitched. "Eleven ducados!" he would answer with barely a pause. "New shoes for all my girls! And perfume! Colored candles! Shawls! I'll take you all to market, and you shall have what you like!"

When checked, his calculations were always correct; any written mathematics were simply for the delight he took in making numbers on the flat hearthstones, of using a charcoal and then wiping his makeshift slate clean again with his forearm. He could not read but he did know his numbers, and he looked almost frantic as he figured, his mouth moving along with his hand and sweat running from the hair at his temples.

Once a week perhaps, Papa would walk up the hill and past the mulberry grove to the silk house, where his father lived with the worms. My grandfather was a cantankerous old man who ate his meat and bread with us but said nonetheless that he preferred the noise of his worms chewing to the clamor of our family at table. He swallowed his food as fast as did the worms and then he took up his staff and made his way out the door and up the hill, back to his spot in the silk house, which was kept evenly warm by a small fireplace in each of its four corners. By one of the hearths Grandfather had his own chair with a high back and a footstool. There he smoked his pipe and snapped the occasional order at Dolores and me when we fed the worms. He used a sweet, heavy tobacco, the smoke of which sat upon his head like a fantastic hat, and after a bowl or two he would doze. It was peaceful in the silk house, and were you to close your eyes to their ugly jaws, the sound of so many worms chewing gave the impression of rain falling steadily onto the roof.

Each week Papa would undertake to persuade my grandfather to move ahead with the times, to try new ways to make us rich, to plant new trees or feed the worms differently. To add madder and indigo and cochineal to their diet, so that they might produce colored silk, which would require no dyeing and would fetch, my father was sure, a high price at market. To feed the worms on leaves soaked in wine, which was said to result in cocoons that were larger and more loosely spun, and in that way the silk filaments could be more readily unraveled and reeled. To forsake killing the worms by the old steam method and instead bake the cocoons in a clay oven. To fertilize the mulberry with oil cake, as they did in China, and to prune them more severely each autumn. To paint the trees' bark with warm tar and to spray their first buds with the milk of a newly kidded goat. He had no end of ideas, my father.

Every year at market time, Papa attended a scientific gathering in Epila. He belonged to a society dedicated to the advancement of agricultural arts—a "convocation of cuckoos!" proclaimed Grandfather—cuckoos who "filled his head with all manner of rubbish." But my father wanted to try every innovation and improvement of nature of which he heard tell. He argued ceaselessly on the behalf of progress, but my grandfather said it all came down to avarice, he accused Papa of not being interested in knowledge, he accused him of being motivated solely by a love of money. Grandfather said the people who held such meetings as my father attended were greedy, too. "But at least they are smarter than you, Félix!" he went on. "For they have figured out a way to make a living from fools. Fools like you who pay money to trade in worthless talk!"

"Señor," Papa would say, for he addressed his father thus, "why be averse to a small speculation? We could invest, say, a mere five ducados and make a return of ten times that in as many years. We could—"

"Nah!" would spit out my grandfather, and he would remove his hand from his better ear, which he cupped in compensation for its deafness, catching the words from the air and directing them down its bristly, winding canal. That is, he would cup his ear when he wanted to hear what was said, but not even for the sake of conjecture would he entertain such thoughts as newfangled fertilizers or improved trees or wine soaks or whatever it was my father suggested. He listened only so long before he turned his face to the wall, his head like a bishop's under its miter of smoke. Then my father would curse and set off back down the hill, casting dark looks at the old trees, which, though they had clothed and fed him for all the years of his life, he had begun to disdain as inferior.

Silk growing is not as easily accomplished in Spain as in the Orient—or even, it is said, in New Spain's province of Tehuantepec—but for generations now the silk produced at home has been favored by our countrymen, for it bears no stain or scent of infidels, no contamination of some Buddha or Vishnu or Allah or whatever gods there are to whom savages bow their heads. People who bought imported silk cloth complained that it smelled of the Orient—a smell, they said, almost as bad as that of Jews. So there was always a market for Spanish silks, which made it nearly sane to cultivate mulberry trees in a climate as harsh as that of Castile, where we lived and where the snows from the Pyrenees blow sideways in the winds and the mountains are more rock than soil. Everyone knows that no matter where it is accomplished, silk growing is an art for the stubborn, the patient, the foolish.

A new strain of mulberry was the innovation that eventually took hold of my father's imaginings; it occupied more and more and more of his thoughts. Available each spring at the market in Epila were crossbred trees from a farm even farther north than

Quintanapalla, where they had been tested by that part of Castile's terrible climate; and each year that he did not buy them my father was sure would be the last of their availability, that he had missed forever his opportunity to make us rich. He argued with his father tirelessly in the new trees' behalf, and for years my grandfather resisted his son's attempts to persuade him to replace half—or a quarter, or just one row—of our trees with the new strain. Papa promised this new strain was in every way identical with the old: the leaves were the same shape, and like ours they were bright green and shiny on one side, lightly furred on the other. The sap, only the sap, was different. While ours was white like milk, the new strain's was a slightly different color, a sort of gold like honey, and it was thicker, sticky. The trees, called *Mirabile,* were resistant to drought and untroubled by pests such as red beetles and the bindle worms that sometimes ate a year's profits along with the bark of the trees; and to produce more leaves with less care and water would indeed have been a miracle in Castile, which has a drought every decade at least, the rains coming only after we choked on the dry dirt that the winds had blown out of the empty fields.

"Nah!" my grandfather yelled on one occasion. "You are lazy, Félix. Nothing comes from nothing. No shortcuts in the making of silk. No easy way. No geese with gold eggs." He went on, speaking in such illustrative abbreviations, many of which I later learned were taken from the tales of a wise man named Aesop, and how my grandfather knew of them I cannot guess. A great noise of thunder interrupted their argument, and Grandfather jumped up and grabbed a pair of tongs. He took a coal from the nearest hearth and, moving with unsuspected agility, ran through the silk house, waving the live coal between the stacked feeding trays filled with worms.

"A storm like this is the Devil's work!" he said to my father, shaking the smoking coal under his nose. Papa merely folded his arms and snorted. But, Devil's work or not, thunder will stop the worms from feeding; and it was said that a burning coal waved in the air would calm them.

"You should use vinegar to settle them," my father said. "Sprinkle the floor with vinegar."

"Bah!" said Grandfather, *bah* being his one variant of *nah*.

"The coal does no good. It is only superstition," said Papa.

"And what is vinegar, Félix? When I'm dead, you sprinkle your vinegar!"

I crept from my hiding place by the door and watched my father stalk down the hill. Rain was falling heavily, but nothing in his walk suggested he was aware of it. He did not hurry, nor did he seek the shelter of any tree. And later that evening, when Dolores tattled that I had been eavesdropping, he hardly took notice of her.

Their next confrontation would come at the worms' spinning time, when every year my grandfather insisted that only the fumes of fried garlic would stop the worms from eating and cause them to begin to spin. Just as a good smell like that of lavender, and all the other herbs we used to keep the silk house smelling fresh, encouraged the worms' appetite, so would a greasy, acrid smell put them off their food.

On the appointed day Grandfather would insist that my father fry garlic over each of the silk house's fires. But Papa wanted to do it scientifically, with quicklime and magnets. Or what about cold air currents to make the worms feel like spinning a warm mantle about themselves? At every possible opportunity my father and grandfather fought.

My grandfather did not own so much land, for we were the poorest branch of the Luarca family and the northern branch. Some of our blood did live in those Andalusian castles of which we only dreamed, but, as Grandfather said, what land he had he did own. We were not tenants like most, and by Castilian measure our land had good soil. Our grove was just big enough that standing at the top of our hill on a bright, windy day, we could watch the shadows of clouds pass over our trees, shading one and then another row of them. The rocks had been cleared away for many years, and the mulberry grove was terraced on a slope that did not descend so precipitously that water, carried up in buckets on yokes, ran down to the bottom before it could soak into the ground. My grandfather raised the silkworms as he had for as many years as he had lived, and he saw no reason to change anything. What he said was true: the family was living well enough in a time when many went hungry; and he cautioned my father that as God was so good to us, it was a sin to want more than we had.

Nothing good comes from greed, he insisted, and he would recount long tales of ruin resulting from avarice, like that of my mother's brother, Ernesto, whom I never met, because before I was born he fell into a ravine and died when he forced his donkey to travel on a moonless night and carry him to the market in Epila. There Ernesto had expected to get a lot of money in trade for his plague coins, little circles of lead that he made by heating and pouring the soft metal into a tiny mold with a likeness of Saint Eulalia and the dove that had flown out of her mouth on one side; and on the other, Saint Sebastian, the plague saint. The coins were meant to be carried in a pocket or purse, a little something to buy off the Devil for another year or a day.

"Well, they must have been of some value! At least Ernesto didn't die of plague!" my papa shouted back at his father from the doorway, heading back down the hill. He always walked out before the end of any argument. Disputes were concluded by means of distance. That is, when the two of them could no longer hear each other, then they stopped arguing. My father's referring to plague was not purely spiteful. Many of our family had been taken away in the dead carts, seventeen in the last generation, not including those six or seven of them who were babies and christened at the last minute, fever evaporating the holy water of baptism right off their heads.

Opinions over exactly what had befallen my uncle varied. Papa said that his reasoning had grown ever more confused from handling so much of the poisonous lead, and that he had walked off the cliff in a fit. Mama said that it was not insanity but that her brother had had a vision of the Virgin motioning him to step into a coach carved from an immense pearl and pulled by twelve lionesses.

When I asked her how it was that she knew a dead man's last vision, she gave me a look that made me wish I had remained as safely silent as my sister.

The next day she told me that Ernesto had visited her in her dreams, and not only her but his other sisters as well. He had told them all the same story. What's more, it wasn't just a story; didn't everyone know that his body was never found? Only the corpse of his crazy donkey was collected from the ravine. Ernesto had gone off with the Virgin.

"But I thought *he* was crazy from the lead," I said, "not his ass." And she looked at me again.

In the winter, when temperatures dropped suddenly and water trapped below the pond's freezing surface made a keening, moaning noise, I told Dolores it was dead Ernesto imprisoned beneath the ice. I frightened her so that she would not walk near the pond but begged Mama to take the long way to market. "What on earth for, in all this snow?" Mama asked, but Dolores only shook her head and held tight to Mama's hand. "Not by the pond! Not by the pond!" she begged.

I hated to share even a morsel of my mother's love, hated to see Dolores's hand in Mama's, and out of jealousy I was often cruel to my sister. As crazy as she was for weddings, I told Dolores I had had a dream that Papa was ruined and her dowry chest empty, and that the family was forced to give her away to a man with the head of a dog.

"Oh, don't worry, he did not eat you," I said to her, and I pulled her hands away from her ears so that she would have to hear me. "But his tongue was long and red and wet and he poked it into your throat!" My stories made Dolores scream, and often she cried until she lost her words, she cried until she could not tattle, and then our mother would look at me with sharp suspicion but with no evidence with which to decide upon a punishment.

Though I had but few years, though I was no taller than the church's altar rail, people believed whatever I said, and sometimes even my mother was frightened by my tales. When she looked at me, frowning, it was as if she knew my dreams were real, clairvoyant; that much of what I said would come to pass.

Dolores never married a dog, but Papa was ruined; and just as I had imagined it, afterward he slept and slept and slept before he died. Not in the bed I had dreamed for him, however, and never wrapped like a worm in layers of silk. Mama did learn to read, but I had never imagined that she would go away to a palace to be taught; nor could I have then anticipated the one who would take her place in my desire, and who would educate me in matters beyond reading; or how the ability to interpret the marks on the page might admit me to paradise and then, like fruit from the tree of knowledge, cast me out, far further from happiness than Eve, the mother of us all.

My father's downfall was his belligerence toward his father. As Grandfather had observed would be the case, their arguments over the silk trees ended only with my grandfather's death.

By then my grandfather had been installed against his objections in our house. Papa had carried his father, who was too weak to fight him off, down the hill to the bed Papa shared with Mama, carried Grandfather with his money and his Bible, both of which Grandfather insisted Mama fold into the bed linens. He couldn't read, not his Bible or any other book, but he could count well enough, and he rested his head on the Gospels while he stacked up coins and muttered to himself. "Thirty-four ducados, thirty-five, thirty-six . . ." He did his calculations when he thought we were not listening. He was so infirm that his legs could no longer support him, and at night he spoke roughly to his feet, telling them how they should obey him the next day and carry him back up the hill.

"I'm not so heavy and I haven't so much money that you won't be able to manage it," he told them. And perhaps he would have been able to climb back up the hill, had he not worn himself out practicing all the night, swinging his thin shanks over the edge of the bed, placing his gnarled toes on the floor, standing with the help of his staff and then falling to the ground. Finally, my mother took his stick and put it away and tucked him in bed so tightly that he might as well have been bound to the pallet. The following night he did not try to stand. Instead, he died.

Papa rolled him over before his body was cold, turned my grandfather so that his face, set forever now in lines of disapproval, was to the wall; and my father began immediately to count the money Grandfather had saved. The coins were warm, for Grandfather had slept right on top of them, deeming any discomfort worth the solace of intimacy with wealth.

My father made six neat stacks of coins on the table where we ate. He counted them and recounted them; he put aside one stack for taxes and two for the tithe. "A full half to our masters, both earthly and eternal," he said grudgingly. "And this is what we will live on for the next three years." He gathered the coins from the remaining stacks into a little leather purse and placed it in Mama's hands.

That same afternoon he burned the old mulberry trees down, burned them all, those trees that had required so much care and irrigation: in the dry season, hundreds, even thousands, of trips up the hill with heavy buckets of water. Wading through the mud and muck into the shrunken river to scrape each bucket's lip under the dying trickle of water, trudging back up the hill to pour it over the roots of the trees. My sister and I were too small to carry the water buckets in their yoke, but we would watch Papa and Mama as they struggled with them, and we used to help in whatever way we could, taking on the earliest feeding, when the sun had yet to rise and the picked leaves were cold in their baskets and had to be warmed before the worms would touch them. Dolores and I would set the leaves before the fire Grandfather kept burning, and then the three of us would feed them as Mama and Papa rested in bed a little longer.

Not only had the ceaseless quarrels with his father failed to convince Papa that his idea of planting another kind of tree was foolhardy, but they had made my father more and more stubborn, word by word locking him in a prison of recalcitrance, so that instead of the more cautious plan that he had outlined to my grandfather—that of preserving half the old trees and replacing the other half with the new strain—Papa destroyed the entire grove that his forebears had planted. The night my grandfather died there had been the uncommon celestial conspiracy of a full moon and two planets describing a triangle over the nearby city of Burgos, igniting the cathedral spire like a torch. Along with seven dead frogs in the water pail the previous week, this augured to my father that a new age was upon the Luarca family. He took this as permission to lose what reason he had.

It was December, the pruned mulberry trees were bare and gray after a dry autumn. Papa walked up and down between the rows of sleeping trees, and he carried a burning pitch and lit them on fire. They caught fast, it was amazing to us, Mama, Dolores and I. We stood in the doorway of our house and looked up the hill at a vision brighter and more festive than any evening celebration for Saint John. The trees blazed up like fireworks against the dark afternoon sky. Later, we learned that Papa had traded one of my grandfather's coins for enough lamp fuel to leave an oil-soaked rag in the branches of each tree; nothing in nature would ignite so readily. It was on the shortest day of the last month of the year, the solstice, that he set the old trees on fire, and as it was a windy night the fires burned better than they might have otherwise. Walking around and around the perimeter of the grove to be sure that the burning was contained, Papa watched the flaming trees.

They say that when Hernán Cortés arrived in the New World he caused his men, every last one of them—or however many of them had not died of seasickness or sun blisters or fallen overboard or been killed by savages or tropical ailments—to quit their ships, and Cortés ordered those three hundred soldiers to watch as he burned them. They stood on the rock port of Vera Cruz, and the ships, which were good ships and large, took a long time to burn and to sink. By nightfall they were not yet consumed; one mast remained, rising out of the waves like a monument to their leader's resolve. So they knew, then, that they should either conquer or succumb to the wiles of the savages, for there was no turning back.

In the morning, when Dolores and I came outside, there was nothing but a field of black limbless stumps, some as tall as men, and standing so still, like an army that had been stopped by some evil enchantment. My sister began to weep, and in the cold morning her tears froze. Dolores never looked like a child. Sharp-featured and pinched, there was nothing about her adult face that had yet to announce itself; and even then, as she wiped fiercely at her tears, a girl of eleven, no more, she had the aspect of a miniature woman, one whose life would offer nothing but hardship.

We watched as Papa chopped the burned trees down to stumps and set about trying to dig up the roots. Of course, they were too strong. He could not clear the old land for the new seedlings.

It seems surprising to me now that he had not anticipated this, that he had believed he could tear the old trees out of the earth, even though we did not own even one ox. But Papa was crazy with stubborn, willful determination—another Luarca family weakness—and he would prove his father wrong, even in death.

Without the restraint of Grandfather's presence, Papa's nightly musings took on an increasingly feverish character. Even I no longer dreamed aloud with him, for he had ventured into a place of fantasy that I did not want to visit. His dreams of how much silk he would raise, of the bounty it would buy, became more and more unreasonable, so that I worried he had become like one of those rapt fools who set out for the New World, so certain of the mountains of gold that awaited them there, so dead set on their shining future that even as they lay perishing of fever or of a savage's arrow, still the vision of a city of Incan gold burned before them. El Dorado in his gilded skin, his eyes mad, incendiary orbs of gold, his hair a golden flame, danced and shrieked at them as they writhed. Papa was no different from these men, nor from his father's father's father's father, Victor Luarca, who had left his silkworms to go with Cortés and who had come home in a box in 1527, his journal on his moldered breast. Family legends had it that the last word written in Victor's account was *gold,* just as one day the last words on my papa's lips would concern silk.

Anyone who listened to my father talk understood that he now fancied himself a sort of silk emperor; he controlled all the guilds and the workers and every detail of the great industry— the wash works and dye works and the fashionable colors and patterns, the weavers and their apprentices who labored to set the great looms, every detail down to the last greedy, chewing worm. He shook his head, made a sort of disapproving noise with his tongue, and as the evening wore on and the fire dimmed, he took to looking fixedly into one corner of our home, to a spot at which he muttered and cursed and occasionally gestured as if in argument. One night I saw his father there.

"Grandfather!" I said, and I started toward the figure, but he shook his finger at me.

"No closer, child," he warned, but he smiled through the smoke wreathing around his head. In a moment he had vanished.

When the old trees' roots would not let go of the earth, Papa said that anyway they had polluted the ground to which they clung, and he set to work terracing and tilling a new grove, on land that we owned but had left unused and untenanted. "The bean field," Grandfather had called it, for each year we intended to cultivate a crop there. But each year the worms and their feeding took all the time and strength we had. In years past, the plot had been leased. In such times as we now found ourselves no one had any money to pay for such things. Everybody was so assured of being caught by the Church in some misdeed—for a crime as small as failing to observe one holy day of obligation—that families clung to whatever coins they possessed, saving them so that they had money for the inevitable fines. If they could pay them immediately, then they would not incur more of them, and they would never end up in one of the prisons of the Inquisition, or so they hoped. For it was said that once the Church took a bite of a man or a woman, once it tasted even one maravedi, its appetite was such that only the whole body, the whole fortune, would satisfy it. So, people saved their coins, no one leased our land, and Papa set to work to reclaim it from the briars and weeds.

Even in the winter with the ground frozen so that he was forced to chip and chip with his hoe and even then made almost no progress in a day, my father worked without cease until there was a new grove laid out beside the old. He planted the prepared soil with the seedlings that he had bought, paying fifty maravedis for each of them, and soon the trees were tall and healthy. So healthy! They grew on nothing, they needed less water and, as if enchanted, they blossomed, they budded, they thrived. In three years, they were taller than I.

My father could not contain his delight. He nearly danced among the new trees, and I believe they gave him even greater pleasure than they might have were they not planted next to his father's ruined stumps. Well, for a time, anyway.

My great-great-great—oh, too many generations to count—grandfather was among the first to cultivate silk in Spain. He had sailed the trade routes for as many years as his legs and back remained strong, his balance good, and then he retired from the sea just at the time when silkworms and mulberry trees and the art of making the lustrous fabric had come to Spain from the Orient. This ancestor, Sandoval de Luarca, returned to his home in Castile with crates of mulberry seedlings, and after the trees took root and grew to sufficient size (they are a fast-maturing plant) one spring, now generations past, Sandoval awaited the docking at La Coruña of a ship bearing silkworm eggs from China. The eggs were transported by sea in a small chest kept cool by its proximity to a great block of hewn river ice packed in sawdust. Once in Spain, they traveled by Sandoval's mule cart, also in the company of ice, not cold enough to freeze the eggs, but just cool enough to prevent them from hatching before their arrival at the lodgings my great-great-and-so-on-grandfather had built for his worms, at which point, having dripped steadily away on the roads to Castile, the carefully packed block of ice had been reduced to a pile of wet sawdust.

Good silkworm eggs are very expensive. No one buys Chinese eggs any longer, but the worms that spun the first silk in Spain came from eggs transported on the fast-sailing ships that brought other perishables from the Orient, everything kept cool by ice: aphrodisiac ointments made from the hooves of one-horned river horses, ginseng-root cures for dropsy, hot sweet peppers from the province of Hunan, tiny Chinese oranges favored by King Philip I and his court. Sandoval hadn't any money for the eggs; he obtained them by collecting on a debt of incalculable value.

At sea, years before, he had saved a man's life by drawing a great splinter from his neck and sucking the wound clean with his own lips. "He spat the pus into the ocean!" my grandfather had told me, and from this grateful trader, ever eager to recompense for the miracle of his life returned, Sandoval accepted the silkworm eggs as a gift. Thus, it was by a twist of fate—a stranger's misfortune and near death—that we became a family of silk growers. Since we were not Moors as most silk growers were, we were not tortured or exiled. But, still, perhaps it is inauspicious for a family's good fortunes to proceed from any accident, even one that did not prove fatal. Certainly my father later attached significance to the story of Sandoval and the splinter, saying that my ancestor had spat out the pus but swallowed seeds of an ill fortune that would inexorably return; but by then Papa's reasoning was not what anyone could follow.

While he waited for the new grove to mature, Papa entered into a partnership with a silk grower named Jorge Encimada. Together they raised an experimental generation of Señor Encimada's worms, feeding them leaves treated with an extract taken from the shells of the kermes insect that lives on oak and feeds on the sweet flesh of the tree just under the bark. Papa had Dolores and me gather the bugs, and he paid us one maravedi for every ten that we caught. We had to strip off their shells, too, ignoring their scratching kicking legs, and set their little suits to soak in vinegar. Sometimes I would drop one down Dolores's collar when she was not looking, or into her hair where its legs would tangle, and then she would scream so that Mama came running, half amused, half angry.

"Don Pascual!" she would say, but not loudly. No, she would only mouth the name of the Inquisitor General. "Come with your cart, Don Pascual, and take this naughty girl away!" And then I would put my head in her skirts and hide.

After my mother died, I wondered whether she was taken to a place with any view, and whether she saw when it came to pass that one day I was collected by an officer of the Inquisition and thrown into a cart like those we joked about. I hope she did not. Yet some say that the reward of heaven is precisely this: the chance to observe from above the torment of the damned. That the righteous enjoy the punishment of sinners, even those who were their children, and in life their beloved.

Could my mother have guessed, when I was a child, what a sinner I would turn out to be? At home with my family I was obedient enough, especially with the incentive of a reward. No matter the quarreling or the unappealing nature of the jobs our father gave us, Dolores and I both pursued money zealously; we were sorry when Papa told us we had gathered enough kermes bugs. He took the last basket from me and bent down until our eyes were level.

"Your papa is a very clever man," he said, and I nodded, but I saw the ghost of my grandfather standing at his side and shaking his head. I heard him, too. *No te rejis,* he said in disgust. Don't blow your horn.

Papa and Señor Encimada's experiment—their intention was to raise red silk—was not a success.

The cocoons that the worms threw off were of a color that must have been a pale pink mockery of their dreams. Still, they did sell them at market, not for much, but a Dutchman, thinking them a local curiosity, bought the lot of them. If only Papa had taken this modest failure as some sort of caution, then our lives might have turned out quite differently, but it seemed an evil spirit had attached itself to him.

My father was a true son of Castile, of our homeland in the bleakest and most fearsome of all the regions of Spain. In his rock-gray eyes I saw the windswept, wind-whipped plains which drop suddenly from the Pyrenees, which fall tumbling down from the Cantabrian Mountains, which plummet, crack and crumble and then work their peculiar bewitchment. A magic of altitude, of precipice, a magic of gulch, gully and chasm. A magic of something high brought suddenly low. A dizziness, a loss of balance. Blood's memory of soaring, and a tendency to dream of that which is far, far above your head. Remember Quixote, fever-addled, finding giants in windmills and princesses in peasant girls? My father could not read that romance, but in Quintanapalla, not far from the birthplace of the Knight of Sad Countenance, he fell under the sway of visions as potent as Quixote's. My father was a true Castilian, a man who would risk everything for the sake of his dreams, even what he loved best. And I am my father's daughter. I am a daughter of Castile.

In the spring of the year of our Lord 1667, my papa, Félix de Luarca, bought eggs from the old man in Soria who bred the silk moths. There were others who raised eggs closer to our home in Quintanapalla, but it is best to buy eggs from a tested, trusted source. Healthy silk eggs are a luminous blue-gray color, like slate. Dead eggs are yellow. It is not unknown for unscrupulous vendors to wash dead eggs in wine so that they take on the slate color; then they sell them. If there was one way in which Papa would not cross my grandfather, even in death, it would be to go to a new egg vendor.

So he made the trip to the old family vendor in Soria; he was gone for three nights. He returned on the fourth, carrying the tiny wood caskets of eggs packed in straw. On the way home, he told us, he had stopped at the shrine in Queranna and there he had poured out an offering of oil—the finest he could buy, from the first press of the pick of last year's olives—over the feet of the miraculous Virgin there. He was sure, he said, that all would go well for us, that the fortunes of the Luarca family were about to change. He seemed, to Mama, Dolores and me ex-changing secret glances, drunk with optimism. He sang as he opened the tiny boxes—more eggs than we had ever purchased before—and he sang as he transferred them to the goatskin pouch used for hatching. He pulled the strings tight, and Mama undid her bodice, as I had watched her do each spring. It was the heat of her flesh, the murmur of her blood, that would incubate the eggs, awakening them from their chilled slumber; and when he handed her the soft little package, Mama tucked it in the warm hollow between her breasts. Before three Sabbaths had passed, the eggs would burst and discharge a hungry army of worms.

The hatching of silkworm eggs is timed carefully, for it must coincide with the opening of the buds on the mulberry trees. Silkworms and mulberry leaves mature together, of necessity. The tiny worms with their weak jaws feed upon tender new leaves, and as they grow older and larger they eat older and tougher foliage. Papa hoped that with the new trees he would eventually be able to produce two generations of worms each year, something that was done in the warmer climates of the Orient but had never been accomplished in our part of the world. It required cutting the trees all the way back at midsummer, just as one generation had stopped feeding and commenced to spin. The Chinese, so Papa had learned at one of his meetings, left just a leaf or two at the end of each branch to draw the sap and keep the tree alive, thus forcing the tree into new leaf for a second time in one year. I saw Mama wince as he explained the process to her, his eyes hot and bloodshot as they always were when he set to scheming; he seemed focused on something no one else could see. "But not yet," he said, "not this season or even the next. The trees are still too young."

Mama walked carefully through her chores those two weeks. Each morning she gently turned the bag that hung between her breasts, checking its contents and safeguarding, next to her heart, our family's livelihood. My papa used to boast that every egg he placed between Mama's two tits hatched. That not one failed, and that there was no silk farmer so fortunate as the one wed to Concepción de Luarca. Then, if he thought we were not looking, he would open Mama's bodice and quickly kiss each breast and the little bag hanging between them. Seeing that, I wanted to kiss her as well. My mother was a taste of something of which I never had my fill.

The worms hatched at Eastertide, exactly as the buds on the trees were unfurling. We brought the worms their leaves, which looked quite like the leaves from my grandfather's trees, but as they matured they grew even better, bigger and shinier. We carried in baskets and bushels and crates of leaves, Dolores and Mama and I. Papa fed the worms three times during each night, while the rest of us slept, for silkworms eat through five Sabbaths without stopping, pausing only once each week to burst and shed a skin. We brought baskets of the shining waxy green leaves into the silk house. We spread them on the trays. For a time everything looked promising.

Growing worms eat steadily. We watched as they grasped the

new leaves in their front feet and chewed. We held our breath at the first molt, that dangerous period when the worms sink into a torpor for a day or so, their flesh growing pale and cool as they cling to the trays. Then the black spots appeared on their heads, and the old skin cracked from that point and split, just as it should. Each worm wriggled out in a new ill-fitting suit that would soon fill out and burst in its turn; the worm ate its old skin first and then went on to eat the leaves. All appeared to be well.

I alone believed that they were doomed. Our worms, my worms. My partners in the rich work of making one thing from another. Waking and sleeping, I dreamed of their death. When I told Mama of these visions, she did not scold me, she embraced me; she pressed my face to her bodice to stop my prophecy. We clung together, holding each other tightly, long enough that when I pulled away I saw how my breath, so close and wet, had left a dark stain on Mama's dress.

In the silk house, on the hill above our little house, the worms stopped eating. Not all of them at once, but gradually, over the course of the week between the second and third molt, the better part of our silkworms stopped eating. They died, and with them most of our investment.

It wasn't like any plague we had endured before, nothing like the yellow disease that makes the skin swell tight and shiny before yellow bile oozes from their mouths as they expire. And not the scarlet disease, either, in which, after the fourth molt the worms emerge in a red skin and die. This illness had no dramatic manifestations. It was a simple loss of appetite. The worms would not eat; they would not eat the new leaves. They would rather die than eat them. Their jaws stopped moving, and we knew when they did so that they were finished.

In the morning, before Papa was awake to see it, Dolores and I would run up the hill and into the silk house. We'd gather up the dead worms and throw them on the ground outside. The birds alone profited from my father's scheme, the crows grew fat that spring. The few worms that did eat the leaves grew slowly, and the cocoons they spun were inferior and small. Too small to sell. On the night we killed them, placing the trays over the steaming rocks and turning the cocoons with a large spatula until the worms had surely smothered and died, my father was genuinely drunk, drunk on spirits from a bottle and not those born of enthusiasm. He was still drunk the next day when we took our harvest, not enough to fill even a quarter of the baskets from the previous years, to the silk market. There we learned that by the stipulations of the guild the cocoons were of insufficient size to sell.

My father took his case to the guild master. He lowered his asking price. He tried to bribe the guild constable, an old friend of his father's. But it had not been a drought year, and high-quality silk was plentiful. On our way to market we saw other carts whose baskets were filled with big white cocoons, the sun touching them and making them shine even as we whipped our mule so that we could beat our competition to market. I stood with Dolores and the mule outside the guild office as my father begged, and sacrificed his pride, all to no good. Above us the trees were filled with hawks who awaited the dispersal of the crowds at dusk. Then they would descend to gorge themselves on the piles of scraps left by the butchers. The birds turned their heads at us and blinked slowly, and pitilessly, or so it seemed to me, and I felt myself cloaked in shame.

The guild remained obdurate. It would not yield to any amount of wheedling.

Papa closed the office door quietly behind him, and before we got back into our cart, he threw all the work of our worms away. Each little spun white house with its dead occupant he threw onto the great stinking heap of offal outside the butchers' stalls in the plaza, and there, as well, did he leave his dreams to rot.

From this time forward, with my grandfather dead and Papa ruined, the fortunes of the Luarca family would be left to the ingenuity of its women. Hardly a bad thing, on the face of it, as Luarca women lacked for neither talent nor tenacity. In fact, my mother was soon discovered to possess a rare gift, and it was this gift that provided her passport to the palace. It was this gift that would save us for a time, before it also brought destruction.

cissoque corde, ut dixi, anima mea fuit ab hac carne soluta. He spoke softly. He touched my eyelids with his tongue.

How can it be that I was in his arms so briefly? A hundred afternoons, no more. Once each week a few hours stolen, and finally at night, by cover of darkness, each embrace made hot and holy by the risk we took in bedding each other.

"Scissoque corde—" I repeated.

He put his hand over my lips. "No," he said. "Translate." His fingers smelled of incense. The man who taught me to read, who licked words from my eyes and tore grammar from my throat, was a priest.

As he spoke I heard—I thought I heard—the creak of a carriage axle outside. But who would be afield at such an hour? I turned to the window's blank eye. I could not make out any sound of wheels. It was said that officers of the Inquisition wrapped the rims of their carriage wheels in rags, wrapped them to ensure silence in their approach. So stealthy were they, it was said they wrapped a horse's hooves, too, and slit an animal's vocal cords to prevent a whinny or a nicker, any noise of warning. Inquisition begins in silence.

"Listen!" I said to him.

A reflection of the one candle burned in each of his dark eyes. "I hear nothing," he said. But perhaps the blood pounded in his ears, drowning out the sound of danger.

"Blow out the light," I whispered. "They came to Rubena last week."

They had come to the neighboring town, and they had taken away the tanner. They left his empty shoes by the door of his house, to prevent his wife and his sons from the sin of hope, of believing some other fate had befallen him, that he had gone off with a mistress or been chased by a bandit. Without that unmistakable sign, the people of Rubena might have thought the tanner's disappearance the work of love, or thievery, or witchcraft. The hide over which he had been working was still on the table, his broad knife dull and sticky with the flesh he had been scraping.

What had this tanner done to attract the notice of the Holy Office? He was said to have been in the practice of changing his linen on Saturdays. At a fiesta he was observed refusing a dish made with pork. He was, someone reported to the Holy Office, a secret Jew.

"Please," I said.

He snuffed the candle with his hand. "*Scissoque corde.* Francisca."

The dark was filled with sighs. Whose? Were we sighing? Was I?

I began to try to sort out the verb form. I spoke slowly but did not falter in my translation. My aptitude for language would later count against me, as literacy is held to be a common sign of witchcraft.

"My heart, as I said, split open, and my soul was liberated from this flesh," I translated.

"Yes," he said. "*Bonissimus.* Very good." His lips breathed words onto my palms. Palms that burn still from his kisses, and that itch with longing.

"Who said this?" he asked me.

"Saint Catherine of Siena."

"When did Saint Catherine die?"

"She did not die. She never died."

"When was she born?"

"In the year of our Lord thirteen hundred and forty-seven."

"And when were you born, Francisca de Luarca?" His breath came in short gusts and broke up the words. *Fran cis ca.* We were lying together on the floor beside the table where just that afternoon we had read from the *Legenda* and the *Acta Sanctorum,* accounts of Saint Catherine's life, written more than three centuries ago by Raymond of Capua, her confessor.

"I was never born," I said.

"When were you born, Francisca?"

"I have not yet been born."

Burning. But not the sting of a coal, not the sizzle of nettles or the shriek of scalding water spilled upon you. No earthly burning, this, but how light might feel were it to enter you, were flesh to become literate in senses other than touch.

And of course flesh does, it does—flesh learns everything. Blood flows toward consciousness, bones apprentice themselves, a body's very skin sets itself a course of study. The only truths worth knowing, the only ones we remember, are those we learn by the flesh.

Where did the burning begin? Wherever his tongue first touched. Yes, *there,* then. Why would he not begin there, and right away? I did not hesitate to open my legs to his tongue. We had no time to squander on modest kisses. Besides, it mattered not where he began, it was as if he touched me everywhere at once. The soles of my feet blistered, and flames licked between my fingers in his hair.

Trying to remain still under the tutelage of his tongue. Its tick-tick-ticking followed by a calculated, expert, teasing pause. He was the clock that made a mockery of time.

My inner eye saw only sky. Despite the late hour and the darkened room, on my back I looked up to a bright day, a day flooded with light. He touched me, and I saw one filament spun by a worm, one almost invisible thread cast between two branches and hung glistening in the air. Bowed by a breeze but impossibly strong. Why did it not break? As soon as I asked the question, *snap,* the strand was gone. I was gone. I was what gave way and snapped.

He pulled away from me. "When were you born?"

I gasped. "Now," I said. "I am . . . being born . . . now."

He touched me, my belly, my shoulders, my face. I touched him, too. Were we truly there? Was he? Was I? "*Bonissimus.* Yes," he said. "You are being born now."

I felt the night sigh all around us, with us, through us. His lips seemed fuller when I could not see them, when I tried to know them by touch. I counted his teeth in the dark, I dug my fingers into the soft, wet well of flesh under his tongue. I pulled him to me, into me.

"Oh, please, I beg you. Please." Arching toward them like a bow, trying to divorce my spine from the rack to which they make me fast. "Please. Further. Go further. Kill me. Split my heart, please. I am begging you."

They do this in the light. In the bright light. Standing near to me, making fast the ligatures, their robes are so long that they drag on the floor. Their hoods obscure their features, and all I can see of my tormentors is an occasional glint of light reflecting on the wet surface of their otherwise hidden eyes.

The robes they wear and the hoods that preserve their anonymity are made of the most wonderful and lustrous silk. Silk so beautiful, so like the silk of which I dreamed when I was a child, that I find myself wanting to touch it. I wonder how it might feel under my fingers.

Their robes are black, but a black that light reveals as containing all colors, a black that shimmers and glints red, green, purple: every hue. Their hoods are white, most of them, and a few are red. Those in red hoods are in charge, they direct those in white. One of them, one only, the one who asks the questions, is the head of this prison. He wears a purple hood.

They do nothing in the dark, of course. They need light to see, they need light to write down what I say, to record my confession. But I can close my eyes. I need not be here, with them.

Scindite cor meum. Split my heart.

I am remarkable for sheer mortal stubbornness. My flesh will not succumb, and its insistent clinging to life enrages them. Is interpreted as a sort of insolence. But it worries them, too: how can so seemingly frail a creature survive all this without the help of some higher, or lower, power?

We begin with the rack, as usual we begin with the rack. After one White Hood secures my ankles and wrists in their shackles, after he turns a crank until I am stretched as taut as a harp string, another stops up my nostrils with wax. Wax he has kneaded with his fingers until it is warm and pliant, until the feel of it is as intimate and terrible as that of his fingers themselves. When my nose is sealed, he forces water into my entrails through my mouth, pouring it from a little height, enough that it courses through the funnel jammed between my teeth. It's either swallow or drown, suffocate.

As they do not want to kill me before they hear what I have to say, they stop after a jug or two, which I generally vomit, and then the Purple Hood begins his questions, after the caution that silence will likely result in further encouragements to make me speak.

I've confessed to everything. I have confessed to too many things, so we keep starting over.

Or, as they say, we "continue."

My unfortunate tendency to laugh under duress also results in continuations. No one can be tortured twice, not for the same accusation—that is the law—but tortures may be continued, as mine has been, for months.

My priest is dead, and my mother, too. Yet they gather evidence against each of them. After all, it is never too late for sentencing, never too late to decide the fortunes of an immortal soul. I am the one in whom truth is hiding: the Purple Hood must suspect this. He asks me questions. About the priest: Had he ever betrayed any disbelief in the sacraments? What was he looking for in those texts? Whom else had he tutored? About my mother: How many times had she been with child? What happened to the bodies of the babies who were stillborn? What sex were those dead children?

Though I was arrested three years ago, it was only last summer that they began to question me. A clerical delay, possibly, for this prison is full enough that most of us die before our records of arrest are reviewed, before even a plan of interview is decided upon. But in my own case, I think it more likely that the Purple Hood's questions reflect a palace preoccupation.

The court is in a paroxysm over witches. Witches are found everywhere. When the *Bellavente* sank last season off the coast of Málaga, twenty women were burned in that port town, burned without trial. Rumor has it that their hearts were gouged out and cooked separately in a big pot, the same in which their accusers said they had stirred up the storm that sank the unfortunate ship. And those twenty women died a hundred leagues away from the palace, a full three weeks' journey from Madrid, where last August King Carlos made his official statement. Stood quavering on the royal balcony in the Plaza Major and read his words from an unrolled parchment. "The failure of Queen María Luisa to get with child," he said, "is due to sorcery." His voice was weak, his words had to be repeated by an official crier. The crowds, faces tipped up toward their king, were strangely silent. After the proclamation they dispersed without the usual rioting and commotion, without the ordinary noise of assembly that is carried down through the cobbles until the prison's locks and hinges whine.

The next day seventeen witches were found in the royal residence and brought directly here for questioning. The cause of the queen's failure to bear a child would be discovered. The records of all persons in palace employ from the year of Carlos's birth until the present were reviewed, my mother's included among them. And I was moved from my original lodgings to this corridor of cells reserved for witches who have threatened the royal family: a consideration conferred by heredity; for in conjunction with my own not inconsiderable mistakes, my mother's connection to the palace was of such intimacy and power that it mandates my being treated as a special case. I now occupy a cell between the queen's translator and her secretary: one more woman in a row of malign maids-in-waiting, of deviously conspiring dwarfs, laundresses whose soaps bore curses, of chambermaids whose bosoms heaved with diabolic desire, wet nurses whose tits leaked liquid spells. Oh, every trade that serves the king and queen has its representative in these exclusive quarters.

Maybe the carriage with its mutilated, silent horse did pause in the street that last night. Maybe it brought its rag-wrapped wheels to a slow and very nearly silent stop on the one cobbled street of Quintanapalla, the same that ran past his lodgings. Perhaps on that night when I returned to him against all caution, and when we let a candle burn a moment too long— But what of it? There is no law against light. He often studied all the night. Still, perhaps someone saw, or merely listened to my unortho- dox catechisms. Stood silent under his windowsill, just as I had once stood there waiting to hear the sounds of his quill, the whisper of pages turning.

Was he afraid of discovery when we were together? I was, but fear only inflamed me further.

Returned to my cell from questioning, I awake to a stir between two departing guards. I hear the queen's name, followed by an ugly laugh. Something is happening in the world above, but what? I crouch by the grille. Someone will have heard some- thing. Someone is waiting to share what she knows.

We are not allowed to talk in here. We wear tongue locks, some of us, iron rods extending from jaw to collarbone that prevent a lady so adorned from opening her mouth. In this way the inquisitors think they can stop us from spreading heresies, one to another, like disease. It is difficult to drink water while wearing a tongue lock—you have to plunge your head into the bucket and suck the water up through your teeth. As for the crusts of bread they give us to eat, we poke them into our cheeks with our fingers, and when they are sufficiently moist they, too, can be sucked slowly through whatever teeth we have left. The tongues of false witnesses and incorrigible blasphemers have been cut out, of course, which makes sucking and all sounds but moaning impossible for them. But still, rumors multiply.

Messages traced by a finger onto the clean slate of an open palm. Those of us who know our letters—and, being witches, the prisoners in this lowest catacomb constitute an uncom- monly literate collection—have the solace of silent communica- tion, fingers conversing through the grilles. Or just the grasping of a feverish hand, that is enough for certain messages, a greet- ing or a taking of leave.

When the guards depart, taking their one lamp with them, the cautious hush of those prisoners who are awake and conscious slowly gives way to a rustle of gossip, conjecture. It cannot be that María Luisa has dared to pretend another miscarriage. For it is common knowledge—in this corridor, anyway—that until her accomplice was caught, the queen had feigned several doomed pregnancies over the last two years. How better to appear to satisfy the one obligation of her position? The one undoable duty of the wife to a king whose impotence must never even be hinted at? A miscarrying queen is, after all, in less danger than a barren one.

A false miscarriage. It could not have been any business for the fainthearted, not the way I imagine it. In the early dawn hours, before the undercook's apprentice had roused himself to set water to boil, before he woke the little scullery maid (boxing her ears when she did not stand quickly enough and frightening her so that she was out of the door and collecting eggs from the hens before she even stopped to rub her smarting flesh and think, Ouch! the bastard!); yes, before anyone had stirred, someone, some secret ally of the queen had smuggled pig's blood from the kitchen up to the royal bedchamber. This loyal if trembling accomplice—the same who in preceding months had discreetly removed evidences of the queen's monthly flow, hiding some bloodstains in preparation for others—had already on several occasions helped the queen to pour pig's blood over her nightdress and bedclothes, on her secret parts and in the chamber pot and all over the floor by the bed. Then the friend stole away, and María called for her maids. Screamed so that the doctor was summoned immediately and an examination made. And as the queen wept and moaned, the sad tidings were delivered; bells tolled to announce another lost heir to the empire.

I lick my lips and let my head rest against the wall, cold against my scalp; I reach to feel what hair is there. I was shorn a week ago, not more. Not a good job: two cuts on my neck and another at my temple for this assurance to my captors that no diabolical writings emerge on skin hidden by a growth of hair. Still, there are compensations. Though my captors surely do not intend it, their routine wielding of the razor provides some little comfort: I can gauge the passage of time by the length of my stubble. And vermin find me less attractive—my head, anyway. Of course, I am in a position to be grateful for anything. I am happy to be small, for I need that much less to eat, and when I sit up straight, there is room enough in here to stretch my legs.

As for the dark, the impenetrable and unremitting dark: that is the best place for dreams. For the dark is not empty forever, no. Try it sometime. Close your eyes, or better, cloister yourself away from the sun, away from all light.

The dark is quickly peopled.

HE QUEEN IS THE SAME AGE AS I, EXACTLY THE same, María Luisa, *Marie Louise de Bourbon,* the princess from Paris, the queen of Spain. When I saw her for the first time, she was like a vision from the days when we believed in the future wealth and happiness of the Luarca family. As if arrayed in my dreams, she wore a gown of the finest watered silk—lengths of silk, and layers of silk: silk petticoats, silk pantaloons, silk hose, silk slippers, all beneath a silk skirt that swelled out as vast as a tent, from a bodice narrow as a sapling. She was tall, too, she rose a full head above King Carlos.

I saw her, and it was as if before me stood the work of a hundred thousand worms. I saw the leaves of all our trees shiver over her in the wind; I heard the jaws of our worms, chewing, chewing, like the noise of a great storm. It had not rained for all the months of summer, but in the weeks preceding the royal wedding it had poured, an autumn deluge that had washed the dust from our one glass window.

The first news that had come home to us from the palace was of María. "Francisca," said a note at the bottom of a letter from my mother, who could now write as well as read, "the prince Carlos is betrothed to a little girl in France—a princess. She is the niece of King Louis the Fourteenth. Her name is Marie, and she is exactly the same age as you, my daughter, exactly. Same year, same month, same day."

We could not read the letters Mama sent—it would be years before I found my teacher—so we had to rely on others to tell us what they said. The innkeeper, usually, who read so haltingly that I guessed most of the words before they found their way out of his mouth, or his wife, who was even slower.

"Do you remember what your grandfather used to say?"

began another letter. " 'Even a cat may look at a queen.' Well, here I am, and I shall tell you everything I see in the palace."

And so my mother filled my head with details of the court, of Prince Carlos and of his mother. Of dwarfs, dresses, of quarrels and betrothals. Mama described what I thought I should never see for myself. But time passed, fate worked its own bewitchments, and one day I found myself in the company of the very princess of whom my mother had written—a woman who, by then, had long been visiting me in my dreams.

Ten years ago I was eighteen; ten years ago she was eighteen; and ten years ago María was married in Quintanapalla, the town where I was born.

Marie Louise de Bourbon. The witch. The whore. The saint. The stranger. The same girl for whom that familiar taunt was invented, the rhyme the mobs were shouting when she first arrived in Madrid, and which they still scream at her, only more loudly. So loudly that the stones of this prison ring with their jeering. So loudly that lately the queen has taken to riding doubled over in her carriage, her hands covering her ears.

> *"Parid, bella flor de lis*
> *Que, en aflicción tan extrana,*
> *Si paris, paris a España,*
> *Si no paris, a Paris."*

The new queen did not understand what the mobs were shouting as her coach rolled slowly through the palace gates the morning of her arrival. How could she, for she spoke no Spanish.

One fool slipped past the barricade and leaped upon the coach she shared with her translator, the coach immediately following Carlos's; the king shared his with his confessor. The man clung to the vehicle's side lamp and leered in the window. *"Parid! Bella flor!"* he hissed, and then a soldier shot him, and, instead of the next line of the rhyme, blood came out of his mouth.

María, holding tight to her translator's hand, shook those perspiring, fear-clammy fingers, she wrung them. *"Comment!*

Comment!" she said. "What! What are they shouting!" The foreign queen held the young woman's fingers so tightly that her rings cut into them.

Her translator hesitated, then explained. *Parir* was the verb meaning to give birth. Paris was not only the premier city of Europe, the city of the queen's birth and of her happiness, but it was also *paris,* the second person singular of *parir. Parid,* the imperative: *You give birth.*

The translator bit her lips, and tears came to her eyes. Only a month before, she had been living in a convent, unaware of how luxurious was the calm of transcribing holy manuscripts. Above her forehead, her cropped brown hair was still flattened from having been long squashed under a black habit.

Parid, pretty queen. Give birth!

A male heir, that is what the whole country wanted, that is what it wants now. A successor to the throne, a healthy male of sufficient intelligence and will to control the corps of manipulative ministers and hidalgos, grandees and bishops who were snatching every day more and more power from this greatly hoped-for scion's father, King Carlos. By the time he was married, a boy no older than his bride, Carlos had already dried up the treasury, crippled the armies and was losing each month more territories to France, to the Netherlands, even to the savages in the colonies. To save Spain, Carlos's heir would have to arrive in a hurry and come to power quickly—before the child was twenty, before he was ten. He would have to be an extraordinary child, a messiah.

So, from the beginning, Queen María Luisa knew what was expected of her.

On the morning of her wedding, I looked at María Luisa, and beyond her crown I saw our silent orchard of failed trees burn with bright insistence against the sky. I looked at her and remembered my mother's back growing smaller as she walked down the path to the road where the black carriage waited, the carriage bearing the king's coat of arms on the door.

Run! I whispered. She was standing before the bishop with King Carlos. In a moment it would be too late, she would be married to him, to the man who took my mother's life. *Run into the woods, hide among the trees! I will come and find you, I* promised. *I will bring you a common cloak and hood of wool. I will take those clothes which would betray you. I will burn that silk gown which would give you away.* But of course, María Luisa could not hear me. And even had she wanted to run, a woman could barely walk in a dress like that.

The wedding of Don Carlos José, príncipe de las Españas—Carlos Segundo, or, as he is called in some attempt to explain his ill luck in all things, *El Hechizado,* the Bewitched—to Marie Louise de Bourbon demanded the princess's translation from French to Spanish, from Marie Louise to María Luisa. And not just her name, but all of her was to be changed—a conversion marked first by the ascension of her dress collar some ten inches, from bosom to throat, those warm breasts so recently displayed like the dough of two rolls bursting sweet and fragrant from her bodice forced flat and apologetic like the unleavened bread of the penitent. Other changes, too, were forced upon her. There was the concurrent taming of her black curls.

"It is to a woman's long hair that the Devil clings," said Carlos's mother, Marianna. And she made sure every ringlet, every handhold, was removed.

Never once in her entire life had the princess's hair been straightened, but was rolled each bedtime in a hundred crackling curl papers such that each night became an ordeal endured for beauty. Yes, in France, Marie Louise had worn it as a veritable cataract of hair, like water flowing, like the tale sung by the poet Ovid of the nymph Arethusa changed into a fountain before Alpheus could rape her: *Dark drops rained from all her body,* the great poet said. Oh, María Luisa had hair like no other princess, and for her wedding it was dressed and bound with ribbons of gold, with gems and garlands and clips of tortoiseshell. For her wedding her hair was pulled back so tight that her eyes offered their own bright jewels.

Eighteen years old, María had dreamed of Spain, had been dreaming of this country for years, even as I had been dreaming of France and of her. María was betrothed to King Carlos when she was five, when I was five, and when our worms were still alive, still chewing, still spinning. Still making clothes for princesses. Dresses so immense and so many-layered, of silk so thickly brocaded and decorated with jewels, that once she was dressed it took all a woman's strength to stand upright.

After dozens of parties, Marie left her mother and brother and father in Paris, and set off for her new life with her maids and six ministers. It took almost an entire season to journey from the middle of France to Castile, it took so long because Marie was in no hurry. She traveled on horseback for as long as the weather permitted, cantering around and behind the three carriages full of ministers and maids. On horseback, describing circles and serpentines, exploring creeks and ponds in the flat farmland around Paris; meandering south, where the land buckled into rolling, hilly vineyards, where the wind shook the grape leaves and made all of France into a vast green sea, rocking, rocking. Marie Louise rode until rain turned to sleet, until, two months after leaving Paris, the three carriages reached the boundary between France and Spain, a border marked by the little river Bidassoa.

In the tiny river-port town of Orhy, a ferry waited for the princess's transport, a flat blue boat with a new canopy of snapping red and white, flags of France and of Spain bristling from each of its four corners. One of the thirty-seven onlookers assembled pointed at Marie Louise and said to the child sitting on his shoulders, "Look! Now you can tell your grandchildren that you saw the queen of Spain!"

The ferry was dragged over the water from the French to the Spanish shore by means of pulleys bearing ropes wound onto two giant spools turned by oxen, one spool on each riverbank. Marie Louise and her maids and ministers boarded the boat; and with a great squeal it began moving across the foaming water. The tide was fast, the wind sharp, and the boat pulled against the ropes. Midway across the river, one ox kicked another, there was much bellowing from animal and master, and in the ensuing struggle to separate the beasts the ropes snarled. The ferryboat stopped, and the journey was delayed an hour, the whole party paused in the neutral territory of flowing water. The relief of the princess occasioned by the reprieve of one hour was so great that, for the first time since leaving home, Marie was forced to admit her fear. What did she know, really, about Spain, about Carlos? About being a queen? It was cold on the water, but a rivulet of frightened sweat ran from her neck down her spine.

Too soon the ropes were untangled and the misbehaving beast replaced by another, more congenial one. The boat continued, pulleys squealing so loudly that conversation was impossible. The one maid-in-waiting who had complained in days previous that the motion of the carriage made her head ache discovered that the motion of the ferry had even more objectionable effects. She vomited over the side rail until nothing more came up, only strings of mucus that shone silver as they stretched and broke in the breeze, then dropped into the water. When finally the ferry reached the Bidassoa's Spanish bank, she disembarked before María. She ran from the boat in flagrant violation of the rules of etiquette, and of state, for it had been determined and contracted that the French retinue might accompany their princess only so far as the border: they were not to step on Spanish soil.

"Back on board immediately!" cried the ministers, almost in unison, and the poor girl was pulled, weeping, from the shore back onto the ferry, where she fell to her knees and began immediately to retch again. "Maman! Maman!" she begged, and María, standing now on the shore of her new home, found herself beginning to cry as well, not so much for the maid's misery as for the girl's helplessly calling for an absent mother.

"In all likelihood," Marie's own mother had said to her in Paris, tears washing the powder from her cheeks, "we will not embrace again in this life." And they had held each other tightly, so tightly, until there was the small snap of one whalebone stay breaking, and then they had begun to laugh. "Yours or mine?" Marie had said, wiping her eyes, laughing and crying at once. "Mine, I believe," said her mother. "Ouch, yes!" She held her side where the broken stay had poked her.

On the Spanish shore, Rébenac, the French minister who had come from Madrid, kissed one and then the other of the princess's gloved hands as the other French ministers watched from the ferry. Water slapped over the deck, ruining shoe leather and spraying the still-sobbing, retching maid. The pulleys began to squeal, the boat withdrew, the sobs grew faint.

In the midst of the corps of Spanish ministers was Marianna, King Carlos's mother. She came forward. "Here is your translator," she said in Spanish. "She is a good, chaste girl, and well versed in your tongue."

At a little push from the queen mother, a young woman came toward María. She curtsied, and translated Marianna's words exactly: "Here is your translator—"

"But do you not have a name?" the princess asked.

"Esperte. I am Esperte."

The party set off south into Spain. Northern Spanish roads would break up any carriage wheels, lame any horse, and so the future queen was carried with her translator in a litter, carried by the legs and arms of men. Strong legs, and noble, too. Each kneecap, each shin and sinew and toenail could follow its pedigree back to King Ferdinand: lesser legs would have been an affront.

If such transportation seemed to bear María backward into centuries past, as far away from Paris in years as in miles, at first she was glad of it. She was young and excited by the romance of inconvenience, when inconvenience was a novelty. Besides, she was more and more wary of reaching her destination. The Spanish king, it was rumored, was peculiar. María knew he had been an invalid, of course, but still she pictured him in good health, recovered from whatever had plagued him. Tall and if not handsome, exactly, then at least vivacious. He would play games as the young men in Paris had. Perhaps he would teach her new ones.

"Have you seen him?" she asked the translator.

"Only from a great distance."

"Does he ride?"

"I think not."

"Oh. Well, does he play croquet?"

"Croquet?"

"Yes, with the mallet and the . . . Is there no croquet here?"

The translator shook her head. "I have not heard of it."

When the litter stopped to change bearers, Rébenac, the

French minister, cleared his throat outside the curtains. "I think perhaps you might occupy yourselves with a Spanish lesson," he said, but as soon as he drew away from the litter, María pressed her translator for more gossip, more details.

"They say His Majesty sleeps upon a bed of relics," Esperte whispered. "The bed's posts are made of thigh bones, and the knobs are skulls. The canopy is the hide of Saint Epipodius, who was flayed when the lions would not devour him.

"They say he has no teeth and does not eat the usual things kings eat.

"They say he suffers bad dreams. He sleepwalks. He still takes milk from the breast."

"*Assez,*" María said. Enough. She motioned for Esperte to stop talking. *I am in a coffin,* the princess thought suddenly of her litter borne aloft by six footmen. The walls of its curtains swelled as if to crush her.

Perhaps she *was* dead. Perhaps she'd suffered an accident in France and now was dead and on her way to hell.

The impassive face of the Spanish minister of etiquette bore an expression that certainly could grace the observer of a never-ending funeral. Not an hour after their introduction to one another at the border, he had told Esperte to instruct María that she could not be seen riding, she could not be seen eating, she could not look out of the curtains of the litter. On the few occasions when she might be seen, she must be careful to let no unseemly passion derange her features.

Défense de manger. Défense de sourire. So, she might as well have been dead already and lying in state. Visitors would see a cold, set smile, for it appeared that Spain would not tolerate any signs of life in its queen.

María Luisa, worn out by fits of panic, slept during much of the trip, and her translator did, as well. Each girl was so shocked to find herself in a new world, a new life, that unconsciousness alone provided relief. They found themselves yawning helplessly. They fell asleep midsentence, and their heads nodded in time with the pitching of the litter and sometimes came together with a smart crack that woke each girl from her dreams: Esperte's of the library in the convent, her sleeping fingers drawn together as if around a quill; and María's of dances, endless dizzy balls, which kept her feet twitching beneath her skirts.

"Do look out of the curtain," said the princess, holding the side of her head, where it had bumped Esperte's. "And tell me what you see."

Yellow grass, gray rocks, blue sky, gray sky. Twisted olive trees with foliage so dark that they looked black against the dry grass. Towns like dirty beads upon the coiling silver string of a distant river. Endless stone walls coming down and falling into rubble, sheep grazing among the boulders. Farmhouses disgorged a few puzzled peasants as the litter and its entourage passed. The common country folk had no notion of a king and queen. They knew not even that they were Spaniards. They paid homage to the weather and the Virgin and little else.

Occasionally, the litter's curtains swung apart to reveal a flash of her bearers' boots, and María saw the dust of the road come up under their heels. It blew into the litter and settled on its passengers. Grime crept under her fingernails and between her breasts. The princess blew her nose, another thing never done in public, so she made sure to blow it well behind her curtain each time before she was called to emerge. The mucus came out blackened with dust, like a tiny augur of death there on the white linen handkerchief, and she hid it under a cushion.

The entire trip María's throat ached with loneliness. She felt the pressure of unexpressed grief behind each eyelid, eyelids swollen and stinging from the sand that penetrated the curtains of the litter. But María did not cry, because the first and only time she began to weep—unfortunately on the occasion of a ceremonial dinner—the minister of etiquette leaned forward, one eye made grotesquely large by the lens of his quizzing glass, and said, as Esperte translated, "Do not cry. Crying will bring you bad luck. If you cry for no reason, God will soon give you one."

"Shhh!" said Carlos's mother. "Why frighten the child any more than she is?" But the queen mother gave the princess a sharp look of disapproval even as she patted her hand. "Do not worry," Marianna said. "You shall be with Carlos before long." And Esperte translated this, along with the explanation that the king was in Toledo, attending the traditional prenuptial bullfights.

María stopped herself before the welling tears could fall down her cheeks. But perhaps she didn't catch herself soon enough, perhaps God had noticed. Perhaps it was He that made the wind blow so ceaselessly through the hills of Cantabria and over the plains of Castile, going from a sigh to a moan and then back to a sigh. Perhaps, once upon a time, the wind had cried for but a little reason, and then God had made him unhappy forever.

Beyond the litter's curtains, the bearers huffed, chuffed, stumbled, and occasionally even fell with exhaustion. As they approached their destination, the meeting of the king and his queen at Burgos, ministers set to waxing their mustaches and duennas occupied themselves with looking glasses and tweezers. María took advantage of everyone's distraction, once even daring to poke her head right out of the curtains, just as the litter wobbled past the lazy Arlanzón River. The water was green and choked by vegetation. On its oily surface, grasses rippled like the hair of a corpse caught in the rocks.

The nuptials were to take place in the cathedral at Burgos. Where else than in that greatest church in all the kingdom, and in whose shadow our town of Quintanapalla took refuge? But in the days preceding the ceremony the bishop of Burgos made as if to die; the court found itself without sufficient moneys to buy enough kindling to properly heat the cold interior of the great stone structure; the young king grew impatient for his bride; and María suffered a mysterious paralysis, a stricture which rendered her quite unable to move her neck and which confounded the court doctor traveling with them. At least, he said he was confounded, for it would have been too impolitic to voice his impression that the princess was stiff with fright.

A dying bishop, lack of money, an amorous king, a frozen princess. All of these and more were put forth as explanations for the very unlikely occurrence of the wedding of a king in Quintanapalla. For years, the townsfolk would talk of it, and these are the sorts of things they said. But none of these was the real reason.

Even then, so fearful were Carlos and his mother (and all the court) of a hex undoing the grand plan of the Hapsburgs, the wish that a prince be sired, and so determined were they that María get with child soon, that the royal family dared not allow the public spectacle of a state wedding. Crowds would offer too many hiding places for witches; and, as everyone knows, witches attend weddings for one purpose only: to cast spells on the secret parts of bride and groom. Obscured by a neighbor's back, hidden beneath a shawl or plunged into a basket, their profane, red-knuckled fingers would be busily twisting up lace knots, those infamous lengths of catgut, of horsehair, of wool, of linen, or of shining silk. Knots that, when tied during wedding vows, would sew up the mouth of the womb, shut it up as tight as a drawstring closes a purse, and prevent the unhappy couple from ever getting with child.

Of course, the villagers were not supposed to know of this hurried sacrament, for that would have defeated the very point of it, would have issued an invitation to local witches. The ceremony was to occur secretly in the hacienda of that obsequious, flattering, foppish hidalgo, Santiago, an estate owner whose not inconsiderable vanity was further swelled by such an honor. A very commodious and well-appointed structure was Santiago's home, and well built, better than most. But built of wood, not stone, it caught fire as the wedding party assembled. A spark dropped from a censer into a drapery, and instead of purifying that presumptuous building with the scent of the saints, it sanctified it utterly. There was a holy conflagration, a fire that was everywhere at once, licking at doublets and dresses, singeing feathered hats, tasting the possibilities of a silk cape even as it ate up the carpet and chairs. The wedding party ran outside and into the courtyard in full view of the townsfolk. We had gathered, of course, in clots of gossipers, fearful and conjecturing about the meaning of so many black carriages bearing the king's coat of arms.

"They must be burning a witch in there!" came the cry, as smoke began seeping out not just from the hidalgo's chimney but from all the windows as well. For it is not just the royal family who fears sorcery.

"Ten witches!"

"Fifty!"

Having decided on so dramatic a ceremony as that required for the punishment of fifty witches, the appearance of the shrunken king and his stiff-necked bride was a disappointment to their incidental audience. At least it was disappointing to those like my sister, Dolores, for whom the smell of a burned witch is the most exalted of perfumes.

The afternoon sky was bright. Clouds moved before the sun and then floated off, so that shadows of the wedding party appeared against a wall or a hedge and then just as quickly disappeared, giving the impression of some ghostly chorus of witnesses: playful spirits, one minute revealing their presence, then suddenly diffident and vanishing from where they had stood.

And among the onlookers, Francisca de Luarca, dressed in felt, dressed in linen, dressed in wool, shod in wood—not a thread of silk on my person—watched the wedding of my king to the princess from France.

I stood alone, without companions murmuring beside me, a woman of just eighteen, already accused of witchery, interrogated and warned by the Holy Office (though not yet were my crimes seen as connected to my mother, my mother was not yet viewed with suspicion). I was young to have arrived already at notoriety. I wore a *sanbenito*, a smock that hung down as far as my knees and covered my dress. On its yellow front was the double cross stitched in scarlet and accompanied by a quill and scroll, indicating an appetite for letters that had taken an unacceptable turn. It was joined by one other image: a breasted serpent, symbolical for lust. On the back of the smock, which I was not allowed to remove, even as I slept, a Devil fed a little woman to a flame with his pitchfork, lest those who could not read miss the point the Holy Office wished to convey: here is Francisca, suspected of heresies and under holy quarantine. Still, I was free then, I felt the air on my face. If I did not count myself among the happy, then I did not yet know how unhappy it was possible to be.

As for María Luisa, for her wedding day she was dressed,

decked, ribboned, corseted, sashed, shod, veiled, and plumed in unhappiness, just as surely as she was covered, every inch of her, in silk and gold and jewels. And her gown of misery was every ounce as heavy as her wedding dress.

His Majesty, King Carlos, stood beside María Luisa, holding her lace-gloved hand in his own. Behind them, on the hillside, grew fourteen rows of twenty mulberry trees, their yellow leaves burning bright, reflecting the autumn sun. As promised, over the years the trees my papa planted had thrived on nothing, had grown ever taller and more lovely in their natural symmetry. Uneaten by any worm, the useless leaves dropped onto the black earth like so many coins spilled there, the only riches we had. The queen of Spain was wearing silk, but not our silk.

She was young, she was my age. Though I well remembered my mother's letters, every word of every one of them, at that moment in the ceremony when the date of María's birth—the fourth day of February in the year 1662—was read from a scroll, I started. On that very-day, eighteen years previous, two female infants were delivered of their mothers: one in France, at a castle just outside the great city of Paris, and one in Spain, in the modest dwelling of a silk farmer in Quintanapalla. We each survived our births and the subsequent ills that take most children. We each budded in our time, surviving the so-called green-sickness that claims its tithe of virgins. And now here we both stood.

It was said that María was the most beautiful of all the princesses in Europe. Melancholy brown eyes, a long nose, a mouth whose Cupid's bow was well defined. White skin, a bit sallow, or perhaps just pale with fright; for every second that she breathed, every second from the moment she was betrothed and given by decree to Spain, Marie Louise, María Luisa, began to lose her life.

The princess had spent the morning before her wedding on her knees, saying over and over the one word she had promised herself to forget. *Maman,* she prayed again and again, forsaking God for a creature she loved better. *Maman, Maman. Je t'en prie.* I beseech you.

"Come," a maid-in-waiting said, and she held out her hand to

María. She spoke and the translator translated. "Your mother cannot hear you," the maid said. "Your mother is far away, and the ministers are calling. Come, you must get up now."

I saw her in Santiago's courtyard, and I took a mirror, a small round looking glass that I was in the habit of carrying in my hand, and I shined a circle of light, sent it bouncing over to her: her face, her eyes. What did she see? Nothing, perhaps. Nothing more than a little flash of light playing over her veil. She turned her head toward me, briefly, but still, she overcame her supposed paralysis. I shuddered. Her veil put me in mind of my mother's winding-sheets.

"They shall kill you, too," I whispered, and then I put my hand to my lips. I did not want to curse her. "Well, perhaps not," I lied.

Beneath that veil, before the consecration of the kiss, María had her brief spell of privacy, one of the few her new life offered. Naturally, she thought of her home. If she tried, María could recall the smell of the gardens in Paris. At her wedding, her hands were empty. *Is there not one flower in all of Spain? Not one for a bride?* she wondered.

She missed flowers—for ten years she would miss flowers, because Castile has few—just as she missed the ornamental lakes, gondolas so full of minstrels that they routinely sank, players wading through the chest-high water bearing viols and flutes and lutes and zithers, oboes and ophicleides, clarinets and pianettes, all overhead and well above the splashing water. Midnight suppers of oysters and ices and cakes. Childish games of romance played by all, even widowed comtes and comtesses—especially they!—crouching in their corsets until their faces were red and breathless, adding up the dots on dominoes to determine the recipient of a kiss. Dancing, of course: dancing on blisters and on blisters' blisters. And gazettes smuggled in by the maids and read under the counterpane, so that they caught the draperies on fire routinely. María missed everything, but she missed her mother and the flowers most of all.

Every year that he did not wage war on the Netherlands, Louis XIV imported four million tulip bulbs. Dutch tulips, and night-scented stock, daffodils, narcissus. Pear trees by the thousands dropping their white blossoms in a carpet over the lawns, a carpet so thick that it gummed up shoes and disrupted croquet as petals withered and stuck to the rolling balls and made a slippery paste on the ends of the mallets.

By the time the pears were ripe, summer had arrived on a wave of honeysuckle that broke cloyingly sweet over the château and her grounds. Even the industrious bees sank in the air. They flew in from the fields and gorged themselves on the king's flowers until their hind legs were lost under packed yellow plunder, until their flight degenerated into drunken, sinking spirals.

Was it possible that just last season María had been Marie, laughing with the other girls? Running through the long allées of maple trees, slipping beneath the canopy of leaves and into that mysterious, deep shade of summer afternoons. Tumbling on the grass and ruining silk dresses, staining them forever. The laundress sulked and scolded, the dressmaker came with his sleeves full of pins. There were always more dresses to be had, more summer days to squander on giggling. María began to weep behind her veil. Her plight was suddenly as clear to her as the action of a sandglass, future hope transformed directly to past regret. Unexpectedly, she found she knew what an old woman knows, that there is no present in which to take pleasure. That minutes are as two piles of coins: those spent, and those about to be spent. There is no other currency.

In Paris the perfume of the flowers had grown stronger and stronger until the kingdom reeled, and then, at the height of this orgy, ten ministers from Spain arrived. It was time to finalize a bargain struck years before. In exchange for certain diplomatic concessions amounting to an adjustment of borders, a loss of land, Spain would receive one marriageable, fertile, pure-blooded princess: an expensive girl, and a girl whose dowry of jewels and of silk was nothing against the hope of what treasure her body was expected to produce. The ministers from Spain brought with them a physician who examined those parts of the princess which most call secret, but which were to be secret no longer. When this doctor was satisfied that María could breed and could bear, then for one week the ministers met with King Louis in the morning. In the afternoons, they privately reviewed the progress of their talks as they walked in their black breeches through the gardens, watched the ladies promenade around the ornamental ponds. Watched the carp rise through the water, their greedy mouths imposing a pattern of endless O's upon its black surface. Watched an occasional bug skate across, each appendage dimpling the water's bright mirror. The French ladies peered into the ponds as well, and the water cast back at them their perfectly rouged cheeks under a blue cloudless sky. The ladies, Marie's mother among them, played cards under the trees, they ate tiny tartines, and when they could think of nothing other than lying down they returned to their chambers and slept away the afternoons so that they might be refreshed when it was fully dark and time to dance and gamble. The ministers from Spain, however, walked in the heat until they were exhausted, and then retired just as everyone else was getting up. They missed the midnight revels, the capsizing gondolas, the laughing and dancing and all the happy nonsense. But they would not have liked them, anyway. At the end of the week, meetings concluded to the satisfaction of interests both French and Spanish, the ministers took away a recent portrait of Marie Louise, along with a written promise that the princess herself would follow as soon as a proper trousseau could be collected.

What in María's old life could have prepared her for her new one? Everyone from Madrid wore enormous jeweled spectacles, an enhancement to dignity rather than eyesight, as the princess learned when she peered through a pair of *oculares* left behind at a banquet table and found that the lenses were of plain glass. Spanish ladies wore earrings that hung down as far as their shoulders, tiny clocks bobbing on the ends of gold chains where they could not even see them to read the time. And, while last season in Paris heels had been high, the Spanish nobility's desire for loftiness was so intense and so literal that aristocratic women balanced on stilts—the higher her rank, the greater the elevation from which she gazed. When María's lady-in-waiting brought her the bridal shoes in their mounts, the princess fell back on her bed, her hands to her mouth. "But what on earth are those!" she said.

Beneath her wedding gown (which weighed a stone at least),

beneath her thirteen petticoats and the hooped armature of wood and wire that held up the tower of fabric (another two stone), María rose above the bishop, who got a crick in his neck when he looked up to see the face of this newest and most reluctant lady of Spanish rank.

Had not such elaborate scaffolding forced her to remain upright, the princess felt she would have fallen down dead. But once she had her stilts firmly placed next to Carlos (who in his own elevated boots rose as far as her shoulders), María discovered she could relax a little, planted as she was in the sod like a fantastic jeweled umbrella. Perhaps this was the key to surviving the public functions of her new position: she would always seek out spongy ground.

On the banquet table, set under a canopy of royal purple, were twelve roasted peacocks, their feathered necks stretched prettily from their cooked breasts, their glorious tails reattached to their naked hindquarters, still smoking from the oven. They looked like a row of gargantuan ladies' fans shivering in the breeze. The food, carried from the hacienda, must have grown cold quickly, and the smell of burned, wet draperies—the fire having been extinguished with water saved in casks from the late storms—rose up the hill to the peasants watching there, dampening appetites aroused by the sight of so many delicacies.

After the servants had packed up the remains of the surprising feast (the vision of which, together with the wedding, was so unexpected that each witness must have questioned his sanity); after the last noble's carriage rolled out of view, the townsfolk of Quintanapalla ran down to the courtyard and searched the ground for any forgotten scrap. They took home stray peacock feathers as souvenirs, proof of the astonishing visitation, a wonder of which they would tell their children and grandchildren. Those feathers, having graced such an august occasion, would undoubtedly prove powerful amulets with which to ward off evil eyes. Indeed, such tail feathers looked like eyes themselves, each one like the oily eye of a courtesan.

I did not get one. It was understood that a woman in my position—a woman marked as a heretic by the Holy Office—had forfeited her right to press forward to claim any windfalls; and I had no desire to feel a stone in my face. Still, in the waning light of that strange day, after the crowd had dispersed, I walked the packed ground where the new queen's tables had been set. Like Thomas, that apostle of doubt, I pushed my finger into a hole, a puncture in the earth left by one of the queen's tall stilts. Yes, there was the proof, it had all really happened.

The wind picked up, tore at the trees on the hill, and the yellow mulberry leaves came down. They rained all around me like gold scattered in the wake of royal carriages, and I caught one from the air, I held it tightly in my hand.

The queen of Spain sees yellow. She presses the heels of her hands into her closed eyes, and she sees yellow circles falling like leaves. The sun has filled her room. She cannot delay consciousness any longer. *Where is the page on which the fate of every soul is written?* she thinks. And then she thinks, *Oh God, it is too early in the day for thoughts like that.*

She eats too much upon rising. Hot chocolate before she even creeps from between the covers and then pastries downstairs at table. Pride tarts, so called because their crusts are filled with air; and Saint Agatha buns, two small round loaves, each with a currant in its center and served glued together with honey or treacle, the sweet bread thus calling to mind the martyr's amputated breasts presented on their platter. María's dowry is long spent, and the kingdom is poor, shockingly so. No longer are *viandes* served at every meal, or even at any meal. No pheasant or fish steaming on silver-lidded chafing dishes. No eels, no venison, no lamb. No dates or any other imported delicacy. Only eggs and whatever can be fashioned from eggs and flour. When currants run out, the Agatha buns are served without nipples.

María leaves Carlos at table. He eats so slowly, she cannot sit forever waiting for him to finish—although she ought to wait with him through his breakfast even were it to last until dinner, or so the courtiers whisper behind her back. From the day they were wed, she ought to have sat and been glad to sit there beside him, his slack lips on the rim of his bowl, his fingers trembling as they held it to his mouth.

He lives on a child's diet of bread sopped in milk, this exalted monarch, on an invalid's meal that does not require him to chew anything with teeth so misaligned they do not allow his lips to meet. Not ordinary bread, though, but bread of the Eucharist, which Carlos himself watches as it is taken from the tabernacle, blessed and re-blessed. And not milk from a cow, but human milk, which—thank goodness—he takes from a cup. His sole smiles are wide and gummy, like an idiot's leer. His kisses unspeakable.

The first time she saw him undressed, she gasped, she could not help herself. Gasped and then pretended the noise she made was due to some other cause, a phantom cramp.

"Are you all right?" Carlos asked, in his terrible French. He moved toward her, naked, and she nodded, mute, speechless, her hand still covering her mouth. The ceremony was hours behind them, they were in Burgos, at an inn. Without clothes or cape to disguise it, his shambling walk looked worse, as if he thrust his head forward and the rest of him followed. Were he fat, he would look like a pigeon, but he was not, he was terribly thin, and white-skinned. The king was remarkable in his pallor, María had never seen any to equal it. His lips, even, were without color; and except for his knees and elbows, inflamed with a patchy red rash, he looked as if he had no blood in him at all. His testicles were small, and they hung low, like an old man's. Engorged, his organ was sickle-shaped and veered decidedly to the left.

The new queen had never before seen a man unclothed, but surely, she thought, surely, they did not all look like this.

The king undressed his bride shyly and slowly. He pulled at her corset strings as gingerly as if they were fuses, as if he were afraid she might go off like a firework. When he was finished, he took up a candle and held it so close to her breasts that she could feel the flame's heat. He said nothing. Then at last he said, "You look better with your clothes off." María did not answer.

He frowned, searching for the words he wanted. He shook his head, looked away, looked back, spoke. "I know that is not true of me," he said. María sat on their marriage bed and began to weep. If only he had not acknowledged his ugliness, then perhaps she might not have had to, not immediately anyway.

From the time of the marriage of Carlos and María, the king's potency was questioned by all of Europe. His amorousness, however, was unaffected by whatever physical incapacity he suffered, and his appetite for María did not diminish with the passage of time or the spreading of her flesh from that of lissome princess to fat queen. María did not return his desire, she never did, not from that first night when Carlos disrobed before her. In fact, in the first months of matrimony, even though she was well aware that she was to get with child, and quickly, the new queen tried to spend as many evenings as she could at card games.

Hoping to delay as long as possible the hour of wifely obligation, she remained cheerful under a barrage of criticisms from her new mother-in-law. Marianna was impatient with María's slowness to learn the rules of trocero and piquet. Or perhaps the queen mother was impatient with María Luisa in general, and with her failure to conceive, and her impatience found its expression in card games. Each evening as she shuffled the cards, Marianna interviewed her daughter-in-law minutely as to her health and diet. "Perhaps fewer fruit ices in the evenings," she would say. "They are chilling to the womb." She suggested clove tea, cinnamon, pepper creams and poultices: anything to heat the flesh. She dealt the cards with her wrists flicking furiously, sending them scattering over the game table. Her explanations of the games' various rules—in Spanish, translated to French by Esperte—were so fast that the younger woman could not follow them. And though Marianna wanted María to teach her fashionable French games like lansquenet, their rules, which María had mastered a season ago, jumbled senselessly in the young queen's head. It seemed not only that María could learn nothing new, but that she had forgotten all she had previously known.

Was she stupid? Was the new queen entirely, even willfully, naïve? Without betraying any worry, María began to misbehave. She did things for which she would not be forgiven. She made the wrong enemies. Some people do.

She cheated at the card games her mother-in-law took so seriously. "Do hurry," Marianna would say to her daughter-in-law. "We might as well not play if you are going to take so long." The queen mother fidgeted, sighed and fanned herself with her cards.

María's eyes were not weak but she squinted at whatever she had been dealt. She used to like cards, she had liked them in France. Liked the sound of her mother's expert shuffling and the way Maman's cool hands had restored order to the unruly pack. Cards with her mother had been fun, but here, whatever game they at last agreed to play lagged and dragged and lingered on, which was part of their purpose, she reminded herself, the strategy of delay. But even so, these games of chance could not protect the queen indefinitely.

As soon as Carlos began to fidget, Marianna urged María to go upstairs; and anticipating his new wife's avoidance of the last contest of the day, Carlos would begin yawning pointedly—and unattractively, but he could hardly help that—soon after dinner. By ten o'clock he would stand from the inlaid card table.

"I am going up to my apartments," he would say. "Would you like to accompany me, María?" Even if he spoke in Spanish, the queen did not have to look to Esperte for confirmation of what he said.

"Yes. I'll just finish this game," she would answer, avoiding his and the queen mother's eyes. Her skirts lay heavily in her lap, where she had hidden a card, an ace of hearts.

"I am going up to my apartments," Carlos said. "Will you accompany me?" Esperte translated his words in a whisper.

María murmured her acquiescence in French but did not look up from her hand. The jack was useless, she thought. Or was it? How could she possibly keep the rules of so many games straight? There were simply too many, and too many exceptions as well. No point in asking again. When Marianna got angry, her Spanish accelerated until it seemed to María that her mother-in-law's jaws were snapping like castanets. María sucked an errant black lock of hair that had willfully escaped her coif. What should she do? She had to go upstairs. She had to get with child. If only it would happen tonight—then she would be safe. For a year, anyway. God help her. Why could she not remember anything? It must be nerves. Was it only the king who was exempt from a trick, or the other face cards as well? She'd have to retrieve her ace now. But, no, she couldn't pick it up when her mother-in-law was looking so fiercely at her. Perhaps she should just play the jack. After all, what was another scolding from Marianna? "I'll just be another—" she began, but Carlos cut her off.

"I am going up now," he said. "Will you accompany me?" María looked up. He was displeased, his eyes narrowed and watered, squeezing out tears of pique.

"Yes. Of course, Carlos," she said. Now what was she to do? She couldn't return the ace, she'd have to let it drop under the table as she stood. María lay her cards, face down, on the gaming surface, and rose carefully.

"You play my hand, Esperte," she said. "Perhaps you will be lucky tonight." The hidden ace slipped down her skirt, over the toe of her shoe and onto the floor. Before the translator even approached the gaming table, Carlos's mother picked up the hand María had laid on the table and continued the game with her daughter-in-law's cards in her left hand, her own in her right.

As María left the gaming room she could hear the energetic click of spoons being stacked and restacked—for lack of coins they played with flatware—and the rustling sigh of cards being laid down. "Ah! She's won!" said Carlos's mother. "Or she would have, if she'd had the sense to play her hand as I just did. Which I very much doubt."

María paused in the hall, listening to her mother-in-law as Carlos ascended the stairs before her. When she tried, she could understand Spanish better than she let Marianna, or anyone besides the little translator, believe. "She would not have had the sense to play her jack," Marianna was saying. "She isn't her best with games of strategy." There was the sound of cards being shuffled, like a series of impatient snorts, but no response was audible. "Ah, what would you know, coming from a convent?" Marianna said to Esperte. Carlos climbed, his valet at his heels, and María hung back in the stairwell, her heart beating too loudly in her ears to allow much more eavesdropping.

"I'll just have a round of solitaire, then, if you're not going to play." A murmur from Esperte, only too glad to be excused, was obscured by the slap of cards on the table, as Marianna began to divide them into their suits.

"Why, there's no ace of hearts!" came the inevitable exclamation, and then the sound of silk skirts rustling, of chairs screeching back over the marquetry. Two pages and Esperte were ordered to search the room, and Marianna's heels made a cross, percussive sound on the boards beneath her shoes, as if she were punishing the floor for suspected complicity. María peeped around the corner to see Esperte's hips wedged under the card table, Marianna rapping them with her fan.

"Here it is!" the translator said, her soft voice further muffled from its origin under the table.

"By the breath of the Sainted Virgin!" said Marianna, snatching the errant ace. "This is the second time since she's come that we've found a card on the floor." She looked at it, turned it over in her hand. She turned it upside down and then right side up. "I believe she's cheating," she said at last.

A murmured response, a sigh, a cough, and the sounds of cards resumed. María scrambled up the stairs at the sound of Carlos's third call.

Eleven o'clock. Were she home in France, the night would just be starting. Aperitifs, then a midnight supper to which she had been looking forward, pheasant or duck or quail, so tender that the meat parted from the bones with a little sigh that was echoed in the contented sounds of diners. Instead, she had indigestion, the taste of eggs rising with each belch. Was it possible that in Spain they ate eggs every night? Lying on her back, she tried to remember the past week's dinners. Monday: eggs with coriander. Tuesday: eggs dropped in boiling soup stock so that the white threaded through each mouthful and hung from the spoon like strings of mucus. Wednesday: eggs with pickled turnips, a bilious combination served with a spiced condiment that made even her eyelids perspire as she ate. Thursday: a hard-cooked egg hidden, shell and all, in yellow bread dough and baked into a small round loaf, one on each plate. Now, who could imagine something like that? Her Uncle Louis's chef would have fainted, and swallowing hard-cooked eggs always made María's back hurt. She felt them descend slowly, like mouthfuls of clay. Friday: a soufflé in the shape of a fish. And then tonight's disaster, eggs *à la française,* an omelette in which strange little brown lumps were disguised. Lumps of what? Sausage? After chewing one, María had chosen to swallow the rest whole.

Throughout each meal Carlos peered over his bowl of milk-soaked body of Christ. María avoided the sight of his plate, conjuring as it did for her the vision of a corpulent, melancholy team of wet nurses voiding their dugs into a basin, making what living they could before they were inevitably dismissed (and on two occasions even put to death) for causing one of Carlos's myriad ailments.

In bed Carlos thrust at her, a motion accompanied by the sound of glass breaking.

"What is that!" Carlos said, but the queen only shrugged.

Upon learning that her husband had disallowed, by decree, the use of looking glasses in the palace, María had hidden all her hand mirrors between the mattresses. Carlos was afraid of his reflection, she guessed, of the revelation of his ugliness and frailty. Or he was worried about the possibility of a mirror breaking, about more bad luck and bewitchments, which—if one was superstitious, and she was—would follow from their having cracked one now.

His hands on her breasts, the king kneaded them like dough, first making as if to flatten them and then rubbing them around and around, as if trying to re-form them into balls. Such love-making might have made María laugh, in anyone but her husband. She could feel him hard against her leg, but he never made it up between her thighs before his excitement grew such that it came to its inevitable conclusion, wetting her legs and nothing else. He murmured, sighed and rolled over on his back. His avid attendance at so many bullfights, dog fights, cockfights, even bear fights did not inspire his own manly prowess. All his watching of cattle breeding and of his stallions taking their mares—his insatiable enjoyment of all manner of masculine display—taught the king nothing. Even the little cocks, who attacked each other's eyes with their painted, gilded spurs and who climbed flapping on the hens until they screamed, even a nine-ounce bird was more intelligently manly than the king of Spain.

"Have you had your . . . your things removed? All of them, I mean?" he asked. At least that is what she thought he wanted to know. Perhaps he wished to blame his failure on some obstructing, nonexistent undergarment.

Sometimes, even if María understood Carlos, she pretended she did not. Either that, or she pretended too great a modesty to allow her to answer even delicately posed questions. Any words she did not know she tried to commit to memory, and the following morning she would ask Esperte their meaning. For a girl interrupted en route to becoming a nun, the translator was surprisingly forthcoming.

Fortunately, as the nightly debacle was initiated only after the candles had been extinguished, María did not have to see Carlos's face, nor disguise her own torment. He sucked at her breasts, and the touch of his lips provoked such revulsion in the queen that she felt her scalp draw tight with rage. She found herself wishing that he would take his nourishment directly from his ridiculous wet nurses. Then perhaps he would let her nipples alone and engage in a more profitable activity.

But he did not, and before even a season of married life had passed, the queen despaired of the king's ever making her pregnant. Carlos never managed to get himself inside her, not the part of himself that would matter. He stuck his fingers in her, stuck them in without removing his rings and moved them around searchingly as if he were examining her prior to any more daring entry. But he did not once put his organ inside her. He sucked her nipples and he wriggled against her and sprayed semen over her thighs like a huge and gangling baby. He even mewed like an infant in her arms. The noises he made were useful in that they obscured the sounds of her weeping.

When she asked him to do it, when she whispered in halting, mispronounced Spanish, "Put it in"—"I think actually you said 'Put it on,' " Esperte told her the next day—when María gave her husband directions and tried to lead him, he went soft in her hand. He quit her bed and bedchamber.

AS IT A MEASURE OF OUR WICKEDNESS THAT
we preferred to do it on our knees?

The Church forbids us the posture of dogs,
of cattle.

The Church reserves our knees for sup-
plication. The Church requires that a man and woman face each
other, that they lie down together.

Did it make us that much more bestial that we could not see
each other's eyes or mouth, nor any feature that might separate
us from the animals? Our hairless skins.

On my knees I saw nothing. Eyes open, I looked forward into
darkness; I used my hands to support me. My hands held the
wall, the floor. Or I might close my eyes; I might duck my head
and go down, breastbone to floorboard.

If he pulled too far out of me, I protested. *Don't,* I said. I
wanted him in, further and further in and never out. Were I to
betray any pain, were I to whimper, biting my lip, he would
stop, and I would turn on him.

No! I would say.

But I cannot while I hear you crying.

I am not crying.

Sometimes he did not touch me at all—not with his hands.
Other times he might put both of them around my neck. I would
imagine him strangling me, then; it would have been easy
enough to do.

When I thought of this, I found myself surprised that the idea
did not trouble me.

HE FIRST TWO BABIES WERE BROUGHT TO OUR house in the week of the feast of the Annunciation, though no angel came to foretell of their arrival. Rather, a dirty man with a leather vest came to our house with a paper none of us could read and asked that my mother sign where he pointed. At his feet rested a large basket with a stout handle and two greasy little heads poking out, one on each side, from a tangle of swaddling that had once been white but now was covered with dust from the road.

Standing next to Mama and holding tight to one of her legs beneath her skirts, I looked at the babies. They were in bad need of a bath, they smelled, and their eyes were crusted shut. The man produced a bent goose quill from his pocket and dipped it into a small glass bottle of ink. According to this messenger, the contract, which bore at its head the insignia of the Monasterio de la Encarnación, said that in return for Concepción de Luarca's suckling these children, she would receive nearly two hundred maravedis per week per child, a sum sufficient to allow us to buy what we then, with no worms, no income, could not provide for ourselves. Like the rest of creation, we grew beans and raised pigs and could trade for our flour, our eggs and salt, but we needed candles, soap, we needed clothing and shoes, and we had almost no money for such things.

Mama did not set out to be a wet nurse, of course. She had had two children of her own, as well as her share of stillbirths and of children who had died in infancy. All boys, in answer to the Purple Hood's question. *Ahh,* he replies. "Nnnn Hnn." When he is thinking, he often puts his hands under his hood to rub his face.

A year after my birth, my mother had taken in a neighbor's child whose wife had died in childbed. It was easy enough to suckle two, Mama had said. My mother was small but she had a lot of milk, so much that she complained that the bodice of her dress was always wet, and her breasts, hot and as hard as bricks, ached.

After that first baby, Mama often helped to feed a child whose own mother was sick or hadn't enough milk. It was a thing she could do easily, nurse a child, and so she never stopped, her milk never dried up.

"What if someone falls ill?" she would say, more to herself than to anyone else. "What if some child's mother dies?" So when there was not some unfortunate babe in her arms, she kept herself flowing by squeezing her tits into a cup. I would catch her with her back turned, milking herself in the corner and then throwing the cup of cloudy, pale yellow liquid out the door. It made a little rivulet that ran quickly down the packed dirt path, as if hurrying away from our house and into the world. The milk was sweet, evidently, for ants came to drink of it.

In the four years since the death of my grandfather—four years since we were silk growers and relatively prosperous among the people of Castile—our silk house had stood empty. Papa sat in the same corner where his father had sat, but instead of looking upon the industry of the worms or, like my grandfather, closing his eyes that he might hear in their jaws the sound of rainfall, always so rare where we lived, Papa occupied his hands and eyes with the manufacture of whatever trinkets he could sell at market. Hair combs with each tooth painstakingly carved, and toys for children: wooden tops painted bright colors and balanced so well that on a flat stone they would spin for whole minutes, dolls with dyed hair of wool from the one sheep we kept for that purpose. And a little jointed man strung up between two sticks. When you squeezed the sticks he executed a series of little flips that had his legs folding over his face, a face that Papa had painted so carefully, each eyebrow arched with fear—that emotion perhaps occasioned by the toy figure's tenuous position in life, forever strung between two tight ropes.

Or maybe the doll's face expressed the fear that other faces would not. Not the usual fears that were always with us: of plague, of drought, of poverty, accident, of bad luck and evil eyes. No, the greatest fear in those years of my childhood, a fear not spoken, a fear I sensed before I could name, was of Inquisition. For a small town, Quintanapalla received an unequal measure of attention from the Holy Office, undoubtedly an accident of geography, as Quintanapalla lay along the road between Madrid and Burgos, two bastions of the Church, and suffered the constant traffic of Church officials, who were always looking out for another sinner to feed to the insatiable prisons, another mouthful of fines to pour into the holy coffers.

One spring, two houses—the house of the mason and that of his retired father-in-law—were emptied in the night, their inhabitants collected from their beds. One day they were there, and the next they had disappeared, empty shoes lined up outside their doors. It had long been feared that the mason, flagrant in his refusal to observe holy days of obligation, would attract unwelcome attention, but no one had imagined that his wife, her aged parents and young children would also be taken.

I walked with my sister past little Antonia's empty house and I saw her blue shoes there, also empty, and whatever sympathy I had for her was tainted by my desire for those ownerless blue slippers with a bright tapping silver cover on each toe. I stopped to stare, clearly acquisitive, and my sister tried to pull me on down the street.

"Look there!" I said to frighten her. "There is Antonia standing in her shoes and she is covered in blood and her hair is on fire!"

Dolores dropped my hand and ran home, and I crept forward and took the little slippers, something no one else in Quintanapalla would have been so brazen as to do. But the street was deserted, and I wanted those shoes. I kept them hidden in the silk house, and I wore them when no one else was around. The lie I had told to frighten Dolores affected me, though. I could not wear the shoes without imagining my own hair catching fire, and eventually I threw them into the pond.

It was said in those days that children taken into the care of the Holy Office were not sent to asylums but were forced to join the ranks of a children's crusade. Each year an army of Holy Innocents, as the forcibly rehabilitated little sinners were called, was dispatched south to the Moors in hopes that God would be sufficiently touched by our country's proselytizing zeal to once again smile on Spain, now generations past her Golden Age of military triumphs and colonial wealth. Well, whether God cared or not for the Innocents' Saharan fate, the Church's disposal of them was pragmatic: the children perished and removed the need to feed and clothe them.

The years after the failure of our worms were drought years in Castile. Our small garden dried up, we had only a few onions to show for our trouble, and we grew sick of thin soups flavored with nothing more than a sliver of salted pork.

Plague as well as famine emptied half the houses of Quintanapalla. Persons whose faith was strong said it was God's right to watch or not watch over the people, and only He knew why such blights came upon the faithful. And those whose faith was weak, if they were smart they kept their mouths shut, lest the black carriage of the Inquisition come silently one night to take them away to a place where they would be encouraged to voice their opinions to a scribe.

We heard rumors that in Madrid whole quarters of the city were abandoned to the plague. The rich people left first, piling whatever they could into their carriages and whipping their horses north to where the air was better. Whatever beggars still lived moved into the empty houses of rich men, ate cured meats from their plates and drank wine from their cellars, only to die weeks later in their beds.

The dreaded white avenues of death. My mama's papa had briefly held the job of spreading lime in the gutters of cordoned-off streets. A soap maker by trade, his business evaporated when plague came, people foolishly caring more for godliness than cleanliness. "Wash yourselves!" he would yell at people in the plaza. "Save yourselves!" But the people hurried past, his wares went unsold, and he was forced to hire himself to the city of Madrid, which paid him well for his work. There was a choice of occupations offered by the desperate city: to spread lime from a cart, to ride a donkey and check the cordons blocking off diseased areas, or to go on foot catching the contaminating rats with a prong and dropping them dead or as good as dead into a wheeled barrel of vinegar. My grandfather determined that the farther he was above the dirty streets the safer he would be, so he signed on as a lime thrower and he stood up on the driver's seat of the lime cart. Every night he washed himself with his own soap, as much as four times from head to foot, but still, he died after a few months, black spots like coins—the Devil's currency—all over his limbs. He took handfuls of lime from the sack and rubbed it on his skin until he burned as if he were in hell already, but it did no good.

Plague ravaged all of Castile, and the death of so many workers meant that fields and fields of wheat rotted. Flour costs rose so high that for the first time in Dolores's and my remembrance we found ourselves hungry at night—not so much that we starved, but when we lay down in the dark we felt empty and when we slept we dreamed of eating.

My papa came home one evening from the market and set his basket of toys on the hearth. "Concepción," he said, and he went to my mama; and when she turned around he put his large hands on her cheeks and held her lovely face between them. "Concepción, I have been with Enrique, and he has told me how their family gets by with Ilena now taking in children from the orphanage in Madrid. She suckles foundlings, and the family gets good money for their care."

Sweat made a dark shadow around the brim of Papa's hat, and he smelled of wood smoke and the Portuguese wine he drank with Enrique. My mama's black eyebrows came together as she waited to hear what else he would say. She took his hands from her face and she held them as she looked at him.

One after another, things had gone wrong for my papa. To discourage evil spirits, we slipped charms under his pillow at night as he slept, we filled his shoes with clover. But nothing helped. His fortunes had turned sour, perhaps, Mama said to us, because he had not respected his father. Not long before, our last pig had escaped into the woods, and while trying to chase it home, Papa had been treed by wolves eager to make dinner of both him and the pig.

After watching the wolves eat up our winter provisions, Papa hung in the tree all night; he stayed there long after the pig's last screams, too frightened to move even though the wolves grew bored with waiting for him to climb down and wandered off. Papa remained hanging in the tree until his nerves were permanently affected, shriveled, as he described the feeling, by exhaustion and fright. The only relief he got, he said, was from the bottle. His hands shook badly, then, so badly that it took a good deal longer for him to make his toys, and he could not paint such engaging little faces on the dolls and soldiers as before, and so he sold fewer of what had become more difficult to make.

"Concepción," he said to Mama, "you could do that. You could take in a foundling or two," and she looked at him. What he was asking was different from taking in a child as an act of charity. To hire herself out, that would be a shameful thing, possibly. Something that might lower the family and jeopardize her daughters' chances to marry well. Mama looked at Papa, she said nothing but she let go of his hands and she sat on the bench by the hearth. I knew that she was figuring in her head the few coins she got for eggs and how they disappeared before she ever had enough to buy Dolores or me a pair of shoes. She didn't answer Papa's question that night, or for two days more. At supper, on the third night, she set a poor soup on the table and Dolores and I made faces as we dipped our spoons in. We made noises of disappointment, we sighed. She looked at us. "All right, then, Félix," she said and she nodded at Papa and he looked down at his plate.

She took in two and then three at a time, she had such abundance, it was like children's stories of cups that never were emptied, bowls of porridge that overflowed. These are the tales that hungry people favor, of course, but it is not just the twist of my memory, the same that makes childhood hay lofts seem as vast as ballrooms, no, Mama did have a genuine gift as a wet nurse.

We did not find this ability surprising, for we all knew of Mama's generative powers. She made us, and gave us suck; and she had given the silkworms their life, too, keeping the eggs safe in the holy warmth bounded by those two warm globes of what, it seems to me now, was love. The silkworm eggs had ridden about where I wished to be, nuzzled as Mama walked, the quiver of her flesh calling the worms to *Awake! Awake!* just as now her body said to the orphans, *Sleep. Eat. Grow.* Mama had that kind of flesh—and soul; she gave what was needed.

I was a girl of nine. I had not yet taken my first communion, my portion of the body of Christ, but I was old enough for chores, which I did quickly so as to be done with them. And I was young enough that I yet preferred my mother's company to that of anyone else. I liked to stay at her side, to watch as she sat with one of the babies by the fire. Sometimes her milk came down so hard that the suckling coughed and pulled away from her nipple, which was dark and lovely and so big that it looked to me like a fruit separate from the rest of her. A fine spray of milk would arc into the light from the fire, and I would see how it fell on the baby's head or right past the baby and onto the hearthstones, where it evaporated in an instant from the heat, as if it were a magic substance and not one to remain before mortal witness. If I was fast enough I could trace my finger through the steaming drops.

It was lazy and warm and safe by the fire, the orange light made us as rosy and pretty as ladies in paintings, and the babies' dark greedy eyes stole sparks from the flames. The milk, too, came into the corners of their little sucking mouths and shone in the light. The babies' eyes rolled up into their heads in delight as they suckled, and sometimes I wouldn't be able to stand it, just playing quietly with a doll at my mama's feet. In mimicry I held the doll to my own flat chest, but then I flung it away and jumped up from the warm stones, trying to force my jealous head between my mother's breast and the babies' busy mouths. Afraid, I guess, that they would eat her up and leave nothing for me.

Does love bring out the good in some people? It always seems to have made me my worst. I began to hate the babies for taking away my mother's attention. l began to wish them ill.

One day Mama left me with a sleeping child. She went to market with Dolores and asked me to stay behind and watch the baby. I played for some minutes on the hearth. I lined up broom straws. I took a bit of cheese from the larder and with it tried to catch a mouse. I looked in my sister's little wood box and touched all the things she would not let me touch. And then I drew near to the cradle by Mama's bed.

The baby was sleeping on her back. Air whistled softly through her nose. Her lips—still shaped in a greedy O—moved as if she suckled even in her sleep. I did not approach the cradle intending the child harm, but I found myself pulling the cover up over her sucking lips and whistling nose. I watched for a minute as the baby's breath made the cloth quiver. Then I put my hand over her face, and I did not take it away, not even when I heard a voice in my head—Mama's!—say to me, "What are you doing!"

But then the baby moved, and the feeling of her struggling beneath the cloth was an awful squirming that I had felt once before, when Dolores and I had trapped a mole under one of my mother's aprons. Suddenly I saw that mole, dead, and it frightened me so that I jumped back, away from the cradle. When my mother and sister returned, the child was screaming, and I was curled miserably in the opposite corner of the room.

"What's happened!" Mama said. At her side, Dolores looked smugly innocent.

I did not admit what I had done, for my sin was so dreadful I was afraid confession might result in the very thing that had led me astray; I was afraid Mama would stop loving me. So, I kept my torment to myself, and soon an outraged infant joined the ranks of those who peopled my dreams. Her cheeks were red and fat and filled with fear and condemnation; and my shame was such that whenever I saw her I covered my eyes. I tried to hide, for now my dreams had turned on me.

Meanwhile, the one surviving son of King Philip of Spain, Carlos, was taken with another of his everlasting illnesses. A sickly child from birth, his health was deemed even more precarious than that of the older Prince Baltazar, who had died the previous year. Though Prince Carlos was the same age as I, he was not yet weaned. An infirmity in his legs, aggravated by troubles with a delicate digestion, meant that this boy of nine years was still carried in arms and still attended by a veritable army of wet nurses, their court-appointed position representing the highest honor for a woman of my mother's new vocation. As King Philip was too ill to sire another child, it was essential that his one remaining heir survive.

Mama smelled so good. She was clean, she washed herself. She never had the sour smell of some wet nurses. The children she suckled, who arrived sickly and small, bloomed and grew at an enormous rate. They came scrofulous, they came with fevers and boils and eyes sealed shut under crusted scabs. They arrived still and cold in their rags, only their mouths moving, sucking and sucking at their wizened thumbs. A month or two with Mama and the babies were saved, their rashes and fevers and discharges all banished. They smiled and laughed, their bellies were round, sickness did not take even one of them. The following spring, the orphanage requested that my mother be installed in Madrid; they wanted to take her away from us and have her all to themselves.

But, instead, with her growing fame as a curer of children, Mama took in the child of the duque de Pastrana, a wrinkled weasel of a baby whose little blue fingers grasped at my mama's neck and left red marks there. As soon as she arrived, her screams filled our house and kept us awake for six nights straight. But the money was good enough that we all had new dresses and ate meat from the butcher's—no squirrel or rabbit for us—and on the seventh day the infanta settled into Mama's side and stayed quiet there. Mama went about her chores, she carried Mercedes in a shawl tied around her shoulder and left her dress unbuttoned, her tit exposed. The baby suckled all day and all night, and how I hated that, but within a fortnight she was not so ugly a child. The following month when the duque's servant came to check on her progress, only a distinctive mark on Mercedes's forehead (one that all the duque's family bore) proclaimed that the child was the same as the dying brat he had left with us. The report was made: Concepción de Luarca was blessed with a holy milk, and it was not long before this was known by all the Spanish court, including Queen Marianna, one of whose ladies-in-waiting was the duque's sister.

Now, the crown prince Carlos Segundo had, by that spring of his ninth year, used up two hundred wet nurses, all of whom had conformed to the royal standard written in a book containing the wisdoms of the court obstetrician and bound in blue leather. I saw this book myself (and read it years later), because Mama was issued a copy of it and two other medical texts and later brought them home with her. A royal wet nurse must be not less than twenty years old nor more than forty. She should have borne two or three children of her own. She must be healthy, of good habits and of a good size. Of course, she must be chaste, modest and sober without being subject to fits of melancholy. There must be no Jewish or Moorish blood in all her ancestry.

To administer the last of these tests—Mama had passed all the rest—an old crone was employed by the court physicians. Her name was Constanza, and she had a wig made of alpaca to cover her bald head. When the powers came upon her, she told my mama, all her hair had dropped out with fright. To make her prophecies, this seer consulted an ancient book of curlicued Arabic writing. Although she could not read the strange and foreign letters, they helped her to see the truth of things, or so she said. Of course, such writings were condemned by the Church, and an ordinary person would be burned for their possession, but Constanza was kept free of the prisons and never examined by any Inquisitor, and this was because she had the power to smell the blood of infidels, especially Jews.

Now that she is so old she is almost dead she is retained by the Inquisitor General. She goes bald because she is too weak to hold up her head under its wig, and she is fed the food of Saint John the Baptizer, honey and specially raised locusts. Her advice is sought only in the most stubborn of cases. They took me to her just last month, and she passed her great, quivering nose over my neck and into my armpits and behind my knees. No introductions were made, but I knew it was she, for I remembered my mother's telling me that when she arrived in Madrid she was presented naked before an old woman who picked up each of her tits, holding the nipple between gloved thumb and forefinger, and she looked underneath and smelled the fold of skin there. And she smelled her undergarments and her more private places as well. In this way, Constanza determined if there was even a little drop of Jewish blood in a person's heritage. But she found none, not in either Mama or me.

After all inquiries were made, after Mama was summoned to the court for a week and then returned to us for a fortnight, we received notice that her services were commandeered to suckle the child, His Royal Highness, Prince Carlos. My mama was collected by the royal carriage and taken to the palace in Madrid, where some three dozen substitute nurses were kept handy in case of emergency—for almost anything could indicate the advisability of a change. By the time Carlos was weaned at age twelve (weaned from the tit but not from its product) the palace had employed three hundred and ten wet nurses. How many of those actually gave suck to the king, I could not say, but any upset, no matter how distant from the prince's delicate digestion—from a pimple on his ass to a chill in his knee—was apt to be blamed on his current nurse, so it was not a job without worry. Mama had never given a thought to what she ate or how she slept, but, under the direction of the court physician, Mama's meals were restricted to unseasoned gruel, to lamb and to eggs and to that part of the neck meat of a bull that is said to make flesh strong and regal. They lifted up her skirts to see if she had her monthly flow, there was fuss and interruption without cease; and her milk, with so many annoyances, could not have been as good as it was at home.

I missed my mother when she was gone, but then it was peaceful, a relief, really, to be rid of the babies, and thus of my guilt and jealousy. And, too, Mama had become increasingly thin and distracted when she was nursing the future duquesa. Her temper had grown short, she laughed less often, and when she did the sound she made was easily confused with crying or coughing. Before she left, she smoothed our hair behind our ears. "Be good, Dolores and little Francisca," she said. "Cause no trouble to your papa."

The money she earned came routinely, delivered four times a year by a man dressed in palace livery. Quite a lot of money, it seemed to us: fifteen gold pieces in a little black kid bag whose cords were kept tied by a squashed red berry of wax stamped with the king's seal. Papa bought Dolores a doll with a china head and he gave to me a little necklace of red stones. He took to smoking the same tobacco that his father had smoked, and it hung sweet and blue over our heads after supper.

HEN THE GROOM CAME TO THE QUEEN'S room, the winter sun had risen just high enough that the draperies were outlined in silver. By the orders of the court physician, Severo, the queen had been given nothing to eat since the fall from her horse, only barley water, and she was dreaming of all the foods that she most liked and had not eaten in the years since her arrival in Spain. She closed her eyes against the sun and let them wander under their lids. Her fingers twitched slightly, as if she were trying to hold on to something being drawn from her grasp. The groom waited, and when the queen stirred, her maid Obdulia nudged him, and he held up a long switch of brown hair.

María said nothing, but *How pretty!* she thought, and she remembered the long fall of hair that she had worn as a girl, when dressed for a dance. Her hair had grown so quickly and so thick that she had had it cut one hot summer, so that it had hung only as far as her waist rather than to her knees. Her nana had saved the cut hair so that she might pile it that much higher for the following winter's balls. Or she could let a long plait hang forward over one shoulder, its last curl dipping coquettishly into her décolleté. She could have it crimped, ironed or waved. She could tie it with ribbons or catch it up in a chignon. Oh, there were a thousand ways to wear such a switch of good hair, her nana said, and it was sent in a box to the seamstress, who gathered it at one end and stitched it so tightly together that it would never come apart. It was put safely away in her dressing chamber, where it lay coiled in a velvet-lined cedar chest. Each week, whether she had worn it or not, her maid brushed it out and laid it away again in its powdered chamois cloth. When María came to Spain, she had brought it with her.

The queen held her hand out to the groom and beckoned him toward her. How odd that Ignacio should bring her hair to her. She couldn't have left it at the stable. She rarely wore it, and never to ride. She did not have a life of such festivity any longer that she needed extra hair to pile up, and that reflection made her feel like weeping. That was the trouble with opium, it made her as sad as it did happy. But why did Ignacio look as if he were crying as well, his eyes swollen and red-lidded? And little Esperte, standing in the doorway, her brown eyes were spilling over down her pale cheeks.

María beckoned to Ignacio again, and the groom stepped toward her bed. The hair he held was gathered at one end, but instead of binding to keep the strands together, María saw that there was blood there, dark and clotted, and the long chestnut switch smelled of the stable.

The queen looked into her groom's eyes, and knew what it was he held out. She might as well have seen Rocinante, his neck slit just minutes after his last bucket of oats held for him by Ignacio. Slit so deep that a mouthful of red-stained grain came out with his good, faithful blood, spilling down in a curtain, darkening his coat and making a red lake of his loose box. His beautiful white-blazed forehead sinking like a falling star, the white stockings suddenly crimson. His lovely, great, wet eyes looking in confusion at the groom, who, sobbing, had cast the blade into the straw and fallen to his knees in his charge's blood.

Ignacio had not let anyone else carry out the king's terrible order; he had trusted no one but himself to be sufficiently merciful, to kill the animal manfully, to cut deep and fast. So, like an overzealous lover, the groom had thrown himself at the horse's neck and stabbed him in a clumsy last embrace. Rocinante's legs buckled in a moment, and as the animal sank to his knees, the groom reached out for him. They lay down in the straw together, Ignacio's arms around the huge, warm neck, his breeches stiffening with the beast's still-flowing blood.

Lying in her bed, her fingers caught in Rocinante's tail, it was as if María heard her horse's hooves in the acceleration of her heartbeat, steady and drumming faster. Saw herself on his back, the two of them growing smaller, more distant, the whisk of his tail as they disappeared around a hedge together.

"No!" she screamed. *"No no no."*

For María Luisa, who married the king whose life my mother had saved, the days in the royal residence had passed, one after another, with the same heartless monotony as the meals. A year went by, two years, three and four.

It was because the queen was bored, I imagine, that she made the mistake of forgetting the minister of etiquette's most oft-repeated advice, to *watch* herself. Her strategies at the games of court were worse even than at those of cards, if she could be said to have anything as sophisticated as a strategy. María could no more remember whose favor it was important to curry, whose protection was essential, than she could whether aces were high or low. If her detractors—and there was no shortage of them, according to my prison neighbors—could agree on anything, it was that it was hard to believe that the queen had been raised at Versailles; for this was a place that to the Spanish imagination was built as much of intrigue, both romantic and political, as of bricks and mortar, a palace gilded more by flattery and pretense than by precious metals.

Inauspiciously, María made a fast friend of the court jester, a dwarf of the grand old line of dwarfs from Peñarroya, that lead-mining city where each family could boast an idiot or two, a limbless prelate or a raving baker, twelve-toed tanners, blind chandlers and salivating spurriers with spittle-flecked lips hanging loose and wet. Why, the people of Peñarroya were so thoroughly poisoned that a normal birth was a remarkable occurrence, and sent everyone scurrying to the church to give thanks, not only relatives and friends but every citizen who heard tell of the miracle.

Unnaturally diminutive, Eduardo Zarragoza was the sole child of his mother to have been born with his heart on the inside. All his other brothers and sisters, both before and after him, were buried in a single grave, which was reopened at the terrible conclusion to each of his mother's confinements, reopened to receive into its depths another tiny corpse with its heart hanging like a strawberry on the outside of its ribs. Like some terrifying, catechizing painting come to life, the little bleeding hearts beat but once or twice in the cold air of earthly incarnation.

Eduardo was happy to come to the court in Madrid when he was fifteen and there join the palace freak show. It was nothing like the one María had known at Versailles, where the Sun King's eclecticism gathered all manner of unusuals. King Louis had only one bias—a fondness for multi-breasted virgins, their little tits lined up and trembling under his august attention like those of nursing cats: two, three, even four pairs ranged down a gauze-draped abdomen. But these were merely the crown jewels, so to speak, of the French collection, an army of entertainers that required its own 117-room dormitory on the opposite bank of Versailles's ornamental lake, a low building just hidden by the birch grove. Unlike the French, the Spanish are not generalists; their passions are narrow, fixed, unswerving. They favored dwarfs to the point that the royal family collected no other miscreations, and Eduardo had made the seventh of seven.

He suffered migraines, all the dwarfs did, and the queen mother doled out headache powders and laudanum each week. The supply of pain medications to the dwarfs was contractual. It allowed for crooked spines and bandy legs to cut capers, turn cartwheels, and it encouraged mirth over melancholy, courage over cowardice. For the laudanum, dwarfs sought out palace employment. More than an addicting drug, it was a change in unhappy perspective, a miniature revolution: seven lives made bearable.

Each week they went to Marianna—Eduardo and Pedro and Domínguez; Escobar and Diego Valdéz and Diego Zarragoza (a cousin of Eduardo) and Juanito (another from Peñarroya). Not to Dr. Severo, the palace physician, but to the queen mother, for Marianna wanted the dwarfs to feel that measure of loyalty to her and to her alone. She wanted them to think of her as the one who relieved their suffering. After all, she needed to be somebody's saint, and more, she insisted on some measure of control over every member of the court, and laudanum was her lead rein over the dwarfs. So each Sabbath after they had remembered her pleasingly at vespers, Marianna received the dwarfs in the west wing's audience chamber, where she sat in her black gown, her soft chin folding over its collar, the beads of her rosary spilling from her lap, and she called them one by one, alphabetically, and they came forward. They kneeled before her and she gave them each the little paper of headache powders (which, useless, they discarded immediately) and the vials of laudanum (which, priceless, they guarded more carefully than they would have coins, were there any coins to be had).

Of the dwarfs, only Eduardo was not addicted to the opiate. No, by the fifth year of her reign, it was María who depended upon his ration, who waited for it each week, her sleeping draft. Her sleeping eating talking laughing breathing draft. The queen and her dwarf—for by then that was what Eduardo was called: *her* dwarf—had places where they met, a different one each week. They passed in a hallway, by the grotto, the map room, the reliquary. He dropped his vial into her hand, her muff, the top of her riding boot.

Laudanum was what allowed the queen, month after month, to bear the strain of her now famous, if only assumed, infertility. To permit, without screaming, the humiliation of having her private parts made public. Of Dr. Severo taking samples of her monthly flow, of his plucking out pubic hairs for alchemical study, of his washing her thighs, her bottom, her every crack and intimate fold of flesh with stinging solutions of astringent herbs meant to increase the sanguinary circulation.

Why, the application of a few drops of laudanum made it possible to lie still under Carlos's repeated attempts to get her with child, attempts now witnessed by physician, by confessor and even by the occasional expert called in for consultation.

"He is doing it correctly," Severo always concluded, for who could criticize a king's lovemaking and remain confident of keeping his head?

"Yes, but are you praying as you do it?" asked the king's confessor.

Experts nodded, mumbled, squinted, then retired to the guest apartments to write unintelligible reports.

Bobbing on a narcotic tide of tolerance, María worried that Severo would notice her wide-pupiled eyes, but the physician was so completely focused on her failure to procreate—a failure that threatened his position almost as much as hers—and so intent on his examination of her nether parts; and, perhaps, so embarrassed by the requirements of his profession, that he never looked above María's neck to those eyes, eyes as wet and as wide with grief as with laudanum.

In the only privacy Queen María had—that is, when she relieved herself—she would unstop the little vial and peer into its blue glass throat as she sat on her commode. She carefully administered the opiate drop by drop onto her tongue.

Each vial of laudanum contained exactly and invariably seventy drops: ten for each day of the week. If a certain day required more—the day of an audience, a festival or some other long torment—then María made sacrifices to accommodate that occasion, the day preceding or the day following one of necessarily restricted solace.

"That old beetle!" Eduardo called Carlos's mother. Always wearing black mourning—Carlos's father had been dead for fifteen years, but she found it suited her mood—Marianna's shiny-tight bodice of iridescent silk shimmered green in some lights, blue in others; and when her feet in their heeled slippers made their clicky-clicky sound; and when, as she had a nervous tendency to do, she scuttled down corridors and disappeared into doorways; well, it all conspired to make Marianna seem to the fanciful queen and her friend like a great beetle hunting smaller prey throughout the palace. Behind the queen mother's back, Eduardo would wiggle his short fingers over his head, affecting antennae to make María laugh. Foolishly, she sometimes did. Even more foolishly, as the years wore on, and as the queen never bore any children who might have satisfied her playful nature, Eduardo and María began to play other tricks as well.

The queen mother was superstitious. She kept a little shrine in her room where she kneeled before the Virgin and told her her troubles. One afternoon, when Marianna was closeted in another wing with the ministers of finance—a monthly meeting whose purpose was to undo those disasters that Carlos weekly wrought—María crept into her mother-in-law's room with Eduardo. Together they looked at the little Virgin of Sorrows.

"Do you suppose the effigy answers her?" said María.

Eduardo smiled. "We could see that it did," he said.

"Yes," María said, eyes shining. "It would almost be a favor, would it not? Think how happy the beetle would be that the Queen of Heaven had time for the queen mother of Spain!"

A master of ventriloquism, the dwarf could project any voice at any pitch. Even a celestial-sounding one was not beyond his abilities. Later that day he hid himself under the bed, beneath the counterpane dragging on the tiles, and when Marianna asked the Virgin for her guidance that evening, he gave it. The Virgin's voice sounded sweet and lilting as she suggested to Marianna that she cut off all her hair and eat nothing but raw white of egg for nine days, as a sign of devotion.

The next day, Carlos's mother's hair joined the piles of long plaits and the masses of curls at the cool marble feet of the Virgin in the national cathedral. When times were bad, devotion increased, and already that season the church caretaker had made three trips down to the little room below the nave where he deposited such tokens of affection: Crates of hair and sacks of hair. Silk wigs, too, barrels of them. Walking sticks and shoes, spectacles, jewels, capes lined in fur. All left for the Virgin, that she might, with such evidence of faith, shape a happier world.

At supper that night, María tried to avert her eyes as Marianna struggled with the clear, viscous matter in her bowl. It slithered once and then again from her spoon. For a moment María contained herself, but such control depended upon her not looking at any other face at table. When she saw Carlos's puzzled countenance she began to laugh.

"What is that, Mother?" he said. María put bread in her mouth and choked on its crumbs. Once she began to laugh, her mirth so intoxicated her that her scalp prickled, her cheeks flushed red. She could not stop. Her buttons popped and her stays flew apart, she wept and wheezed with glee.

The queen's behavior was diagnosed as hysterics. She was

sent back to her rooms, and Dr. Severo came and dosed her with cathartics until she was too weak to laugh anymore.

Eduardo came to visit her, clambering into the chair by her bed. He looked very grave. "We must be more careful," he whispered. "In the future I shall not let such silliness carry me away. I apologize to you."

"Oh, I don't care!" the queen said aloud. "It was worth it!"

"Shhh," he cautioned, and he pointed at the maid standing by the door, her ears sticking pink and eager from under her cap. María paid no heed.

He sat silently by her bed. "I shall be very lonely," he said at last.

"Lonely? What do you mean?"

"Because you will be sent back to France, if you are not careful."

"Oh!" she cried, sitting forward, the bedclothes falling immodestly about her. "Do you think I could do something so dreadful that I would be sent home?"

He looked at her. "No," he said at last. "You would only be sent home if that is where the courts of both France and Spain agreed you were to be buried." They were silent then, he looking out the window, she looking at him.

"María," he said at last. "It is getting worse. The talk in the kitchen today was of nothing else." He examined his fingernails, his overly large head lowered in concentration, his abbreviated arms bent in an uncomfortable-looking angle that called attention to his short-fingered hands. Eduardo's bowed legs ended in small, delicate feet, which he kept expertly and extravagantly shod. He was vain about his pretty feet, and about his large expressive eyes with their brows arched high.

"What do they say?" María asked.

"That you are barren, and—"

"I am not barren! No woman in my family was barren, no—"

"No, of course not." He smiled. His red lips were framed by a well-barbered beard. "But it is either your fault or the king's that you have no heir. And given that choice, who do you think will be blamed?" María was silent. She folded her arms.

"You know that if Spain is not to succumb to France and lose what little power remains to her, she must have a healthy male heir to her throne. And whether or not you find politics a bore, you cannot afford to ignore them." Eduardo whispered, but his voice was adamant.

"Do you not see," he said, "that if it is officially decided that you are responsible for the lack of issue—and we are almost at that point—then you will be eliminated?" He sat forward. "Do you not understand what that means, María? You will go mad, perhaps, and have to be locked up. You will be declared consumptive and sent off to the Alps. You will succumb at last to despair, and when days of weeping go uninterrupted by a smile, you will be examined by experts and exorcised, or worse.

"You will, perhaps, be poisoned."

María looked out the window at the cheerless gardens, unrelieved geometries of box hedges, one plant pruned into a wall enclosing another and another, nature forced to express endless confinement. "Oh that," she said, attempting ironical cheer, but the words came out too high. They both fell silent remembering a severe and unexplained illness she had suffered the previous season.

"You will be sorry, will you not?" she said to him after a moment. "A little inconsolable?"

The dwarf sighed, he looked at the ceiling. Sitting back in his chair, his legs stuck out absurdly. Only the dwarfs' apartments had chairs and beds and tables scaled to their size. In the rest of the palace they had to adapt, and the queen's furnishings seemed to mock Eduardo's somber mood, making dignity impossible. But, in truth, grief does not suit dwarfs, they are hampered by always appearing comical.

"Eduardo," María said, and she held out her arms to him, as if she were a child and he her shrunken father. "I know I am vexing. How tired you must be of trying to educate me."

The dwarf sighed again. He got down from his chair and came to María's side, he let his head rest on her bed.

Eduardo found his mistress mysterious. As a man whose sole genuine talent was for survival—all the double-jointed, voice-throwing stunts were mere parlor tricks in service to that higher artistry—he knew that he would always do what he had to do.

María, on the other hand, was she indifferent to survival? Would she not settle for anything less than those girlhood dreams she had shared with him?

The seasons passed, one after another, and largely without incident. Seven winters, seven springs. Seven summers, seven autumns. The trees my papa had planted years before were now so tall and so full that their leaves, each autumn, made a solid canopy of gold between the sky and the earth. By this time I was in my final home, in prison and exiled from all that I loved. No longer could I wander amid the mulberry as a wind blew, or lie on my back and look up as it shook the yellow leaves. With my head resting on the black earth, the trunks of the trees rose solemn and columnar, like legs—like my mama's legs disappearing under a full yellow skirt—and sometimes I would turn onto my side and put my arms around one trunk. My heart quickened as the wind parted the finery of the leaves above and revealed a glimpse of heaven. When I put my hand before me in the dark, the rough stones of my cell seem like the bark of trees. Sometimes they do.

The riding accident occurred in the autumn of the seventh year of María's reign.

The day of the accident began like any other. The queen returned to her chamber after breakfasting. Though it was almost the noon hour, her maid Obdulia knew she would return to bed, and, as always, she was slipping the warmer between the sheets, chasing away the cold that had crept from the stone walls under the heavy counterpane.

Queen María Luisa, back in her nightdress, her morning gown discarded and her hair unbound again, crawled beneath her heavy covers and slept, a plump fist to her mouth. She was sad, so she slept. But, sated with sleep, and not yet having had the day's first dose of laudanum, she was fitful and kicked under the covers. She started awake with a cry as the bell rang terce, perspiring, with her hair sticking to her cheeks. She sat up in bed and called for Obdulia to dress her in her riding habit. She did this as a somnambulist, ringing the chime on her nightstand. When the maid appeared, she held out one pale arm so that she might be pulled to her feet. Her toilet did not require her attention: she had sat patiently, passively under the hands of a maid so many times, so many thousands of times, her curling black hair pulled straight by the comb.

It was rare that María desired conversation from her maid— she saved confidences for Eduardo and Esperte—and Obdulia was quiet as she worked. After all, the maid knew her place: that was the first requirement of her position. Any lady who cares to wait on a queen must have a highly refined perceptivity. She must provide palace gossip when in her mistress's gestures she reads an invitation to chatter. But if silence is demanded, that, too, is something she must understand from the subtleties of posture, the communication of a sigh. She should direct her attention only to the part and never to the whole woman. Manicurists must focus on the cuticle; hairdressers converse with the curl behind the ear; dressers attend an ankle, a button, a tie on the stay. Each day, few people actually looked at María, whose vantage, whose *highness,* allowed her to look at whomever she pleased and for as long as she cared to. She stared and searched their features, she let her gaze rest on their downcast eyes, and there she looked for clues as to what happened out in the halls, what the queen mother was up to and whether Carlos would come that night to her chamber. Dutiful, the king was yet human, and had grown tired of failure, as tired as was María. He was no longer aroused casually; now he required certain dresses, certain perfumes, even certain words. A sure sign of an impending visit was the arrival of her tightest corset, a request conveyed, humiliatingly, from valet to maid-in-waiting. King Carlos liked his bride to have the waist she showed off when still a princess, a waist he could span with his trembling-fingered hands.

When he had come to her the night before the accident, the favorite corset had not worked its magic, and, unable to feel manly, Carlos left after an hour, no more. He did not speak sharply, he never did, but he had taken the corset off María and tossed it aside roughly. It still lay on the floor under the stand bearing her washbasin, and María looked at it as the maid combed out her long, long hair and dressed it before placing her riding hat on her head.

The undergarment looked so small and so constricting, how was it that she hadn't suffocated the previous night? The movement of the hairbrush tugged her eyes away from the corset. Still in a state of sleepy fretfulness, when she was at last all buttoned and laced, combed and gloved and booted, the queen walked down the long staircase of the west wing, followed by a footman carrying her riding crop.

"Oh!" she said suddenly, and the footman stopped. "I must return to my apartments. I'll be no longer than a minute. I will meet you at the garden's south gate." He frowned. "A call of nature," she explained, and without waiting for a response, she left him and ascended the stair. At the landing she turned left (not right, which would have taken her to her apartments) and slipped into the map room just as the bells for nones sounded. Eduardo stepped out from behind a large rendering of the territory of Tejas, its boundaries filled with colored pushpins indicating the location of each incident in the rich history of slaughters of Spaniards by the Nasoni, the Apache and Comanche and Tonkawa. A duque merited a pin with a blue head, a grandee got a purple one, hidalgos blue, caballeros green, and so on down the ranks of intrepid explorers. There was no marker for a dead savage, but he would probably care little for the slight, his only real adversary being smallpox, which wages its wars without maps or pins.

The queen took the vial from the dwarf and they parted, but only after she had applied exactly two drops of the amber liquid to her out-thrust, eager tongue: not enough to induce any narcotic effect, just that required to offset her addict's nausea.

María rejoined her footman at the appointed gate, and together they traversed a path through the box hedges, currently in metamorphosis as they were reshaped from pure geometric design into a clumsy representation of an armada of green ships incapable of motion. Already, six years before the event—but "Plants cannot be rushed, they cannot, they cannot," said the head groundskeeper—gardeners were preparing for the bicentennial celebration of Columbus's discovery of New Spain, assuming that in 1692 Old Spain still had enough plundered Incan gold for any sort of festival. María and her footman walked silently along the perimeter of a topiary maze that the queen had never once essayed. "Why should I," she once asked an insulted hedge trimmer, "when the palace itself affords more labyrinths than anyone could hope to penetrate in a lifetime?"

At the stable, Rocinante was waiting with his groom. Rocinante, amber-eyed, frisking at the noise of the queen's boots on the cobbles. Rocinante, named after the steed of the Knight of Sad Countenance, the same as in that most popular novel by Cervantes. The footman helped the queen to mount and then collected his own horse and followed ten lengths behind María, two equestrian maids another few lengths behind him.

The queen was a better horsewoman than any of her servants, and she lost them after a few minutes. She gave her horse his head and went from a canter to a gallop. As usual, María Luisa was careful not to truly wake until she was in the saddle, until a mile had passed beneath Rocinante's hooves. Only in flight did she fully regain her wits, the black earth flying up in clods from under her mount's hooves, wet leaves sticking to her boots.

Exercise made her ache at first, or perhaps consciousness itself made her ache, but then it felt good, she felt good. As her hair tumbled down her back, as her hat blew off to be retrieved by the surly footman, she felt a sudden bursting joy, and the autumn sun seemed to grow so bright and so penetrating that it filled her uncovered head and poured down over her heart. The queen's life, stripped as it was of almost every pleasure, her every indoor moment burdened by her failure to fill the royal nursery, her life yet offered her the pleasure of riding. The movement of her horse offered María some compensation for her own restriction. She had at last mastered the stilts she wore for public occasions—not only the highest in the land, they were the highest in history—but even the most gracefully athletic woman would find herself crippled by Spanish-court clothing.

And, too, there was the embarrassment of the queen's occasional falls, induced by laudanum. Encouraged by the contents of the little blue vial, María had perfected the trick of sleeping with eyes open through most ceremonies; she nodded and gestured automatically at appropriate points. But the cost was that on occasion she had tripped, stumbled, fallen.

On this day, just as she was beginning to laugh—she felt that happy—just a few lengths past the middle of the meadow where the sun had seemed to blaze so brightly, María lost control of Rocinante. Afterward it seemed to her that the saddle had slipped; perhaps its girth had been left too loose—perhaps, as Eduardo had warned, someone did intend her harm. Or perhaps, as the dwarf had also observed, the laudanum made her a less attentive horsewoman than a spirited mount required.

Rocinante tossed his head and skittered sideways. The queen lost one rein, pulled hard on the other, but the horse did not recognize the clumsy gesture as his mistress's attempt to slow him down. He began to gallop. Young and—though castrated before he grew mean—excitable, Rocinante's whinny issued from deep inside his lovely, glossy throat and made a sort of laughter. Once out of the stable and off the palace grounds, this horse danced on his hooves; around obstacles and over logs, his shoes made music on the stones. He was inclined to jump, it is true, but he rarely took a step that was not conscious of his rider. His only failing was a fear of snakes, at whose sight he would lose his head, skitter and bolt.

María jerked the rein again, she tugged it as hard as she could. Confused at having his mouth pulled in such a rude manner, Rocinante reared. Or perhaps he lost his footing. Or he saw a twisted stick, something that looked like a serpent. Whatever the cause, and no one could ask him, he reared and then stumbled, going all the way up and then all the way down—down on his knees, as if in sudden bestial prayer. María fell forward, an undignified slide off the sidesaddle and down his neck onto the ground. She was not able to rise. Her stays were laced so tightly she could hardly breathe, let alone move, and she remained on the ground until her maids and footman caught up with her and helped her to stand.

Rocinante, having cantered off toward a hillock, came back, ears pricked good-naturedly forward, and María took his reins. At her direction, one of the maids checked the girth, which was a bit loose, but not enough, really, to indicate any intended harm to the rider.

The queen stood with her cheek resting against the surcingle, breathing as deeply as her corset and tight habit allowed. The sky refused to move back to its rightful position; to her eyes, it tilted and threatened to push the trees into the lake. Her side hurt so that she was afraid she could not remount, and she asked that her footman excuse her and her maids, so that they might get her out of her habit. As they unlaced her, María leaned panting against her horse's wet hide, and his smell filled her head. The intimate perfume of the horse, so familiar and evocative of her childhood, of a past of no worries and only bright expectation made her cry with sudden and unexpected vehemence.

The footman cantered off to the stable on horseback and re-turned with a carriage to collect María and her maids from the fields. The vehicle's wheels jolted back to the palace over grass and clods of dirt. With each bump the queen's side pained her sharply.

Severo examined Maria in her apartments and diagnosed a fractured rib. To Carlos, he recommended that the queen have bed rest and, he regretted to say, a period of abstinence from marital intimacies of not less than eight weeks.

"If God had intended woman to go about on four legs, He would have given her as many," Marianna remarked at dinner, an observation that was unoriginal, even for her.

"Severo says that some fresh air is necessary for health and, uh, fertility," Carlos said.

"Then let her walk, when she is able," his mother replied.

In the stable, the groom, Ignacio, finished bandaging Roci-nante's legs. He stroked the horse's nose, and the pretty beast nickered and thrust his velvet-soft lips with their surprising prickle of whiskers into Ignacio's neck. "Stop!" the groom said, laughing at the feeling, but his tone grew somber. "You are in trouble, my friend," he said, his hand on the horse's warm neck. Rocinante turned to him. His long eyelashes trembled as if he understood the groom's words.

The next morning, after Mass and an hour in private with his confessor, Carlos proclaimed, by royal decree, that the accident was all the fault of the horse. By then, Ignacio was removing the bandages and fetching his boot grease. He began to erase the white blaze and stockings from the horse's coat, working the dark stain of walnut oil into the hairs, rubbing and rubbing. There were fifty-three horses in the royal stable, only four of which had white stockings. Soon, thought Ignacio, only three would be so distinctively marked. But he was interrupted in his work by the arrival of the king's page.

On the second day after her fall the queen was still in a great deal of pain, enough that Severo had prescribed a tincture of opium much stronger than that of the laudanum the dwarfs received. María felt herself floating pleasantly above her bed. Her side hurt her fiercely, but this struck her as unimportant. Even the fact that she could not get with child—the great vortex of worry and sorrow and shame that swallowed up more and more of her life—seemed less dire than usual. She wondered if she could claim some chronic distress that would merit infinite opium treatments.

She got a double dose after the groom came with Rocinante's tail. And then she got another half dose on top of that—for only then did they manage to unwind her horse's tail from her hand, unwind it in spite of fingers that clung so tightly that the coarse hair cut into her soft white flesh. The opium did nothing, however, to stop the queen from screaming. She screamed until every last soul in the royal residence made his or her way as far from her apartments as possible, until pious Marianna began to blaspheme and Carlos to cry; until the chickens stopped laying; until cats scratched their skins and dogs chewed their paws; until the desperate cook plugged his ears with gobs of cold lard that melted down his collar; until one wet nurse lost her milk and was dismissed and another quit outright, saying not all the gold in Spain could make her stay.

María screamed until nightfall, until she had no voice, until Severo was ordered to overdose her into silence.

"Why?" she begged her maid the next morning, her voice ragged, almost unrecognizable. "Oh, please, why would anyone do such a thing? Do they want to kill me?"

"It was His Highness," said Obdulia, wringing her hands and straightening the bedclothes in one confused gesture. She bit her lip. "He decreed that the horse that had thrown the queen be destroyed. It was his order on the day after you fell. He suggested that Ignacio bring the tail to you, Your Highness, that you might know your accident was avenged." The little maid tried to grasp María's hand to stroke it, but her mistress pulled away.

Now there is one less reason to try, the queen thought, now there was one less pleasure to make her lonely life bearable.

She said this to her maid—she said it standing in her bed, her legs tangled in the counterpane. She said it with her face swollen with weeping, and with one hand holding her broken rib, the other bandaged where Rocinante's tail had cut it. She said: "Between me and them, between this French queen and her Spanish persecutors, there is a war." She said it in French, *la guerre*.

She stopped crying and began to laugh, a high, horrible, hysterical, gasping laugh. "I declare this war and I declare that I would rather be dead than capitulate to such monsters as would murder my horse," she said. And then she fell back into her bedclothes, weeping and laughing at once.

It is true that my countrymen do not easily tolerate the vision of any woman astride a horse, and certainly not their queen, the princess who learned to sit a horse at seven. Riding through the woods of Versailles. Snowdrops and muguets just emerging from the earth like patches of spring snow yet to melt, the blossoms of a thousand cherry trees raining down, pink and fragrant like the tears of cherubs. Sometimes hail was falling; it bounced off the slate roofs of the château, and Marie could not go out but was trapped inside, a girl wandering the long halls. There were bowls of wooden fruit with skins of gold foil, and she liked to leave the mark of her teeth upon an inedible pear or peach. Chairs the color of pistachio ice, vast carpets of chartreuse silk, a red and purple counterpane, and endless galleries of mirrors, mullioned windows throwing light into their depths. The whole château ate light, drank light. Her uncle, the Sun King, beamed within.

There were seven galleries between the dancing master's studio and her mother's apartments, and she ran through them, stopping suddenly to slide on the kid soles of her slippers, sliding through the bars of light falling on the warm wood floors. The light was pink in France, or so it seems to her now. The green gardens were laid out under pink curtains of light. Why, the very sun had shone at the command of the French king. All planets revolved around the sun, the first lesson in her study of natural science, and all the world revolved around Louis XIV, also a lesson for a neophyte, for even his swans, gliding clockwise around the looking-glass lake, knew that Louis was the prime mover, the mainspring of the vast clock that was France in the new era of so-called Reason, the age that marched witches to the gallows, one a week or more.

And the witches, they too became part of the movement of the terrible clock. Their legs swung like pendulums back and forth above crowds cheering their death. Marie went to hangings, everyone did. After the fêtes, after dinners and dances and the latest drama from Racine, a hanging was the best entertainment. Marie and the other princesses begged bouquets of mugwort and marigold and angelica from the gardener.

"Very fine against witches!" Monsieur Clément said. "And make sure to get some thistles!" he called after them. "And here is a bit of purslane for your carriage!" They threw their bouquets on the gallows. If it is true what they say, that yellow flowers trouble those who practice dark arts, then perhaps before they swung, the witches trembled.

María was not so amused by the public sentencings in Madrid. Even the last and grandest of them—the next and last celebration at which we were both in attendance, the queen and I—did not appear to please her. Of course the smell of a score of heretics burning is not so festive, I imagine, as the jaunty ticktock of a pair of wicked ankles.

The grand auto-da-fé, now three years past, on the twenty-first day of what was the hottest June in memory, Saint Paul's feast day, began at dawn and continued late into the night of that longest day of the year. Heretics were collected from the whole of Spain for sentencing and the humiliation of public punishment. Jews, witches, bigamists. Harlots, adulterers, blasphemers. Simoniacs, panderers, falsifiers. The prisons of Madrid and nearby Toledo were packed with sinners, but not enough of the most flagrant and spectacular transgressors for this display, so more and more were dragged to the capital from every wretched corner of the country. From dank prisons in Seville, from the infamous floating asylum off the coast of Málaga, from salt mines in Badajoz and from the dungeons under the Alhambra. Miserable, ragged corps of the damned, made more miserable still by weeks of travel in tumbrels, packed in like sheep bound for the butchers' stalls. Those who died en route were fortunate.

On the twenty-first day of June, the sun blazed with a febrile intensity that well represented the rabid, nay-saying apostle Paul. Lengths and lengths of crimson damask draped the outdoor theater and its piled balconies. A full eight sagged with ladies-in-waiting, another ten groaned under grandees, and the scores of hidalgos were packed so tightly into their observation galleries that they had to stand rather than sit. Everyone sweated in costumes made heavy with a holy brocade of religious symbols stitched one upon another. The Inquisitor General sat in his chair above them all.

Having been arrested a month prior to the grand auto, I was held until that date in a relatively spacious chamber of the same underground prison I inhabit today. There were sixteen of us witches in the one locked room, shackled ankle to ankle in the dark. Whispered introductions revealed that we were, in sum, six midwives, two wet nurses, five sluts and three crazy widows. So here you have an accounting of the dark arts: birthing babies, suckling babies, fornicating and going mad. Of course there were witnesses against us all, those who attested under oath that we had bewitched their cattle, that they had seen our faces burning in the fires on their hearths, that they had taken fits when they crossed our paths or that droughts had begun when we moved to town. They did not lie, no, they believed absolutely the words they spoke against us.

Upon arrest we were stripped by White Hoods and our bodies were then searched for Devil's teats, which, not surprisingly, we

all were found to have. I stopped struggling against such profane inspection when I understood that the White Hoods would
sooner break my arms and legs and neck than let me go without
searching every fold of my skin, looking for that hidden nipple
where every witch is said to give suck to her master, the prince
of dark arts. My knees were forced apart by a special brace they
have for that purpose. For that or for any other reason a man
might have for keeping a woman's legs spread.

"That is no tit!" I said, uselessly. The White Hood had pried
open the flesh of my secret parts with the toe of his boot, he
would not touch me with his hands. The scribe stepped forward
with a lantern, he shined it on me, he wrote down what he saw.

For the auto, we witches were robed in our underground
chamber while it was yet nighttime, and breakfasted in the
night, too—lest we faint and spoil the procession. A piece of soft
black bread smeared with goose grease, a big piece for each of
us. We were led from our temporary cell before the bells rang
lauds, ascending a wet stone staircase to reach a triple-gated
door between two shops, a baker's and a casket maker's—two
businesses whose services might have complemented the
prison's, had anyone, any average citizen, any common baker or
funeral master, known what lay beyond and below the gates.

But even were I to tell you where we find ourselves, I and all
my company of witches, were I to explain to the best of my
knowledge where it is we live: two hundred and eighteen paces
north of the Plaza Mayor, a hundred and forty-three west and
then score after score of steps descending down, you would
never find us.

The prisons of the Inquisition are secret, they have no address, they extend without boundary under the city of Madrid.
Below bullrings and parks, under the opera house and the great
mercado. The citizens of Madrid are always treading and working, supping and fucking, talking, singing, bathing, sewing and
sleeping over a vast labyrinthine metropolis of the damned, a
world equal to the imaginings of a Dante. Those housed and
those employed by the prison do not enter and leave by any one
gated passageway. No, there are countless accesses throughout
the city, each invariably a modest door bearing no sign and

squeezed between two busy merchants. Everyone has seen such doors, passed one en route to the barber, the glazier. Wondered briefly, what is that unnamed portal just beyond the apothecary's? That locked gate by the tanner's? There are so many, they need not be used twice in one week. Unlocked but briefly and under cover of darkness, when streets are empty, when no one is there to see a few cloaked figures, heads bent, eyes averted.

Our band of sixteen, plus guards, left on the morning of the twenty-first day of the month of June in 1686, while it was yet dark. And as the sun was just beginning to rise, we joined the procession heading toward the Plaza Mayor.

My eyes watered all day from the brightness of daylight. I had not been outside for a month, a time that seems laughably short to me now. But then, at one point, when it occurred to me, I pulled up my sleeve to examine the skin of my arm in the sun. I had not seen myself in long enough that I had to touch it to make sure it was mine.

We tottered under the heavy robes and pasteboard hats bearing inscriptions of our crimes. We swayed after an army of soldiers bearing bundles of wood to the stakes, already set in the plaza, set and ready to receive their damned. We excited fury in the spectators, and they spat on us, some demonstrating a quite astonishing marksmanship. For the occasion of the grand auto, Madrid had been closed to carriages and to all horses save those beasts that had the honor of bearing the Inquisitor General and his holy army. Some onlookers had had to walk miles to reach the Plaza Mayor, but, after all, attendance at this spectacle granted a greater indulgence than even a hundred novenas or a thousand self-imposed lashes. As for those who were trampled to death en route, I guess they went straight to heaven, having been sacrificed with newly whitewashed records.

For so great a display as this grandest of public burnings, the court must have gone into considerable debt. Swooning under my hot, heavy robes, I wondered dully what person could have advanced such sums as must have been required to buy what looked to be a silk carpet ten leagues long, a path for the august Inquisitor General to walk between his balcony and that bearing King Carlos and Queen María Luisa. More interesting, what sins must have paved the way for such generosity?

Had I been a man, and as rich as my papa dreamed of becoming, then I, too, could have taken my pleasures and paid for them thus. As Papa's father might have remarked, God helps those who help themselves.

Perhaps the saved congratulated themselves on their virtue as they stared at us poor damned—stared as though before their eyes we had been dredged from the burning lake—but I tell you that the shrieks they gave were little different from the profane yowling that fills the prisons of the Inquisition. "Burn them!" they cried. "And no strangling first! Burn them alive!"

My little company was not there to be included among those incinerated at the end of that day. No, our appearance was merely one of the many appetizers for the holy consummation that would take place only after bigamists were burned, blasphemers made to lick coals, the foreheads of falsifiers branded with their crime and the thighs of harlots scalded with boiling holy water.

As part of one act in this interminable drama of foreplay, I marched—stumbled—in my robes depicting hellfires, beneath the canopied box of royals in their velvet upholstered chairs. One of sixteen, together making a living tapestry of caution: Do not dare to do as these wretches before you! All told in pictures on our robes, stitched prettily in silk twist. Mine was a little long, it dragged. On my bodice a diminutive couple fornicated in such a position as only a chaste and virginal needleworking nun might have conjectured. Around our necks were lanyards bearing knots, one for each hundred lashes we would receive prior to imprisonment. Each of us paused in our procession as those sinners immediately before us heard their sentences read.

A band of seducers dressed in robes of red with three-horned hats heard that their genitals would be publicly scalded with melted wax, and then on the following day they would be ridden around Madrid from dawn to dusk on the backs of mules, so that everyone could get a good look at what was left of those parts that had led them astray. At least that is what I think was to happen to them—the sobs of the relapsed Jews behind us made it difficult to hear the sentences. The Jews carried un-lighted candles, evidence of their stumbling in spiritual dark, I would venture. Whoever had planned this spectacle had fully indulged a passion for symbol. The sexual offenders were led off to the cauldrons of melted wax, and my party of witches ad-vanced to the sentencing arena.

I was insolent enough to glance quickly at the king and queen as they looked down at us. I knew it was hoped that God, even as used as He was to heaven's boulevards all paved in gold, might be sufficiently impressed by such an extravagance of piety to bless the royal couple with an heir, and I looked at the child-less mother of our country.

Yes, again it was by chance that I saw our queen, some seven years after her nuptials, and still on rations of opium following her riding accident. Severo was having trouble weaning her from the milk she chose to suckle. This time it was not any hur-ried, secret ceremony I witnessed; the queen was displayed like a jeweled chalice on an altar at the end of a long beautiful corri-dor of silk and more silk. To my eyes, unused to color and light, such finery seemed to burn and burn and never be consumed, like that celebrated biblical bush. María Luisa looked a good deal fatter and more unhappy than she did as a bride. And Car-los, he looked thin and unhappy.

Our names were read aloud, and together we witches were sentenced to life imprisonment. Those nine whose tongues were to be cut out were separated from the rest of us and led away. I saw the queen watch them. What did she think of it, this pecu-liarly Spanish display of religiosity? As far as I could see, Her Highness remained composed. She turned a little in her seat as the deceased criminals passed by, each represented by a box of bones and a placard bearing his name and likeness.

My priest was there among them, in one of the boxes. A monk carried his bones, provided the legs he no longer had, so that he could ascend to the stage and be hung on a post to hear his crimes recited by the Inquisitor General. We were together that day. What flesh we could still claim was reunited. The like-ness over his remains did him no justice, but I knew it was he when the great robed judge read his name and his history of transgressions: heretic, seducer, irreligious priest.

The French might view executions as a form of entertainment, party tricks only a little more importunate than conjuring birds from cloaks or pouring water from an empty cup: a kind of hocus-pocus, here-and-then-gone. The French might gather around scaffolds with song and flowers, but no one in the Plaza Mayor threw bouquets at these condemned. When the bishops of Toledo and Granada and Madrid stood up and in unison excommunicated those they had judged unrepentant, a cry went up from the crowd. The sound of self-righteous fury was so loud that those condemned to be burned jerked in their shackles, and as God knows, the lot of them looked dead already.

Those nobles rich enough to have bought a place in the ceremony each led a criminal to the circle of stakes set with tinder. Twenty-two were burned that night—as the sun went down, heavenly fire eclipsed by hellfires. Each at a stake about twice the height of a tall man, with a little plank seat nailed almost at the top of it. Each criminal was handed by a nobleman to a pair of priests who escorted the damned up a ladder and chained him to a stake. The priests exhorted each sinner one last time to confess, repent. The four who did were given clemency and strangled before their fires were lit.

As for the rest, all relapsed Jews, on this, their last hour on earth, they were past caring about anything; their last sobs were behind them. Had Christ himself descended from heaven to light their fires with his flaming heart, they would not have betrayed any surprise. After a trumpet blast to ensure attention, the fires below the little seats on the stakes were lit. Set with a good amount of dry straw below the wood, they caught quickly. The windows around the plaza, rented for at least a ducado an hour for the privilege of viewing the burning at close hand and unmolested, disgorged arms waving handkerchiefs and flags and standards, any scrap of fabric.

My band of witches stumbled off, encouraged to step lively by a lash that whisked at our ankles. We were marched three times around the plaza, our pretty robes having been removed so that they would not sustain any damage from the crowds who hurled stones and garbage at us; and then we were whipped and led to our cells in bloody underclothes. One long day of unshaded sun had been sufficient to burn our faces so that we had many subsequent days' worth of entertainment picking at the blisters on our cheeks.

Stripped of my holiday attire and returned to the netherworld of prison, the dark exploded before my eyes for hours, showing me all the colors again and again, colors of which I had but dreamed for a month. The vision of the silk threads of my robe, which on that everlasting day I had had ample time to examine, stitched up the dark making it red, yellow, green. It mattered not whether I opened or closed my eyes, a fantastic fabric wove and rewove itself before me, silk binding everything up together. For the first time I asked myself, was it shameful that it had been my family's trade to raise the worms that spun such robes as Inquisitors forced their victims to wear?

As a child I never considered such matters, for then the machine of the Inquisition was far less real to me than any of the machines of silk production—the mills and the cumbersome looms, the great stone presses that force the red, blue, brown from madder root, woad leaf and walnut. I was so filled with dreams of a fantastic future, and all of us were so thoroughly under the spell of my father's hopes for wealth that we did not even care whether or not, being working people, we were denied by decree the very fabric we helped to create. If you were a person who earned his bread by the work of his hands and were caught wearing silk, the fine was never less than triple the cost of that garment: in other words, never less than what you could not afford.

Even so, we all did wear a little bit of it. All silk workers do for luck, for pride, for defiance. Privately we would not comply with the silk laws, and those rough clothes that the world could see had inside them secret pockets lined with silk. Empty of coins, perhaps, but filled with a rich weave of purple, green and gold. Or we wore little belts of silk, like the red sash that used to lie next to my mama's skin, hidden by her skirts, or the black one my grandfather had had on him. There had always been one blue silk ribbon threaded through Dolores's and my undervests, knotted tightly over our hearts.

HEN MY MOTHER CAME HOME FROM MADRID, I thought: So this is the woman who has suckled a king! For she was so small, and her hair was suddenly gray; she was not at all as I remembered her. I suppose I had grown a little, and she had shrunk. But even so, what I had feared had come to pass. Another child—a king, no less!—had gobbled up my mama.

I was eating an onion when she came in the door. Dolores and I would take one from where they hung twisted into a rope, pull it down when Papa was out, and then lay it on top of the coals from the night's fire and cover it with more coals. They were big, sweet yellow onions, and the juice seeped out and turned to sugar as they cooked slowly. We squatted on the stone hearth and waited, and after what seemed long enough Dolores would poke a sharp stick between the embers and into the heart of the onion. She would draw it out of the ashes and cut it with the long knife I wasn't allowed to use, and we would each have one half; though, being older, Dolores's was the first choice of the better or bigger portion.

I could never wait to eat my share, and I would burn my mouth on the hot open skin of the onion. I had a crack in the middle of my bottom lip that would not heal from burning it so often, and I was just touching my tongue to that place where my lip stung when I looked up at the noise of the door, a scrape of wood against the packed dirt floor.

My mother had been gone for nearly three years, and her hair, hair that had swept the floor as she combed it sitting on the bench before the fire, the very color of her hair, even, had been sucked from her head, which was now gray and drooping on the tired stalk of her neck. When I was very young, my mama would dress her hair as she sat on the hearth, warming her back with it

gathered before her in one long swaying rope, her fingers flash-
ing white through the dark locks as she braided. After she was
done, she would pull the loose hairs from her comb, and they
would drop onto the floor, and, as it was my responsibility to
sweep, I would pick up the long black strands later and look at
them. I saved them all coiled together in the box where I kept my
few things, and on the night Mama came home I went to that
box and took out the hairs. While she was sleeping I compared
the old hair to the new, and it wasn't the same at all; and I
wondered, was this really my mother?

The mediums say that it is prudent to keep a lock of hair and
a few nail parings from the dead, especially those of your father
or mother, because in them lives the spirit of your family; that is
why the hair and nails continue to grow even after the rest of the
body's life has fled. So when your papa and mama die, they tell
you, keep these little snippets and shavings, hide them in a safe
place by your hearth. Called by these slivers, the spirits of your
ancestors will return and keep you safe.

In our house was a box made of rosewood with little carvings
on all its sides, designs of stars and suns and moons. I hated to
open it and see the contents, hair and fingernails all tangled together, too many generations to count, and whose was whose?
It was impossible to tell, and the smell of unfamiliar bodies was
concentrated inside and distasteful to me.

Papa told us that when he married Mama she had danced a
hole in her shoes. They were new and black and polished with
beeswax to shine like a mirror, and Papa could see his face on
her toes shining back up at him as he said his vows. He kept his
head bent not because he was not proud to take such a wife, he
told us, but because he was humble; he did not take my mother's
hand for granted. After the wedding Mass, said by a friar who
used to come to town on horseback, in the days before Quintanapalla had its own priest, the villagers drank wine and
danced all the night, and no one danced longer or harder than
our mama. She danced the first dance, the "dance of the grandmothers," as it is called, when the gray old mothers of the town
cast off their years and hold one another's hands. And Mama
did not stop after that, but went on dancing. Everyone played

something, even were it only an instrument as crude as a stick on a bottle or a spoon against a tin plate—they all beat time as she danced.

At last, when all the wedding guests were tired out and drunk and sleeping (the old horseback-riding priest drunk and snoring, too), Papa wanted to take Mama to bed, but she would not stop, she had to keep dancing. When I think of her now, it is as if I see in my inside eye the last of her girlhood: her dancing and dancing and not stopping until the sun came up. For that was the last night of a girl's life, her wedding night; the next day would come housekeeping and the next year childbearing. Mouths to fill and pots to scrape and shine, grain to carry to the mill, and no one ever asked a girl to dance again, no young man brought her a sweet or a flower. The day after her wedding Mama's feet were covered in blisters, she couldn't get up from the marriage bed, and she never wore those shining black shoes again. Dolores has them still, I guess, Dolores who has never danced a step in her life.

I looked up from the onion, my tongue just exploring the burned place on my lip, tasting it, and then Mama was inside the door and I dropped my half of the onion. It rolled under the table, and when I bent to pick it up it was covered with dirt.

"Francisca?" said my mother, Dolores already in her arms. I could see that she was hurt by my reluctance to come to her. When I did at last embrace her, I felt how small she was under her clothes, and how her bodice, which once had split its seams trying to hold her abundance, that bodice seemed almost empty now.

After she greeted us, she went to her bed and lay down upon it, right away, because she was tired and ill, and I could see then that her chest was indeed as flat as a young girl's, as flat as my own. She came home spitting blood, and she did not live long after that, whether it was weeks or months or a year, I cannot say, all I know is that to my childish greed, it was short, too short. Nothing. An afternoon.

All the time that she lay in bed, she told us stories of the great stone house where the king lived, the king who was only a boy, as young as I, younger than Dolores. The king's house in Madrid was so big, Mama said, that a hundred of our house could fit inside, and I sat with Dolores beside Mama's bed and tried to imagine a house of that size.

Of course it was in the king's house that one of my dreams had come to pass: now my mother could read. There had been hours each day at her disposal, and Carlos, whose physical health was so poor that his studies were endlessly forestalled, made but little use of the tutors assembled. So they and my mother passed the evenings in her lessons, and she came home with a box filled with books, making ours the only household in Quintanapalla to have such a thing as a library, and causing suspicion to fall upon us.

For spoken words are uttered and then gone: orphaned, disowned; but recorded words are evidence. Who could know if our books reflected heretical thoughts? If one could not tell what was written on a book's binding even, how could that person know if it was a forbidden text? How could a body trust that an Inquisitor would not come and kill everyone in the house for inviting the Devil to live under its roof? No matter that my mother told those few who did come to call that she *could* read and that her volumes were safely pious, the women of Quintanapalla looked nervously at her books. They would not touch them, they drew back if she so much as flipped through the pages. Mama's friend Pascuela, carrying her first child, and on this account very nervous of evil eyes and other dangers, covered her ears when Mama tried to read a story to her. There was no one else besides her two young daughters with whom my mother could share her last enthusiasm.

Despite the fears of the women of Quintanapalla, the books my mother brought home to us were not dangerous works. They came from the king's great house, after all, and were the *Lives of the Saints* (most of whom we had not heard of, for they were foreign saints like Patrick, who chased all the snakes off a green island) and *Confessions* of Augustine, along with guides to prayer and contemplation written by some holy persons from Castile, including Teresa of Avila, of course, and *The Imitation of Christ,* by a man called Kempis—that one was in Latin—and some medical and chirurgical texts on midwifery and the care of infants.

Mama wanted to teach Dolores and me to read, but she was not strong enough to sit up, and the lessons, which she began the very evening of her return, made her breathless. She pointed to the letters and made their sounds, and she tried to show how it was when they were strung together. But when the letters kept company, one with another, their natures changed in ways she could not explain, and the languid movement of her thin finger trying to chase them down on the page made us yawn with frustration and then weep with fatigue until, finally, we fell asleep in the bed with her.

After a few tries, Mama decided to forgo explanations and simply read to us herself, so that at least she could pass on the learning contained in the stories. When she grew tired of reading, she would close her eyes and simply talk, so slowly sometimes that she made me impatient and I would nudge her or even jump on the bed and rumple the bedclothes, reach out and tug at one of her hands. What was it like? What was it like? I wanted to know.

Carlos was only eight years old when King Philip died, and then Carlos was king, but still, Mama told us, King Carlos put his hands down his breeches and scratched his asshole like any other child with worms. He put his fingers in his mouth and into our mother's, too, until she began to be troubled by the same itching. "Don't think the rich courtiers are so different," Mama told us. "Everyone in the palace has worms."

Mama said that Carlos jumped and jerked his limbs about, any tiny noise and he would startle, she had never had anything like him; he made Mercedes seem like an angel. He had been baptized, she knew, but, just for good measure, she had taken him again to the church and poured water from the font over his head. But it did no good, he trembled in her arms, and if a cup dropped, a casement slammed, he would scream as if he were being burned alive. For a child of nine, he was greatly stunted, his legs would scarcely support him and sometimes she had to carry him like an infant.

Mama's milk improved Prince Carlos's strength, and while she was in the palace he learned to walk and to laugh; but she could not cure him, not completely, and she said to us that perhaps it was true, the talk that all the Hapsburg family was bewitched. She would try to shove her nipple into his wide-open mouth, just to shut him up, but sometimes it would not work, he would choke upon it and cry harder. The windows of the nursery were lined with layer upon layer of wool felt to protect Carlos from any unwanted noise or draft. What little light did come into the prince's apartments seemed to disappear, sucked into the thin, high wail of the boy, as if his crying were some kind of rent in the fabric of the day, a hole into which all sweetness, all substance, all flavor disappeared.

The prince preferred my mama, demanded her; her smell was the only thing that might make him stop crying, and so no one ever would take him from her embrace, and my mama was enslaved. Each day she looked forward to one thing only, Carlos's falling asleep and giving her the chance to make progress in her studies. Then she could bring home to us her books and her knowledge.

Before she died, Mama read us every book she had; she died the day she finished the last page of the final volume. After, I tormented myself, wondering if only I had been able to borrow books indefinitely, would she not have lived as long as there were new words to read? But in the moment I was happy, I did not look ahead. I had a particular fondness for stories of martyrdom, and in the afternoons, after Mama would fall asleep, Dolores and I remained on the floor by our mother's bed, and I told her how we might contrive to get martyred ourselves. We would travel, I said to my sister, to places far away and filled with infidels on horseback. I saw them with wild snarls of hair hanging down their naked bodies, and they sat their horses without a saddle or bridle, just holding the beast by the mane. Rogues who would assuredly try to compromise our virginity and, when we protested, run us through with their great lances until we were transported to heaven in raptures of ecstasy.

Well, I was young, my blood was hot, and the stories had not the effect on me that my mother had hoped. I tossed in the bed I shared with my sister, suffering nightmares of Saint Lucy with her eyes in a dish, followed by Agatha's breasts in a bowl and Eulalia stumbling with her head on a plate—a legion of women all dismembered with their parts displayed on the kind of fantastic gold dishes I imagined must outfit a palace.

I rolled about on the floor by my mother's deathbed talking nonsense, and sometimes I would see her looking up to the ceiling, and she might smile as she heard what I said to my sister. I comfort myself that perhaps it was a diversion for her as well. At least she could rest her voice when it grew weak from reading. Perhaps she was happy to see that, ill as she was, these stories were yet something she could give us.

All pious stories, of course, dwell particularly on the idea of *eternal reward,* and I puzzled over this idea. *"For ever and all eternity,"* I whispered to myself as I wiped the table, repeating the stories' common refrain as I did my chores. And I would wonder how it was that Saint Lucy had *traded time for eternity,* never dreaming that I would come to such a place as this prison, which has taught me the sense of such phrases. The stories my mother told assured me that *eternal bliss* was very desirable, but I found it not nearly so exciting as the martyrdom that preceded it.

The big black book containing saints from all the lands had illustrative engravings of their torments, and I teased Dolores until with me she enacted these tableaux, once earning for my trouble a beating when I rent our dresses by forcing sticks through the cloth (so as to better indicate the arrows that pierced Sebastian). Papa was in no mood for martyrdom, he felt Mama's and his own pain too keenly.

Perplexed by this constant talk of death and transcendence, Papa asked us not to say such things as made his flesh creep. It was bad enough that Mama was so ill, without my daily imaginings of how we, too, might depart; but I could not stop myself. I persisted, I led my sister astray until that day our father punished us severely, and so frightened Dolores that she never mentioned such things from that day forward. I am not sure what she continued to think privately, for she never again would whisper a word of our game, not even in Papa's absence.

But, for my part, I continued to dream of raptures and martyrs, perhaps even more feverishly once it became my own private realm.

Saint Teresa was my favorite. Having lived only the century before and been born not so far from me, in Avila, she seemed close enough to be real. She died a virgin and was not martyred, but she suffered other torments, and I prayed for any sort of vile disease that might mortify my flesh to the benefit of my soul. My spirit then would burn so prettily, like a little lamp of virtue. The *Life of Saint Teresa,* written by Herself, was filled with intoxicating accounts of how prayers had transformed her flesh and caused her to float up toward heaven even as she clung to chair legs and doorframes. The next day her bones would be all wrenched out of joint and she felt as if dogs had been chewing on her heart, but this did not seem too high a price for flying.

There must be some price paid for the transformation of matter—think of all the dead silkworms, after all.

TOUCH MYSELF TOO MUCH. YES, THAT IS what I'm speaking of. I do not have the strength to stand, but I have strength for this.

Of course, I stink, and when I give myself pleasure I shiver and sweat and stink that much more. Self-pollution is the name they give it: this sin of solitude, sin of longing. By any mortal measure my transgressions thus far are sufficient to cast me into the eighth deepest, coldest circle invented by that ingenious Italian, so what do I care if my soul is fettered by one more small self-indulgence? I have no use for mortal measures, not even Dante Alighieri's.

I do it to help me call back the past, that I may take some solace in the memory of what provided passport to this prison. And how it was worth any price.

A sharpening of longing and frustration—it's as bad as the teasing, bobbing circle of light cast by the guard's lamp as he passes. That moment when the door to my cell is outlined in silver. Not sun, but the memory of sun, just as when I touch myself I suffer the memory of physical love. Greet that memory, no matter how dim.

Passion. It does not exist in time, it erases the past and belittles the future. My love was willful and unreasoning; it was like a stone cast into the still pool of my life, waves reaching back to touch the far bank of my childhood even as they traveled forward to the opposite bank. It feels as if there were never a time when I did not know him. I see him at my birth and at my death.

Alvaro! I call his name some nights when my tongue lock is off. I call him, and my neighbors try to silence me. They kick their bars to obscure the sound of my voice as I beckon him. *Venite ad me!* Come to me. Oh, lie close with me! *Dormi supra me et sub me.* Lie over me and under me. *Proximus me.* Next to me. I speak in Latin, I use the words he taught me. Words of the Church, language of the saints.

"I'm praying," I tell the White Hood if he comes. "Surely prayer is encouraged in this place."

Venite ad me. I don't call on God. I care nothing if Christ comes. It's Alvaro I want and I make my miserable flesh raw trying to remember how it felt to be with him. But the trembling twitch of response rarely does better than mock me and my desire.

Our bed burned, it burns, it always will burn. Sometimes we were fucking for four or more hours in a night. We could not stop, we could not wait until the door was shut behind us. We tore the clothes from each other.

His hands shook. It was as if every little hole that nature gave my body, he would try to get into me that way, so that the two of us might live together in one house of flesh. He crammed his tongue into my nostrils, his fingers up my asshole, his cock in far enough to touch my heart: he wanted to be that close to me.

I did not speak, but yes, *Open me,* I thought. I could not unlock myself by myself. I would begin to cry out to God. *Christ, Christ, Christ. Savior,* I would say. It would feel as if I had waited for him all my life, my every breath drawn in anticipation of this suffocation.

He was a fucking, sucking, licking dog. Yes, he was the man with the head of the dog, he was the terrible suitor with whom I had threatened my sister. He poked his red tongue into my throat and made me scream.

He wanted me so badly that I knew I was treasure, a galleon of gold from New Spain. He would sink me, he was a great wave breaking over me, making me gasp. He began by thinking he was the sea, the endless ocean, but he drowned in me. Swallowed me like a salt wave, gagging, but he wanted to die that way. We all want to die that way.

The pleasure of the flesh used to wash over me like a flood tide, a great black wave upon whose crest were borne fragments of my past—as if the carnal knowing were a storm, a great deluge after a dry, dry drought to end all droughts. The waters rushed through my papa's house, battered down the doors and swept everything away.

Under him, I lost my reason, I thought I saw what wasn't there, my father's clogs, his chair and pipe, cooking pots and kettles, the ladle kept hanging by the hearth, blankets from our beds and the remains of the previous night's supper. I saw it all in a jumble and turning over and over in the foam and spit on top of the curl of a great wave, and I would laugh sometimes until tears streamed into my ears, Alvaro's hand over my mouth, "*Tacete! Tacete!*"—Be quiet!—and the cold tears filling my ears.

"What! What!" he would ask, and he would shake my shoulders as if to dislodge some explanation. But this was nothing for which I had words—not then, anyway—just my surprise in how his body in mine had the power to break up the very chairs at my father's table, carrying them off over our heads.

I returned home long after vespers, the sun dimmed, the bells of the cathedral now silent, but ringing still in my head. I would come into my father's house, where he sat before the fire, Dolores tending a pot of something with no savor, chickpeas or bacon boiled until nothing but salt remained—the table my sister set was one whose guests dined on the taste of grief—and I would reach forward to touch the wall to see, was it there, any of it?

Dolores and Papa looked at each other as I made a slow tour of the room in which we lived, touching it all that I might believe in it again. I would pick up some trifle, a cup or a candle, turn it over and over in my hands. "Is this new?" I would say. "Did Papa bring this home from market?"

"*No,*" Dolores would answer. And then to Papa, "See, it is as I've told you."

I paid no attention to her, I did not see how it was that my sister tried to turn my father against me. Made sure that he took note of every odd thing that I did.

"You'll go to the wash works," she said to me.

My grandfather once told us that when he was growing up in Quintanapalla they used to call the prisons of the Inquisition by that name: the wash works. For the method of the Church in the cleaning of souls was not so different from the process of the wash works. The Holy Office wrung a body out, boiled and bleached it, trying to get a good confession. Of course, people could make such jokes then, more than fifty years ago. They even dared to speak them aloud, for when my grandfather was born, in 1611, Spain was not so troubled a place as it is today. The Inquisition's hold on her countrymen was not so fearsome, and people were not so poor that for a few coins they would bear tales against a neighbor who did not say his prayers, or, worse, said the wrong ones.

If only a soul were so easily laundered as a hank of silk.

"Your mother killed her sons."

"My mother's sons were stillborn."

"Your mother killed her sons and she ate them."

"My mother had children born dead like every other woman in every other town and they were buried by my papa. You can find them if you dig, you can go and find them, they are in a row. They have gravestones, each of them, they are in a row next to my papa's silk house, there are four stones. My mama never killed anything in her life, not even a rat."

"Your mother killed her male children."

When I put my hands over my ears, the White Hood smears the soles of my feet with grease, he builds a fire before them. As I am always so cold, for a minute the heat feels good.

"Did I say that?" I used to ask the Red Hood when he read me the transcripts before I signed them. *Release me and I'll tell it. I don't know. I do know. I didn't do it. I did. If you say that I did, I did. I did whatever the witnesses say that I did. Tell me what to say, I shall say it, God knows that I will. Only tell me what I am to say and how. . . .* They go on like that for pages. And it seems that a person is capable of conversing entirely without intent or even consciousness.

The silkworm has been enslaved for many centuries. It cannot walk. Its legs do not support its body.

And the silkworm used for breeding, the female that lays those eggs my papa used to buy, her wings are unable to lift her.

In nature, a silkworm lives in the tree off which it feeds. It eats the leaves, and in the autumn it spins a cocoon around itself; it binds its hidden self to a naked, stripped bough.

Sometimes, as the Purple Hood speaks, I have a vision of myself suspended by a strand of silk and swinging from a bough of a mulberry tree, one of many planted in a grove. The sun is bright, and hanging in the tree, I see the white light of the sky above, I feel its warmth. The trees are tall, they were planted many years before. *How black their tops are against the bright, white sun,* I think. *How implacable and mysterious. They are too high, too far away to know them.*

A playful breeze picks up. It catches my strand of silk and then drops it. Leaves me swinging: back and forth, back and forth. I swing outside of time, my whole body held in a smooth arc of motion.

My heart beats. It is the only sound in all creation.

Then, suddenly, I am blown off course, and the strand of silk carries me into the trunk of one of the trees. I hit it and swing backward into another. This happens over and over in time with the crashing beat of my heart.

The treetops disappear just as I awake to understand that these collisions *are* the noise of my heart, so loud that each beat threatens to annihilate me. And just as I think *No, I cannot stand any more,* the strand breaks and I fall. Fall but never hit.

Fall like water dropping from a precipice so high that it evaporates before it strikes the ground below.

All the while that I am consumed by this curious vision, I am speaking, evidently, I am answering questions. I used to believe that the transcripts were false, made up. But certain of the statements contain phrases that sound too much like my own to have been fabricated by another person.

The Purple Hood is increasing his persecutions. He is after something. A secret he wants from me before I die. But what? I would tell him anything, I have told him anything, whatever I can think of. That is the problem. I have contradicted myself. In my cell I think up perverse and damning crimes to attribute to my mother. In my cell I plan to give him what he wants. But then, when I am questioned, I forget the false accusations I have rehearsed. I cannot utter them.

It is growing more difficult to hold on to what is left of Francisca de Luarca, daughter of Félix de Luarca, failed silk grower, and Concepción de Luarca, wet nurse to the king.

When the White Hood brings me back, the dark throbs in time with my pulse.

"I am a worm," I say to no one. "I am a silkworm," I say to the dark.

ONSIEUR DE TROUVER, WHO OWNED PARIS'S largest shop dealing in exotic animals, was enjoying a very lucrative year. Not a week went by that he didn't sell dozens of lovebirds, and when a shipment was late, carriages of tearful ladies stretched for a mile up the street from the place of his business. Each morning, when he arrived for work, Monsieur de Trouver raised the shade in his shop, sliced an orange in quarters and dropped it into the cage where the marmosets sneezed. Then he put his hand in the big basket of birds, his thick forearm squeezing through the little trapdoor at the top. He made a face as he groped for dead birds on the foul wicker bottom. They were so light and frail that if he grabbed a live one by mistake it died of fright, as if he had tried to clutch an angel, a creature so sweet and elusive that his rough mortal touch had caused it to vanish.

Les anges, he said to Marie Louise, when she made her first visit to his shop. He invited her to peep through a hole in the wicker at the bright beating color inside. *Vraiment.* I am telling you the truth.

Marie was fifteen. She had come to the market in Paris with her father. She was a princess and could have anything she liked, her father told her so. And while all fathers say such nonsense, this one, brother to the Sun King, spoke the truth. Yes, Marie was a princess and she should have any creature that might amuse her. Except the monkeys, which carried diseases.

Les oiseaux d'amour. The tiny lovebirds were imported by the thousand for the pleasure of French ladies. Bought in Venezuela, traded for beads or mirrors or worthless stones dug out of the banks of the Rhine—that cold and twisting river worlds away from the steaming Orinoco—the little creatures were packed in baskets by savages and loaded onto Portuguese ships in Cumaná. Suffocating in the hold for the better part of a summer, most of the birds perished by the time they reached the markets in Paris. But if only three of every hundred birds survived the journey, they made a nice profit for their dealers.

It was the rage that year in Paris for fashionable ladies to have a lovebird and to teach it to sing. The tiny, brilliantly colored birds had a naturally plaintive call and, so far from home, so homesick, the sounds they made grew piercingly sweet. The duchesses and marquises, the comtesses and princesses who bought the little birds devoted hours to their tutelage. The ladies changed their cages, one after another, to make sure their pets were housed in a musically conducive environment. Cages of birch wood, of wicker. Cages of gold or of bamboo with silver leaf. They bathed the little creatures in spirits of alcohol and massaged them with scented oils. And if the birds survived these treatments, they fed them fruit ices and put spirits in their water dishes: a drop of vodka made by royal appointment to whichever Romanov was currently the Czar—the bottle said Alexis, but hadn't Feodor ascended? Well, no matter, whoever caused the potatoes to ferment, the vodka was quite effective in loosening the lovebirds' tongues. And why not (for resistant cases) a tiny drop—oh, just a breath!—of alcoholic suspension of opium? Laudanum: that did the trick. Some of the birds sang most beautifully. Others fell silent, perhaps dreaming bird dreams of their faraway homes. A few fell dead from their perches and were replaced.

"Five louis for a creature weighing less than an ounce!" Marie's father rapped his walking stick against the big basket, and the resulting flurry of constricted flight was such that a few bright feathers leaked out from gaps in the wicker. Monsieur de Trouver did not cower. This might be the king's brother, but the laws of fashion and of commerce were entirely on his side.

"Five louis," he repeated.

"Very well." Marie's father shrugged. *"Vite, Marie, plus vite."* Just be quick about it. He was impatient, he wanted to go to the perfumer's.

Four years later, on a Wednesday afternoon, at a quarter to three—Queen María was returning from the stable—her father died in the rare-animal dealer's shop. He was picking out a matched set of tortoises for his brother Louis's birthday. If he had them gilded that afternoon, they would live for another week, they would last through the festivities. His heart stopped as he counted out the money.

But that was four years later. On this afternoon, the duc d'Orléans was impatiently swinging his silver-headed walking stick with one hand, adjusting his wig with the other. His daughter was on her knees beside the basket of birds. Monsieur de Trouver busied himself watering the animals with a polished copper can whose long spout he poked into the cages, replenishing empty dishes. The marmosets sneezed without stopping. Marie picked a lovebird with a little crest of rosy feathers sticking up from its head. She tried to touch one tiny pink quill, and the bird bit her. Back home, in the château, she had her maid hang its cage by the window. The lovebird sat on its perch without moving. A month later it was dead.

What must it have been like in the trees by the great rivers of the jungle? Air warm and soft and flowers of so many colors. Then caught in a net, packed in a basket, held in a ship's hold, and at last, dead in France, where the sun did not shine so often. Dead and then replaced, one bird after another.

The first Friday of every month, the marquise de Montpellier hosted a competition for the most piercingly lovely birdsong. She held it in her salon, and it was the most coveted invitation, but no more than thirty ladies with their birds and their maids could be accommodated by the marquise's salon of chartreuse and pink brocade. They came by carriage, and the owners of the little creatures, feathers drooping, berated the driver at every sudden jounce or turn, at every motion that might upset the bird swinging in its cage from a hook in the ceiling of the coach. At the marquise's salon, they played endless rounds of cards, reversée or trocero, to determine the order in which the birds would sing, all the while sharing those infamous imported pink cigarros (one part tobacco, one part cloves and one part coca leaves) upon which all revelry depended, and which they smoked with the aid of long ivory and gold holders (to keep the fumes at such a distance from their painted faces that they would not cause their eyes to water and wash off their artfully applied cosmetics, their gummed-on black beauty marks).

It was because of those cigarros that the entertainments reached so immodest a pitch, just as the cigarros were to blame for the previous spring's excess, when one and then another of the ladies took to wearing naughty golden lockets. They would press open the little catches so that out tumbled the contents: not miniatures but locks of hair, and hair not from a lover's head, but from somewhere else. These curls were tight and wiry. A game evolved: based on the minute examination of but one hair, its exact shade of brown and the tightness of the curl, who could guess the identity of a certain paramour? One springy red sample gave away the duke of Fife, but others were more challenging.

That was much too vulgar and risky, decided the marquise. The birds could hardly get them into the kind of trouble that came from the lockets, all the tedious duels and their tiresome result—balls that were ruined for lack of men who could dance.

The ladies soon discovered that though the lovebirds sang nicely in cages, their performance improved if they were let out into the room. For, though they called piteously for their release, the birds were terrorized by the ornate furnishings at the marquise's, and they flew around and around the salon, inevitably lighting on the chandelier, where they sang most beautifully until they were either recaptured or they expired. Some burned to death over a candle flame (the stench of singed feathers was dreadful!), but most dashed themselves against the illusory escape offered by one of the hundreds of mirrors.

Adding to the frenetic quality of the first Friday of each month was Mademoiselle de Toquetoque (the same whose teeth had gone prematurely black from too many of the pink cigarros) and her unfortunate tendency to overexcitement. At nearly every competition she climbed up on the chairs in such a fashion that some bit of her attire—farthingale, hoop, lace pantaloon— caught upon an armrest or spindle and caused her to topple to the ground in a tangle of ribbons and teacups, little iced cakes stuck all over her voluminous skirts. While the craze for birdsong lasted, Mademoiselle de Toquetoque sprained one ankle and both wrists, broke her collarbone and exhausted seventeen lovebirds, all of whom she had buried between her favorite rose trees, claiming ever after that the blooms thereon grew prettier and more colorful with each added corpse.

It was cruel sport, the marquise de Montpellier thought, but enchanting nonetheless. Or perhaps enchanting because cruel. She would have considered hosting the competition two Fridays a month instead of only one, if it hadn't been a rather untidy entertainment, what with the scramble to catch the birds and the unavoidable evacuation of their panicked bowels. Even though they were so small, they could make quite a mess. And the frantic pitch of the afternoons—after the cigarros, drugged ladies chasing drugged birds, climbing chair backs in their fetching but quite unstable gold slippers, the birds each a quick blur of red or green that came to a sudden stop at the mirror over the great fireplace and dropped softly to the floor. The feel, so light, of the finally stilled body, when one stooped to pick it up.

The sun in the queen's apartments in Madrid shone gray and wan and reminded María of the faint beam that fell on the first bird that died, its feet curled and pulled up into the soft feathers. Marie had taken her chance then, she had touched the crest of pink, stroked the little corpse. The marquise's had been no place for tears, though, and she left with her maid before anyone noticed. At home, she was out of her coach almost before the horses had stopped, the dead bird hidden in her muff. She ran down the galleries, she put her head in her nana's lap, *Pas juste, pas juste.* It isn't fair. She was behaving like a child of five, not a young lady of fifteen. Nana put her hand under Marie's chin and lifted her face. *Whatever made you think that life was fair, child?*

The bird was replaced the next afternoon with another even pinker than the first, which, after the example of Mademoiselle de Toquetoque, came to rest in the garden, but without palpable effect on the flowers. Of course, the king's roses could hardly be improved upon, they were already fertilized with fish from the Caspian Sea, with the blood of lambs and the bones of pheasants and all the other sacrifices made in the royal kitchens.

Had her father known what passport the purchase of lovebirds would arrange, he might have considered them even less desirable gifts than monkeys, hydrophobia notwithstanding, but the marquise's entertainments, along with the pink cigarros filched from the marquis's hidden stock (what a boon that her absentminded husband couldn't remember where it was he had stashed them!) were a secret carefully guarded by ladies and their maids. If the men were to learn of such revels, they would have put a stop to them, as killjoy fathers and husbands always did.

Yes, girls hide things from their fathers. They grow up, then, and keep secrets from their husbands.

The queen began to consult witches because of infertility. Not the unfortunate souls who ended up my neighbors, not laundresses or nursemaids, but admitted sorcerers and makers of potions. Beautiful women, some of them, they earned enough money off the superstitious court to dress in such silks as nobility could hardly afford. They did nothing for María except to take her gold coins, seven ducados for a little copper hand wrapped in coltsfoot and bound up with hairs from Carlos's pillow. She was to wear it only when they lay together, wear it next to her heart. She told the king it was to protect them from sorcery, and of course he approved of that. Around his own neck he wore a paper folded seven times and secured in a locket made of leather from the ear of a hare, a fragile pink leather. On the seven-folded paper were the words *In nomine patris et fili et spiritus sancti,* followed by a long roster of saints' names and angels, and lastly the names of their highnesses written in what was said to be ink made of nuns' blood, then *Christus ab omni vexati me diabolicae perversitatis te Carlos et Maria defendat. Amen.* Very bad Latin, but then most witches are not so well tutored in their Latin as I am.

After the two state weddings—the proxy at Versailles and the hurried affair in Burgos—Carlos and María had a third wedding. A colleague of Carlos's confessor arranged it in great secrecy, lest anyone find out, especially his mother. The king and queen went cloaked from the palace at midnight, after Marianna had retired. They were guided by a hooded person, whether man or woman they never learned. They carried salt in their pockets and coins in their shoes. In the church of San Cristóbal, in a dark chapel near the north entrance, they were greeted by a cleric who also was cloaked and hooded. When directed, the queen removed her wedding rings and Carlos made his water pass through those gold and jeweled circles three times. The cleric prayed in a language they could not understand, he doused them with waters sacred and profane, and then the couple was returned to the royal residence.

Such nocturnal rites are, of course, forbidden. Their performance is reason enough to hang a common person like me. But in his fear of impotence, Carlos has been attended over the years by many upon whom the Church would frown. In the wake of initial disappointments, Carlos and María were fumigated with a special magic fish upon retiring, something caught from the great river Amazon in the New World and brought home to Spain packed in tamarind bark. And for one month, each evening upon retiring, Carlos's royal member was anointed with hypericum juice, with wine and honey. In all, the king was better seasoned than a state dinner, the cook could have taken lessons from the witch. After that, Carlos's manliness increased, and, excited by the fumigations, he decreed that he and María were to be exorcised weekly: stripped and rubbed and beaten with holy switches, splashed with water from a font. Untoward spirits were exhorted by holy men who screamed into their navels and ears and assholes, trying to rout them out. A hot stick was shoved into María's nostril to smoke out the devil, and morning and evening, Carlos enjoyed enemas of holy water.

Not only the illiterate daughters of silk growers and soap makers are impressed by the written word. Evidently, spirits are not immune to such power as that conjured by symbols traced on parchment. The king's and queen's names were written everywhere, on hundreds of bits of paper sealed into tiny envelopes and worn next to the skin of pious nuns. A whole convent wore their names, nuns prayed each hour for their fecundity. Two hundred friars walked to San Sebastián under a banner asking that God send their highnesses such evidence of his love as could only be indicated by the queen's pregnancy.

Though blame was generally placed on María, there were many who suspected that King Carlos was unable to get his queen with child. María's own uncle, King Louis, was the worst for curiosity about Carlos's manhood. The Sun King's spies stole so many pairs of the Spanish king's drawers to inspect them for emissions that the king had to be re-outfitted monthly by the royal tailor.

Poor Carlos. In spite of excitement over scourging and fumigations, in spite of eating quantities of Severo's potency pills, in spite of praying while fucking, nothing worked; and Carlos began to suffer fits of melancholy so deep that for days he would not eat or speak but lay inert in his bed. The moat of relics heaped around him grew so wide that even his valet could not step near, and his gloom spread over the kingdom until almost all of the flowers in the palace park ceased to bloom. On those days on which he rose and allowed himself to be dressed, his mood was as fragile as one of the remaining sickly blooms: one discouragement would knock the frail pink endeavor from its stalk. Either that, or the cumulative disappointments of the day—the dismal reports from the financiers, the news of outbreaks of plague, the sinking of ships and the inevitable discovery of another family of Jews hiding under the Academia de Historia—it all wilted his spirits so that by evening he was hiding again under his hair shirts and martyr's knuckles.

When María Luisa recovered from her broken rib, she was summoned to the king's audience chamber and then she was told by Carlos, Marianna standing nodding behind him, that she could not ride again.

"Never?" she said. "Surely you do not mean never?"

"It is too great a risk," Carlos said. "Severo concurs that another fall could compromise whatever hopes we have of your conceiving a child." His little speech sounded rehearsed, an impression supported by Marianna's nodding. His mother had coached him, María guessed.

"I see," she said.

Her one pleasure taken from her, María returned to her bedchamber and brooded. For a month she sulked. She looked out the window past the grille and watched the swallows over the pool as they flirted with their reflections, coming within a hair-breadth of their shadows on the water. The reflected bird, the illusion, lived and shimmered, breathed and flew just as the living one did, disappearing into the deep black water. Diving down, then surfacing. Reality, illusion. The bird in the air looked no more real than the one in the water. She watched and watched them until she was in a trance some days, there was nothing else to do. Slowly, an idea began to form. A plan.

When the court traveled, as it did each June, to the Escorial, that prison called a summer residence, Marianna took her daughter-in-law on a more complete house tour than any she had given her before. They went through libraries and solariums. They toured the pastry kitchen and then they descended into the crypt below the palace church, not the gold-and-black mausoleum that was famous all over Europe—no, that place was only for the remains of kings and of those queens who produced heirs, Marianna said. She showed María a neighboring chamber of all-white marble: floor and ceiling, walls and sarcophagi. Lamplight shone prettily on the white surfaces of eternal sleep. "Queens without issue," said Marianna, and she looked sharply at her daughter-in-law.

That night, María Luisa asked Eduardo and Esperte to help her. She told them of her idea, a drama she would like to enact. They listened, they considered. Finally they agreed.

That summer, the dwarf and the translator managed, between them, to spirit away the little cloths upon which María spilled her monthly blood. Eduardo's long tenure as a jester was helpful; years of prestidigitation made his tiny hands quick. And Esperte, well, that particular subterfuge was less dangerous for a woman.

The queen of Spain's two friends secreted her bloodstained cloths on their own persons. In her apartments they took them from her and they put them in their underclothes. It was not without risk, and on one occasion the bloodied bandages were discovered on Eduardo by the palace gamekeeper. The accident involved some dogs: as Eduardo hurried away from the estate's grounds to the thicket where he burned María's cloths, one of the king's hounds caught the scent of ripened blood. Joined by two more, the animal easily overtook the dwarf on his short legs. Together they caught him and tore off his hose and breeches, exposing drawers filled with red-stained cloths. Afterward, Eduardo suffered an unpleasant course of cathartic treatments to relieve the hemorrhoids he said tormented him.

"Is this not chivalry?" he asked, laughing between spasms of intestinal cramps brought on by enough strong senna tea to make a regular-sized person quite ill. María sat by his bed.

"I would tell you it was the best example I have seen in this country, but that would not be much of a compliment," she replied, shifting queasily in her chair. All summer Esperte brought the queen emetic herbs and fed them to her in secret after breakfast so that María could pretend the sickness that comes with carrying a child.

When they returned from the Escorial to Madrid, it had been three months—June, July and August—since the observed and documented cessation of the queen's monthly flow. Carlos, Marianna and all the court were ecstatically happy. Bells rang nonstop. One thankful novena commenced before another was concluded. María set about trying to crochet a little silk cap for the pretended baby.

"How flat you remain," Carlos said, his hand on her stomach. "You are not being laced, are you?" he said, his small eyes made smaller as he squinted in worry.

"No," she said, and in the privacy of her apartments she opened her bodice. "See, no stays." She patted his arm. "A woman does not show a child so soon," she said to him.

Severo examined María. It mattered not, he told Marianna, that the queen's breasts had not yet swelled as an expectant woman's should. In time they would. Anyhow, he said, what sort of queen would give suck to her own children?

"None, none," agreed the queen mother, shuddering fastidiously at the notion.

The pig's blood was intended for the manufacture of blood pudding. It was delivered to the royal residence on the evening of the third Friday of every month. Delivered in a large crock made fast with a doubly knotted cord, it sat in the kitchen overnight, for the cook did not begin to make blood pudding until Saturday.

The dwarf's fingers, though practiced in parlor tricks and juggling, were so short that to untie the cords was difficult for him. He panted with fear as he crouched in the dark kitchen. When at last he got the lid off, he dipped a ladle into the blood and took out as much as he dared, filling María's chamber pot to the depth of his first finger's second knuckle. He put the dripping finger in his mouth and sucked it clean, then replaced what blood he had taken with water and stirred it into the crock. He retied the knots of the cord.

Step by silent step from kitchen to María's apartments. Careful not to spill even a drop. One hundred and three stairs.

The blood was cool, even cold. "Ugh. My God, my God," the queen said as Eduardo stood watch and Esperte poured it over her thighs, between her thighs. When she stood from her bed, it ran down her legs, and María carefully made footprints to her chamber pot and back to her bed. The smell of blood filled the room. Esperte, a little squeamish about such things, felt ill as she watched that first time. When María was back in her bed, lying in her blood-soaked nightdress, Esperte stood back and looked at her mistress with her hands over her mouth.

"All right. Go. Go!" said the queen. She gave Esperte and Eduardo a quarter of an hour to return to their beds before she began to scream.

KNEW THAT MAMA WOULD LEAVE US, WOULD die. I knew it even before the parish notary arrived to draft her will, for though she could make her own letters and sentences, it was the business of the Church to oversee a testament. Mama made her confession of sins and of faith, and the death tithe was paid from the coins she had brought home from Madrid. Then, one night, Papa went to fetch the priest from his lodgings, the new priest who was tall and had good leather shoes, the same who had occasionally read her letters to us. Alvaro.

Yes, my Alvaro, though I did not know him yet. I was still a child.

Mama was hemorrhaging after a fit of coughing. There was blood, a lot of it. It spilled all over her and us. Dolores and I had been quarreling—we were unmindful of our mother's deterioration in that way children have of not seeing obvious dangers. Oh, I suppose we were frightened to see her so thin and to hear the coughing, but we didn't think about it. Instead, we went along as usual and that evening we fought. When Dolores reached over Mama's legs to slap me, I caught her hand. Mama sat up as she had not for days and she tried to separate us. She began to cough and the blood came up, spilling down her chin and neck.

We stopped, stunned, and watched as it soaked into her nightdress. She was sitting up in her bed; and her nightdress, a new one of bleached linen, was white, very white. Her face had that beauty peculiar to the dying, as if already she partook of the spirit. I guess I always believed my mama was holier than Mary, above even the Queen of Heaven, who stands with her feet on the moon and stars. When I saw the blood and watched it soak into her gown, I was frightened, but I was also awed, as if some mystery were unfolding.

She lay back, and the blood spilled out of the corner of her mouth, and her face grew more and more lovely, her eyes bigger and more beautiful. To a child inured to the ugly stink of plague, of people's swollen armpits and lolling tongues, of pus and black swellings in their groins, swellings so close to their secret parts that it seemed as if they must have been some punishment for concupiscence, there was something mysterious and beautiful in my mother's dying, something that must have come from the everlasting talk of the Church, of blood redeeming souls. My mama looked to me as if she died in a fountain of holiness.

After Papa left to fetch the priest, I stood waiting by the window near Mama's bed. She roused herself suddenly and took my hand. "I dreamed nine dreams," she said, and she told me that there was a cat sitting on her chest and he was so heavy she could not breathe. "Chase him away, Francisca," she said, and then she said no more but only tried to live a little longer.

From the window, I could see nothing. It was a moonless night, and quiet, as quiet as if all creation held its tongue. We spoke not a word, and Mama breathed so slowly and shallowly, but she was not resting. No, her attention was keen, and her hand held tight to mine, and I knew there were many about her bed waiting—her mama and her papa, her sisters and Ernesto, and all the little sons who died. Together they cried for her to hurry to them.

Then, all at once, her breathing grew fierce and loud like an animal's. So loud that it seemed to catch hold of me, to take me in its teeth and shake my bones. I covered my ears with my hands, but the noise itself tore them away and forced me to listen. I tried to find the place on Mama's arm where Dolores had showed me her pulse beating, I wanted to feel the language of that heart which loved me best. It had been steady on the morning of that day, but now it was so erratic that the beats scattered under my fingertips like spilled grain. As I sat beside my dying mother, holding tight to her arm, something happened to me.

Did I swoon? I felt an unaccustomed lifting. I know I used to fill my head with nonsense about saints and all manner of feverish ravings, but that night—I cannot say for how long or by what power—I truly felt myself plucked from the material world and from the ordinary minute-by-minute march of time.

I found myself in a secret chamber of God's unknowable heart. I had a certainty that life held a beauty and an order which I could but dimly perceive, and which at that time I compared to the teasing appearance of unreadable words on the page, an unknown key to human understanding and happiness. Perhaps it was no more than the shock of being once again parted from my mother, my life, this time forcibly and finally. Perhaps it was the ecstasy accompanying that annihilation. Whatever it was that came over me, the fit passed quickly, the thoughts remained but their potency evaporated, they became ideas as dead and as cold as my mother was soon to be.

When I came back to myself, the house was still. Even the fire burned without a pop or crack, and I could hear Father Alvaro's cassock as he walked toward our house. His cleric's robe, a little long, hissed over the cobbles as he and Papa approached.

Dolores let the men in, and the priest wasted no time with us but kneeled immediately by my mama's bed. He began to pray, and when he wiped her mouth before he anointed her, I thought to myself, *He cannot help himself, he cannot resist touching her.* The Latin of the viaticum was mysterious and beautiful. It flowed from Alvaro's lips and all around us, and we, too, kneeled as Mama was anointed. Long after her whispered profession of faith, he went on praying, invoking the Virgin, *Mater pulchrae dilectionis, liberos tuos adjuva.* Mother of fair love, help your children.

I heard an owl call softly and mournfully, as if the great bird of night also listened and grieved. It was late, I was young, I swayed on my knees. I sat back on my heels, and, finally, it seems to me, I slept, although I did not lie down.

When I awoke, the priest had left, my mother was dead. There was wax on her eyelids, and I knew that she belonged to us no more now, but to the priest and to the Church.

Dolores was busy throwing out all the water in the house,

which you must do when someone dies. For this is what people believe, that the water takes into itself the spirit of death and must not be used for drinking or any other purpose, not to wash off a plate or to put out a flame. And you must be careful where you throw that water, for if it soaks into the earth where the roots of a tree are hidden, well, those roots and perhaps the whole tree will die.

Even that day, even directly after Father Alvaro's visit, I found I remembered little of his being there. I recalled the odd detail. I remembered that his hose, when he bent over my mama in her bed to anoint her lips, were dark purple, the color of an eggplant. *Requiescat in pace.* Peace.

"Mother of God!" Mama would exclaim when she was angry with my sister or me. "Only when I am stretched out with dirt covering my eyes, only then will I have *peace*," she would say. The vehemence with which she said the word, spat it out. *Peace.* Now the priest had come and had given her what she had so wanted, proclaimed it in the language of the Church.

We had not enough money to pay for mourners or for a sin-eater to sit by her body with his plate of cold mutton, chewing away at whatever transgressions might keep my mother in purgatory. We did not have enough for friars to carry her from our house to the church, but neighbors helped, and despite Papa's expulsion from the guild of silk growers, my mother did not go into the charnel trench. No, Concepción de Luarca was allowed burial in the church of Quintanapalla, where my grandfather rested beneath our pew, as did his brother and all our family (except Ernesto, whose body disappeared, and the little dead children of my mother and my aunts, whose flesh had to be content to wait outside until such time as Christ would come to wake them).

The slab covering the Luarca grave had a hole in it where the gravedigger could put his crowbar to pry up the block of slate, and around the hole was a design of eleven silkworms making a circle and, below that, the letters for the name Luarca. It was eleven worms because it was from eleven hundred eggs that my ancestor Sandoval had begun the Luarca family silk business. We set Mama in her tomb, and the slab slid into place with a gritty, regretful sound—a sigh, if stone could sigh—and I wondered if she had at last the peace she had said she wanted.

When my mother left for Madrid, three years before her death, she took comfort with her, but so long as she was alive, I believed comfort existed in the world and I believed in its return. When she died, comfort died too. I was tormented by memories of her sitting by our bed, of her singing in the evenings as we fell asleep. She knew many songs; I cannot remember more than a verse of any of them, but they were songs of love and romance, of young men who went out in the world to seek a wife and the trials they endured for the women they wanted.

When Mama died, Dolores was a girl of about fourteen. Not yet fully grown, neither was she a child, and to her fell all those duties that belonged to women. Dolores made a mockery of the idea of a home. She knew how to tend a pot, but the meals that came from hers were without taste. Whatever she cooked might have been good except for the lack of an onion or a clove of garlic, things that were not unobtainable. No, something easy, something hanging by the hearth. Something she withheld.

The character of my life without my mother became such that I survived, certainly, but there was always the rebuke of whatever was missing. Buttons off dresses, hose not mended, fingernails ragged, cups chipped. Everything was clean, my frocks and even my underthings, hidden from the world, had no stains; but there would be one unmended seam and my hair left unplaited. To me, these were shameful announcements to all that our mother was gone; and when I went out in the world I felt that people looked upon me as one insufficiently loved.

Dolores must have grieved after her fashion, but I was the only one to cry either at Mama's death or after it. My sister held her back straight and set her chin. Papa became distant and vague, except for brief fits of rage, which were almost always directed at me. For I wept, and my crying drove him wild with anger.

He would begin by begging. "Stop, Francisca, *stop*," he would say. "Please stop, child. It doesn't do any good, this crying." And he would tell me how it troubled my mama up in heaven, never letting her spirit go easily to its reward. Or how the weeping would wear out my eyes until I was blind, how he would apprentice me and send me to live with the weavers in Epila, and on and on. But nothing he said could check my tears, even when he resorted to threats, saying, "Stop! Or I'll turn you out of this house, I will, for I cannot stand another minute of it, Francisca!"

Finally, he beat me. He would cuff the side of my head so that I would fall to the floor. I would cover myself, and he would kick me, even, while Dolores remained silent and stolid. She stepped around us, continuing her chores. When he stopped, I would crawl to him and climb like a tiny child into his lap, for when the fit had passed I was not frightened. My father was a gentle man in all other ways and times, and something in me understood that his striking me was just his way of railing against fate. His rage was the only thing that could purge us both, me of my grief and him of his anger. I have fond memories of our sitting quietly together with him rocking me.

Mama left behind a small chest of belongings. Cures, they were, herbs and other things as well, things that were condemned by the Church but in which people kept their faith, and it was not any slight to God to use them because whatever power was in them was put there by God, so what was the harm? Was there any difference between an amber bead to ward off the evil eye and a relic of a saint or a scapular with a holy image? They were all the same, my mother said, but she kept her amulets secret nonetheless. It was not possible to be too careful when any harmless thing might be considered evidence of witchcraft.

After Mama died I kept her chest secret from all eyes, I found a place where it was safe and spent a part of every day going through the contents, although I knew them as well as the back of my hand. A necklace of shells from the sea to prevent children from foaming at the mouth; those gray donkey beads taken from just under the forelock of some animals and used to make a foul-smelling poultice. Glass beads, and that yellow compound taken against jaundice. Powerful words written on small papers sealed in wax or velvet pouches. Dried herbs in little leather bags tied with horsehair. The powder from the white hellebore roots we collected in autumn and dried on the hearth, and which we used on the floor beneath our bed to keep fleas and lice away. Dried hop flowers, too, which we gathered wearing gloves and a kerchief tied around our mouths and noses, otherwise it would cause us to sweat and have palpitations. Senna, and monk's rhubarb. Savin for the kidneys, and deadnettles for the monthly time, and the five-fingered grass that stops diarrhea. Silverweed seeds for spasms of the womb. Orpine for pus. Dried arum berries, which I had eaten once as a small child and which had taken me to the point that I could hardly breathe and nearly expired, for the berries are poisonous when fresh and uncured. A headache powder I used to watch her make from equal parts goose grass, sapodilla and the thorn weed, which never grows in the same place twice but which—required as it was for every woman's larder of cures—had to be tracked down each summer when it flowered and released its nauseating odor.

I opened all the little bags and inhaled, as if breathing their contents would heal me of the sorrow of which I believed I should die. For it seemed impossible that my mama, whom I loved without measure, was gone and had left me with all that love for her still in my heart, yet with no place to go. I tried every cure she left behind, but there was nothing that could help me. I was so wretched that I stopped growing taller. How could I continue, how could I change, unwitnessed by my mother?

Dolores was three years older than I. Wherever we went she was in a great hurry and she held my hand tight. I took three steps for each one of hers, but still I tripped on the cobbles or on a stick. Or I just tripped on air, it seemed.

"Clumsy!" she would say, and she would pull my arm with impatience until it began to hurt me all the time, my left arm.

"Quiet!" she would say, at least a hundred times a day. "Quiet! Or I'll tell Papa to feed you to the wolf."

Now that it had fallen to Dolores to be my mother and to

discipline me, she would try to contend with me as I did with her. She invented a wolf who lived in the old silk house, and she threatened to let it out so it should catch and kill me. Well, though my sister's bad-temperedness and constant rebukes may have been as ready to eat me up as a slavering beast, I knew she did not quite believe in her wolf, so I decided to help her.

"Have you seen him, then?" I asked. "He came last night while you were sleeping. I didn't wake you for fear you would scream and then he would kill you for certain.

"It is not me he wants," I told Dolores. "He stood here, by your side of the bed, and look where he scratched a D on the door." I pointed to a clumsy letter I had made in the wood with a sharp stone. Mama taught me that much, anyway. When Dolores looked at the door, I could see by her mouth drawn into a small circle that I had frightened her, and she gave up on the wolf and on turning my own tricks against me.

When I could, I would go to my friend Natalia's home. Natalia's father was a wine merchant; they lived over his shop, which had in it casks and barrels and jugs of all sizes. I was greatly taken with Natalia and enchanted by her nimbleness. She was a pretty child, and I knew that were she to walk with Dolores, she would never stumble, she would skip daintily by her side. Natalia would not cry and thereby grieve her papa; and were I only like her, my life would be different. And so I studied Natalia, I tried to move as she did, I practiced taking graceful steps, balancing on the stones behind our house. When we played together I would beg to try on her shoes, which were not like my wooden clogs (the end of our mother and her work was also the end of leather shoes for us) but were kidskin slippers her papa bought her. They had designs pressed into the tops of them, designs that looked to me like writing, magic words that I imagined formed some spell that kept her from tripping.

I wanted to coax my toes into those pretty slippers, but my feet were too big. "You will grow into them," Mama had said of my feet. But then she died and I decided not to grow any more. Natalia's little feet disappeared into my clogs as she laughed. We spent many afternoons in the wineshop, underfoot, but her father did not mind our being there, nor did her mother. If it was cold outside or if it rained, we could always go there; it was better than at my house, where Dolores spied on our games.

One day I went to Natalia's papa's shop and he told me I had to go home. Dolores took me back a day later; they had Natalia lying in a box on a table where I could not see her. My sister picked me up and held me over the box. Natalia was wearing a white dress, and there was lace on the collar. Beautiful lace like the kind that comes from Brussels. Wedding lace, the lace she had shown me among the other things from her mama's dowry. "Oh, Natalia!" I breathed, "you are wearing your communion dress!"

She was dead. I must have known this, for I was not such a young child and I had seen my dead mama just a year before; yet it seemed to me that Natalia was asleep. Her hands were tied together with a long strip of white cloth, and I asked why. Was she a sleepwalker?

Dolores told me that Natalia had turned into an angel, and that the following day all the people would take her to the shrine at Queranna.

"Will we watch her fly up out of the box?" I wanted to know. All I remember about going to Queranna was the mud where so many had trampled the earth outside the shrine. That and the backs of people taller than I. But I did begin to regard my life a little differently. Now I have a friend in the sky, I thought, and I wanted to die, too, so I could fly up and be with Natalia and Mama. But I was frightened, too, and the fear of death, of Mama's and Natalia's being dead, settled into the color white. Anything white—not just winding-sheets, but a lily, even, or a white chasuble on a priest, the dresses we were to wear for our first communion. The color white thrilled me, it made me tremble.

As if, even then, I guessed the place I would end in, this place of White Hoods.

The first time I came to Madrid was with my father. In the year after Mama died, Papa made a trip to this city to collect payments owed to my mother from the palace, and I accompanied him. The throngs of people, the noise and heat and dust of that summer following Mama's death, the vendors wiping their wares ceaselessly, keeping them free of the dirt that blew along the roads in the wake of carriages. Constables and soldiers and hawkers and beggars, women with young children. The unceasing calls of people selling soaps and candles and knives and sweets, wines and orangeades and sandals and scarves. I had never been in such crowds before, and I clutched my papa's arm. Despite having begged to accompany him, I felt I was being dragged somewhere against my will and was sure I would die in the heat and dust. There was a protest over some tax or another, and we were held up by a great throng in the street and forced to wait outside a city tanner's business, much bigger than the shop that had been in our town, so big that a full dozen men scraped meat from hides with broad knives. They made long swipes with the blades and then drew them against their legs before the next pass. The smell of lye was strong and sickening.

An unearthly music interrupted my watching them, and I turned to see the approach of a party of lepers ringing their bells. Their faces were white and fleshless, and I found them curiously beautiful. To my eyes their rags seemed like lace, and I asked my papa, holding on to his hand, "Are they angels? Are they coming to tell us something about Mama?"

"No!" he said, and roughly he pulled me to the side of the road. "Why are you so given to strange fancies!" he hissed, but I paid him no mind. I watched how easily the lepers got through the crowds that had delayed us almost an hour. The people parting to let them pass only further convinced me that they were holy visitors, spirits who might tell me of my mother, and I tried to escape Papa's hand so that I might follow them. When he would not let me go I felt tired and ill and suddenly defeated in everything, and I made as if to lie down on the ground.

"How you hinder me, Francisca! I wish to heaven I had left you with Dolores!" Papa said, and, at the advice of one of the men at the tanner's, he ended up entrusting me to the care of the Monasterio de la Encarnación, the same whose charitable offices had first hired my mother as a wet nurse. The friars gave me a cup of water and left me on a stool in their library, among all their books and two monks studying there. I looked to see that my hands were quite clean and then I asked their leave to touch the books, to take them down and examine the marks on the pages inside.

I wanted so much to be able to read, I felt that this ability which my mother had wanted to give me would, like the ringing bells of the white angels I had just seen, clear a path before me. If I could read, I might also tread as an angel, unhindered.

 *ou be my book, my prayer book.*

He said this, and he pushed away what we were studying. Not the Bible or *Lives of the Saints,* but a book of magic stories by a man called Ovid. A book of women turning into trees, of a god become a bull who rapes the daughter of the king, of a lover going down to hell for his bride. Of many nights of passion written in the language of the Church. It was the sun in his chariot, and the son of the sun dying in that burning heavenly conveyance. It was the head and lyre of a poet, Orpheus, floating down a river, still singing, the tongue and the strings together.

You be my book.

That is what he said as he opened my legs. His tongue was silver. Clever, yes, and when it touched me I changed. Like alchemy, like those verses written by the poet Ovid, but I was not turned into a tree, no, I was nothing earthbound. If Daphne became wood, I was that wood thrown on the fire. I was the spirit that rises heavenward: invisible, escaping.

I was the tremble in the air that you can see above a bonfire.

He would embrace me and put himself between my legs, touching the inside of my thigh up high near my sex. *This is what silk is, Francisca. This is the silk that no worm can make.*

When he came from behind me, when he put his hands around my waist and pulled me to him, I felt how small I was. I felt his thumbs almost meet over my spine. I felt his fingers on my hipbones as if he were holding two handles of a bowl. Sometimes he would drink from me. And sometimes I was a cup he would take and dash to pieces on the floor. I felt myself break up and fly apart. It felt good to be freed.

I rose until I was above the cares of all the people I knew, until each person was so small I could not make out the color of a dress, the features of a face. Sometimes I might recognize a body by its walk.

Up high, the sun shone with a fierceness. There was no wind. The birds that seemed to dart so quickly when viewed from underneath revolved slowly below me. There was no loud noise: no voices, no tears, no speeches or clamor of any sort. Only a thin hum of collective sighs and curses, prayers and imprecations. No individual cry rose to where I found myself.

In heaven there are no errands, no duties, no obligations. Even a great city like Madrid is rendered small and incidental. Far, far below: a tangled weave of activity, as if in the great mortal loom the heddles had snapped and threads took directions of their own. Some formed a lovely tapestry, others a dirty trodden carpet.

Sometimes I began to weep, for there is grief in altitude. Sometimes I would wonder, how do the angels stand it?

HEY WERE CAUGHT, OF COURSE. HOW COULD such a ruse continue? They were as cautious as they could be, but palace guards kept vigil on all the stairs, and Carlos was a fitful sleeper. The king was known to walk in his sleep, in which event he was never woken, he was followed by his confessor, the two men silently slipping through the dark halls. Once the sleeping king had ventured as far as the map room. And it was not only nighttime exposure that threatened their subterfuge. The cook complained that the butcher was cheating the royal kitchens by delivering thin blood, and Severo's continued examinations of María Luisa's breasts left him puzzled. Why, he mused to the queen mother, did the queen's milk flesh not swell if she was pregnant? Why did her nipples remain that palest pink?

To get away once with the deceit of a staged miscarriage was possible. Twice, unlikely. Three times, remarkable.

Almost five months into the queen's fourth feigned pregnancy, the dwarf Eduardo was apprehended on the west stair, just before dawn. In his arms was a chamber pot containing blood. A guard stepped out of the shadows, and the sound of his boots echoed through the cold stone corridors, echoed and multiplied, sounding to the dwarf, crouched in the shadows, like the approach of an army of tall men. Eduardo, small hands slick with sweat, dropped the chamber pot, and it broke on the stairs.

By the time the queen mother herself saw the spilled evidence, the pig's blood had dripped thickly, slowly and deliberately down to the landing below. Away from the queen's bedchamber it dripped, as if trying to avoid the scene of the next intended crime, as if in loyalty to the co-conspirators.

As Marianna looked at the blood on the stairs, María and Esperte waited in the queen's apartments. The sun was just beginning to rise. "What can have happened!" cried the queen. Esperte was helplessly wringing her hands and walking from bed to window, from window to bed, when Eduardo—forcibly escorted only as far as the door by the guard—entered the room. The flame of the one candle burning on María's nightstand trembled at the sudden draft of air and set all their shadows leaping. In the hall, the king, queen mother and guard stood silently, hidden from view.

"Why, you've spilled it!" María cried, seeing the stain on Eduardo's sleeve.

The dwarf made no answer.

"Is there no more left?" she said. "Where is my chamber pot?"

Eduardo shook his head. He said nothing. From behind him, Marianna and Carlos entered the Queen's bedchamber. Esperte covered her mouth with her hands.

"What are you doing here at this hour?" Marianna asked Esperte.

"I called her," said María quickly. "I could not sleep. I wanted company."

"Why not call your husband, in that case?" asked the queen mother.

"I wanted female company," said María. She did not look at Eduardo or at his sleeve, its darkening, stiffening stain of evidence.

"Well, then," said Marianna, "you could have asked for me," and then she said, "Daughter." At that word, spoken so venomously, María Luisa sat suddenly down on her bed.

No one said anything for a minute, two minutes, more. Esperte lost her nerves and fell to her knees weeping. Carlos, his face still pale and flat with sleep, began to cry as well. He made no noise, used as he was to disguising grief held inappropriate to majesty; but tears fell down his cheeks.

"There was no baby?" he said to his wife. "There never were any babies?"

The queen put her hands to her face. She shook her head.

Interrogated downstairs, Esperte admitted her part in the deception. She admitted that she had brought the queen herbs to help her pretend childsickness. She admitted spiriting away the cloths bearing stains of María's monthly flow. She admitted that she loved María and that she would have done any evil thing for her mistress.

She admitted she was a wanton, undeserving slattern, and she agreed to the queen mother's suggestion that she had cast spells and made potions. When Marianna asked if she had fashioned little dolls of wax, Esperte laughed and laughed; she could not stop. She did not deny it, nor any other accusation. The translator, whose usefulness had long been outgrown, who had been retained as companion to a lonely foreign queen—for what harm could a convent girl cause?—suffered such hysterics that her teeth chattered. She heard herself calling Marianna a fat old spider, a snake, a cow, and possibly even worse things, which she subsequently forgot. Eduardo had no chance to say good-bye to Esperte, for the little translator was removed from the royal residence that very afternoon and thrown into the cell next to mine.

As for the dwarf, there was no disciplinary action taken against him. At least not immediately, not obviously. Carlos and his mother remained closeted in their respective apartments. For some days they even ate in solitude, away from the courtiers, and away from the queen, who breakfasted alone at the long, long table, who lunched alone, too, and went to bed before sunset, without any dinner.

María was afraid. No one spoke to her, not one person, but all the people who touched her in the course of a day, all those present only by the actions of their hands—dressers and hair-dressers and maids and manicurists—grew kinder. Now that it was clear not only that María Luisa would not produce an heir, but that she had tried to deceive her husband the king and must therefore be doomed, those serving hands no longer pulled the queen's hair and dressed it so tightly that her head began to ache within the hour. They did not pinch her as they fastened her stays. Indeed, no longer did they exact any cost at all for her high-and-mightiness. As if in recognition that now they had such power as she did not—the power of the living, of the safe, of the loved—they stroked her. Affectionately they tucked stray locks behind her ears and caressed her neck. They kissed her almost, these sympathetic hands, fingertips lingering at her waist, her toes and aching temples, for they were not so cruel that they would deny small comforts. Not when the situation had grown so desperate.

The queen's flesh recognized their pity, understood what it meant and tightened with fear.

The scent of her doom wafted down the long corridors after María. It was a strange odor, it was like that of a stale floral arrangement: the sweetness of withered petals overcome by the smell of stems rotting in a slime-slick vase. The smell entered a room before María Luisa, it announced her arrival. At meals the servants took note of it and set her plate before her with excellent silence. They arranged every morsel so artfully that each bite might have been presumed her last. Her breakfast chocolate—which in the old days had been served cold enough that María had had to lift a skin from its surface with her spoon—was served hot, and steam curled prettily from the cup. At last María did not have to take up her spoon to break that unsavory and yet implicitly hopeful milk skin, lifting it from the sweet surface and leaving it to congeal and adhere to her saucer.

Two weeks after the dwarf's capture on the stairs, Carlos appeared at table across from Queen María. He greeted his wife for the first time in a fortnight and was seated. The familiar sight of Carlos's sopped bread made the queen feel nauseated, as usual, but she ate her one bun and, on the morning I am picturing her, three Chinese oranges. A visitor had brought an entire crate of these as a gift.

María had company. A week after Esperte was taken away, the comtesse de Soissons had arrived in Madrid. She came from Versailles, to stay for a month, before going on to her winter residence in Majorca. She was a lively guest, she offered many diversions besides the hamper packed with fruit and chocolates and marzipan and candied ginger, all manner of delicacies carried over the border from France. The comtesse was as delicious as all of these, and she did her best to cheer up the queen. Despite having been forced to leave the French court early and at the height of the fall season (a little matter of a love spat with the king and a subsequent paroxysm of jealousy by Madame de Maintenon), Olympe de Soissons's spirits were irrepressibly high.

Of course, none of the Spanish livery would wait upon the comtesse, at least not after the second week of her visit, for rumors of arsenic caught up with the pretty visitor.

"She killed the king of France's mistress!" the queen's maid Obdulia had whispered to the dwarf, her dropsical eyes bulging even more than usual.

"Don't be such a fool as to believe everything you hear!" Eduardo retorted.

But rumors about Olympe did include those that she had gradually eaten poison for years: arsenic distilled from apricot pits, which she had taken in higher and higher doses until her flesh was immune. In France it had been whispered that she had made her body into a vessel bearing death. That one kiss and her lover would die. At least, that was what was said late at night, after the confusion of too much wine, the dizziness of too many dances—the hour when people will say anything to keep their audience.

La Jolie Araignée, the pretty spider, they called her.

Olympe was mysterious, she was beautiful. All her features were so sublime, and yet it was as if they were slightly blurred to her admirers' dazzled eyes. Her pliant mouth, her nose, her mutable eyes, all encouraged the comtesse's lovers to see in them whatever characteristic they favored. Her eyes: were they blue or gray, or were they violet? Monsieur de Vendôme said that her nose was sharp; his brother called it a button. To the comte, her lips were as full and sweet as dark cherries. Why, he married her on their account, he said. But the prince of Langlée said they were drawn as sharp as an arrow from Cupid's quiver, he said they lacerated his heart.

The comtesse's personality, too, was as changeable as the shifting pigment of those tiny lizards that creep from leaf to petal, going green to pink to green again. With the prince de Conti, Olympe was brazen and loud and adored playing cards. With his consumptive, bookish cousin, the duc Charles, she became an intellectual, volumes of philosophy slipping from between the folds of her skirts. Her skills at self-alchemy made Olympe de Soissons a great social success.

As for her clothes, the money spent on them might have dressed all of Quintanapalla, spring, summer, fall and winter. Her skirts were the widest in the land. At a masked ball in Paris everyone joked about what might transpire beneath such dresses, for the comtesse de Soissons favored hoops so extreme that her skirts were like tents. After Olympe had sacked her the previous season, the maid who used to dress her at Versailles told that the comtesse's skirts were wide enough that they required three extra lengths of silk, and that her mistress easily hid one lover beneath them while answering the door for another.

And, what was more, her clothes did not always stay on, the maid said. She had once removed all her garments, even her pantaloons, at the premiere of an opera by Quinault and Lully. This was before King Louis had thrown her over, and when he had taken up with the star of *Proserpine*, who was singing on that evening of the comtesse's disrobing. Before the arrival of a gendarme, Olympe was assured that every opera glass in the house was trained on her, and that talk was so loud no one heard the sweet soprano of Juliette Mérival.

When the fascinating Olympe de Soissons arrived in Madrid, the situation she found there was hardly more congenial than that in the Paris court, which had just expelled her.

"Why, what on earth has happened!" she said when she greeted her old playmate Marie. For the queen was in a very nervous condition, one that she said she could not explain until later, when they might be assured of privacy, and when no one would frown at their speaking in French.

Clearly everyone was out of humor. Maids burst into tears at any provocation, and meals were so strained as to cause dyspepsia. When at last they appeared at the same dinner, Carlos and María sat at opposite ends of the long dining table; and the queen mother, forever dressed in her black habit, sat at Carlos's end. The king and queen and queen mother and their guests were outnumbered two to one by the corps of tasters. When dinner was served, plates were passed and traded until the food grew cold.

Carlos, María Luisa, Marianna, the comtesse Olympe, the French minister Rébenac, along with Vasco da Melo, a Portuguese alchemist visiting from Lisbon, and the Austrian minister, Von Richsberger, watched as eight men and seven women gingerly lifted their spoons to their lips and swallowed. They waited until grease congealed on their plates and until the sauces separated into their components. When no one gagged or grew faint, then Carlos began, and Marianna undid her corset and she, too, began to eat.

Fear destroyed the queen's appetite. Each day she awaited some word from Carlos or from his mother, each day she awaited a summons to the audience chamber and there a formal response to her scandalous attempt to dupe an entire empire. But there was nothing. For a week she kept herself buoyed by the hope that she would be returned, in disgrace, to France. She wrote letter after letter to her uncle, King Louis, to her mother, to her brother, to anyone who might be able to help her. She entrusted these to Rébenac, but he returned them to her, saying that it would be best for her to wait.

"Assez! Ça suffit!" he observed. "You have done quite enough. Now let us see how much I can undo."

But Rébenac had had nothing to report for over a week, and so nervous was the queen that she found herself unable to eat in the company of Carlos and his mother. She pushed her eggs around on her plate. Carlos sipped milk from his cup, milk that after it was collected from the wet nurses had been taken to the kitchen and boiled on the stove for twenty-four minutes precisely, twelve rotations of the sandglass and no more, no less. Cooled to room temperature, strained with a cheesecloth, served in a goblet.

The king, to whom common folk ascribe magical powers, to whom lepers pray and whose carriage is mobbed and touched that some power might rub off it, the king has no magic in him, not even the workaday alchemy of a healthy body. He is afraid of illness, of illness and poverty, of woods and horses, of choking and of being poisoned. But, after all, everyone in every court is afraid of being poisoned. Why, the office of taster is the one profession whose ranks swell and whose salary increases.

Long before the palace's staircase was baptized with pig's blood, King Carlos had been afraid of stairs, and of dwarfs. He had dreaded any celestial manifestation. Now, afraid of his wife, as well, the untimely appearance of a comet in the week after Eduardo was apprehended caused him to shut himself in his apartments and hide under the cloak of Saint John of Ortega. He wrapped his belly in the hair shirt of Saint Inés and piled manuscripts—copies made by monks of Saint Teresa's reflections—around his bed, the same in which his father and his father's father died, their bedclothes turned to winding-sheets before they breathed their last. The comet passed on, it singed the sky with its angry tail, and Carlos lay upon his grandfather's bed and asked that God please spare him. That even if María had so displeased the heavens that an angry bullet had shot out of the sky, God must know that Carlos had had no part in his wife's offense.

"What shall I do?" he prayed over and over. And when God forbore to suggest any discipline for a treacherous queen, Carlos decided to leave the whole mess in his mother's capable hands.

Marianna looked across the dinner table at the various guests. Since Olympe's arrival in Spain, the wanton comtesse and María had spent many afternoons together. If Olympe did not actually accompany her daughter-in-law on her walk, then María would return from the royal park and go directly into the comtesse's sitting room on the third story. They drank chocolate together, and maids reported that the comtesse would send all servants away so the two of them could speak French without anyone frowning. She was a fast piece of baggage, that Olympe.

The royal marriage would have to be dissolved, somehow. Von Richsberger, who had arrived just last week in the midst of the disgraceful scandal ensuing from the capture on the stairs, had brought with him several miniatures of the princess Anastasia, who, ill-favored as she was, was the only unwed princess in all Europe. *Marriageable* seemed like flattery, but she would have to suffice. The subsequent alliance of Spain and Marianna's homeland, even if not the long-wished-for reforging of the Hapsburgs, might make a dynasty strong enough that

Austria and Spain together could someday rout King Louis, shove the Sun King's prepossessing light under a barrel.

A dangerous person like that Portuguese alchemist Vasco da Melo, who claimed he could revive dead birds with silver salts, might be useful. In Lisbon, da Melo had built up a thriving business in harmonizing incompatible marriages by transfusion. He sucked the blood out of the quarrelsome husband and piped it into the testy wife, and vice versa. In this way, if they did not die, they stopped arguing. Da Melo's Spanish was not understandable. He seemed to think Portuguese should be good enough, and he hollered all his comments as if amplification could correct for whatever differences there were between his native tongue and Spanish. Then he waited, blinking, for a response. He did not seem even to realize he was eating at a king's table, so bumptious was he. But if he did not do them all in accidentally, if he did not blow up the palace, he might be useful.

Despite the diversion of the visit from her old friend, the queen did look miserable, almost as miserable as she should look, thought Marianna. Maids reported that she was suffering nightmares and slept almost as little as she ate.

In truth, fear had seeped into María's bones like a chill. She complained all the time that she was cold and talked of her hair, which used to lie over her like a warm cloak in the days before she was forced to wear it up on top of her aching head. How her head ached, how it ached all the time, she said, and she stared out the windows and talked of the fires in France.

Of smoke spiraling, twisting, dancing heavenward from all the château's chimneys, a fire burning in every hearth. Each long, long evening after dinner, María Luisa sat in her cold apartments with Olympe and the dwarf. Eduardo listened as aloud the queen remembered happier times. Imagine: almost seventy fires constantly burning in the French palace. And enough servants to tend them, making sure that they never burned low.

HAT WERE THE NINE DREAMS THAT MY MAMA dreamed on the last night of her life? I try to think of what they might have been. A mother's waking dreams are not hard to guess. She wants at least nine good things for her children, she wants nine hundred. But what does she dream while she is sleeping?

Nine is not an unlucky number; it isn't nineteen. Or thirty-nine. Once I made a study of such matters. After Mama died, and then Natalia, I became fearful as I had never been before. I made the sign of the cross on myself often, and I turned around twice to the left and once to the right before walking over the threshold and entering our house. To go out, the reverse: once to the left, twice to the right. Even though she was not without superstition herself, Dolores slapped me whenever she caught me in these actions; she did whatever she could to make my life more miserable.

My sister was always bossy, but she became more so after Mama died. She took advantage of my unhappiness, which was so great that I could not even begin to defend myself, and she was always telling me what to do and treating me for ailments she said I had. For melancholy she had me drink only rainwater. She fed me capers against worms and celery for headaches. I could have no rabbit or chestnuts or cheese, and the quantity of fennel that I swallowed for my eyes delayed my monthly flow so that I believed I should never get it. I ate quince and sycamore and pomegranate until I suffered continually from colic and the flux, and until I stayed abroad at all hours, preferring not to eat at all to being fed by my sister.

Dolores would tie me to Papa's big bed, she would tie my hands to the post. I could have gotten away if I had wanted to, but I was too proud, so I would close my eyes and dream, whether or not I was asleep. Especially on rainy days; it seemed Dolores was forever tying me up when it rained, maybe because she did not want to have to go looking for me in the wet. The streets of Quintanapalla were not paved, most of them, and when the rain came, it came all at once and made holes where you could not see them. You would be walking along the wet road and your leg would suddenly disappear up to the knee in what looked like a regular, shallow puddle.

From where I was tied to the bed I could see the rain at the door, see how it made all the world a slippery, undulating sea, and hear it come down on the roof. It was peaceful and solemn, and it smelled like trees, instead of the old smells of fire and of food we had eaten the night before. It sounded, of course, like the silkworms eating, and that sound made it easier for me to dream, to believe that Mama had never gone away and that my grandfather was still among us—and that I was yet a child imagining illustrious fates for the work of our worms.

When people sleep and dream, their spirits wander afield while their bodies rest, and the trick of dreaming while awake is not so different. With my eyes closed, breathing in the rain, I dreamed that our house had six windows made of glass like the house Natalia had lived in. I dreamed we were both angels now and that we were in a glass box together all wrapped up in white cloths like those they had put around Natalia's wrists. Our mamas and papas took us to the shrine, and there were many people there, as at a big feast day, and all we could see was the backs of people's heads. And then bells began to ring and the glass casket burst open and all the little cloths like magic began unwinding from our arms and legs and stomachs. When we were unwrapped we were naked, but our skin was gold like the angels in the great cathedral, gold like El Dorado's, and we flew up above everyone else, not with wings, but like Saint Teresa made buoyant by prayer. I looked down at Mama's mouth open in astonishment. But then I could not see her anymore, for we were over great smoking clouds of incense and all we heard was people's voices, Mama's among them, saying, *Angelitas!*

When I opened my eyes, Dolores would be shaking me. Sometimes my sister said she had shaken me for an hour, and then she was angry and slapped me, but I didn't care. I could always escape her in my dreams. I did not dislike her any less than when Mama was alive and I felt she stole some love that would otherwise have been mine. No, now that death had proved Mama's love to be finite, I begrudged even more whatever Dolores had gotten of it. When we spoke we spoke of nothing but chores, of a dirty plate left on the table, of how much I should give the baker for a loaf. "And no more!" she'd say, pushing me out of the house. We never talked of what was in our hearts.

By this time I was twelve, the year that children made their first confessions, the year that girls became women and boys, men. At this age we were considered old enough to understand the meaning of sin, but still young enough to be innocent of the sins of the body.

In a dream Mama talked to me of this day, telling me to remember that I was to be a good and worthy vessel to receive the body of Christ. "Do not run or shout on that day, Francisca," she told me, and in my bed, lying as far from Dolores's body as I could, I felt Mama touch me. I felt my mother's hands on my face, on my neck and chest and over my heart.

"Obey your papa and big sister," she said, "and make a good confession. After you eat the body of Christ, hold yourself still. For you will have Jesus in you then, and you do not want to lose Him."

I pictured myself as some drinking cup, a vessel to be filled with holiness and then held carefully, so carefully, for the rest of my life, lest I spill it out. And yet I knew myself—I was the child who knocked over her cup at every meal. The way I saw it, either I would dribble and slop the love of God away or I would knock it down and lose it all at once. It would be impossible to remain filled with holiness.

Nevertheless, when all the children of twelve years went to confess to Father Alvaro, I stood in line with them. Waiting to talk to the priest, I remembered how his purple hose had flashed from under his cassock as he had leaned forward over Mama in her nightdress, for I had not been so close to Father Alvaro since that night long past.

After Milagros, the wheelwright's daughter, went into the

confessionary, there was no other between me and the little house built inside the church. The confessionary looked like a tiny chapel in the big church, it had a pitched roof and a little cross on top like some celestial weather vane, and two doors, two wood benches, two stones upon which to kneel, all divided by a wall with a window hung with a red cloth.

"It is dark inside, you can see nothing but the red square of cloth, and all you hear after you close the door is the priest's voice," Dolores said.

I felt dizzy waiting my turn. I wasn't without transgressions, but I kept thinking, *What shall I say? What shall I say?* I did not even consider betraying the one sin that troubled me. I suffered immodest dreams. What could I do about that? Either Mama came to me in the dark and asked me to be good, or the Devil came.

Just the night previous I had dreamed that I heard the sound of a bird calling out fiercely—it shrieked as if a cat had got it— and when I rose from my bed, I saw a man and a woman and they were naked, and when he touched her she cried out like a bird. I could not keep my eyes away from them, they were so tiny that I had to bend down to look at them where they stood together at my feet. Suddenly there was a carpet on the floor such as only rich people have, a beautiful carpet woven of silk of all colors, and underneath a squirming lump. *Bite it!* commanded a voice in the dream. *You must bite it.* But I did not. I watched the wriggling lump under the carpet, until at last I turned back the edge, drawing it up by the fringe, and underneath the little man and his consort were taking their pleasure one with the other. When I looked more closely at the tiny female I saw she was myself.

That was not all. There was something worse than the dreams. Dolores would leave me at the well when she went to have our corn milled. She said I was so slow that she would not walk with me the whole way, she would just as soon let the old women at the well watch out for me and relieve her of me for an hour or so. But as the women talked, I slipped away. Though I was old enough that I no longer had the freedom allowed to children, and though I had the beginning of a woman's body and was to be watched, I had a talent for making myself invisible. I was not like some of the other girls who ran hoping to be chased, and when I stole away, no one stopped me. I made my afternoons my own.

The tumbledown house by the smith's had a room at the back, a place easily overlooked by those who did not know of it. But the Devil always knew where to find me.

One day I squeezed myself behind an empty cask and put my eye to a place where the boards were warped and parted, like a skirt, to reveal the chamber beyond. There was a woman inside, uncovered, her bodice undone. A nurse, I, like an idiot, thought at first, but there were no babies there. Men came in and took off their belts and buckles straightaway in front of the hearth. From where I was hiding I saw things falling, hats and shirts and occasionally a slice of naked flesh, white and soft.

I returned again and again to spy. I did not care that it was wrong, I slipped away from my chores. It was concupiscence that drew me. Concupiscence that made me feel the way I did when I woke in the morning from my dreams, that made me feel as I had when a younger girl, hearing about saints and having lustful raptures.

I would not tell the priest about this sin of mine. He would tell me to stop, and I did not intend to. So, there in the little dark cage in the church, on the occasion of my first confession, I began to lie.

I made up sins of disobedience and covetousness, I fabricated whatever seemed likely for a girl my age—jealousies, gossiping, small thefts I had not committed. I fell under my own spell in there, telling stories, only the hard floor under my knees reminding me of the world. It was easy to lie in the dark, there was no one's searching eyes to avoid. When I was done, I stopped speaking and waited for the words of absolution, but there were none, not immediately. I heard what I thought was a sigh, and I felt my face burning in shame. Suddenly it seemed to me that this Father Alvaro could see through the wall and into me, straight through to my heart, which he knew was stained and not yet ready to come into any knowledge of Christ.

As for that heart, it began to beat so loudly that I could not have heard any mortal voice. I got to my feet, stumbling, and I quit the confessionary and ran. I remember the faces of the other children as I passed them—they hung before me in my mind's eye, pale and trembling as if I saw them under water.

That night in my father's house I became ill. A sickness began in my head and spread down into my hands and belly. My eyes closed shut with fever, and I found myself dizzy and tormented by strange dreams of having stolen my sister's old doll. Dolores no longer played with the doll that Papa had bought when we first got money from the king, but she was too mean to let me have her. She had given the doll a beautiful name, Margarita Isabella, and while I lay in bed I saw myself get up and go into the little box that Dolores kept under our bed and I took out Margarita. I touched her head made of glazed porcelain, her pretty red lips and her eyes that were blue like a foreigner's; I stroked her dress with its pinafore and bows and touched the little shoes of black leather that Dolores used to slip on and off Margarita's feet, as if nothing were more wonderful to her than those tiny black slippers. Even then, I knew that Dolores loved the doll because in her clean dress with its tiny, perfect buttons, Margarita was like a little piece of a past that was happy, of a time when our mother's abundance was so great that it took her to a king and bought for us such presents as we never had again. I knew it and begrudged my sister that little evidence of better times, of the possibility of happiness.

In the fever, I saw myself strip off Margarita's clothes and then take the naked doll, leaving only the dress and the shoes in the box. I went to the back of our house where the dry earth was packed from everyone's walking in and out, and I sat and dug a grave in which to hide the doll. I dug it with my own spoon for eating, a wooden spoon that my father had made. Then, as I laid her in the hole, suddenly Margarita was not a doll any longer but that baby whose mouth and nose I had smothered many years before. In the dream I believed I had killed the child, and I wanted to hide her body before Mama could find it.

I was lying in bed with a fever, at least I know my body was there, but my eyes would not open, there were sores on my hands and feet and in my mouth as well. The skin all over me felt dry and tight. It seemed to me that it took days to cover the dead baby, to bury her in the hard gray dirt. Though I was very tired, I walked back and forth until the dirt was packed so tight that no one would ever be able to tell I had dug a hole there.

After the dream, I heard the voices of my father and the cu-randera talking together, and she said, "Well, if Francisca lives, she will surely be blind." I felt her fingers on my face, I felt her bathe the crust from my eyelids. The wash she used had the astringent aroma of rue, reminding me of Mama and making me cry all the more. She pulled one eye open and she was right, I saw nothing.

The curandera told my father that she had a powerful tea made of devil's cherries, the same that come from the bella-donna plant, and if I grew worse he was to give it to me. But he boiled it up as soon as she left our hearth—he did not wait to see my condition—and the bitter draft burned the sores in my mouth and made me cry until the tears took the skin from my cheeks.

In the sickness I tossed, I walked in my sleep. I fought my papa and suffered more strange deliriums. I thought a midwife was after me with her tongs. Not long after Mama died, Dolores had taken me to Pascuela's house to be present at her childbed. This was the same Pascuela who had been a friend of our mother's—the same who was afraid of Mama's books—so it was not odd for us to be there, we came in Mama's stead, since Mama would have been there. That was what was right, Dolores said. At Pascuela's, the blood came out of her, but not issuing from her mouth, from lips like my mother's that spoke and kissed and told of magic palaces. Pascuela's blood came from between her legs, more blood than there ought to be at a birth, much more. Her screams were loud and terrible. She cursed her poor husband and said she would know him no more, she called him a pig and a toad and a foul lying lizard who had crept between her sheets. Her sisters sobbed with fear. This was to be Pascuela's firstborn and she was a narrow portion of a woman married to a big man. So fate overtook her, the baby was too big. She and the child died before the midwife had a chance to take off her cloak and unpack her child-bringing tools.

My fever would not abate. I saw the midwife at the altar with Father Alvaro elevating the host, and I had thoughts of how the body of Christ Jesus had been born of flesh and thus soiled by the impurity that comes from a woman in her childbed. I worried about such things. Even though I never knew I was thinking of them, they must have lain in my mind to bother me like that when I was ill. Or perhaps I had had some premonition, then, of how passion might one day take its due.

The fever made me thirsty, so thirsty, as if all the dust I had dug from that hole was in my throat. Believing that I had hidden my terrible crime, I prayed for Mama to come back to me, the way that she used to come to our bed at night, when Papa was busy with some chore or another, adding up imaginary wealth or planning arguments against my grandfather and his obdurateness. On such nights I was almost never asleep, although I pretended to be, breathing slow and deep and even. I was waiting for Mama to come. She said things to us when she thought we slept, brushing the hair from our foreheads, finding an ear in which to whisper—she said things she would never say aloud during the day. "Francisca, child, your mama loves you, oh, you cannot know how much!" She would whisper these words of affection in a tone she did not use while we were awake, and she kissed the tips of my fingers, each one, before putting my hand under the blanket. Thinking of it now, my fingers ache with the memory of those kisses.

Her words came low and urgent and she apologized for her short-temperedness, her punishments. Nothing grave, nothing that ever led me to doubt my mother's love. But she must have felt some sorrow, for she put her head in her hands, and sometimes she wept. Whenever my mother cried I remembered the girl my papa spoke of, dancing at her wedding in the shining black shoes. My papa said he leaned against a wall and watched as she danced alone. With an angel, a devil: someone or something no one else could see.

"I was not patient with you today, Francisca," she would say at our bedside, her mouth pressed to the blanket, "but it wasn't how I meant to be, it never is. I raise my voice and an instant later I think how sorry I am. How, if only I had a little time, I might be kinder." They were two different women, the day and night mothers, the day one sometimes distracted and short-tempered, and the night visitor whose throat I could see in the moonlight, her head tipped back, her cheeks wet, and her smooth neck glowing while she cried.

Perhaps, while I was ill, my night mother did come, as I prayed for her to. Perhaps she pulled my hot head into her lap and kissed my eyes and cured me, because when the fever finally passed and I sat up and opened them, the curandera had been wrong, I could see.

My papa was not a pious man, but he brought us up not to go looking for evil, he told us that there was trouble enough in the world that would come after us, whether we wanted it or not. After I recovered, he told me that if I had any bad thoughts I must pray, and I did. I tried hard to be good. I got into the habit of penances that I inflicted on myself without the help of any confessor. I did not wear a shift for all that winter or the one after it. But it was a while before I went back to the priest.

HOUGH DEAD FOR MORE THAN A CENTURY, Juana la Loca has her box in the Teatro Real. Not everyone can see her, of course, but when the queen and Olympe take their seats in the neighboring balcony, María starts, she stumbles back and drops her opera glasses.

"Why, what is the matter!" says Olympe.

"It is nothing," says María. "Nerves. Only nerves." She sits down carefully in her chair, but she cannot take her eyes away from Juana.

Juana, the mad queen. Daughter of Ferdinand of Aragon and Isabella of Castile. Great-great-great-great-grandmother to María Luisa, and to Carlos, as well. Juana was mad from birth and then further undone, some say, by more education than the female brain can withstand. Ten languages, and mathematics, too. She could converse in Greek and Latin. Long before her own passing, she made herself an expert in every dead thing. Others say the lessons never hurt her, that her husband, called Philip the Fair, made her crazy with his philandering.

When Philip died in the north in the year of our Lord 1506 and had to be transported home, Juana walked behind his coffin for forty nights. She walked with him because she did not trust her handsome husband. At every stop she had the casket opened so that she could kiss him, that she could see he was still inside, faithful in death if not in life. When the mourning party stopped to rest at a convent, she would not suffer his casket's being carried inside that cloistered, female place, but sat beyond the walls of the nuns' dormitory with her hand under the coffin lid.

Everyone has heard the tale that Juana once took a pair of scissors to the cheeks of one of Philip's mistresses. She roamed the castle naked, covered only by her long hair, always holding tight to a pair of golden embroidery scissors. When her ghost comes to her box in the theater, she comes naked, she brings her scissors.

"You must not allow your nerves to get the better of you," Olympe scolds María. "And, for the love of the saints, do stop fanning before you blow all our hair off." The comtesse smooths the high curls of her wig.

María Luisa drops her fan in her lap, she wrings her empty hands. "I am sure they are deciding what to do with me," she says. For Carlos and Marianna have remained at home, they refused to go to the theater with the two women.

In the weeks since the dismissal of the translator, there still had been no action taken against either the queen or her dwarf. "I do not understand it!" María cried to Eduardo that morning. "What can it mean!" The dwarf shook his head, his eyes watering.

"Something will happen to us," he said at last. "Something will."

Olympe smiles at the queen now, she takes her hand. "I hope they do decide," she says. "Then it will be over with. And how wonderful it would be if they decided to turn you out! You could come to Majorca with me." The comtesse draws the queen's hand to her lips, kisses its palm and lays it against her cheek. "We could enjoy the sun while everyone else in Paris and Madrid sulks in their cold, dreary castles," she says.

"Yes, perhaps I shall be exiled," says María. She tries to concentrate on the stage, holding up her fan to block the sight of naked Juana and her tangled hair.

The court playwright, a mediocre talent, was busy all fall concocting this farce about a lady and her maids, a highly unlikely tale of intrigue and poison, in which nobody dies, nothing much happens, and no one is punished, excepting the audience.

During the intermission between the second and third acts, María, sitting between her maid Obdulia and Olympe, her back to Juana, feels a sharp pain in her side. "Oh!" she says to Olympe, holding her side where it hurts. "I feel so unwell, suddenly."

"Indigestion, perhaps," says the comtesse, yawning. "It certainly cannot be that you were laughing too hard."

In fact, the comedy is so tedious, and the queen so nervous, that in the privacy of the royal box (and behind her fan) María has only just resorted to a drop or two of laudanum, which she has lately taken to keeping with her at all times. As she swallowed it she said a little prayer to the drops, asking them to dispel the ghost and her glinting scissors.

Olympe offers María Luisa a digestive mint from a little tin she keeps in her reticule. But the mint does not help, and the queen feels ill enough that the three women decide to return to the royal residence. They go downstairs to wait for their carriage.

But just inside the doors of the great theater, María suffers a spasm of pain so intense that she turns to her friend with tears in her eyes. "Something is wrong!" she says. She complains of a burning sensation in her mouth, her throat. She says she is afraid she will be sick.

"Tell the footmen to hurry!" she begs Obdulia.

Olympe pulls a small silver case from her reticule. Under her thumb the jeweled catch springs open. Inside: two tiny vials. "Triaca," the comtesse says, identifying the antidote that was so popular in the French court that all Parisian ladies carried it with them. "Take it quickly."

"I haven't been poisoned!" says María, and then she vomits on the marble floor of the theater's grand vestibule. She begins to cough, and to sob.

"Perhaps not," says Olympe. "But take it anyway."

But before she can, the queen collapses.

The carriage arrives just as Obdulia is unlacing María's stays, and the three women depart, two guards carrying the unconscious queen from the theater. A small party of curious onlookers, who saw the queen leave her box and then followed her and her companions down the stairs, return to their seats. They talk to their neighbors, and their neighbors talk to their neighbors' neighbors, and soon everyone in the theater is whispering excitedly, paying little attention to what transpires on the stage.

The queen's driver whips her horses around the circle in front of the theater and pulls the carriage up so sharply that one of the horses stumbles and cuts his leg on another's hoof. As the injured animal screams shrilly, a corps of palace militia arrives and hurries into the theater, just after the palace livery boy. They barricade all the exits from the theater, even as the queen is loaded unconscious into her coach. Actors and actresses continue with their performance, but no one is in his or her seat.

"Where is the French queen?" someone calls out, pointing to her empty box. "Where is María Luisa!"

"Poisoned!" calls a voice from the third balcony, and instead of laughter there is a shocked silence in which opera glasses rove all over the audience, their lenses reflecting light from the chandeliers.

"Parid, bella flor de lis!" someone screams, and then, in this late autumn, when King Louis's forces have routed the last of the Spanish armies, when everyone has attended more funerals than concerts, when the harvest is poor and when tales of the French queen's shameful pretended pregnancies and staged bloody miscarriages have already spread from palace to streets, a riot begins.

"Where is the French harlot!" come the cries. "Give her to us! She shall be whipped in the plaza!"

"The whore María mocks King Carlos and all of Spain, all her citizens! She mocks every one of you!" yells a man standing on the wall of the loge. He brandishes a broken chair leg in his hand and then hurls it into the great chandelier in the middle of the ceiling. It sticks there and begins to burn. Candles drop into seats below, a fire quickly spreads.

When the audience discovers it is locked inside the theater, the women begin to scream, all of them, and the men to fight. People take up chairs and throw them from the balconies. Seventeen people are killed outright, countless others trampled.

By order of the command of His Majesty's forces, the audience is held inside the theater in order that its members can be searched, questioned and released one by one. They would be there tomorrow, most of them, but for one lady's maid who observes to her mistress that, as all the actors and actresses seem to have disappeared, perhaps the trapdoor used in the first act really works. In an instant the entire audience disappears down the secret stage stair, and drains like wine from a broken cask out the back of the theater. They leave Juana alone in her box, naked and staring at the burning chairs below.

When the king's guard looks inside, pokes his head inside the barricaded theater to call the next suspect, he finds that the great, smoking room is empty.

Some of the audience go home. Anticipating a siege of unrest, the few more cautious souls want to count their money, bar their doors and lay in some provisions. But how many are this provident? At least two hundred people run directly from the theater, down the Calle de Arenal and on to the palace, picking up rabble as they go.

A huge crowd gathers at the gates to the park surrounding the royal residence. From the gatehouse, the guards watch the people milling around. Fires are started. Small at first, over which hands are warmed on a cold night, by dawn they are bonfires into which the crowd throws whatever it can find: a walking stick snatched from an old man, broken chairs carried from the wrecked Teatro Real, papers from the gutter (including that seditious publication *El Hechizado,* which fills the squares, finds its way under every door, but whose authors and whose press are never found—mysterious, in that it cannot be easy to hide something so immense and loud as a printing press). Dry boughs from a dead chestnut tree on the Calle de Arenal, refuse from the dump at the marketplace, a tattered cloak, seven doublets reeking of wine and three pairs of boots left for the destitute on the steps of the Monasterio de la Encarnación. It all burns in the fires. One enterprising man has already set up a little brazier over which he heats a punch of oranges and cloves and some spirit so strong that it burns the nostrils. For two maravedis a cup, he ladles it out, and those who partake are sufficiently warmed and emboldened to climb the gate and call out over the strangely silent grounds. "María Luisa!" they shout, and others take up the cry "Ma–ría! Lu–isa!" until the queen's name resounds throughout the city.

Dawn. A time of quiet, usually, but the stones of the prison ring with the queen's name, and with the rhyme. The terrible rhyme that the queen must hear, too, as she lies in her bedchamber.

Give birth, beautiful flower!

The queen of Spain sees a shower of sparks when she closes her eyes. The sight is pleasant, not alarming, and she keeps them closed, thereby ignoring the unusual assembly in her bedchamber: her maids Obdulia and Jeanette, the physician and his assistant, Marianna and Carlos, Olympe.

A few ministers mill about in the hallway. Their ornamental spurs jingle with merry discordance on the tiles.

Dr. Severo puts his broad thumb on the lid of María's left eye and lifts it, her brown eye with its black pupil dilated so fully that it almost obscures the ring of brown. The white of the queen's eye is unnaturally clear, a side effect of a poisoning agent, Dr. Severo posits privately. But in such a climate of panic and hysteria he dares not make a diagnosis of poison, not unless he is very, very sure. And for that he will have to make an analysis. To learn which it is—arsenic, alkaloid, antimony: these are just the A's from an alphabet of poisons—he will have to make many tests. He peers more closely at María's eye. Not the tiniest vessel is visible on its surface, and it rolls slowly in its socket, so slowly.

A healthy eye moves quickly, darting from one subject to another, but this royal organ of sight travels in a barely perceivable orbit. Since returning from the theater, María has drifted in and out of sleep, of consciousness. She has had brief periods of lucidity, and longer ones of confusion.

To the king and queen mother, Dr. Severo makes a tentative diagnosis of cholera morbus, and administers *agua de la vida,* a quack decoction of cloves in vinegar. It produces a warm sensation, stimulating to the digestion, and the queen retches and coughs, spraying the remedy, which went down clear and comes up pink, over the physician's starched collar. He shakes his head. He'll try sweet almond oil, perhaps it will help a little.

"What did she eat?" he asks again. "Tell me exactly what happened!"

"I do not know," says Obdulia for the third time, and repeats all that she said before, all that she does know. "Her Highness complained of a bad pain in her side. We were in the box at the theater, we were accompanied by Madame Olympe. The comtesse, thinking that Her Highness had been seized by an attack of biliousness, gave her a digestive remedy, but it did not help, and so we left the box and went to get our carriage.

"Then, as you know, Her Highness vomited, and she collapsed just inside the door of the theater."

Severo nods. "Dinner?" he asks.

"The same as everyone else, sir. Omelette. Bread. Apple tart."

"What besides a pain in her side?"

"A burning in her mouth. And more vomiting." Obdulia points to a basin resting on the vanity table and covered discreetly with a cloth.

He lifts the cover. "Is that all of it?" he asks.

"The first time was in the theater, sir. There was no basin."

"Did no one collect it? Did no one even look at it?"

"It looked like egg and apple only, sir." Obdulia gestures nervously, cupping her empty hands as if they bore the vomited dinner.

"Is it not understood that all palace vomit is to be analyzed in my laboratory?"

"Yes, sir. But—"

"Obviously, you may consider that your position is in jeopardy." His mustache quivers with importance. "There will be an inquest," he continues. "You will have to speak."

"Yes, sir."

Dr. Severo nods, and Obdulia falls back into place beside the other maid, Jeanette, who looks at her own feet. Severo leaves the royal bedchamber followed by his assistant bearing the covered basin. The ministers scatter, spurred heels jingling.

The omelette, was it the omelette? And what about that digestive mint? The comtesse's bag, including the mints and the remaining triaca, have been confiscated and taken to the laboratory. Downstairs, everyone reviews all the details. The queen was in her box at the theater, she felt a pain in her side, she left her box, she collapsed. She vomited in public.

It was an attack of biliousness, the courtiers are saying to the corps of foreign ministers, a crowd of them gathering in the king's audience chamber, collecting this latest and most interesting of international developments for their own kings waiting back home. This is the news that all Europe awaits: *The queen was taken ill at the theater. Spain's French queen is dangerously ill.* The foreign ministers are dispatched to their various offices and apartments, where their secretaries scratch at parchment with goose quills and burn their fat fingers on hastily melted sealing wax. So seldom is there any real news to send home! Spain is teetering, toppling, and as soon as she finally tumbles, France and England, Austria, Belgium, Portugal, the Netherlands will carve her up among themselves.

Yes, *She was taken ill at the theater* is the news the courtiers instruct the ministers to convey, but after they are alone together, they eye one another suspiciously, and the word among themselves is *Poison!*

"Someone has poisoned the queen!" It is as if the very walls of the palace whisper the words back and forth. Floorboards moan, staircases shudder under the lightest tread, and the heavy draperies hang more disconsolately than ever.

After she quits the clot of alarmed observers around the queen's bed, Marianna keeps to her chamber until the next morning. In a panic, Carlos summons his confessor, the cloak of Saint Eulalia and the bell jar under whose glass is preserved the last gasp of Benedict, patron saint of poison sufferers, a breath exhaled between seizures caused by mercury and trapped under glass in the year of our Lord 543. So crazed with cracks is the glass bell that any soul less credulous than Carlos might suspect that holy Benedict's last gasp has ascended to a more rarefied atmosphere than that of the royal reliquary. But Benedict's last exhalation is one of the prizes of Carlos's collection, even though today it does little to calm him.

The king vomits from fear, and then, further frightened that he too has been poisoned, commands that a special Mass be said while the basin of his half-digested breakfast is sent down to Dr. Severo in his laboratory. There it takes its place among basins of the queen's, already undergoing examination for malign chemical agents.

María Luisa's maids change her nightdress yet again. The almond oil does nothing for the retching. It has gone on all night. What can stop it? It is like the action of some terrible regret.

Regret not of one meal, one dose of poison, but of an entire life.

She retches and retches. She is ill enough that she is out of her head with her sickness. Her bedchamber, her curtains, her hairbrush and water glass and the rings upon her fingers, they are all less real to her than her dreams. When the spasms of nausea abate, her mind returns again and again to the woods.

Beyond the Sun King's lake, beyond the ordered, barbered trees are woods, and in her bed, with its two mattresses of batting and one of feathers, María Luisa dreams of riding trails. Of willow trees in new pale leaf, stone cottages and daffodils, tulips, clematis, the wet branches of a peach tree, so dark they look black. Pink blossoms against a bank of dark clouds with the sun bright silver behind them. The smell of the earth in her nose as her horse's hooves tore into the wet ground. What was the name of that first little horse? The one only twelve hands high? Lucie? Yes, Lucie. Lucie with the funny, bouncing gait. Her trot was like the rocking of a nursery's toy horse.

The night her cousin Berthe died, all the fires in the château went out. Berthe had been poisoned, a certified case. When they opened her up, her liver was white.

Is my liver turning colors? the queen wonders. But she cannot think about that. Think about something else, think about something pleasant. She'll think about Lucie, her little mare of long ago. Not of riding sidesaddle as she had been forced to do in Spain, where she was not allowed to have her legs parted, open and astride an animal, but was trussed up in a heavy habit of velvet, complete with plumed hat and gloves to the elbow. No, she'll dream of riding in boy's breeches on a real saddle. Of France. Of lingering at the stable after her ride and watching as the livery boys lifted her saddle from the pretty chestnut back. Underneath, Lucie's coat would be dark with sweat, a silhouette of the princess's saddle drawn on the animal's back.

EVERO IS NOT AN UNSOPHISTICATED MAN. HIS degree—purchased from the University of Leyden after five weeks of study, the vellum scroll signed by the great scientist and physician Sylvius, and bearing engravings of Hippocrates, Bacon and Paracelsus—guaranteed that he had been tutored at great expense in various arts of medicine: mucus analysis, glandular function, ferments and gases, advanced underwater chirurgical techniques to prevent sepsis from the contact between organs and parasites borne on air currents. It said that he knew the use of the Huygens Calidometer, whose long tube of glass—its case as tall as Severo himself—bore a serpent of volatile mercury far more exact in its measurement of temperature than any human hand. That he had mastered atomism, mercury fumigations for skin ills (both venereal and allergic), Harvey's findings on the movements of the heart, Fallopio's circulation theories and his investigations into secret female parts, as well as all the many branches of iatrochemistry. That he was well versed in the art of cautery, and could use a heated knife blade to staunch hemorrhage and to cure hernias, migraines and gangrenous furuncles. That he was an alchemist, and though he had not yet turned lead into gold, he had had as much success in the endeavor as any other great thinker.

In Leyden, Severo witnessed chirurgical procedures to correct such congenital misfortunes as a cleft palate, an eleven-toed foot and one unfortunate child's arrival without an anus. He saw broken heads put back together and whole ones taken apart. The procedures were largely unsuccessful in that none of the patients survived more than a fortnight, but as the infirm were all volunteered from Dutch prisons and asylums (and either came to Leyden while still living or died in their cells and came as cadavers), it was no loss to society, and the sawmanship and stitching techniques were unparalleled. Severo also learned of many new places from which to take blood, places that doctors in the low countries of Spain and Italy had never tried. Why, as it turned out, you could get a good deal of blood from almost any part of the body, and Severo came home from Leyden with a chart of forty-seven of those locations.

At the lecture halls, Severo attended a two-day congress on the values of bleeding from the side of the disorder versus bleeding from the healthy side, and a series of dinner talks by Francis Glisson himself comparing the benefits of emetic purges and cupping to those of fomentations and enemas. He stood until he grew faint in the great anatomical theater where the cream of Netherlands society came to picnic, drawing from their hampers cold joints and soft-crusted loaves of yellow bread, and drinking champagne as they watched the correction of a harelip or the transfer of blood from a sheep to a prisoner, whose own body had been nearly emptied of its sanguinary fluids that it might accommodate the beast's. He saw the removal of a live baby from its dead mother's belly; he saw a hundred kidneys preserved in vinegar. He watched a heart beat outside its body for whole minutes; and, on no less than seventeen volunteers, he improved his technique for repairing hernias until he could accomplish the procedure in under a quarter of an hour without sacrificing either testicle. Yes, Leyden had an undeniably reputable program, with peerless teachers and scientists. And, for a foreign collective of learning, it was very particular, excluding as it did unconverted Jews, the sons of hangmen and all bastards, even those of noble birth.

At the end of these varied and exciting colloquia, Severo went home to Spain, but not before he visited Leeuwenhoek's workshop in Delft, where he purchased one of the great man's microscopes, a tiered contraption of no fewer than ten lenses, which used a new screw method of focus—no more old-fashioned draw-tubes—to provide magnification of three hundred and seventy times the power of the naked eye. The microscope offered surprises: that minuscule worms wriggled in blood, that muscles were made of bundles of hair, that Severo's own toenails provided generous accommodation for no less than thirteen different organisms, five rooted like a tiny garden, and eight capable of independent locomotion. As far as the doctor could judge, these were all revelations that the eye, mind and imagination together would never have been able to forge. And for no extra charge—for the microscope had literally cost a king's ransom—Leeuwenhoek gave Severo a marvelously ingenious spring-loaded knife that dived into gum boils and abscessed wounds before the patient ever had a chance to see it, much less cringe.

When he slept, Severo often dreamed of the Netherlands, where he had learned all he needed, bought all he wanted and had dined exceptionally well. He could still taste those beguiling little cheeses the Dutch served for breakfast; and, though it was well known that strong-brewed coffee thinned the blood, he still missed the Dutch blend he had sampled some twenty years ago.

Carlos's father, King Philip, paid for Severo's passage to Leyden in 1665, and for his degree, in hopes that the young doctor would learn something to arrest the gouty necrosis that had already crept from Philip's toe, on up his ankle, and from there to his shin. And, too, Marianna, then queen, had hoped there were Dutch wisdoms that might safeguard the health of her son, at eight years of age still spindly in his wet nurse's arms, still unable to stand. (About to be in *my mama*'s arms! About to take what was mine!)

Alas, Philip expired before Severo had even crossed the border into France, and though the doctor made inquiries of every teacher he met, there were no known cures for any of Prince Carlos's ailments. Once home, Severo tried mercury fumigations, once each season, but each time he worried that the child would choke to death, and—to poor Mama's dismay: "The pain is very bad," said one of her letters—his wet nurse's nipples broke out in blisters.

Now, years later, Carlos having survived countless ills and treatments, Severo is having little better success in treating the king's bride. With his microscope the doctor searches in her vomit for one of two suspects: an invading organism, which, according to one text, looks like a bent, furred stick, and which would support his first diagnosis of cholera morbus, or some toxic substance, which might not look like anything he could recognize.

By now, basins and basins of María's vomit have been analyzed. From basin number one, Severo heated the fetid liquid and skimmed the fatty substance off the surface. Inspection of this, through the stacked Leeuwenhoeken lenses, revealed it to be the remains of the sweet almond oil he had himself prescribed to quell her retching.

Severo then distilled the contents of basins two through four, yielding a quantity of putrid-smelling water, but nothing he added to this distillate told him anything he needed to know. Sulpheride made it stink all the more. He sprinkled in copper oxides, and it turned a pretty blue. Jasper made it red. He went on to stain it all the colors of a cathedral's windows, and made his laboratory look like an artisan's workshop, all without learning a thing. Of the remaining basins (allowed to stand for four, six, eight and twelve hours) none had yielded any precipitate.

Even more confounding, María Luisa's bodily acids have an unexpected effect on the medicaments he prescribes. Mithridatic administered in a base of clear, raw egg white comes up literally white, as if she has cooked it internally. What is more, her tongue is peeling as though blistered, and likewise her gums, thin ribbons of flesh hanging. Her pulse is so erratic that it eludes his fingers like leaves before a wind. And as soon as her breathing settles into a quiet, regular cadence, it devolves into rasping, gasping and choking. Clear fluid drips from her nose.

If only the University of Leyden had offered a curriculum in poisonings. But that would have been impossibly vulgar. Only an Italian college would present such scandal.

Dr. Severo dips two fingers into the contents of one of the standing basins. He rubs them together, noting the thick and almost oily quality, the tarry color. It reminds him, suddenly, of his dinner two nights ago. Of that dish the cook prepares but once each month. Of the queen mother's favorite dish, and of the one Carlos does not like to even see on his table. The one meal which some look forward to and others dread. It reminds Severo of blood pudding. It reminds him of blood. The acidic humors of the stomach could render blood dark and foul and viscous, could they not?

Dr. Severo sends his assistant to request a special evening audience with the king and queen mother. "Her Highness is vomiting blood," he tells them.

"Blood!" says Marianna.

"Blood?" Carlos looks back and forth between the doctor and his mother. He is confused.

"Blood," Severo responds with a conviction he does not feel. But he must provide some definite diagnosis of the queen's ailment. If it progresses as it has, the queen will die. He must take some decisive action. He clears his throat. "Either Her Highness has a surfeit of the sanguinary humors, or some toxic agent has settled into her circulation."

"Toxic?" asks Marianna. "There *is* a poison?"

"Perhaps. Analyses are in progress."

"Then María does not suffer from germ agents inside her?" Carlos says.

"Your Highness," Severo says, and to prevent further questions, he pauses to collect vocabulary that the king will not be able to understand. He clears his throat again. "Palpation has not yielded the discovery of any petrification that might indicate a septic inflammation of the viscera," the doctor says.

Carlos nods, frowns. His features fall into the practiced expression of simulated concern that he uses each morning when he listens to various ministers' reports. Marianna frowns as well, says nothing. When the silence grows uncomfortable, Severo continues.

"I would ask Your Highnesses' leave to bleed Her Highness, beginning early tomorrow morning. Perhaps if I could purge her of this bad blood, help her body to rid itself of what troubles her, then she will recover."

Carlos looks at his mother. She nods at him. "You have our leave," says the king.

HE TORTURER, HE IS A LOVER, TOO. SOMEONE
who cannot be satisfied by words from your
lips or by the assurance of your captivity.

Someone who wants the secret inside you,
who wants to open your flesh and read it like
an oracle, expecting truth.

The torturer—he has no name, he wears a white hood—asks
that you believe him to be the ally of your soul. The enemy is
your flesh, your corporeal life. Together you and your torturer
conspire to force this stubborn mortal flesh to reveal those secrets that it has kept from your soul. Together, you persuade the
flesh not to be so withholding.

It is not hard to believe this. No, there is nothing easier to
believe, it seems obvious and true. And I sometimes have a vision of myself as an egg—an egg with a stubborn shell. Inside
me, we know, my torturer and I, is a golden orb of truth: my
heart, my pith, my yolk. And if only we can conspire together to
break me, then the truth will flow forth.

I want nothing more than to give way. I have not been silent,
I have spoken pages. My confession fills chest after chest, and
they gather dust, waiting for my final sentencing. I have testified
endlessly against myself, against Alvaro and against my mother.
Like an old woman who knows that death awaits her impatiently, I have tried to divest myself of all I have: of every
thought and memory.

After I have been made fast to my seat, after each wrist and
ankle has been shackled to a rung so that I will not wriggle
away, and when the White Hood is occupied with the quiet
chores of setting tinder and painting the soles of my feet with
grease, I can hear the rabble, the shouting from the streets
above. I can hear the queen's name, an endless singing taunt,

Ma–ría, Ma–ría, Ma–ría Lu–isa, sounds of rioting and confusion.

The Purple Hood comes in. He asks me endless questions about my mother. I will never be able to tell him enough, for this one fateful consanguinity will sentence me to endless interrogation: the king of Spain and Francisca de Luarca drank from the same tit.

The sorry bewitchment of the king and queen of Spain, the reason for their not getting with child, the reason that the queen will be destroyed—all this has been traced back to my mother's milk. No matter that Mama might well have saved Carlos's wretched life along with those of countless other children. No, her ability to cure damns her—and me as well—more than any other fact of her short life.

"What did she do with the sucklings that died?" says the Purple Hood. The White Hood stands by the tinder, but he does not light it, not yet.

"None died," I say.

"None?"

"No, not one."

"And of her own children?"

"I told you. They were buried by my papa."

Every time the Purple Hood asks about my mother, he returns to this notion of dead children. It is said, I know, that witches use the fat of infants to smear on their legs and arms so that they may fly.

"Did the people of your town find your mother unusual?" the Purple Hood asks.

"She was unusual."

"How?"

"She was better than they were. She took in foundlings and saved their lives."

The White Hood rocks on his heels with boredom. He wants to light the tinder.

"They were impressed by this?" says the Purple Hood.

"Everyone was. Why else would she have ended up in the palace in Madrid?"

"And the priest, Alvaro Gajardo, did he know she was a witch?"

"My mother was not a witch."

"He heard her last confession, did he not?"

"Yes."

"And you heard it as well?"

"No."

"You attended her death with your sister Dolores."

"I was a child. I do not remember what was said."

"What do you remember?"

I say nothing.

"What do you remember?"

When I still do not answer, the Purple Hood makes a slight motion with his right hand and the White Hood steps forward. He nods, and the White Hood lights the tinder.

The flame creeps along a dry stick, and I watch its progress.

"What do you remember?" the Purple Hood asks again.

I remember everything, and nothing. I remember my heart was rent. In the same way that Saint Teresa wrote of her raptures, after it was over, my heart felt as if it had been chewed by dogs.

"She said to me that she dreamed nine dreams," I say. "That was the last thing my mother told me."

"Dreams of what?" says the Purple Hood.

I shake my head.

Have I squandered something in giving him this secret? Something that had been mine and mine only? A memory that had meaning only for me? This is nothing he could want or value. I see my mother on her deathbed, conjured by the flame in the room with the robed Inquisitor, the scribe and his quill, the torturer and the bored physician. My mother seems suddenly small before this audience.

This is how they conspire to break you, the fire whispers, and I am silent, listening.

Yes, I am talking to you, it insists. *I am eating you up, I lick you like a lover, I consume you. They think I shall convince you of their wisdom and power, but I am betraying them to you.*

Do not give them everything, the fire says to me. Does its voice issue from the sticks as they snap? Is it gas in the wood, popping and hissing? A coal's collapse? The grease as it drips from my feet to the stones below? The fire's voice is persuasive. It is soft, learned and irresistible.

Your love for your mama and papa, your quarrels with Dolores. Alvaro and what time you had with him. They will make all of these seem small and pathetic to you. Everything, it insists, and falls silent.

All of us in the room are silent. The torturer puts his hand under his hood to scratch his face. I have a brief spell in which I begin to cough, and unable to draw a full breath because of the smoke, I think I shall suffocate. When the fit passes, I find that I understand the fire's message.

Exaggeration of punishment diminishes temptation. Their reasoning, what the Holy Office hopes to make clear, is that *nothing* can be worth such anguish. Thus all human desire— everything that tempted you—is reduced to folly.

At the advice of the fire, eaten by the fire, I determine that I will never speak of anything I love or hate. But I will betray my promise.

It is very difficult to keep your secrets under such conditions. Do you know why? It is not as simple an answer as *pain*. It is because you want to love your torturer, too. Yes, that is easier than hating him, it requires much less strength to make him your final passion, to die of love for him.

But this is how he will destroy you, whispers the fire.

What does it matter? I argue back. Any momentary enlighten- ment is likely to be obliterated by the next trial.

The Purple Hood's questions go on endlessly. Which herbs did she use to cure an ague? Did she keep a cat or a bird? What were the things she said to us as children?

"Did she know her Paternoster?"

"Of course."

"Her Ave?"

"Yes. Yes."

"How often did she say the Credo?"

"As often as anyone else."

Whatever I say, the scribe writes it all down. Sometimes, on a fortunate day, at some point during the encouragements, I find myself in a bright field of the past, one of the terraced plots where the mulberries grew, and it is just as it was one afternoon so many years before. A lifetime before. One winter afternoon I went outside and found what I thought was heaven.

Snow, so quiet. White.

Such snowfalls we had the winter I became a woman. Enough snow to silence all creation, to shut up each gossiping tongue and cloister every spying eye. The town of Quintanapalla slept all winter long.

I walked up the hill to the silk house, past bare winter trees, past ice twisted into fantastic shapes in the place where we daily spilled our well water, slopping it out of our buckets because the cold made us that clumsy. I walked and each footfall was smothered, the cold leaked into my shoes, the only sound was the creak of ice under my feet. Against the dangers of such weather we used to tie the pruned branches of the mulberry trees, tie them so that the wind could not snap off a frozen limb. Rabbits perished in their dens that winter. They curled tight into one another and they slept their lives away. The beasts of the field tried to burrow into the haystacks to keep warm, but they died, too. A merchant traveling from Madrid stopped in our town's inn, and, sitting with my father as he warmed himself before the fire, he told Papa that in the royal residence a fire blazed high on the kitchen's great stone hearth, but still the room remained so cold that spirits froze in a glass left on the mantel above.

Alvaro made pastoral calls on the day following the Sabbath. He was out, everyone knew, so no one came looking for him. Even if some soul required a priest—the birth of a sickly baby, its death, or the last rales and rattles of its grandmother—no one came slogging his way through the cold to his lodgings. As for me, I was always afield even in the worst weather, no one ever looked for me. Dolores had long since given up any pretense of sisterly guidance. She took no credit for whatever virtues I exhibited (she saw none, either) and accepted no blame for my flaws (of these she could list many). And she no longer expected that I would be home at any particular hour. So on those silent, white winter Mondays Alvaro and I met in the silk house. We knew we were safe there because if my papa was out, he was at market, and Dolores would be tending the hearth or visiting some pious gossipmonger, letting her feet, wet in their hose, steam before the fire as they discussed with relish the eventual damnation of the majority of townsfolk.

Walking through the silent snow, feeling the heat of my flesh burning under my very clothes, I was on fire, enough to melt the very winter and banish each drift. Flakes balanced on the boughs I passed turned to bright drops and fell winking into the snow. On fire. Feverish. No, better to say I was *fever* itself. I came to him like a disease, and he caught me up in his arms.

Each time, the first embrace so tight as if we meant to crack each other's bones and suck the marrow. I would pull him toward me, and everything would grow confused in the heat of my desire for him. Like looking at a vista beyond a bonfire, all that I saw was distorted, trembling and merging. One body ran into another. Sometimes when I closed my eyes I was Teresa wedded to Christ as recorded in the journals she kept. He came and put his lips on her, and she burned, too.

Venite ad me. He spoke to me in Latin, the language of the Church and all her saints, and when he called me to him with those words our union existed not only out of time but beyond ordinary and profane human conversation as well. We became sacred together.

Venite ad me. Come to me, Francisca. His eyes as hot as his tongue but lacking its focus.

We were trapped together in the silk house one day, then another and another. A blizzard left our absences undiscovered. She is in some barn, she has found shelter with a shepherd and his flock, I imagined Dolores saying. The snow trapped all of our town, and perhaps all of Castile, in shuttered houses.

We drank snow from the drift outside the door. My handfuls slaked his thirst. And what did we eat those three days but each other? What fire did we make beyond the burning of our bodies?

Suspended outside time, speaking in Latin together, tracing my letters on his body. Long and leisured love poems spelled out

in the language of the saints, *A m o r e s   m o r t u u s   s u m,* I
am dead of love.

We lay together in his cloak lined with fur, my face tipped up
into his neck, feeling the pulse in his throat under my parched
lips. I felt the whole silk house rise into the storm, the wind
picked it up with us inside, and I shook in his arms even as
timbers rattled and trembled.

When we returned to earth, when the storm was over, I went
outside into the snow and walked down the hill and toward my
father's house in the little valley. I saw each tree standing snow-
laden in fantastic garb of ice, and as if I had happened into a
group of lovely, lace-dressed dancers, the trees shimmered and
waltzed through my tears. In the afternoon's light, so bright and
clean, I became blind with the white all about me, I saw nothing
but white light. As if I had waked from our bed in the silk house
and walked into the bright fire of heaven. So cold that my skin
burned, I felt that I was consumed by God. I heard angels sing,
my head rang with celestial voices.

How lovely to have died in my sleep and to have been taken
up to heaven. The sparkling streets of heaven, the white fields. I
believed in heaven as a child.

When the scribe reads me my confession, he stands with the
light coming from behind him, over his shoulder, so as to see the
pages he holds, he stands and he reads to me what it is I have
said. And kneeling there (for someone pulls me to my knees,
someone forces me into a posture of supplication), kneeling no
higher than the scribe's boot tops, the light looks so holy and his
features are invisible: just the dark outline of a hooded man. It
looks the way I always thought Judgment would look. This
angel has the light, and I float in the darkness at his feet.

Did you say, Francisca de Luarca, that you had knowledge of
spells, that you sought to enchant, that you made figures from
wax, that you set a spell on your father's silkworms, that you
bewitched your sister and dried up her womb, that you . . . Oh,
it appears that I agree to anything, I believe anything, under
duress.

"And do you now abjure this statement, or do you agree that
it is the truth as best you could reveal it?"

You would be no different. The scribe holds forth a quill for signature, and you would take the quill, kiss the quill, you would be only too happy to put your mark to such a document, your confession, which will send you to heaven. For you believe in whatever this angel says, so mysteriously black, his face obscured to you and his white hood bathed in the celestial light of the torch. You want this angel to save you.

REED, SLOTH, ANGER. GLUTTONY, ENVY, pride. The course of any other of the deadly sins is easier to chart than that of lust. For lust is as a mirror to your soul. Until you know who you are, you cannot know whom you will desire.

When I was a girl of fifteen, I went to see the priest for the first time since the illness in my eyes, and I told him that I was afraid. That, though I had recovered my health, I was troubled in my soul.

"Confession?" he suggested. He shrugged his shoulders. It had been three years since Mama had died, but, standing near to Alvaro, I felt her presence, I thought that I did.

I remembered how his sleeve had brushed her forehead, her neck. I found myself wanting to touch his cassock. That was what we shared, after all: the witness of her passing.

I did not confess, and I went home. Then I thought better of it and returned. I made my confession to Father Alvaro once, twice, three times and more. Having started, I could not stop. I sought him out each week, becoming more and more scrupulous, and keeping in my head every tiny transgression. Savoring them. Each unkind thought I had conceived against Dolores, each word I had spoken sharply.

I kept myself as clean and as pure and holy as only the wicked can.

I worried over defilement but never over those appetites that possessed me. No, I did not want to. I set about satisfying them.

Without lying, I made my time with the priest last as long as possible. I felt how my blood burned, but I did not admit what my trouble was or how easily (how willfully) I confused the passion of the body with the afflictions of sainthood. *Incendium amoris.* They say the love of Christ can cause the flesh to burn and never be consumed. Martyrs feel it long before they are staked and set afire. How foolish I was to imagine that my common scrupulousness, my delight in every sin confessed might draw me close to the flaming heart of God.

How foolish to think it was God's heart that drew me.

At the door to the confessionary, my pulse would quicken. And after, when he would absolve me—*in pace,* "Go in peace, Francisca"—there was no peace. I was breathless at the sound of his voice.

One day I approached Alvaro in the road after Mass. He did not see me coming, for his head was bent, he was walking while looking at a small text. I caught up with him easily and I asked him without preamble, would he teach me to read? He was learned, he was a scholar, he was said to know many books. I told him I was quick to learn and that I wanted to help him. I suggested that I might apprentice myself to him and then he would have an assistant.

"Francisca de Luarca," he said, and that is all he said. I looked at his mouth when he spoke, not at his eyes. I had made the mistake, in the wake of my mother's death, so dreamlike and holy, of confusing this man with a phantom, a spirit, but when I looked at him now, I saw that when the priest smiled his teeth were strong and white like an animal's.

I struggled with Alvaro's transformation from angel to mortal. Having heard, when I was yet a child, his whispering approach to my mother's deathbed—robes breathing as he walked, the sudden flash of the beautiful purple hose—the idea had grown in my mind that this priest did not walk as others did. Now that I knew him, now that I saw him when he was in a hurry and running with his cassock tangling between his ankles, I found myself surprised at these things. Just as I was shocked when I looked from his white teeth to his hands and saw how the wrists projecting from his priestly sleeves were covered with hair.

I never was sure which Alvaro I wanted, angel or mortal. Both, of course. But could they, did they, exist at one and the same moment?

"What is it you want to read?" he said at last, and I told him how much I had loved the lives of the saints and how our mother had died before fulfilling her wish of teaching Dolores and me to read.

I lied to Alvaro. I said I intended to teach my sister all that he taught me; that for the two of us, it would be an aid to the progress of our souls to be able to study from devotional books, and that winters were long and tedious without such pious occupations. He looked at me, I saw myself reflected in his eyes, two tiny Franciscas caught in those rings of brown. He said nothing for a minute or more, appearing to consider my suggestion. Then he agreed. He said to come to his study on the next Thursday, after the bells that rang nones.

So it came about that each week I came to sit beside the priest at his long oak table, and I turned the pages for him, tended to his quills and blotted his writings, and, little by little, learned to write myself.

Alvaro was tall. When we stood near to each other, my head reached only as far as the fourth button of his cassock. He held himself straight, a matter of training, for he had been a member of the Bóveda, the Dark Vault. Ten months of the year the Bóveda devoted to study; and they were said to be as learned as the members of Loyola's Society of Jesus. But, unlike the Jesuits, who were always concerned for comfort, during Lent the Bóveda scourged themselves, they went without food, they shed their own blood in their search for holiness. The rest of the year was little better, because the order had precepts governing every detail of life, down to the expressions the brothers wore on their faces. It was said that though the Bóveda had been disbanded for some years, a former brother could still be discerned by posture that was more rigid than a soldier's.

Despite this history of self-discipline, Alvaro's complexion revealed a sanguinary nature. His forehead, his cheeks and even his sharp nose were red, as if he had endured long exposure to the sun or wind, and this improvident-looking flush never diminished. His face, though clean-shaven, was shadowed by a heavy beard, and while he was thinking he would sometimes brush his quill against his cheek, so that it made a rasping sound. Later, when he would come up behind me and put his lips to my neck, the scratching of his jaw against my nape would make the hair on my arms rise.

In the beginning, however, in the early weeks of my tutelage, Alvaro's jaw was not in proximity to my neck but over our books, where it moved patiently up and down, making sounds to accompany letters, just as my mother's had so long before. After the necessary tedium of copying and recopying baby words and infantile sentences, we moved on. It seemed to me to take forever, but Alvaro assured me that I was (if too old to be considered precocious) indeed a clever student and the quick one I had promised to be.

I swallowed long lists of vocabulary, I could not eat enough words. I loved the Latin ones best. *Félix,* my papa's name, the name his papa gave to him, meant both lucky and happy, and so I learned that it was a doubly useless way of identifying my father. Good fortune had by no means graced him, and the father I knew was a man consumed either with longing for what he did not have or with sadness for what he had lost. He was never happy. A better name would have been *Fabian,* or "bean grower," just two above Felix in the same week's list of words. On the other hand, *Dolores* and *Concepción* were accurate enough. As for *Francisca,* the free one, well, I would learn of my own name's aptness and irony—those liberties I took being the same that ended in my incarceration.

Words seduced me. I pondered the contrariness of ones like *femina,* being, as it was, comprised of *fe* for faith and *mina* for less. "Why, who could call woman the sex of less faith!" I asked Alvaro. "Of what is a woman's life composed, if not of expectation?" What more would I learn when I read whole sentences, I wondered.

My mama told us that when her papa took his post as a lime spreader, when plague had turned the streets of Madrid into charnels, he could not sign his name to the workers' roster, and this had shamed him. Part of her desire for words came from having eaten her father's insulted dignity. With me, it was not pride. I was inquisitive. Too curious for a girl, my grandfather had said. When he told me the fires in the silk house were hot, I put my hand to the coals to know his meaning. I had badly burned my throat eating an uncured olive. After a flood I nearly drowned in the stream. I licked the cat to taste what that was like. I always had to know. The existence of a world of words to which I had no entrance tormented me.

That the only educated person I knew was the priest—the same to whom I had helplessly granted other magic powers—made reading seem that much more an entrance to some better world, one apart from the sadness in life. And the ability to read made Alvaro seem all the more extraordinary. Reading and the priest, in my head they magnified each other.

What did I want? I wanted him. Him, of course. After the first week I knew that it was thoughts of him that had possessed my head, not holiness. Still, even now, when time and distance ought to make motives clear, I see that desire is not simple. How much of my wanting him was wanting to touch the person to whom my mother had entrusted her last journey, the hands through which she had passed on her way to eternity? I thought that he was like a portal to another world. I remember well the night my mother died. I cannot stop myself from conjuring the past, from listening again for the sound of his cassock whispering over the cobbles as he came to our door.

The books we read were not wicked, but they had magic in them, they did to me. We read of things I never dreamed existed. We began on Scriptures, both in Latin and in translation into the vernacular. But after those and after the usual devotional works—Thomas à Kempis and Augustine, *The Interior Castle,* by Saint Teresa—we read other books. Aesop and Aeschylus and Ovid. Boccaccio. Pedro Calderón de la Barca's sonnets, Mandeville's *Travels,* Sacrobosco's *De Sphaera Mundi* and *Gargantua,* by François Rabelais. Places. People. And stories, so many stories.

Alvaro had in his possession books that had been banned by the Church. They were set aside, marked with a red stamp along the binding and piled on the highest shelf, from which they called to me, as I always wanted what was set out of reach. A few were scorched, their covers black and cracked. One afternoon he selected one of the blackened texts, and I ran my finger along its binding. "What happened to this book?" I said.

"It was taken from the Church's burning of the library at Salamanca," he said.

"But who would do so dangerous a thing as to seize it? Who would not be afraid?"

"I would not."

"But how did you do it? Why were you not punished?"

"Who said I was not?"

I looked at him. He gazed out the window and his face was still in the way it was when he was thinking. His composure was the opposite of how my father concentrated himself. Papa's thoughts seemed to scramble over his face like insects, they made his lips tremble, his eyes squint.

Suddenly Alvaro seemed much older to me than my father. His capacity for physical quietude made my father seem antic and boyish. "I was arrested and tried," he said finally. "I made a case to the Holy Office for the examination of banned texts. I said that if I could study them, I could better refute any heresies they might betray."

"Are you in trouble?" I asked.

"I am not in favor, Francisca."

"Is that why you have been sent here, then? To such a small and insignificant town as ours?" As long as Alvaro had been in Quintanapalla there had been conjecture about this. Before his arrival, our town had shared a priest with Rubena and another place farther north. He had been an old priest, not educated, and he took a fit during one holy week. Then we had no Masses at all for a time. Finally Alvaro came, with his books.

He looked at me. "Yes," he said. "That is why I am here."

I nodded.

We began our lesson. We read from one of the Pseudepigrapha, called "false writings" because they were not accepted by the Church as the letters of Paul or Timothy had been. Some considered these books very wicked because they were a mix of faith and magic, but they were pretty tales. They colored the grim robes of Christ and made his bloody cross burst into flower.

In love with the words, in love with their master, on days when we did not meet, I would find myself helplessly drawn to

Alvaro's lodgings in the road behind the church, and I would have to walk on so as not to attract any attention to myself. The priest in a small town is a public person. More than the baker in whose oven-warm shop people gather, more than the smith around whose fires the men go to gossip; more than the apothecary behind his counter or even the innkeeper at his long table, the people of a town own their priest. They come to him at any hour, his whereabouts are almost always known.

Having been without any priest for the better part of a year, the people of Quintanapalla were inclined to be grateful, and though they thought Alvaro too bookish and too often cloistered with his pages and his quill, like most uneducated people—like me—they were awed by studious occupations. Once it was made plain to them that Alvaro was searching for heresies hiding among all those words in his study, they became respectful of his need for quiet, and people were tolerant even of my setting about to help him. It seemed to them that I was offering my labors in service to routing the Devil out of one of his bastions, and as much as persons were able to perceive my longing to be with Alvaro, they understood my desire as a kind of piety. For a while they did. As long as I was careful, they did. And though his window beckoned me, I would not stand beneath it unless no one was about.

But one week I arrived at the little study early, breathless, and I found that he was waiting, too. He was eager. He must have been, for my knuckles had rapped only once when the door opened. In the sudden draft, as if the very room had sharply drawn a breath, his cassock swayed around his ankles. I panted on the threshold, eyes watering slightly from my run down the hill. I drew a deep breath, smelling all that for which I had longed: the ink's metallic fragrance coming from the open well, the lamp's scent of oil, the odor of charred wick lingering still from when it was extinguished the previous night; the smell of the books he had rescued, slightly damp and acrid like wine cork; the paper upon which we would write together, dipping our quills into the ink.

And in the midst of all these, Alvaro, whose blood, so visible in his cheeks, seemed to exude some yearning or hunger. Or was that my own? I withdrew my hand, still poised in the air between us, ready to rap again on the door, which he had opened. I pulled back and covered my mouth with the hand, and we stood thus for a moment, not speaking.

"Come in, Francisca," he said at last. "You let all the warmth out." I stood there as if paralyzed, until finally he grasped my wrist and drew me in.

"Is there something troubling you?" he asked, when I could not concentrate on the words before us, and I covered my face with my hands. But then, feeling childish, I looked up quickly. I did not answer his question, and he dismissed me early.

I did not return the next Thursday afternoon, nor the two following. Our next meeting was the obligatory Lenten confession. Alvaro was in his dark cubicle, I was one more in a long line of sinners. I began with the usual words, I said I had transgressed and asked forgiveness. But then, "It is Francisca," I said.

My words, whispered, seemed huge in the dark of the confessionary, that first darkness from which all others issued: the dark of his study, lights extinguished. The dark of longing, and of night. The heaving, awful dark of my cell.

Alvaro made no answer, not knowing what I meant by identifying myself. Or, perhaps, because he did know. At last he said, "Go on."

"I have impure thoughts," I said. *"Ad te puto."* I think of you.

I had no thoughts at all for the old women in line behind me, waiting to confess their niggardly sins. No thoughts of Dolores or of my papa or of my immortal soul. My only thoughts were impure, and they were so great as to obscure my notice of anything else. I whispered—I must have, for I was not totally mad, not yet—but what I was saying was so large to me, it seemed as though I must have shouted.

"We must not see each other anymore," he answered, suddenly, urgently, and not in our Latin but in Spanish. "You may not return to my study. The lessons are over. I absolve you. *Cede.*" Go.

"How can you absolve me?" I said.

He made no answer. I waited as long as I could, I waited until

I could feel the old women grow restless, and then I quit the church. The grandmothers looked at me as I passed them lined up against the wall, muttering their Ave's.

I came to his study. He sent me away. I came back.

"Please," he said.

"Please," I said. We were standing in his doorway together. He was trying to close his door, but I reached past it. I touched him, I let my hand rest for a moment on his chest. And I saw it—whatever had let him hold himself apart from me—I saw that resolve give way.

He let me in. He told me that he had mortified his flesh. He knew, he said, that a woman could be the Devil's tool, and he considered the Devil surpassingly clever to have sent so small a woman, one who was a virgin and one who asked for a tutor. He scourged himself rigorously, but every place that he opened his flesh, it was as if he made it burn that much more with lust.

His nose was long and sharp and it would dig painfully into me when we embraced, like a blade against my breast, and when he entered me the first time, my soul flew up above the town of Quintanapalla. Up, up, until I saw the innkeeper's wife with her sticks for her fire slowly walking the steep path to her house, and I thought, Oh! how old she is, by the end of this winter she may be dead. And I saw my father in the silk house, now the workshop where he made little wooden things to sell, and my heart swelled with love for him, for those fingers that looked so coarse yet fashioned such toys as the little acrobat on his wire. I saw all the toys and spoons and hair ornaments that he had carved for me and my sister. I saw Dolores, too, scrubbing and scolding, and our neighbor as he led his cow back through the gorse. And I loved everyone. I felt I was touching all the world.

"You have learned to write on me as well as on the page," Alvaro said once, examining his skin before he clothed himself again. I used my fingernails on his back as if they were quills. I liked to leave my mark on his body. Sometimes, when I was under him, I would bite Alvaro, and then he would pull away in surprise, the red signature of my teeth on his smooth skin.

We read. Each time we began the same way, sitting at the table with words spread before us, until my hand reached for his leg. I was brazen, feeling him hard under his robes. Nothing held me back, I felt him and I burned. The idea of hell was such a poor little fire in comparison.

"Is it for this that a priest wears skirts?" I asked, my hand feeling between his legs. "To hide his sex?"

In the beginning of our bedding together, there was only one question each week. Not whether or not we would fuck—that was understood—but *when*. When would we succumb? We would wait, heads over books, until the question grew, until the always unspoken (but no less audible, no less readable) words— *Fuck me; lie with me; oh, touch me*—had grown so large, it was as though they were spelled out in the air before us, obliterating the lesson on the table.

When we gave in, I would feel light begin to pour through my body. As though I were a vessel, a pitcher, a cup. As though at last this were the Holy Spirit my mother had promised on the day of first communions. Light that I saw only as a silver fire behind the closed lids of my eyes. I could not help thinking of all that I remembered of saints and their raptures. I felt an ache in my throat, like that of suppressed grief, or the onset of illness. I was driven by a sudden shift in the old relation between spirit, mind and body. My senses were enslaved to the flesh. I was sick with desire.

In the beginning it was I, always, who touched first, whose hand reached over the quills and ink and pages to touch his sleeve, to undo one and then another button. It was my question that had to be answered, my *Tui tangere possum?* "Can I touch you?" But then he became bold, too. He would be standing by the door when I entered, he would have been pacing for an hour or more. The lesson would be set out on the table, quills lined up precisely and books open to where we had left off the previous week. We shoved aside its pages, pushed away the opened ink-well. The lesson that day would be written on me. My head came down hard on the table. The ink went over, a spreading black lake of lust.

What did I know of his life? It seems to me now that in the time we had, I told him everything and he told me nothing. He had come from Jaca, in Navarre. He was the second eldest of his mother's four children. When his papa left them, the two girls ended in an asylum—his mother could not feed and keep them all. Alvaro and his older brother remained with her only until they were old enough to go out in the world and learn a trade.

His papa, to hear him tell it, had suffered greatly because, like Carlos's father, the tormented King Philip, he was always struggling between his worry over his soul and a hellish itch to put his hands on every woman he saw. In Alvaro's family it was thought that the sons of Bartolomé Gajardo were each of them half of their father. That Tomás was lust and improvidence, and Alvaro was worry for the soul.

Yes, Alvaro was to be forbearance, he was to be zeal for higher things, and not prey to mortal temptation. He told me that he had never thought before to worry over lust. But, as it happened, the sons of Bartolomé Gajardo were not like the front and hind quarters of an ass, one all head, the other all immoderate balls.

It was true that Tomás had been a rogue, he could not keep any job. Apprenticed to cabinetmakers, to tanners, to chandlers and bookkeepers, he did not last at any occupation. As the two brothers had set out in the world together, their mama crying bitterly, Alvaro stuck by Tomás and followed him from town to town, job to job, always going farther north until they finally reached Paris.

Tomás disappeared into the masses of the city. Alvaro lost him, but he did not go back to Spain, not yet. He remained and got a position in an atelier that made buttons. He learned to make buttons of horn and bone, turning them on a special lathe, and wood buttons meant to be covered with fabric. He made silver buttons, too, which had to be hammered after they came from the mold, buttons made of shell, which broke as often as not before he had finished polishing them, buttons to be stitched upon gowns and waistcoats, stitched with silk.

As I lay with him I liked to think that the work of our worms, years before, had somehow made its way over the Pyrenees, wafting north like a thread of smoke through the air, until it reached the great city of Paris and a tailor there, where, guided by a needle, it pierced the shank of a button my priest had made.

Alvaro made busks, too. Those balusters of ivory or of bone that keep a woman's back straight. "Ladies of the court wear them," he said. "Their maids fasten them into the backs of their corsets." A busk is what lies closest to a woman's skin.

"It touches her," he told me.

Because it did, a busk had become a fashionable means of sending a *billet doux*. Gentlemen ordered them for their mistresses. They paid to have sweet messages and poems inscribed upon them. At his bench, Alvaro etched passionate words into the long, flat tongues of ivory. He began to think of a woman's skin, and of her body.

Alvaro said that he had led a peculiar, solitary life in Paris. He had few friends. He took all his meals in his rooming house; he ate silently and read the gazettes slowly as he drank his soup and chewed his bread. He could read by then; he taught himself French by carefully copying messages from paper to ivory, and by less exotic means. He read gazettes others left behind at table, publications bought by persons traveling through the city and then discarded. Advertisements for lectures at the medical colleges, for theological debates at the seminaries, for the performance of a new drama by Racine. Notices of positions offered to those trained in dentistry and wig making. Warnings of fever outbreaks and lists of its symptoms. Accounts of ladies and their dresses, of who wore what to the prince de Conti's Mardi Gras ball. Reports of how high the heels would be the following season and where to get the best jeweled opera glasses, and an article on how the price of hat trimmings would increase the next fall because of a plague among African ostriches, which were molting so uncontrollably that even those birds which survived were running naked through the sands. He liked to read of the fashionable people who might be wearing his buttons and busks. But two things happened. The buttons and busks began to bore him, and the flesh for which they were intended beckoned.

The Bóveda welcomed those whose minds were agile and keen. In Paris, Alvaro felt a vocation—a call either toward God or away from the button atelier—and he entered the order. He studied in Paris for some years, he believed he would remain there always, but in the year 1673 the Bóveda was cast out of France. If the pope would not discipline them, then Louis would, and the same year that so many witches were purged, the same that Princess Marie threw her bouquets on the gallows, the Sun King disbanded the Bóveda for its study of questionable texts. Alvaro came home to Spain and to further discipline at the hands of the Franciscans, his mind having trifled with wanton books, perhaps, but his body still pure. He had remained celibate in that city famous for its courtesans and dancing girls, for every titillation of the flesh.

"What were you like as a boy?" I asked him such questions all the time. I wanted to possess that knowledge, wanted to bind myself to him even in those years that preceded our meeting. He reminded me of myself, a little—the youthful desire for knowledge, and now I wonder if all mortal lovers are not like Narcissus, ever eager to catch a glimpse of themselves.

Alvaro told me a little, very little. "I had a penchant for sweets," he said, as if that were the sort of answer I was seeking.

"But what did you *do*?" I pressed.

"Well, sometimes we boiled milk and honey until it formed a soft candy that stuck to the sides of the kettle."

"Ugh!" I pushed him away from me. "What does that tell a person!"

He would look at me when I burst out at him. His face would express puzzlement, as if truly he had tried to give the kind of answer I sought.

"That was when my sisters were still with us," he continued. "I dreamed of sweets. I never got enough."

"Perhaps you had worms."

There was a sadness in Alvaro. It drew me to him, and yet it vexed me, too, and made me say sharp things. Some of this sadness was the way he was made, but some had to do with his sisters. He had tried to find them but could not, and the Church was angered by his stubborn attachment to his earthly family. Because of it they almost did not grant him the reader's license he requested, and he was routinely called back by his new Franciscan bishop for questioning. He left once for months on a useless journey, discovering no trace of Tita and Amalia. He knew the asylum to which they had been sent was somewhere west of the place he was born, but he did not find it.

When he told me of the little girls, he said of Tita that she was small. "Small like you, Francisca," and he held his hand out and placed it on my head. I felt that he was seeing her there instead of me. He did not care so much about his mama or papa, all his love for family was spent on those two lost little girls.

I had no breasts to speak of, and one Thursday, with his razor, Alvaro took away the hair covering my secret parts. He looked at me. "You are . . . you look like a little girl," he said. "Just like a little girl." And I could see he liked me this way. His eyes were steady as he looked. "Turn around," he said, and I did. I enjoyed his rapt attention. His pleasure in making me a child and his knowing me carnally as I looked so like a child caused me some uneasiness, but not enough that I resisted him. No, not at all.

I have never known another person with so unwavering a gaze. His eyes blinked less often than was natural. They were so dark, it was hard to discern where the colored part left off and the middle began. I let my head slip beneath the surface of the still, black pool of each pupil. Submerged, there was no logic, no means to question. It was as if I had attempted to speak with my head under water: words bore no discernible shape. Ill formed, they surfaced, popped and evaporated too quickly to interpret.

That first afternoon I had heard my own drowned objection as I reached forward to undo his cassock. When Alvaro allowed me, after so many buttons that my fingers were ringing—perhaps with guilt rather than exertion—when he let me push the robe from his shoulders, I smelled him, smelled the scent that had tantalized me all the while, a scent almost eclipsed by books and ink and the dust of the confessionary. That essence of him, which had come through the grille and the curtain, a salt sharpness, as if all the seasoning withheld from my poor life were there in his flesh, springing forth.

"*Da, Domine, virtutis manibus meis. Impone capite meo galeam salutis.*" Give virtue, oh God, to my hands. Place on my head the helmet of salvation. With these words he had put on his cassock. With a different language I removed them.

My lessons recommenced at the usual hour, on Thursdays, after the bell that rang nones. Time collapsed and stretched at once. Some afternoons each moment hung in the light like a red jewel, like a single seed of a pomegranate: I would be aware of each one breaking under my teeth. Ten minutes became a sea of time and longing. Another day the bells of vespers seemed to follow those of nones without a moment between them, and I would wonder how it was that so many hours had elapsed without my even drawing a breath.

I closed my eyes under him. I closed my eyes and I saw deer running or hands kneading dough. I saw ten spoons in a box, a bottle of walnut oil. I would see a cloud of flies buzzing over a bowl. I never knew what I would see. Paper burning. One page with nothing written on it, clean white, and the flame catching a corner. Then suddenly the whole thing on fire, crumpling.

Some afternoons, as the last light of the sun shivered and disappeared suddenly like a candlewick drowning in melted wax, church bells calling softly through the trees, calling the faithful to drop their earthly chores and turn to God; on such afternoons there came that moment where flesh smothered consciousness and sought its own destruction. Eyes closed, everything black. Feeling him on me, his weight, I'd see Alvaro's broad thumb, just as it looked on Ash Wednesday, approaching my forehead as if to crush reason and sensibility and will. *Remember, Francisca, that ye art dust and unto dust ye shall return.*

"Fuck me!" I would say to him. "I want to be under you.

"Please!" I said.

He pulled back and looked at my eyes to be sure I wanted what I asked for. I nodded, and he did fuck me, hard enough that it hurt, and I liked that, too, his hurting me. I wanted him to reduce me to no more than a shadow, the place where I had lain under him.

He pushed me away, sometimes, refused me. Once he laid his head on the table and I wondered, were his tears soaking into the binding of the books from the great library at Salamanca? But when he looked up his eyes were dry. He knew he could not help himself, or me. I took off my clothes and kicked them under the table. It was cold, on winter afternoons, but I did not feel it. For a long time Alvaro just looked at me, saying nothing, and I was not ashamed. I returned his look.

"Give me the razor," I said. "I will take off the hairs. I like to." And after that, it was always I who did the barbering.

I reached out to him and he caught my wrist. How quick I grew at undoing all those priestly buttons, thirty of them—my fingers flew nimbly over each clerical closure. I undid him and held him in my hand. Pressed my tongue in the little hollow where his throat met his collarbone, licked up the salt taste of him.

He kneeled and walked on his knees to me. And I crawled away, taunting him until he lunged and caught me. One hand on each buttock, he pulled me back to him, my hands catching at the chair legs.

"These are the loaves," he said, biting my ass, and he put his hand between my legs. "And the fishes." *Panis et pisces*. Smelling my secret places.

"Loaves and fishes. And so now you know the miracle of abundance, Francisca. Here is the feast that is never consumed."

Profaning, yes. But what if there isn't any God or gods listening? None at all? Or what if there is, and he likes his creation to take pleasure in its flesh?

What if it is unbearable sadness to find oneself an angel, so much love and no arms with which to embrace?

I N MADRID, IN THE DAYS WHEN SILK WEAVING was the most lucrative and competitive of all the industries in Spain, it was not unknown for a business to disappear outright. A cracking, creaking, rumbling shudder would shake the cobbles loose in the street; horses would shy, but before their drivers could whip them on through the dust, a shop would have collapsed and sunk under the street, its foundation undermined by hidden passages. So secretive and sly were the silk mercers that their district was riddled with underground tunnels, tunnels that allowed workers to come and go without a rival's knowledge.

The richest of these mercers was Catalano, who sent spies to ateliers in Lyon, thieves to workshops in Paris and Marseille: small, mean and desperate men who stole sketchbooks from the best French weavers and brought the season's latest patterns home to their unscrupulous employer. Before a certain weave had even rolled out of the great looms in Paris, Catalano had it draped over his arm and under the nose of some grandee who paid him in gold for his ingenuity and trouble.

This mercer had little competition in Madrid. The only man to stay in business, the only one at all, was Alessandro, a weaver who would not stoop to dishonesties, but whose own fabrics, based on designs he had made himself, were so beguiling that he still made a living, enough to keep him and his one child.

For Alessandro had a beautiful daughter whose name was Ana and who was almost ready to be married. Alessandro had been worrying over her dowry and how he might contrive a good match for her when Ana fell ill with a fever that sapped her strength and spirit. Formerly cheerful, the delight of her father and all who knew her, she lay upon her bed, and when she was not sleeping she wept.

Who would marry Ana now? She grew ever more wasted and sad, and the weaver gave all he had saved to worthless physics and apothecaries, until he had no dowry for her. Not even a peasant would have her, Alessandro worried, for the girl was ghostly, although her beauty had not vanished.

Finally, as there was no cure for her illness, Ana died.

Alessandro was stricken. He cloistered himself in his workshop, caring nothing for himself anymore. He had no earthly desire beyond a fitting burial for his daughter, and he determined to use his loom to make her a dress for all eternity, a dress so magnificent that when Ana rose to greet her Lord she would outshine every princess of all the ages. Lacking any assistance— no drawboy or a single soul to help him—Alessandro was forced to reset his loom alone, and it took him three days and three nights, during which he did not sleep or eat but worked without ceasing.

When the loom was ready, he threaded it with the last silks that he owned. He used colored threads as bright as jewels, and threads of silver and gold thread he had saved for many years because there had never before been any call for such richness.

What Alessandro loomed was not merely a pattern or a design, but a bewitchery of silk, a magic cloth the beauty of which was born of his despair. It was a pattern of bees sipping nectar, of flowers turning their heads to the sun, of birds and deer and every graceful creature. Of all bounty and goodness, of stars and planets, sun and moon. It was everything that Alessandro's heart had known when he held his daughter in his arms, and all that he could not bear to part with. When he saw what he had made, when the last span rolled out from under the reed, Alessandro knew that the wearer of this fabric would steal every heart, just as surely as Ana had stolen his. He knew that it was a cloth that could make him the richest silk weaver in all of Spain, in all the world. But Alessandro would sell none of it, and would weave no more than that required for his daughter's dress.

At the funeral Mass, Ana's beauty caused rioting. Though she lay still on her bier, she was as radiant as a full moon. Sparks flew from her unbound hair, her lips smiled as she wore the dress her father wove. Princes who had flocked from distant cities fell in love with the dead girl. They wept upon her breast and kissed her cold mouth. Mourners crowded so close about the coffin that there was trouble in getting the lid nailed shut, for so enchanting was she that everyone had to touch her, no one could be dissuaded from putting a finger on her breast or tracing just once, just for a moment, the outline of her cheek. But finally, after the last of them were beaten back from her body, Ana was put in the earth, and then her father died, too.

After Alessandro was dead, his goods and all that was in his poor workshop were sold to meet the debts he left, for he left nothing else, no mourners and no kin.

And the rich mercer Catalano came to the auction. He bought Alessandro's loom, just as it was, still set to make the fabric that had created Ana's dress, and he had the loom carried to his shop. He ordered that it be set up with his best silks and his gold and silver thread; and before he commanded his workers to start the loom, he bought himself a hamper filled with the finest wines and sweetmeats, for Catalano wanted to be ready to celebrate the fame and even greater wealth he anticipated. But, as it happened, he never had cause to make merry.

The rich mercer's factory was incapacitated by Alessandro's loom. Drawboys could not hold their threads. They dropped them, and they tangled and caught in the works. It happened this way over and over again, for when the workers looked at the cloth coming from the loom, they went crazy with love, they lost their reason.

At first, Catalano was not deterred. He outfitted his drawboys with blinkers, and when they tore them off, he fired them and hired blind men. Still, even blind workers were drawn to the cloth. They fingered it as it emerged from under the reed; they, too, dropped the threads and stilled the loom. He gloved them, then, but they tore their gloves off and left their posts to touch the fabric, and the loom clacked on untended until the heddles snapped and the warp beam broke.

Catalano had the loom repaired, and he traveled to Cádiz, where he bought twelve African slaves off a boat. He had their hands burned until there was no sense left in their fingers, and he blinded them, too, but to little purpose. They sucked the cloth and died of love.

So the rich mercer went on, spending all he had accumulated over the years, determined to make Alessandro's loom work.

He called in priests and had the machinery exorcised, consecrated. He squandered days of prayer. He fasted until he was a wraith, until he was an utterly broken man, but he never made more than a few inches of Alessandro's cloth, a scrap much fondled, sucked and picked on, which he took with him to his grave.

"There, that is a story that my grandfather told," I tell the queen. "He would tell it at night, that story or one of his other tales, when it was summer and the days were long. My mama would let my sister Dolores and me walk up to the silk house to sit with our grandfather after supper, and that is when he would tell us tales."

Is it true? María whispers.

"I told you, it is a story my papa's papa told me."

Yes, but is it true?

"Do you believe it?"

Yes.

"Then it is true."

She nods.

It must be a very good poison that unsticks the spirit from the flesh, allows it to come and go as it pleases, leaving the flesh to founder alone.

The queen thinks she is dreaming. What happened was this: the retching finally shook her loose. María choked. She coughed, writhed, and then she was free. She left her feverish, aching body in her bed, left it in the company of basins, bandages and useless remedies. She came seeking company, seeking solace. She came and found me.

In the palace, Dr. Severo draws back a cape of silk from María's breast. He feels her arm, looking for her pulse, for some confession of how her heart fails her. He squeezes so insistently that he calls her back. She stirs slightly. "Ouch," she says. The doctor understands almost nothing of the queen's condition, only that it is deteriorating steadily. Her periods of lucidity are shorter and more infrequent. Despite all manner of teas and waters, she grows steadily more dehydrated. Her hands pick at the cape over her as if she wants to take apart the lovely pattern: unloom, unweave all the world.

The poison makes her do it. Makes her fingers twitch and trouble the cloth. The chemical, whatever it is—Severo still does not know—has a complex of effects, and not all of them are unpleasant. She feels cold, it is true, and the cold is a dead cold that creeps toward her heart from fingers and toes, inexorably claiming more and more of her extremities. Her feet paddle helplessly, tangling in the bedclothes, and then they are still.

What an odd dream, she thinks. *That loom. That unearthly fabric.* Why can she not waste quietly away like the weaver's daughter? Why must she suffer so, she wonders miserably. She wants to go back to sleep.

Each time before she vomits she feels her scalp grow wet and slimy with sweat, and the spells of retching are disorienting. It is not possible to vomit so much so often. She watches with stupefied interest what comes up into the basins held by patient hands. *What is that?* she thinks. *Where can it all come from?* It is as if she disgorges meals she has not eaten, a life she never led.

But, afterward, she feels better for a moment. She stretches luxuriously, and with a feeling of sensual pleasure she has never before experienced. The sheets come alive under her hands. What is more, her moments of rapture grow more frequent. There were none yesterday, the day she fell ill, the day she was poisoned. Then her thoughts circled senselessly in a sort of abased pleading. *Help me, God, O God. O God, have mercy. Mea culpa, Mea maxima culpa. Please.* Church Latin yielded to helpless begging, and then to sentimental pleading, *Mother, Maman, please come, take me home, please please please.* But, today her suffering is not so unremitting. There are these curious flights of ecstasy, and these wonderful dreams, as if she were once again a child listening to a story, feeling a cool hand on her head.

"Ma–ría! Lu–isa!"

From her bedchamber the queen can hear the rabble. At the

sound of her chanted name, she opens her eyes to the white winter sky, she sees black smoke coiling heavenward from her east window. What does it mean? she wonders. Is the stable on fire? But what can that matter now? All she wants is her mother. All she wants is to be home.

The queen's swollen tongue feels dry and sticky, and when she tries to ask Obdulia the origin of the smoke, the little maid cannot understand the choking noise she makes. María's body burns in her bed, but all she feels is cold.

"Is there such a fever with poison?" whispers Obdulia to Jeanette. She lays a fresh cloth on her mistress's brow, replacing the one that has grown warm. María's left hand lies on top of her little dog's head, stroking the soft fur. He trembles. "No-o, no, n-o-o-o," moans the queen as the sickness returns, and she writhes a little. She feels so wretched, it is as if her organs squirm like eels in a net. Her liver feels black and damp and cold, her heart shivers, her bowels cramp. Only her stomach is hot. Her stomach burns all the way to her throat. Obdulia holds a cup to her lips and she takes enough water to wet her tongue. "O God, O God," she says, and she turns her head back and forth on her hot pillow.

Just a corridor away, a floor above, Carlos is with Estrellita, pushing aside the little table with its cold cups of thistle tea, untouched plates of omelette and bread, a bowl of custard.

He kneels by her bed. He puts his face in her bedclothes, he feels the heat of her coming through the counterpane. The king prays in Estrellita's company. *Touch me, God,* he asks silently. *Touch me through her. Find me. Please. You are here, I know.* The king's eyes are closed.

They have had Estrellita in the palace for forty-seven days now, in the room just next door to the weeping penitents, twins whose tears fill buckets and in whose lachrymose offerings Carlos bathes each evening. All palace teas and coffees are boiled up in the water they weep, all eggs hard-cooked in the tears they shed. They are greedy for sadness, they have not as much sorrow as they desire, and so they always have reason to go on lamenting.

This is the corridor of the living saints, the wing of the palace reserved for penitential misfits: bleeders and weepers, spectral self-starvers who live on no more than their ration of the daily Eucharist: a thimbleful of wine, a morsel of dry bread. This is the secret corridor whose entrance is hidden under a tapestry, whose servants and whose kitchen are separate from the rest of the palace's, whose inhabitants are so precious that their company is shared with only an honored few.

Behind each door is another miracle. There are the two conjoined boys, who, born to a life most intimate, have between them four legs, two arms, no testicles, twenty-three fingers and one many-chambered heart, which beats a slow song. Their identical heads are turned ever toward each other; they have found their vocation in a never-ending dialogue on theological concerns. When Dr. Severo is confident that their health will allow it, those thornier Inquisitorial questions are presented to them. Their neighbor is fat old Sister Tomita, the one who levitates, her elephantine girth swelling with rapture against her stays, a giant corset, which, empty of her flesh, the laundress who has never seen Sister Tomita believes is some strange military contraption, a sling for hurling boulders, perhaps, or some sort of tent. But why should I wash this? she wonders. Should it not be the responsibility of the soldiery? When the fits come upon her, Sister Tomita's stays must be undone, lest they pop, grommets whizzing. She swells further and further until, at last, she floats.

Unlike most afflicted with charisms, Sister Tomita is not shy, and as she rises, before she even passes the sconces illuminating her chamber, she calls for witnesses to come.

"Intestinal gases!" Doctor Severo has diagnosed.

"Ridiculous! Theatrical chicanery!" snorts the queen mother. Nonetheless, she never misses an ascension.

"Excommunicate her!" wrote the pope to the bishop of Madrid, and his letter was delivered by express coach.

As for little Estrellita, she too has her detractors. "It is a hysterical manifestation," says Marianna. "We must send her home."

"But she is not of a hysterical temperament, she has never been hysterical," argues Carlos.

"Not unless you count spontaneous hemorrhaging as getting carried away," says his mother. Still, she keeps a small square of silk soaked with Estrellita's blood beneath her own pillow. No harm in it, if the child lacks supernatural power or divine connections, and, on the off chance that she is not a holy pretender—well, so much the better.

Carlos cares nothing for skeptics' taunts. He believes, he guards all his living treasures jealously, he values none of them above Estrellita. Each afternoon, before vespers, he is at his little saint's feet. Wrapped in a cloak, her small boots are elevated on a cushion of white silk, a cushion replaced each morning when the night's blood has soaked it through, the sodden one taken downstairs to the royal reliquary.

Today, she was asleep when he came to her. She is still asleep, and dreaming, and as she dreams, her dreams pass through the king. And it feels good to him to be filled, if only for a moment, with the dreams of a saint. All the sweet, aching longing, all the patient certitude of God's love rises from the child like steam off a hot cup and fills Carlos José, the crippled king of Spain.

When he can resist no longer, he reaches for her cheek and brushes it with his ringed fingers. Her eyes open, eyes black and mysterious like the night that brims with spirits.

"My wife is very ill," Carlos says to Estrellita. "I am afraid she may die." Estrellita rests her hand on his head. She strokes it in much the same way that María Luisa strokes the little dog on her bed downstairs.

"I am afraid," he says again with his head bowed.

"You must pray for her," Estrellita says.

"May I look, then?" asks Carlos, gesturing at her feet, and she shrugs. He is her king.

Only Carlos may open Estrellita's boots. To their locking buckles there is but one key, and Carlos wears it on a black velvet ribbon around his neck. The lock ensures that Estrellita may not remove her boots. The lock promises that her wounds are a real and true testimony to the presence of God, and not some trick played on the king. For all of Spain knows that Carlos—like his father and his father's father and all the kings before him—is desperate for any manifestation of the holy. In such troubled times of drought and plague, a family might well drive stakes into the hands and feet of an unmarried daughter, hoping to trade her weight in gold before she found a lover and demanded a dowry.

But Estrellita is the genuine article, Carlos knows this to be true. From inside her boots spills a red redder than rubies, a treasure of bright gems falling to the floor. He wipes up her blood with his royal sleeve. He presses it to his mouth. Estrellita's family resisted her being collected and carried off to Madrid. Unlike the Luarcas, they accepted no bag of gold in exchange for unusual talents, and they pleaded that their daughter might be returned to them by the new year. Estrellita's mama and papa made no more claims for her than she made for herself. She had had no visions in which the Virgin or Christ or any saint appeared to her. She had never been a clever student of her catechism. She was given to pranks and bursts of temper.

As the king busies himself with her dressings, Estrellita stretches on her couch. She looks like an ordinary child waking. Despite her stubborn, ceaseless bleeding, her lips are full and rosy, her cheeks are flushed with apparent health. Wrapped in her cloak, gloved and booted, she eats nothing, sips tea made of thistles. The bandages Carlos removes from her wounds smell sweet like the blossoms of the orange trees that fill the terraces of her family's home by the sea, and Carlos keeps these holy linens, stained with sanctity, in a chest at the foot of his bed. The reliquary with its pile of forty-six cushions (forty-seven, less one that was sent to the pope), smells like the most exalted hothouse. When they are in its confines, the nuns who tend it laugh with helpless joy. They cannot remember the troubles of the world, they cannot recall what keeps them on their knees ten hours of each day.

As for Carlos, it is not only that he desires to be saved, and to save his country. The king of Spain has fallen in love with Estrellita.

He does not want to know her carnally. He would not think of such a thing. It is just that she smells so good. He wants to inhale her. He presses her dressings to his lips, and his teeth ache with longing. He breathes deeply: a lungful of orange blossoms, of blue ocean, bright sun, of . . . Perhaps it is because Estrellita seems so oblivious to him—the king!—that Carlos's love for her grows ever stronger.

She breathes evenly, slowly, and her eyelids flutter as His Highness speaks to her. Perhaps it is not true, any of it. Perhaps there is no God, no heaven—still, faith does transform believers. And perfect faith, a faith such as Estrellita's, makes the blood smell sweet. When she dies she will not rot because, like all the other holies who have expired in the secret corridor of saints, she cannot conceive of putrefaction.

Sometimes Estrellita vomits the tea that she drinks, and it comes up gold like wine. The lame king drinks it, and then he dances. He forgets all his fears. He forgets that he wants to be saved—it is tiresome to worry all the time—he forgets that for him each night blooms with pain, fantastic red flowers bursting from the draperies with every beat of his pulse. His latest ailment, gout, the one that killed his father, is a hot, flaming mortification of the flesh that gives him no rest.

Carlos looks at Estrellita's eyes, her smooth brow. "The doctor says that María is vomiting blood, that she has been poisoned." The little saint does not move. "I am afraid," he says for the third time.

Estrellita sits up on her elbows. She looks at him. "I want to go home," she says. "I do not like it here."

Carlos stares at her. He shakes his head. "I cannot let you go," he says.

The girl lies back on her couch.

Downstairs, Severo is bent over the queen, his ear to her mouth. "I want to go home," María manages to say, her dry tongue laboring to form intelligible words. He knows she is dying, but *I cannot let you go*, thinks Severo, shaking his head. Not without some attempts at healing that appear heroic.

By María Luisa's bed, also, are a clutter of trays, but unlike the little saint's, these bear basins and bandages and salves, lancets of various sizes. Severo is discovering that María does not part with her blood as readily as Estrellita.

The queen is afraid of bleeding, so much afraid that Severo's first three attempts to bleed her have been failures. It isn't that she has not delivered herself into her doctor's care—she is trying to be obedient to his wishes—but her fear is so intense that her flesh refuses to comply. She can feel her veins deny the knife. When Dr. Severo cuts, her heart pumps backward, her panicked blood flows away from the lancet's touch. Now her arms are paining her, burning in the places he has cut them.

"Please, I beg of you," she says. Her voice is terrible to hear, a ragged, phlegmy whisper. "The foot, the foot. Use the foot. Oh, please."

Dr. Severo nods, and he and his assistant each take one leg and gently pull María down in her bed until her knees are bent over its edge and her white feet hang below the level of her faltering heart. The assistant brings the basin and sets it on the tile floor below the queen's toes.

Dr. Severo's touch is cool and dry. He kneels before María's feet, and he takes the left one in his hands. He runs his thumb along the top of the arch where one promising vessel protrudes stark and blue against her pale skin. The assistant lays a square of linen on the floor beside the basin. On it he places a fleam and a lancet kit containing four delicate, bright blades forged in the Austrian city of Klosterneuburg. Partial as he is to spring-loaded devices, Severo prefers to use the fleam, which is equipped with a trigger similar to those on firearms. When he discharges the sharp, one-toothed blade, it makes a satisfying little *chock* and cuts deeply and with surprising strength. On the other hand, the fleam's one metal tooth is nearly the size of a horse's, the marks it leaves unsightly. If the queen should recover, as unlikely as that may be, he might find her displeased by the scars. He had better use a blade from the lancet kit. Doctors have been hanged for less.

From his bag Severo retrieves a piece of lambskin, cut long and narrow like a sash, and, turning the soft fleece side to the queen's skin, he binds it tightly around her leg, just below the knee. He taps her foot when he is done with the tourniquet. "Your Highness, if you would, please move your foot," he says. María wriggles her toes a little, and slowly the vein fills and rises. When the physician takes the foot in his hand again, she flinches.

The prick of the lancet is expert, relatively painless, and on this, the fourth try, her blood spurts out. Each beat of her heart sends a feeble jet that runs down her foot and drips warm as bathwater from her big toe and its neighbor. But blood does not feel like water, and her skin senses blood's heaviness, its almost oily, slippery quality.

Dr. Severo and his assistant step back at the sight of the queen's blood. They bow their heads. It is as if a new presence, some exotic dignitary requiring homage, has suddenly entered the room. And, in truth, the smell of María's blood—like Estrellita's, or anyone else's—carries its own peculiar intimacy.

Nearing death, and brimming with longing for those she has loved and lost, an unexpected, almost embarrassing smell of revelation flows from María's opened vein. Freed from the constraints of flesh, memories and desires carried in her blood crowd about the room. Her heart empties itself silently, but Dr. Severo cringes as if at a sudden clamor, and his boy shrinks back against the draperies.

Who are all these spirits! Mischievous Mademoiselle de Toquetoque, the marquise and her naughty cigarros, María's nana and her cousin Berthe, her dance master, Lucie, Rocinante and a dozen little lovebirds—they are all there in her blood and they fly out for an instant; they mill about, they gossip together. Laughing, and flowing under the bed, splashing the tiles. Horse's hooves clatter on the floor, the lovebirds sing their homesick song, they fly at Severo's assistant's head, and he starts. Over goes the nightstand and its water glasses, almond oil, unraveling bandages.

"You oaf!" the doctor yells at his boy, who scrambles to right the stand. He nervously mops up the barley water with his own doublet.

María opens her eyes, she stares at the canopy of her bed. The very air in her chamber trembles and expands. Above the noise and chatter of the spirits, the piercing birdsong, she hears her own pulse in her ears, she is aware of each breath she draws. Loss of blood makes her fingers cramp, her neck and shoulders suddenly ache sharply. She has the unpleasant sense that her teeth are loosening in their sockets. The thought of her foot, open and dripping her life into a bowl, makes her think of Estrellita. She wonders how the child lives with her terrible gift from God.

When the blood begins to coagulate, Dr. Severo kneels and makes another opening just above the first. María hardly feels this prick. The room has grown brighter to her eyes, as if it has come unmoored and floats heavenward from the palace. Her ears pop, as if she has suddenly ascended a great height. She feels wonderfully cool, the fever is all draining away through her foot, and a strange taste fills her mouth, a sweet taste, as of hope. She is so light. *As if my veins had been filled with lead,* she thinks. *I am unburdened.*

Now she feels she understands Estrellita. Now she opens her arms and prays in the same words her husband uses: *Touch me. Find me.* She too would bleed and bleed, if she could only feel this ecstatic rising forever.

But it cannot last, too soon it will be over. Pleasant memories will forsake her. Dr. Severo cauterizes the wound with a knife blade heated until it glows white. As cool as she is now, in a few hours she will be miserably hot. Her tongue will feel thick and sticky again. It will cleave to the roof of her mouth and render her incessant requests for water incomprehensible. Yes, for the moment, she is improved, she can smile as Severo leaves, and for an hour or more she feels happy to remain in her body, she stops thinking of her mother, stops dreaming of somehow returning to France.

The hour passes quickly. The lovebirds turn to bats, friends to tormentors.

When Eduardo comes to sit by her side, she grasps his hand, she draws him toward her. "I want it over with," she says. "Bring the laudanum. Every bit that you have, all that you've saved."

When he refuses, she begins to weep.

Before the queen had Eduardo's laudanum, her life had been a struggle between two poles: panic and the only means she had to smother it, a willed blankness. Without any rescue, when she first arrived in Madrid, the queen's cheeks tingled with fear, her fingers trembled and she shook so at supper that she was forced to hold her cup with two hands, she could not cut her meat. Such a pitch of feeling could not be sustained, of course, not even for a season, and so she settled into long periods of dullness interrupted by periodic fits of frantic weeping.

Her crying became a source of gossip and conjecture. As María could have told anyone, there was much to be unhappy about, and yet none of what came to pass in a day was the actual cause for tears. It was more that she had become like some vessel left under a steady drip of loneliness that would not dry but steadily accumulated until she overflowed. Weeping became a part of her routine, as regular as her morning toilette. Each morning as the angelus rang she began to cry as if the bell itself broke her heart, the way certain sounds of high pitch can shatter a wineglass or some overly fragile bauble.

"You must try to stop," Esperte said to her. But María would weep until she was summoned to the midday repast and come to table with eyes swollen and face blotched. Her hair, of course, was smooth, but no servant could unruffle her spirit and erase the marks of woe.

Whatever concern Carlos's mother first expressed yielded quickly to displeasure, and María knew her grief was dangerous. Still, she could not stop the feeling, and it was years after her arrival that the queen learned about the dwarfs and their laudanum and asked Eduardo about the drug. "You do not use it!" she said.

"No," he answered, and he told María that she should be suspicious of unfelt pain. Did she like the way the other dwarfs smiled those smiles without mirth?

"Just let me try it," she said, and she wheedled and cajoled and petted and begged until he finally acquiesced.

She knew how to charm him. How could he resist the lovely, lonely queen? In a month's time María was taking the drug each day after breakfast, and again before dinner: one, two, three drops, just enough so that she was cast by the opiate into a deeper part of herself, each day's brief drowning. Six drops spent during the day, the larger dose of four drops she saved for bedtime, for Carlos. With laudanum, the idea that she could perish lonely and exiled from all that she loved seemed somehow less shocking. It was no longer an unthinkable punishment against which she railed.

In fact, at twenty-two, and in those hours of narcotic embrace, she began to long for death. "Kill me," she would say to Eduardo, who invariably doled out no more than the seventy-drop bottle. "Kill me, please. I know you have more. You did not dispose of all those little vials, all those years' worth. I know you saved some." But he would not give it.

"I do not want to feel pain," the queen said. "Not any kind. Not in my body, not in my heart. Nowhere." María never believed her anguish to be some trial that might enlarge her character. Suffering would never raise her up but only cast her deeper into animal misery. Keening like some hound, or mute and wet like a mollusk: nothing exalted. It was laudanum that exalted her.

Mother, Mother, Mother, she thinks now. How can it be that she is dying so far from home? How can she have been exiled forever?

"I am thirsty," she tells Eduardo. He gets a cup and holds it to her lips. The water flows, just a trickle, cool and tasting of the metal of the cup. She has trouble swallowing, it runs down her chin.

She squeezes Eduardo's short, thick fingers. "Where is the blue bottle?" she whispers. "Could I not have just a bit? A little, little, little bit?"

He shakes his head. "No," he says softly. "You are too weak. It might harm you."

She squeezes his hand again. "I don't care," she says. "A drop. Just a drop?"

He shakes his head.

"Talk to me, then. Say something. Tell me something nice." She turns her head from side to side.

Eduardo looks at her, at her hair. So much of it. "Do you remember what I told you?" he asks. "What they say of freaks?" He strokes her hand, her forehead. "They excuse such deformities as my own by saying that our mothers must have had bad thoughts, bestial and monstrous, while they carried life inside them. That they let their eyes linger too long on some terrible picture, that they let their thoughts stray to abominations.

"But your mother, María, each night that she carried you she dreamed of gardens. Of lilies and pear blossoms. She gazed upon roses and candles and pearls. She watched the Seine as it flowed beneath a moon so full that it spilled its silver light upon the river's waves, and inside her your hair grew black and lustrous. She—"

"I want water," says María fretfully. "More water, please. I am so thirsty."

"Wait a little," he says, and she knows he is right. Its taste is no longer delightful; it brings a sudden rush of saliva that wells up from behind her tongue. The taste of metal overpowers, and the retching begins again.

"Obdulia!" the dwarf calls. He keeps her head rolled to the side, preventing her from choking, as the maid holds the basin. Obdulia looks away. If she does not, she will be sick herself.

Eduardo stays with María until the vomiting stops. Her face, turned on its left cheek, is absolutely motionless. "María?" he whispers, "María?" Her eyes are open, but when he passes his hand before them, she does not blink. She appears peaceful, though, asleep, and the dwarf gently closes her eyelids. With her hair falling down the pillows and all around her, she does look as if she were resting on the surface of vast black waters. Her little dog, so old his mustaches are gray, his eyes clouded blue and blind, sleeps next to her. His legs twitch and paddle in his dreams, as if he seeks to outrun some pressing enemy. And then he sighs and lies quietly beside his mistress, his head under her hand. Even in her sleep, she strokes him.

The queen is never alone. When Eduardo leaves, the maids sit near her. For them the time passes with exquisite slowness. The bells ring terce, and Obdulia rises to straighten the bedclothes and to pull a robe over the dog, hiding him from view. The queen mother is expected for a visit.

Marianna is not fond of pets. All the birds that María had sent from Paris that first year her mother-in-law set free, and they died in the cold. For a time the queen could not walk the palace grounds without seeing a bright clot of feathers here and there, where a bird had dropped frozen from a bough. The kittens were drowned, her rabbit disappeared. The monkey that Olympe sent last spring didn't last a fortnight. Only the little dog, in whose behalf Carlos interceded, has lasted. But it is best to keep him out of sight.

When Marianna bustles in, she is followed by her secretary, dripping ink. The queen mother will attend to her correspondence in María's bedchamber. That way she can visit the sick and dispense with her letters at the same time. She hates to waste even a moment, and there is a pressing legal matter which she must resolve.

Last month, after the shock of the discovery of the queen's conspiracy to deceive them with a false pregnancy, Marianna had asked the duque of Valdemoro to advance her the funds required for the transportation of an identical pair of female dwarfs, twins born six years ago, from Segovia. The daughters of a chandler in that city, when they were orphaned their uncle was unable to afford their keep, and he wrote to Carlos, asking if the court might not find so rare a phenomenon amusing.

The king's secretary had passed the missive along to Marianna, who at first threw the letter aside. No more dwarfs, enough is enough, she thought. But then her desire for a grandchild—thwarted as it was by María—found momentary satisfaction in the idea of the two tiny matched girls. Not even the girls so much as all the things they would require. She began to see herself dressing them in identical gowns of pink silk. Of two matching muffs. Two pairs of minuscule kid gloves. Yes, four tiny gloves! And four little pointed, pink velvet slippers, with seed pearls sewn on and a little tassel on the toe of each.

At the first opportunity, at a dinner welcoming the Portuguese alchemist, Marianna mentioned the twins to the duque. She promised him a seat at the next public trial, one in the balcony just below the king's, a seat from which he could bend down and touch the very hair on the heads of the damned. If only the duque would pay the passage to Madrid for these tiny girls, and loan moneys sufficient to dress and keep them, then he would go to heaven, he could rest assured.

She got the money, it came by horse courier. Now the standard contract for palace dwarfs must be revised to address the needs of the little twins. The clause concerning laudanum must be replaced by one providing for an educational allowance. The royal governess would earn her keep again.

As Marianna dictates, her secretary, whose penmanship is unequaled but whose mind is feeble, follows behind her and writes down all that she says, making use of whatever surface she comes upon, vanity tables, mantelpieces, even the floor, if need be. "How are we feeling?" Marianna says to María, and the secretary appends this greeting to the paragraph she was writing, one concerning yearly visits.

"Oh dear," the secretary says softly, realizing her mistake, and she looks up, ink on her lip.

"Not again!" exclaims Marianna. "We shall never conclude this business!" The little secretary curtsies from nerves.

"I'll copy it over. It shan't take but a few minutes." She collapses in a heap of quills and ink bottles and parchments.

As the queen mother approaches María's bed, Obdulia brushes the damp black curls from the queen's forehead, where they are sticking in the sweat.

"She does not look any better," says Marianna, and the maid shakes her head. "Well," the queen mother says, and she sits in the chair near the queen's pillow. She leans forward and, as if María were deaf rather than dying, "What now, then?" she shouts.

María's eyelids tremble but they do not open, and the queen mother reaches forward and gives her shoulder a little shake. "I'll read to you, then, shall I?" she says, and she takes out a volume of patriotic histories. The stories are boring, and her voice lacks inflection. Soon the maids fall asleep, the secretary botches one and then another contract, and, having used up all her parchments, she too falls into an inky stupor.

María twitches, dreaming. When the counterpane slips and exposes her little dog's nose and one gray paw, Marianna looks at it with distaste.

"I must leave you now," she says, though she has not had time to finish even one tale, not gotten even as far as the union of Castile with Aragon. María stirs, opens her eyes. And the secretary wakes and quickly gathers up ink and parchments. The queen mother pauses in the doorway.

"Oh," she says. "Your friend, the comtesse. She has left."

"Left?" María says softly.

"Yes, by night, and without so much as a word. A search of the guest apartments has not yielded anything—nothing that might implicate the comtesse, but Carlos has sent forces after her, nonetheless."

"Implicate her?" María whispers. "In what?"

"Why, in your poisoning, of course."

María closes her eyes.

The queen mother hesitates at the door for a moment, but when her daughter-in-law says nothing more, she leaves. The maids awaken, the little dog's paws twitch. Under closed lids, María falls asleep once more.

In her dreams, Juana la Loca comes and snips and snips with tiny golden scissors.

"I do not like Marianna, either," the mad queen Juana says, and she lays her scissors on María's dressing table, bequeathing them to her.

OME WEEKS IT SEEMED TO ME THAT NOTHING happened, nothing except waiting to see him. The rest of my life was reduced to a tasteless gruel of existence, like the penitential fare they feed us here. There was nothing but anticipation, and by Wednesday, when but one day separated me from him, I was already heartsick, because I knew that it would be so fast, our time so short, then gone and another whole week of nothingness to endure.

Did the week begin or did it end with the day I was with him? Thursday was consumed as if by a bright fire. Then Friday's burnt, dry husk. Seven days until our next meeting were too many to endure, and I began tortured vigils below his window, the sound of his quill scratching my heart.

I lost what ability I had to be careful.

When Sunday offered the solace of going to see him say Mass, even my prayers were profane. I asked God to give me the priest all for my own.

Mama told Dolores to keep the blood of my first period, she would be gone when I became a woman, but she said Dolores should save the cloths so that I might use them later for a spell her mama's mama taught her. A love potion: mistletoe, holy thistle, the little cloths, one hair from the head of your beloved and water passed thrice through a shift worn next to your heart for seven days. Boil them and heat them all together over a fire made with birch wood. Pour the potion they make over your love's meat. Not white meat of a fowl, not meat of a rabbit with a racing fickle heart, but red flesh: mutton or venison.

My own spell was a little different. I poured myself out over his words. We took each other on the table where we read together, we did not move the pages, and I spilled my monthly flow over the manuscripts. My blood stained the story of God's blood. Alvaro pulled back, his fingers wet with my flow. He looked at my life on his hand, he put his fingers in his mouth and tasted me.

Did my spell enslave him? Was it from that point forward that he, too, lost his reasonableness and discretion?

"What do they say to you there in the dark?" I would ask him what sins people confessed. Dolores. My father. And others as well. Everyone.

At first Alvaro refused to tell me such confidences, but now he answered me, he put his hot mouth between my breasts as he spoke. "Whose sins would you have me betray?" he said.

I thought for a moment. There was an old gossip in our town, Doña Petra, whom I did not like because she had caused trouble for my mother. She had said that Mama's dancing so long at her wedding was wanton. When Mama came home ill, she told me that our mother was prideful and that she had finally been humbled.

"What are Doña Petra's sins?" I asked Alvaro.

"You will not believe me if I tell you," he said.

"Tell me anyway."

"She says she is troubled by self-pollution."

"Oh, what a liar you are!" I said. I pushed him off me.

"I swear it to you," he said, and with his breath hot on my neck I believed him. Eyes closed, I saw Doña Petra upside down in her house, her skirts around her head and her fat old legs in the air, her hand between them.

"What about her husband?" I asked. "What are his sins?"

Alvaro sighed. "He thinks the baker is a cheat, he thinks the chandler is a cheat, and the miller, the smith and the wheelwright. Because he thinks everyone is out to cheat him, he steals from them first."

"He steals!"

"Nothing much, nothing that anyone misses, so he isn't caught," Alvaro said. "Or if he is, if the chandler knows of his slipping, say, a length of lampwick into his pocket, then the chandler adds another maravedi to the price of the lamp oil he came to buy."

"So, he is right in thinking everyone cheats him."

"Yes."

"And does the chandler come to you, then, and tell his side? Does he confess to charging too much for lamp oil?"

Alvaro nodded. "It is tedious, isn't it?"

"What about Dolores?" I said. "Her sins must be dull."

Alvaro looked at me. "Why does your sister hate you so?" he asked.

"Is that what she confesses!"

"Yes," he said.

I looked at him. "Our mother loved me more," I said.

He said nothing, and I went on. "I made sure that she did. When I was a tiny child and just learning to speak, Mama saw me walk in circles around and around my sister, who was sitting by the hearth, and I was snatching at the air by her head, her neck, her heart. 'What are you doing, Francisca?' said Mama, laughing. 'Taking Dolores's love away,' I answered.

"Mama stopped laughing. She pulled me from my sister's side and she shook me and told me not to be so wicked. But I did not change. I only grew more clever at getting what I wanted. And, despite my being wicked and unworthy, Mama did love me more." I rolled onto Alvaro, ground my hipbones into his groin, felt him harden. "She could not stop herself any better than you can," I said.

With my tongue in his mouth, how could Alvaro make any answer? But I ought to have listened to what he said about my sister. It should have made me more careful.

Alvaro told me that my father cried in the confessionary. He cried and said that he was afraid of dying. Afraid that my mama was not only not in heaven but nowhere.

"I try not to think on it," he said to Alvaro, "but it is like a great black wall before me, from the earth at my feet to the stars above, a black wall and nothing behind it. No heaven. No Concepción." And he wept.

"Don't tell me any more about my father," I said after I heard that. I did not like to hear about his crying while Alvaro listened.

I was hungrier and hungrier for tales about other people, though. I could not rest until I knew what everyone's sins were.

Most were sad to me—even Doña Petra's was sad after I stopped laughing and thought about it. They all had to do with longing and lonesomeness. My sins, as well.

Now, remembering our conversations, I wonder if Alvaro did not give me everyone else's soul instead of his own. if it was because he would not give himself to me that I wanted to know everyone else's stories. He always kept some part of himself hidden. He fed my desire for communion with other people's secrets. This did not make me love him any less. No, it inflamed me. I wanted him more and more. All the others whetted my appetite for him.

He used to call out while we fucked. A man of such composure with his books, when he was inside me he uttered syllables that made no earthly sense. He spoke a new language, and his speech was not human. Either that, or it was utterly human. He cried out with a grief-stricken sound, an awful, low moaning, a keening, lamenting howl.

"What are you thinking when you make such sounds?" I asked him once when we were spent and lying beside each other. A moment before, he had had me on my knees from behind, his hands on my shoulders. He drove into me until my lips bled for biting them—I didn't dare scream—and when we were done with each other, we crawled under the table to sleep. We curled together, sometimes we slept upon the very pages we had studied and then scattered to the floor in our haste. I would wake first and then look at him, he would seem as if dead, he looked that peaceful, his breaths so shallow, and his face so still. His eyes traveled under their lids, but his countenance was as smooth and untroubled as the village idiot's.

If I did not sleep, I would drift and dream. Words floated into my head, bits of what we had read together. I thought about the knowing of the body. Like the first story in the Scriptures, the man and woman who are father and mother to us all, they cannot keep themselves from this carnal knowing, it is irresistible to them. The Scripture calls it having one's *eyes opened*.

Knowledge, unbearable knowledge, of everything all at once: the knowing that makes you naked. And not knowing with the head, but with the heart.

"What are you thinking when you make such noises?" I asked him, again.

It was dark, and he took so long to answer that I thought he had not heard me. Finally he said, "I think the thoughts that I have been instructed never to think. I feel what the fathers of the Church have told me I am not to feel. I think of *possession*. I think, *She is mine*. I think, *Francisca, you are mine*." He rolled toward me, held me, drew in a breath so close that I felt the air rush cold past my cheek.

"I know that it is wrong," he said. "At least, I know that I have been taught that it is wrong to feel as I do. This is the danger of carnality, my confessor would tell me, but in the moment I cannot regret it. And I wonder who the devil is that he could make wrongdoing feel so much like . . . like a gift from God.

"I am afraid," he said then. "Afraid because I do not want a God who could refuse me this. Who could refuse me *you*. When I am with you is the only time I believe that I will live forever, the only time that I do not care if I expire this day, this night."

I touched him. I put my hand on his belly, always so hard, muscles tensed as if braced for a blow. "I want to hold you until we are dead, both of us," I said, my mouth on his throat.

As a child I always conceived of the world as if it were one of my mama's plates, the earth laid out flat. It never made much sense to me that it was round like an onion, some of us clinging like ants to the sides or the bottom. No, I thought of it the way the ignorant persecutors of Columbus did, and I saw myself as someone running along the rim of the plate. Heaped on the plate like some good meal was the safety of the world and all its comfort. Outside, over its edge, was endless chaos and plummeting down. Each of these—safety and surfeit and their opposite: falling—each held its attraction for me, and it was an equal attraction. Only on the edge, only with Alvaro, was I balanced between the two.

I was not innocent of how it was that a woman got with child, but having always been told that children were the reward of virtue, I had no worries about myself and that matter. After all, I was doing something that was certainly wrong. Had my mama lived longer I might have known better, but as it was, I was surprised when Alvaro said one day that we had to have a grave conversation. What we were doing was dangerous for many reasons, and one was that I could find myself with a problem like that which ruined the Barrancas, all of whom had died of shame, more or less. It was said that Bonita Barranca, as beautiful as her mama, had lain with her brother, and her papa turned her out. After she was gone, he died in his bed, and we heard that her brothers, who went away, died, too. It was plague, I guess. The old women of Quintanapalla said wolves had eaten Bonita.

"I don't care about that," I told Alvaro. "Let them eat me, too. I'd rather be dead than stop."

He was silent. After a moment, he said, "There is something we might try." I could tell he was of uneasy mind about it. Still, since anything seemed to me less dreadful than abstinence, I ended up consulting a witch.

There was a trick that certain healers knew, something that had spread north through Spain, a device of the Moors who used it on their camels so that the beasts should not calve and delay a desert journey. And then they turned it on their women. Well, as the work of Moors, it was held doubly wrong by the Church, but Alvaro and I, we had stepped outside the boundary of holy laws. Harlots used this trick, and it worked for some.

"How does a man of the Church know of such things?" I asked Alvaro.

"I am surprised you did not guess, Francisca," he said. "What teachers do I have besides books, and the confessionary?"

"Who told you, then? Who is as wicked as I intend to be?"

But he did not answer that question.

I had been Alvaro's pupil for some time. The Six Weeks of the Virgin had come and then passed, the mulberry was in spring leaf, and I wanted to be with him each day. Still, we met only once each week. On one of those Thursday afternoons, I did not go to Alvaro's study, but I went on the back of the wine seller's cart to Rubena, and I saw Visita, who did cures in that town.

The wine seller was a taciturn man, who had agreed to take me to Rubena in exchange for some eggs and he said nothing as

I handed him the basket. He said nothing as he drove, and said nothing as he dropped me in the small plaza of the town of Rubena. I asked directions to Visita's from an old woman in the marketplace, saying some lie, that I was coming to fetch a tonic for a cousin with the greensickness. She told me how to go and I walked the three miles to the witch's house.

Visita was a midwife and a healer, especially to women. When I called at her open door, she came to the threshold and looked at me. "Who are you?" she said, and I told her.

"The younger daughter of Concepción de Luarca? The same who nursed the king?"

"Yes."

She looked me up and down. "You are not with child," she said. "And you have yet to be wed."

I told her that what she said was true.

"Then you are here because you are not chaste and you do not want to get with child." She folded her arms.

"Yes," I said, finally.

"How will you pay me?" she asked.

"I have no money, but I am used to work. I will do as you bid me."

She let me stand at her door for some minutes, and then, seeing that she had not frightened me off with her sharp manner, she stood back and opened her arm, inviting me in. Her home was a storehouse filled with more remedies than a person could count. Visita told me she made a practice of visiting shrines and collecting holy things, picking up the grain and flowers and whatever else pilgrims had left, offerings that had soaked up some of the saints' power. She had holy water and the forelock from a cow that had been marked with a sun on one flank and a moon on the other. Charcoal from olive bark, fangs of a dog, licorice and wild rhubarb, fenugreek, ligosticum, marrow from the bones of a paschal lamb. Indigo, birthwort, goldenseal. Sacks of cherry pits dyed many colors, fragrant beads made of sandalwood and cedar, feathers and ribbons, materials with which to make amulets. The sacred takes many forms, supposedly, and it looked to me as if Visita had found them all. On her hearth she had four cats sleeping.

"I have no senna," she said. "I will help you, and you will collect this herb for me." She handed me an empty basket, a big one that would take me some time to fill.

I nodded. I stood among her cats by the fire as she went and pulled a chest out from under her bed. From it she took a little bag of stones of different colors, and she shook the bag and four fell into her hand.

"Which one do you like?" she asked, and I hesitated, for I had no understanding of what they were.

"Some young girls like to have trinkets for their hair or fingers, my daughter wears a ring on her toe, but you will have a special shining stone inside you, just like Saint Eulalia." Eulalia's liver had been like an oyster—when they cut her up, it was filled with pearls.

Visita held the stones out. "Pick your favorite of these, and I will help you to wear it," she said.

I was not sure, suddenly, that I wanted the magic Visita offered, but some power in the woman compelled me beyond my fear. Her two hands were different. The right hand, like any other working person's, was calloused and thick. Even after she washed it, black lines of dirt remained etched into the dry cracks in the tips of each finger. Her left hand, though, the one she called her healing hand, was as if it belonged to another woman. It was as white and soft and smooth and beautiful, as delicate as the hand of the Virgin. And it was unnaturally warm. When she shook the little stones from their bag into its palm, they seemed to acquire an extra luster and to wink there at me.

"Come," she said. "You are taking too long."

I reached into her palm and chose the stone that was the smallest and pale purple. She put the rest of them in the bag, locked it back into the chest and with a great heave slid the heavy box under her bed. The purple stone she put into a kettle over the fire and made her fire blaze high under it. She put in some herbs, too. I am not sure of all of them but I could smell trincilla, and I recognized hyssop and the white hellebore flowers. The steam rose higher, and it began to boil.

Visita led me into a small room with no windows, where I could hear the noise of geese through the wall. Mama used to tell us that witches turned themselves into geese and that they sucked the life out of children. They could stick their bills into a basket with a sleeping child and that would be it, she said. But she also told us that women must be good to their babies and care for them and that if their babies died from lack of care, it was wrong to excuse this as the work of witches who came in through the cracks.

"Lie down," said Visita, and I did. She took my underclothes from me and opened my legs and I was lying with my knees up as I did for Alvaro. Somewhere in Rubena a pig was screaming. The screams stopped abruptly. The next week that pig would be sausages.

Visita was an agile old woman, gentle and her hands were clean, but it hurt me when she put the little stone up so high. She had a wand that she used, something made of bone that held the stone and pushed it farther than where her fingers could go, past that circle of flesh that closes a woman's womb. When she did this, there was a terrible clenching in my belly, and it did not go away, even after an hour or more. I felt cold all over. "You will have to lie here for a while," she said, and she kept her hand on my forehead so I could not rise.

Visita's voice was soothing as she talked to me. She never put curses on people, she said. She could, but she would not. "Why should I go to hell to pay for other people's wickedness?" she asked.

I was sick with pain for hours, I had to lie on my side and keep my knees drawn up to stand it, but she talked and she talked, and it helped to pass those hours. She told me so many things, some to do with me and of the practical sort, that I must always be clean about my person and not let any other man besides my lover know me. "Someday you will have children, too, Francisca," said Visita, "but not yet, for you are just a girl and you have no mother to help you."

By dusk I still did not feel as if I could stand being in a cart drawn by a mule. I could not even sit up on a pallet, so I remained at Visita's for the night and went back to Quintanapalla the next day.

"I went to the priest to find out what had become of you,"

Dolores said when I returned home. "He told me that you had not come to help him yesterday."

"No," I said.

"Where were you?" my sister asked me. "You frightened Papa with your absence."

"I was taken sick," I told her. "I had some trouble with my stomach and I—"

Dolores turned her back to me, and I stopped speaking.

Well, let her think I have a secret, sinful life, I decided, and I was glad she had gone to Alvaro to ask after me and had learned that I had not come to see him. As long as no one connected my straying to Alvaro, I felt safe.

With the weather fine, some days I wandered far from my father's house. I had the senna to gather for Visita, and I took her twice what she had asked, and after that I found more and more excuses to be afield at all hours. I was seen everywhere, I made a point of this, so that the people of Quintanapalla would come to understand me as a wandering sort, and I was so taken up with my own passions that I did not see beyond them to how others might also find them interesting.

As for Visita's cure, it turned out that I was not so unfortunate as some girls, for I learned later that a bad fever could follow from the stones, and it even killed some. But then, neither was I as fortunate as others, for after several months the little stone came out one night, with some blood and water, and it hurt me very much. I had quit the bed I shared with Dolores and gone outside to relieve myself, so at least I was away from my sister and her prying eyes. I looked at the little stone in my hand—it was a summer night, the moon gave me enough light to see—and I decided to say nothing of its coming out to Alvaro. I did not want to go through the pain of another visit to Visita, so I hid the purple stone away in the chest of my mother's cures.

My monthly time was very strong and bloody after the stone came out, and it got worse for some months and then dried up. I thought I was ill, for I felt so weak and tired and I thought how bad it was that the stone had come out and I had hidden it from Alvaro and now was sick. But it was nothing unnatural: I was with child.

I say this easily today, but then it was something that I held inside as a secret even from myself. I mean that I *knew* it, but as it seemed to me something that would change my life irrevocably, I refused to consider it before I had to. I suppose I had a desire to remain myself a child. They say no female is a woman until she is a mother.

I continued to go each week to Alvaro. My pleasure had shriveled, yet I teased him to touch me, to remove my skirts, and in time it became obvious that I was carrying. Alvaro said nothing at first, but he stopped knowing me carnally, and if we lay together, he would only put his hand in my hand, or he would hold me as I slept with my back turned toward him. Finally, one afternoon when I came in, he was standing at his window and when I opened the door after knocking, he turned around and said, "Francisca, come here to me."

He put his hand on my side and he looked at me. "This is my child, is it not?" he said finally. And I looked back into his eyes.

"Yes," I answered.

He nodded.

We stood awkwardly together, and then we made as if to pray, both on our knees, but we rose again quickly. Having forsaken the Church and all her warnings, what purpose was there in returning to her now?

We spoke of leaving the town together. The next new moon, we said, when darkness would aid our escape. But when that night came, I did not do it. I stood for an hour at the door to my papa's house, listening to the sound of his breathing. I could not rid myself of the feeling of his rough palm stroking my head. I thought of Alvaro's telling me how he wept in the confessionary, and I knew that my father held himself at fault for my mother's death and that missing her, together with the blame he took to his heart, made his life sorrowful.

My father took solace in my company that he did not find with Dolores, and this was because I forgave him, as she did not. I did not say to Papa that I knew he had wanted the mulberry to make a better life for Mama and for us, but I did not have to. He knew that I loved him: *him,* the father whose dreams had ruined us. I knew that he could not be any man other than the one he was, no more than Dolores could have been another woman. Or than I could have been a reasonable girl who put up with the attentions of a steady farmer or cobbler or smith. Allowed my betrothal to a dull decent man and had his babies and scrubbed his pots. Papa had to have his silk, and I had to have my priest, and we forsook all else. Still, even as my father's daughter, I did not want to run away in a manner that would cause him the shame of my disappearing with a priest. That would have killed Papa, I thought.

But he would soon know of my state—I could not hide it much longer—and then what? So Alvaro and I planned to leave Quintanapalla separately. We would meet in Soria, we said, on the Feast of the First Martyrs. But then we did not do that, either.

After a while, when I felt better, we resumed our carnal life, we took it up again. Not just I, but the two of us together had begun to dream even while waking. We ignored our approaching fate. We did nothing to avoid it.

ILKWORMS FIND THEIR WAY EVERYWHERE. IN the dark of my cell I catch myself brushing at my arm or my neck, trying to shake off a phantom worm. They crawl among my skirts. The sound of their jaws gives way to the silence of their spinning.

I would take one in my hand when I was small. I would stroke its cool, bluish skin, and it would stop mid-chew, jaws open, leaf held in its front feet. The worms' great eyes are useless to them, they swing their heads as do the blind, their front quarters falling into the ceaseless, serpentine motion they use for spinning.

Having had their food brought to them for more generations than anyone can count, silkworms lie helpless and greedy in their trays. They go nowhere unless their hooked feet catch in the clothing or hair of those who feed them. We found worms in our beds and in our shoes, in our bowls and our pockets.

I used to carry them back to the silk house; I did when I felt tenderly disposed to them, transporting their smooth, cool-fleshed bodies on my flat, open palm, which, if not sufficiently warm, made a worm lie as still as if it had died.

In another mood, I might squash it. Lay it on the ground outside and stand with it under the toe of my shoe, considering for a moment. Then tread on it slowly, so that the chewed green leaves of our trees would burst from its split side. If it was old enough, from just below its stilled jaws, its full silk glands would squeeze out. I would squat down and poke a bit of straw into one of the glands, shining like a tiny silver egg. A silvery mucus would ooze out: unspun liquid silk.

The spring before my grandfather died, Mama fell ill with a fever the same night that Papa came home with new eggs. My father worried that her hot skin would kill the worms before they hatched, but instead the fever hurried the eggs to hatch sooner than we expected, and they burst all over my mama and papa in their bed one night. They awoke to find their linens alive with tiny worms, no bigger than ants.

Mama stood carefully on the pallet. She shook with chills as Papa picked the worms from her long hair and her white night-dress. I remember watching from the bed I shared with Dolores as Mama stood silently, her face pale. I could not see the worms from that distance, and so I did not know what my father was doing to her. On his knees and peering so closely at the folds of her nightdress, the end of her long braid in his hand, he seemed, to my childish eyes, to be performing some curious obeisance to my mother.

After he was done, Papa gathered up the sheet with all the worms inside, and he ran up the hill in the dark to the silk house. Until the mulberry was in leaf we had to feed them osage, and that year we feared that the cocoons would not be the best grade, that they would spin waste silk, which broke when the comb girls unwound the cocoons. But, as it happened, the worms performed well, and the cocoons fetched a good price at market.

Long after the failure of the trees, my papa would talk about the better years that had preceded it. "Do you remember, girls," he might say, "when the worms hatched early and how your mother stood in her nightdress as I collected them?" And he would stare into the fire.

Increasingly, my father became a man interested in salvage, in anything that had been saved. The more dramatic or miraculous the rescue, the better. The year following my mother's death, he entered into the curiosities trade. Not for any profit such enter-prise might bring—though we were poor enough that we had no money for sugar or for candles. Papa traded in curiosities for the comfort they brought him.

The things for which he walked miles each month to Epila were these. A pair of breeches, whole and undamaged, found in the belly of a giant sea tortoise. A hat fashioned of thick wool felt with a handsome buckle that bore the marks of lightning. Its wearer had not been harmed by the storm, "Because of the buckle!" said Papa. "The buckle saved him!" A set of false teeth carved from ivory that survived a fire. Their wearer did not, but the teeth were unscorched, and bequeathed to Papa by his old friend Señor Encimada of the colored-silk experiments—who set his house on fire one night building a device to conserve lamp oil—they provided Papa's entry into the curiosities trade. Papa exchanged the teeth for the hat, which he kept for a month and then traded for a dog that retrieved objects cast into deep water. But the animal had an appetite that matched its exertions, and my father traded it for a wooden bosom, a fragment from a figurehead, the carved lady who had graced the bowsprit of a sunken ship: that much of her had washed ashore. I liked her—I would, being my mama's child—but he traded her away, too. He went through quizzing glasses that never broke though they were run over by carriages, a featherless bird that ate nothing and drank nothing and yet lived, and other odd things. Finally, Papa had the breeches from the tortoise's belly, and those he liked too well to consider parting with them.

I would catch him examining the fabric, turning the breeches inside out to look closely at the seams, the gussets and codpiece. They were silk, of course, they were a gentleman's pair dyed yellow like goldenrod, and Papa would touch the buttons and the knee laces. "See here how they are unhurt," he would muse aloud to himself and to any incidental audience. The breeches were cut for a man of smaller stature than my father, or he might have tried to wear them. As it was, I saw him put them on his person once or twice. He drew them up as far as he could, and he turned his leg this way and that to admire how it emerged from the miraculously surviving fabric. As his father would have observed, the happiness of some is always at the expense of others.

Any person, any thing that had escaped ruin: my father took pleasure in these. On the last night of his life he asked for that pair of breeches, and when I brought them to him, he touched them with his eyes closed, and he smiled.

AST OF THE ROYAL RESIDENCE, TICKET SELL-
ers at the bullring close one and then another
booth. No one has arrived for this afternoon's contest between the celebrated
Avianco, a beast that has this season gored
five toreros and trampled three times that number of picadors
and banderilleros, and Juan de Juni, his latest challenger. In his
stall, Avianco bellows, but no one comes. Señor de Juni and his
entire entourage have joined the masses of citizenry walking
west toward the palace. I can hear them overhead. Their footfalls shake mortar from between the stones.

Outside the palace the rioting has not abated. The original
theater crowd has swelled and gains new fervor with each report
and rumor. "Give María to us!" people scream. "Why does the
slattern hide! Of what is she afraid? Of justice?"

The throng at the gates has grown large enough to interrupt
traffic. The Calle Mayor is impassable, and carriages and carts
are halted as far north as the Gran Vía. With nowhere to go,
horses skitter in their traces and kick at one another. Shrill
whinnies pierce the air.

Though it is not yet dusk, and the hour when on most days
the last frenzied business would have the plaza bustling, the
marketplace is empty. Merchants did not open their shops at all
today, vendors never arrived. Even the rats are nowhere in evidence, and the hawks have forsaken the butchers' stands for the
palace roof.

Below them, the little maid Obdulia enters María's bedchamber with a basin. She sets it on the edge of the vanity table,
pushing aside hairbrush and earrings, a breviary with its spine
unbroken, tortoiseshell combs, combs of silver set with tourma-
line and garnet, combs of gold set with emerald and alexandrite.
Ivory combs. A pair of teak combs inlaid with jet flowers. So

many hair ornaments all heaped together, one and then another falling to the floor. There is no room for the requirements of illness among all the clutter of cloisonné boxes, families of tiny dogs made of silver, baubles and trinkets, bottles of scent, and a wooden toy, an acrobat no taller than her hand, a little man walking a tightrope stretched between two sticks. When the sticks are squeezed, he does a jaunty flip and returns to his pose on the ropes.

The toy belonged to Carlos many years before. It was something that his wet nurse gave him—yes, something that my papa carved. Obdulia makes room for the basin, and the little man falls to the floor. She picks him up. She squeezes the sticks to make him execute one and then another flip before setting him down and turning to Jeanette.

María's maids are trained in matters of ribbons and buckles and curtsies. They know little of medicine or apothecary arts. Why should they, when their flesh is young and healthy? Their sudden immersion in illness—in bandages, basins and purges, in fomentations and diaphoretics, in sweet oils, barley waters and astringents—leaves them shaken, by turns hysterical and subdued. But they do their best. As instructed by Severo, once each hour they try to settle their mistress as comfortably as they can over a large shallow basin, so that she may urinate in it.

This time when they come, María is dreaming that she has been locked, by her mother-in-law, in the works of a great clock. She is standing on one tooth of a cog, which turns slowly, carrying her toward the door to a huge birdcage. She holds a golden key, a key she must fit to the lock on the cage door. The timing is exquisite, she knows she must be ready to get the key in the lock quickly and climb inside the cage. Otherwise, she will fall from her place on the tooth of the cog, she will be ground between gears.

When Obdulia wakes her, María sobs once with fear as she senses herself falling through clockworks. She looks at her maid without recognition. The process of getting the queen over the basin is awkward, and Her Highness slips from Obdulia's grasp so that one buttock fills the china cavity, the other remains on the sheet. Still, it is the best the two maids can manage. Their mistress moans so terribly at every touch that they dare not try to adjust her or center her body over the basin.

It has been more than a day since the queen has passed any urine. María tries, but she cannot, and the effort brings a terrible burning between her legs, as if God had set her secret parts on fire in some unwonted punishment for lust. *"Please,"* she begs the maid, "just leave me be." But in this, her requests are overridden by her physician's. María closes her eyes. Why do they wake her? Why don't they leave her in peace? Even bad dreams are better than waking. She can be awake only so long before the vomiting starts again, as if consciousness itself brings on nausea. Perhaps when they go, she can fall back to sleep. Perhaps her old trick of the orange trees will work.

Each night when the queen went to sleep, when at last she closed her eyes, she would think about the orange trees. One thousand orange trees in silver tubs.

Picture them. They are beautiful.

The tubs are solid silver, polished bright. They bear a design of the sun, of Helios in his chariot, horses plunging around the sides. But unless directed, you would not even notice the tubs, the artist's work would be wasted, because the trees themselves claim all of your attention. In the winter, when streams are frozen, when beneath the surface of rivers there is only the distant and ghostly passage of water, when all the world is frozen into silence, the halls of Versailles are clamorous, are resounding ringing pealing with the sight and scent of orange trees in bloom. Impossible, but the trees bloom because their king desires that they bloom.

The light comes in the countless windows, and the warmth of the weak winter sun is magnified by its passage through the panes. When it touches the white blossoms, it encourages them to release their fragrance into the long galleries down which the princess Marie runs, dodging fat old comtesses in their sedan chairs, their weight cracking the kneecaps of their footmen like so many walnuts.

One thousand orange trees in silver tubs. Each tree as tall as the princess, or taller. The leaves shining, the blossoms white as snow, and the smell so sweet that when Marie Louise put her face to the orange flowers, it was impossible not to weep.

The queen brought three orange trees with her when she came to Spain. Their roots were bound up in wet moss and wrapped in sacks. But when the bridal party was transferred from the ferry to litters there was no one to carry them: they were too tall and too heavy. And so the trees were left to die in the Pyrenees. María thinks of them, gray and leafless. By now, even their dead, dry boughs would be gone, the wind would have blown them over.

Some nights, when Carlos came to Her Highness's apartments, while the queen mother was in the gaming room playing solitaire, the king and queen would read aloud together that tedious first chapter of the book of Saint Matthew. After a year or two of marriage, María could recite it, she did not need to see it before her: *Solomon begat Roboam and Roboam begat Abia and Abia begat Asa and Asa* . . . Forty-two generations from Abraham to Christ. Generations uninterrupted by flood or exile or any other disaster. The holy litany was meant to incite Carlos's manhood, to provoke him to get with begetting himself and continue the endless chain of holiness. To the queen's mind, there were few things less arousing than recitations of Scripture, but it was Carlos's confessor's advice that they recite this little bedtime prayer, or wish. In the dark, after the liturgy, the ineffectual fumbling began. When it was over, the king left the queen in her rumpled bed, and Obdulia came in to dress María for sleep.

As the maid began to brush her hair, María closed her eyes, her head nodding with fatigue and with the gentle tugging of the brush. *One thousand orange trees in silver tubs,* she said to herself. And they appeared before her, and she began to count them. She pictured herself walking down one of the galleries in the château; she willed herself to feel her fingertips brush each branch as she passed. Sometimes María would fall asleep before Obdulia finished brushing her hair, already dreaming as her maid dropped her nightdress over her head.

The queen's happy dreams are always set in Paris, always of

some endless fete, a party in full progress that began days before and will go on for days longer. She dreams of a courtyard full of footmen and carriages, a parterre swarming with pages. Everywhere she looks, someone is bearing trays piled so high with food that they spill over in doorways, and grapes roll along the floor so that guests tread on them. The princesses all stay in bed past noon, drinking dishes of chocolate and eating thickly buttered bread served with violets on top. The small, bright heads of the flowers yield under their sharp white teeth.

The dances begin after midnight, and the princess spins and swirls in rooms whose walls are of mirrors. Surrounded by mirrors, the silk and the lace, the velvet brocade, and the plumes and the jewels, all the layers of finery go on forever, each dancer multiplied a hundred times, each princess become a hundred princesses. Endless sweeping skirts and silk dancing slippers. Not only are French ballrooms built of mirrors, they are built with such marvelous cleverness that the sound of one violin is refracted and refracted until the notes of the single instrument sound like a whole orchestra. But there is not merely one violin, no: there are one hundred. And twelve harps, harpsichords, dulce melos and piccolos.

And chandeliers filled with candles, also reflected over and over until it seems to the hot dancers that the room itself is blazing with stars. Yes! The whole château is on fire, as if comets shoot through the ballroom, making it burn with every incandescence: with velvet and gold, with light and with sound, with improvident whispers and lips made feverish by wine. All this heat growing ever more hot, it set the orange trees on fire. An enchanted fire, which does not consume them, no, but forces them to exude perfume so sweet that it makes everyone drunk— all the princes of the blood and all the princesses, too, they inhale the impossible sweet smell of orange trees that bloom in the dead of winter.

And so each night, every night, even this last night that María is to spend in the somber, guilty kingdom of Spain, where people never dance but only go to everlasting Masses and confessions and penances, where supposed lovers read the most boring passages from the most boring book, each night she counts the orange trees.

Perhaps the princess is vain, or selfish. But as soon as she came here, to Spain and to Carlos, she knew that she had lost what she wanted, that the life that she had as a girl was the one she desired always, that she had no need of a prince, but only her dreams of a prince. She wanted each day to be filled with the pleasures of a girl, the sweetness of expectation—not fulfillment, because fulfillment brought disappointment, like taking home the bright little bird from the shop in Paris and having it die as it beat its bright wings against a mirror and the illusion of escape.

The body of the queen of Spain shudders. She is breathing slowly, shallowly, and her eyelids shine with unguent. A dozen dozen candles burn, and after the maids leave with their empty basin, Carlos orders that the relics be brought in.

Gold-lidded ossuaries filled with saints' knuckles. A splinter of the true Cross kept safe in twelve nesting ivory boxes. The blood of Saint Pantaleon, which remains a dry crust inside a vial until each Good Friday, when it miraculously runs red and livid against the glass. The hair of Saint Clare. The hair of Saint Agnes. The hair of Bernadine, Dymphna, Flora and Gertrude. María turns her head to watch as the trunk is unlocked and opened to reveal shining hair of all colors. Hair curling, straight, combed, tangled. Hair plaited, hair held in a ribbon, hair bound with twine, hair however it was—dressed, undressed—when the saint lost her life.

Who is it that shears off the hair of dead saints? the queen wonders. Who comes with scissor, razor, sword? Who pulls it out? Her own hair is more beautiful than any of the holy hair before her, but no one will keep it, for she is no one's savior. The sacrifice of her life will have meaning for few. In France, her mother will weep.

Persons were poisoned routinely in the Sun King's court. A godmother, an aunt, two livery boys. María's own first cousin, Berthe. She remembers how angry Maman was when Berthe was dying. Her mother came into the drawing room at Versailles. They had been waiting there, she and her brother Henry, for hours. No one had remembered the children, everyone was at Berthe's side, where children were not allowed. Henry was lying on the carpet before the fire. He writhed and screamed. He tore his hair and made gagging gestures, clutching his throat.

What are you doing! their mother had said, and she grabbed him and shook him so hard that when she let go, Henry could not stand but dropped to his knees.

I was playing at being poisoned. Henry was only five, he did not understand that Berthe was dying.

The poisoners of Versailles were without rival for imagination and bold enterprise. They murdered the beautiful princess from Albania. She broke out in sores like chancres all over her face, and at first the court was shocked that a princess of the blood could contract something so vile as the Italian disease. The poor girl died raving in a convent, uselessly protesting her innocence, feeling disgrace more keenly than death. Too late to comfort her, it was discovered that the lining of her ball gloves had been dusted with arsenic. Kid gloves the color of pistachio ice, they were turned inside out and passed on a silver tray, so that all could see where the pink silk linings bore the deadly sparkle of poison. At the funeral, the gloves were set beneath the princess's catafalque.

After that, slippers or gloves or hats were never left lying about. Ladies-in-waiting were instructed to lock everything up. María remembers watching as maids attended her mother, each with the keys to Henrietta's wardrobe kept safe in a little reticule worn under her own clothing. When they undressed Maman, María sat in the chair by the window, a little girl of ten, not more. She watched as layers and layers came off. Where, under there, was her mother?

Four maids to lift the dress, like the shell of a sea creature, up over Henrietta's head. Underneath foamed undergarments, white like her snowy wig. The wig came off last, revealing hair that was curled like little snails against her mother's scalp, still pink where the comb had drawn and parted. Yes, finally, under all those layers, all the false mothers of silk and of wool and horsehair, the scaffolding of hoops, farthingales, corsets, ruffs, bustles and busk, there she was: Maman, quite small and pale and soft. The substance of the woman was much less than that of her garments, she was like an oyster stripped of its shell, soft and gray and swimmy, almost transparent. She was never just naked, Marie's mother, but changing from one incarnation (hostess, dance partner, singer of romantic ballads) to another (overseer, nurse, chatelaine). Under her farthingale, hung from the metal hoops encircling her hips, were little glass vials, like some eccentric decoration, and in the bottom of each was a drop of honey or treacle, something sweet to tempt fleas away from her flesh. They jumped down into the little vials and drowned in the treacle. That was what had made Maman smell so sweet.

HAT ARE YOU THINKING?" I ASKED.

"Nothing," Alvaro said. We were lying together.

"But you must be thinking something."

"No, nothing."

"No one thinks nothing."

"I do."

"So you are empty, then? Just a vessel to be filled with other people's stories? With mine and everyone else's? Little sins, big sins? Love, lust, fear, woe. Anger. Proud follies, greedy, wicked—"

"Why do you torment me so!" he said, and he pushed me off.

I sat up, naked. "I want you!" I said. "Why do you not ask me what I am thinking! My thoughts are unremarkable, it's true. I think of what I ate for supper, or that I need to mend my shift. Things that have nothing to do with God or with heaven or hell or anything else. But I think them nonetheless. They are *my* thoughts, *me*. Do you not want them?

"I think about dragonflies, about the worms in the floorboards, about grease in a pan. Clouds, sheep, door hinges, feather beds. I think of this child I am carrying. I think, Will it be a son or daughter? What will it look like? Should I go to market to buy it a charm? I think I ought to sew more clothes for it, and then I think how it is that I hate to sew and to mend, but sewing for a baby makes it a little better. Then I think perhaps I am going to be less selfish when I have a child, perhaps I will go to market and think only of what I want for my child, and nothing of what I would like for myself.

"I think of all the things at market, of the animals I like to see there. Of that great ox the oil merchant has and how his coat is a red color, redder than any other beast's I have ever seen and how pretty the animal looks in the sunshine. I think of a cut on my leg and of how many rows of onions Dolores and I planted last season—fourteen, it was—and perhaps we should plant twenty next year, for this year we hadn't enough.

"I think of next year. Where shall I be? I think of this year, this month, this day. What is to become of us? I wonder.

"And I want to know the dull things you think, too. I don't want to know only what it is you think of the books we read or whether or not you believe Ovid was a greater poet than Homer. I don't care about that! Why do you keep me apart from you!"

He pulled his hand out of mine. "I am tired of words," he said. "I am tired of words on the page and I am tired of talking. I want you to lie here next to me and be still."

What is desire? What did I want to see in Alvaro? What did I think might be revealed?

I wanted us to *know* each other. I wanted every wish made plain, every memory given voice. I wanted one vein to empty into another, mine into his, his into mine. I wanted the gristle of our joints, his and mine, mine and his, pounded flat so that I could read what was said there.

What else was there for us? For anyone?

Two months before my confinement, Alvaro was arrested, and it was outside my papa's door that the Inquisitors left his shoes. His shoes at the door, and his empty cassock hanging from one of our mulberry trees, hanging from a rope so that it blew a little in the wind, twisting like the blackened body of those criminals they string up in the plaza and leave for hawks and dogs.

The rumor was that I had been taken by some shepherd or laborer. I thought that was the rumor. That poor, peculiar Francisca who wandered about as she pleased, who so grieved for her mama that she took none of the precautions that a young woman ought to take, that Francisca had been raped on one of her strange and solitary pilgrimages. I assumed Dolores had done her part to conceal the truth. Not purposefully, not to protect my sins, no, of course not; but there was not one old garrulous widow to whom she had not gone with tales of how impossible I was, how stubborn, how wayward, how willful and wild. If I was with child, it was no fault of hers, she made that clear.

My sister must have spied on Alvaro and me, and, once she knew what we were up to, gone to the wheelwright. Everyone knew the wheelwright was an informer for the Holy Office. Dolores got some money, then, she must have, enough for a dowry someday. Her treachery would serve her in another way as well, for in the eyes of the Inquisition she had now officially separated herself from me. Later, when suspicion of witchcraft fell on my mother, the Holy Office would judge that Concepción de Luarca had passed her sins along only to the younger of her two daughters.

So Dolores told the wheelwright, and the wheelwright told a Red Hood, and the Red Hood sent a White Hood, and on that last Thursday, when I stayed too late and then returned to Alvaro after nightfall—when we quarreled and then used our bodies to forget our quarrel—someone watched at the window that night. It must have been that night, for it could not have been longer than a day between witness and arrest: no one would allow someone as dangerous as an irreligious priest to go unpunished longer than one setting of the sun. Why, the Devil might come and take the whole town if someone like Alvaro was not punished quickly.

The night they came for him, I had already retired with my sister, my big belly making our bed that much more cramped. We still slept as we did when we were children, back to back, and I do not know that I heard Alvaro's approach. But I *knew* it. My mind's eye saw him coming to me, taking the same path through the wood that I had so often traveled to reach his side. The same branches tripping him, tangling in his cassock even as the night before they had snared my own skirts. Out of the wood, then, and stumbling over the furrows in the field that separated him from my papa's house, the hops field, the last obstacle. The horse would have gained on him there, jumping the ditches where he had to scramble in and out. Perhaps, plunging through dead hops, the horse grew a little intoxicated.

My inner eye saw Alvaro's approach, and I sat up in bed; and

Dolores sat up, too, and looked at me. She did not ask me, "Francisca, what is it?" for she knew. Of course she did. In her eyes I read my sister's betrayal. Otherwise, wouldn't Dolores have asked what troubled me? Was I ill? Was the baby coming? But she already knew what would come to pass that night.

Dolores and I sat together, both of us watching the door. Papa was asleep; he woke only as Alvaro entered. He sat up and looked as the village priest burst into our house and stood before the hearth with his eyes wild, his hair with leaves and sticks in it. Alvaro's face, always red, was white that night. It made no difference now what he did, his fate was certain, and he came to our bed and he pushed my sister from it. She fell to the floor with a bump, dragging the bedclothes with her, and as he pulled me to my feet by my wrists, she gave such a shriek, as if she had seen the Devil, which I imagine she thought she had.

"Listen!" he said. "I have only a moment before they come. Say nothing to them. I will say I led you astray, I will say I raped you. Do you understand?" He shook me in his adamantness.

I reached out to embrace him, but he shook his head, eluded my hands. There was a crash then, and a horse—lathered and with rags falling from its hooves—came in the door with a White Hood on its back. The beast threw his great black head up, tossing it with his teeth apart; yet no sound came from his throat. So I knew it was true, what they say, the horse's vocal cords had been slit, lest he give them away. It was terrible to see the great tongue dripping foam, and the beast plunging side-ways so that he split the doorframe, and not a sound coming from his throat.

Every person in the room stood still in horror. No one breathed. But then, I could not help myself, I went to Alvaro, I buried my face in his neck. He stiffened. This was not part of his plan—I was implicating myself. Quickly, to cover for my mistake, he made as if he were the one who had grabbed me. I felt his hands all over me. I felt him touch me from without and felt his child kick me from within, and the night roared around us as though a terrible storm shook my papa's house, smashed the window and tore the door from its hinge.

"Francisca, Francisca, Francisca." He said my name over and over. *Possessio mea.* His one possession. I felt his lips, cold, on my forehead, and then they tore him off me.

The White Hood and his deputy took him away in the black cart they had waiting, and they remanded me to the care of my father. For a few days there was confusion. The whole town of Quintanapalla had itself purged and bled, so that the evil left by so wicked a priest as Alvaro would be banished. They took senna and mustard and lobelia, they swallowed any noxious herb to make them vomit years of sacraments touched by his unclean hands. A special *sangrado* came to the town, and he filled basin after basin, pouring them out so the gutters outside the barber's ran with blood. Dolores fumigated our house with burnt yarrow, she waved crosses in the air and burned up whatever she could. She made a bonfire of our bed and washed me down with tea made of skullcap. I sat naked in a tub and watched dully as the brown water ran over my swollen belly. Every time I looked her way she made the sign of the cross between us. But mostly I kept my eyes downcast. Whenever I could, whenever she would let me, I slept. My hatred for her wore me out in those weeks. Later, I did not blame her so much. I saw how Alvaro and I had been so blindly foolhardy and indiscreet that we might as well have turned ourselves in to the Holy Office. If Dolores had not spoken to the wheelwright, someone else would have done so.

Alvaro's fate was certain: he would be tortured; whatever confession he made would be recorded. For the sake of his soul, he would be pressed to implicate whatever other sinners he could. But he would not betray me, he would do what he could to save me and our child. After they had as much as they needed, or as much as they could get, the Holy Office would excommunicate him, and the Church would then abandon Alvaro to secular justice. The Church sheds no blood, not even that of denounced heretics and seducers. Spain, however, would take her due. Would burn him, or—as it happened that he died in prison—content herself with burning his bones.

My fate remained unclear for a while. As I was carrying a child, I could not be hanged or even tortured, not yet. And the baby, whom I had expected in a matter of weeks, stayed put in my belly as if he had no intention of abandoning his mama. Perhaps I misjudged the time of my confinement, but my son did not come into the world until a decision as to my fate was reached. The rhetoric was a bit mystifying, the pages of the decision ran to thirty or more—"As thick as this," Papa said, and he held his fingers to show a fair width—but the gist of it was that I was considered to have been abused and led astray by one whom I had reason to trust, a man representing the Church, so the Church could hardly punish me as it might any other harlot. As it had not yet begun its postmortem pursuit of my mother, inherited suspicions had not yet fallen on me.

Still, I was punished by the townsfolk, regarded with suspicion and contempt for the rest of my free days. I could not go to Mass, they barred the church door, and just as well, for it made me ill to be in a church now. The incense was overcome by the smell of so many bodies in one place together.

The day following the decision to leave me free under the care of my father, I went out walking with no guard over me. I was almost at the time of my confinement, I was so great with child that I felt breathless and unwell, I was sick and shocked over Alvaro's arrest, and yet, still I felt some—what? *Joy.* Yes, I was so happy to think that I would be allowed to keep Mateo; I had already decided the child was a boy and would be named so. I had gone to the river and was now walking the long way home, up the hill and through the grove. I began, even great-bellied as I was, to run among the trees and around their trunks. I made loops and loops and eights and naughts, and I felt the baby moving inside me. I was like a child myself with sudden happiness, the child I had not been for so long, not since the death of my mother. My sides ached with the running, but I did not stop. I thought no sensible thoughts, such as that I might bring on the baby with my antics, I just danced and danced. I began to turn around like one of Papa's tops. Around, around. Alone in the mulberry grove, those trees of failed dreams, and so big with life, with *hope,* inside me, and my skirts flying out from my body. I felt as if at last I was dancing in my mama's arms, dancing and dancing the hopeful, hopeless dance of women.

During my lying-in I missed my mama as I never had before. With the first pain came a gush of memory, and soon I was drowning in a sea of the past, wet and tearful, a thousand things that I would not have been able to recall at any other time. Her hands warm on my face when I came down the hill from the silk house. That little pot of clove ointment that she kept on the shelf by the door, and her habit of dipping two fingers into it and rubbing the yellow salve on her dry elbows. How she would touch a little of the grease to her eyebrows and lips to make them shine.

My mother made a soap using the fat of deer kidneys. It took nine days, like a novena to beauty, and if we could buy any musk or civet at the market she would add a little. She had a mold that she got from her own mama, and into it she poured the liquid soap when it was hot. After it cooled, ten soaps came out with a little picture of a deer jumping on each, very pretty, but I saw her make them only once. Of course, she knew how to do such things because she came from a family of soap makers, but she had little time to think on her own looks and comfort. Nine whole days to make a basket of the little cakes of soap. She sold them at market, or Papa did, except for one, which we kept, and with the money she got she bought Dolores a new pair of shoes. That was the year Dolores grew tall, and her shoes were too small. She did not complain—she liked to be a martyr about everything—but her toenails turned black, and the big ones came off from wearing shoes that were too short.

No one was with me when my confinement began. Dolores came home from the mill at dusk, I had been inside all day, not feeling well and worried that something might happen if I were to go too far from home. Then the pains came, and they began hard and fast. Dolores looked at me as she came in, and she dropped the flour she had been carrying on her shoulder just inside the door, and the white dust came through the sack and fell around her shoes.

The midwife in Quintanapalla had made it clear that she would not come, but in the next village was Azima, who was so old that she had not brought a baby since before even my papa's birth. Azima had agreed to come for the price of my birth cord, and she required transportation, she could go nowhere by herself. But we had no cart of our own anymore, so Dolores could not fetch Azima but had to go to the oil merchant who traveled between the towns with his casks. The oil merchant, Raynard, was a widower, and for the price of a ride in his cart, Dolores had baked him bread for a month. It would have made better sense for my sister to stay with me and send Papa for Azima, for Dolores had attended a birth or two, but I guess she did not want to be alone with me. Or with the child of such a malefactor as Alvaro about to make its appearance. Our dealings with each other were polite and distant; we were to each other as we would be to a stranger.

Dolores took a piece of bread and a swallow of water and she went to get the midwife. While I waited, my papa sat on one side of a sheet Dolores had hung for decency and I sat on the other. I tried to make no noise, but every once in a while I cried out.

"Francisca?" Papa would say, and I would answer that I was fine, that everything was all right with me and surely Dolores would be back in a short time. But she had a fair journey before her, and I was frightened. Perhaps the old midwife had reconsidered. Perhaps not even she would risk bringing forth the Devil's child.

I do not know how long it took for Azima to come, but it seemed that it was dark for a great while. The fire burned low and then Papa threw a log on and it was high and bright and then low again, I don't know how many times. At one point he went outside to get more wood. He dropped it onto the stone hearth. I heard one log fall and I could see his silhouette against the sheet Dolores had hung, his strong arms full of wood and then the black shapes of the logs dropping down into the wood bin.

It seemed the house was growing very hot—it was April and not a particularly cold spring—but perhaps that was all Papa felt he could do for me, keep burning more and more wood. I could see his outline as he sat at the hearth and poked the fire, sometimes raising his iron rod and striking the burning wood, one, two, three times until such a flock of sparks flew up, I could see them even through the sheet, and great hot sighs of heat were echoed by Papa's sighing. Now I cannot think of the birth of my son apart from that fire, and it seems apt, since the child was the gift of heat, of improvidence.

I was up as much as I could be, I walked back and forth between the close walls, stumbling a little, but finally I just got down on my knees as if in prayer. Perhaps I *was* praying. Even the faithless pray when they are sufficiently afraid. I remained kneeling on the floor with my head on the bed Dolores and I shared.

I began to believe that Dolores meant to kill me by delaying with the midwife, and in my mind I flew after my sister, down the rutted road to Rubena. I kept seeing the cobbles around the well in the marketplace, and I would get just so far as the portal to the east, so that I could see the black road to Rubena, the moon making wraiths of the trees, when there would be another pain that pulled me back into my body.

Papa made a black shadow on the sheet and all around him was the orange of the fire on the cloth. He was seated with his hands before him, his right hand moving in a continuous even arc, back and forth like the weighted stick in the clock in the cathedral. He was carving a toy. When he was done he would put it—a little man or a horse or a top—in the basket where already he had made others for his grandchild. The house was hotter than the blacksmith's, and I had undone my bodice and taken my arms from my sleeves so that I was unclothed on the upper part of myself and my skirts were bunched wet around my legs, wet with the water that came with each pain. I was thirsty, but though I could see the water bucket, being undressed I didn't ask Papa to bring me a drink. I felt I had done enough to him.

Most fathers would have turned out any daughter such as I had proved to be. But Papa—well, perhaps the death of the silkworms had humbled him, for never once did he act as though he were ashamed of my state. In truth, he seemed happy, and he had spent many hours in the last month making toys. He had no sons, of course, none that lived, and he was sure that his grandchild would be a male, and thus a Luarca, since there was no one else to give him a name. The name Alvaro Gajardo had been removed from all lips, and those who agreed to see me treated my expectant state as a mystery, as if, like the Virgin, I had gotten magically with child.

Dolores came back around midnight. She opened the door and the cold air came in, and I sobbed with relief. "Where is she?" I asked.

"Not here yet. I did not go myself. Raynard said his ass would be faster with but one person in the cart. I have been this long walking back from where he left me by the pillar at the gate." Dolores looked at the sheet. She hung a blanket over the rope so that I could not see through to the fire anymore, so that Papa could not see through to me. She lit a candle on our side and helped me out of the wet skirt and onto our bed. I knew I should keep walking and moving about, but already I was so tired that I wanted only to lie on my side and rest between the pains. Though Dolores had wasted little affection on me in the past weeks, she tried to stroke my head now and she offered her hand to hold but I brushed her away.

Before Mama's friend Pascuela died they had fetched a birthing chair for her, but she could not sit up. Her sisters tried to sit her in it, and then she screamed so, no one could lift her off. "I won't," she had cried, "I can't. Please, no, do not make me." That was the last I had seen of a baby coming, and I knew when we fell into silence that we were thinking back on that birth long ago and how frightened we had been.

My sister talked to pass the time. She sat beside me spreading black bread with salt and garlic, breaking open the cloves so that the smell of it, together with the pain, made me ill. She said her prayers and then she said more for me, endless Paternosters and Credos and Aves. After each pain, I slipped away and rose over the roofs of our town. I saw the smoke rise from the houses, I felt that I cared for nothing, only that this ordeal pass.

When Azima at last came and slipped her hand inside me, her skin was cold from the night outside and the feel of that chill reaching in called me back. Eyes closed, I was going through all the contents of my mother's chest of cures: the different herbs and powders and charms. I didn't care that I would die, I was thinking that it seemed better to die than to go through any more of this. And just as I screamed out—blaspheming, as Dolores pointed out the next morning—crying that if there was any God of mercy he would surely take me, then it was over, my son was born.

Mateo.

His face was blue, the mark of the cord still around his neck as though he had been delivered from a hangman's noose, and the rest of him just a miserable lump of red flesh, eyes swollen shut and mouth open wide and crying. When the afterbirth was delivered, Azima tied a piece of twine around the cord, and then she cut it. My son was so ugly that I thought of the silkworms of years before, and I laughed and cried at once as I held him. Of course he was a worm! He had to be—he was mine.

The midwife swaddled him tightly and laid him in my arms. I heard her say to Dolores that she would accept her payment now. She was well pleased with the birth cord, for it was of extraordinary length and would be useful in treating dropsy and heart pains and lameness. She was careful to say that it was a cure for this or that disease, of course, because the ears of the Church were everywhere and none bigger than my sister's, which, like an ass's, turned to catch every indiscretion. But everyone knows that birth cords are prized for spells, and no doubt Azima had agreed to attend me because of the profane sort of passion that had got me with child. Mateo's birth cord would have strong magic in it.

The rope that had bound me to my child lay in a dish on the floor. Bled white and glistening in the early morning light, it looked to me like the holiest thing. I remembered the prayer that Alvaro had been taught to say as he tied the cincture over his alb: *Praecinge me, Domine cingulo puritatis,* Gird me, O Lord, with the cincture of purity, *et extingue in lumbis meis humorem libidinis,* and quench in my loins the fire of concupiscence. He recited it for me once, that I might appreciate its ironical value. Either that, or the cost to him of our love.

I asked to touch the cord before Azima wrapped it up, and she brought me the bowl and left it on the bed. As she got her cloak I picked one end of it up, slick and smooth and strangely heavy.

My mama used to say that every soul had a silver rope binding it to heaven. After Dolores and I were born, Papa buried our birth cords and planted a cork tree over each, and the trees were growing still. I felt a little afraid of selling my own child's, but what else had I of value to trade for the help of the midwife?

When Azima was dressed, she came back to my side to collect the cord, and she put a colored candle in my hand. "When you are up," she said, "light this to the Virgin." And she gave me three little pieces of paper, each with some indecipherable writing on them. I looked and looked, but for all my reading I could not make out the letters. She said one was to burn over the candle, one to chew and swallow, and the last to put around Mateo's neck. She had a little string with a kidskin pouch for this.

I never did go to the Virgin's shrine. I would have, if given another chance. I would have done any nonsense, stroked any talisman, muttered any prayer to keep him safe.

I dream of nurseries some nights. Of letting my lips rest on a baby's brow, inhaling its soft sweetness. The babies stir but never wake. I touch the amulets on their beds, little beads their mothers have left with them to ward off evil. Spirits are always waiting to snatch a body, and a baby's weak soul, it might be scared off easily. So mothers hide little charms around their children, in their cradles, anywhere they can. They sew them into the hem of swaddling cloths, they make sure to leave a little yarrow under the sheet. Inquisitors might miss these precautions, but evil spirits would know not to draw close.

ROUND THE BEDSIDE OF THE QUEEN A SMALL crowd has gathered. María's little dog has been removed to a basket in the corner, and the only movement from her body is that of her hand as it feebly touches here, then there, feeling among her bedclothes for her companion. Her lips move, but no sound issues from them.

Her face, the face that will be her death mask—set in plaster, then in silver, and at last in whatever Incan gold remains— grows ever more beautiful as she dies. Her eyes become larger, and her mouth smiles now, as if she knows a secret she might tell. Those around her are quiet, Carlos weeping silently and Marianna standing next to him with her arms folded. Everyone waits for the queen's final confession; everyone—almost everyone—wants to hear an accusation against her poisoner. A little wizened man sits on a stool by her pillow. He holds a quill and ink, his hand is poised above his parchment; he is ready to record whatever María says.

Not asleep, not awake. The queen's eyes are open, but she does not see what others see. From time to time, an unnatural tension grips her body, a vigilance, as if she feels the approach of death and resists being taken off just yet.

In consultation with Marianna and Carlos, Dr. Severo has called in another surgeon, Tarragona, famous for thick drinks of cream and egg yolk laced with iron filings. He calls himself a doctor of the science of magnetics and studied in Rome with Baldini and Ferrar. His whole career has been in preparation for such a moment as this, when he passes his little metal wands over the body of a queen. He says he is energizing her organs and calling her back to life.

She cannot last through another day of their cures. All their voices merge into one buzz over her head. The light from the candles has painted her eyelids gold, beginning already her transformation from corpse to relic. When Severo bleeds her again, the blood meanders, each drop hanging languorously from her vein before dropping into the basin held beneath.

Her confessor leans over her, he prods her for a word, just one: that is all an accusation requires. One name: that of her secret, mortal enemy.

There are other theories, of course. The court does not want to believe a poisoner lurks in its midst. Someone says that the queen undermined her constitution long ago with the decadent French foods that she ate. Or what about that fall she took from her horse? It must have injured her in some grave, slow-acting manner.

"Her Highness's habit of sleeping so late and always face-down caused an inflammation of her spleen," says a minister. Hearing this, Obdulia has a sudden fit of hysterical laughter, her amusement quickly taking on that protracted, breathless quality that always accompanies a deathwatch.

Someone always chokes on water, someone always has a laughing fit, someone is always seized with diarrhea. Someone plays cards, someone has a nosebleed, someone pares his nails, and the rest have headaches.

The queen mother looks sharply at Obdulia, who collects herself with some effort. "Bad habits can, certainly, bring on fever-ish inflammations," the maid says, looking at her feet.

The words *feverish inflammations* penetrate the queen's secret dreams. In France the princess Marie had a friend, Nicolette. They loved each other the way girls do, and they played at matchmaking and at weddings together, each taking turns at being the bride or the groom. They practiced kissing each other, so that they would know what to do when the time came for a prince to take one of them in his arms. They kissed a good deal, and so they shared the usual ills of childhood.

One summer they fell sick with a glandular fever that kept them to their beds for months. They were so weak, they could not stand or even sit. Something in the fever increased their propensity to weep, and they would cry over anything: a dead sparrow on the sill, the cook's failure to provide gooseberry fool for dessert. They cried over their little mares in the stable, whose lonely, wet noses must have been thrust forth in anticipation of the never-arriving princesses.

Marie and Nicolette crept into the same bed together. They lay in each other's arms and wept weakly, tangled in each other's hair. Their skin was dry and parched with fever, and how thin they grew. Hours went by without words or thoughts, just a swamp of wet feeling. As if time had slowed to nothing. They turned their heads on the pillows and watched branches toss in the breeze, watched shadows of leaves dapple the bed-clothes and play over their pale cheeks. Sometimes they tried to read a novel together, each holding one side of the book, but then neither was strong enough to cut the pages. And they did not like their ladies-in-waiting to do it, they cried if their maids tried to help them.

When they were convalescing, the girls were carried in their chairs to the park, where they might sit at one end of the grand allée of birch trees. So beautiful those trees were, their paper bark unwinding white in the wind, unwinding and then blowing past their feet. Like love letters torn by some coldhearted recipient, and then cast on the wind. And that idea, too, made them weep. They recovered, of course. The next season they were laughing together at the marquise's salon, shrieking heartlessly with the others as the little birds sang.

As Nicolette's mother had died when she was small, Nicolette was raised by an old nurse, Agnès de Brabant, whom the girls called Bonbon, and who told them the sort of things that frighten girls, though later the two would laugh about them. "Test the man you will marry," said Bonbon. "Tease him, but do not let him put his seed in your secret place." She said women were trees, only upside down, their legs two boughs between which God had set a nest.

"Men want a nice, warm place for their little birds," she said. "But do not let them. Not before you have the gentleman place his seed in a cup. Set the cup aside from one Sabbath to the next, and then look at it. If it has become a tangle of worms crawling, then you know you have been with a man who is evil and you must have nothing more to do with him. But if it is just dry in the cup, a little silver wafer, then you know he is safe for you."

How María missed Nicolette when she came to Spain. And when she weeps now at the memory of her friend, the maids think it is Carlos for whom she pines, and they summon the king to stand close by her bedside, where he fidgets and peels his cuticles. The king is afraid. If only the crowds outside would stop calling his wife's name. Chanting it. Chanting that horrible rhyme.

Ma–ría! Lu–isa! Ma–ría! Lu–isa! The throngs that surround the palace—can it be that they are calling for her death? Perhaps she is taking too long and they are growing impatient. How strange, María thinks under her closed lids, to have come from a place where everyone loved her to one where they hate her. Just the previous month, after Eduardo was caught, after Rébenac admitted that he could do nothing for her, María had sent letters to her uncle. She wrote that she believed she would be killed, and that the illness she had suffered the previous spring had likely been caused by poison. If someone wanted to murder her, not all the tasters in the world could prevent it, she wrote, and she needed his help. *Please,* she wrote, *Let me come home. Send antidotes, send more ministers. Send the army. Send Maman. Anything. Please.*

Perhaps the envelopes arrived without the letters inside, mysteriously opened and emptied in the same way she receives packets mysteriously without content, seals unbroken, paper not torn. She knows that her family thinks of her often enough that they write regularly, but she doesn't know what they think, for every fortnight when María is handed an envelope bearing her mother's looping, lilting script, slanting optimistically up toward the corner, not one has a letter inside. One day she went to Rébenac, sure somehow that Marianna stole the messages. "What can be proved?" he asked. *Rien.* Nothing.

"*C'est atroce!*" exclaims Rébenac now from the corridor. In his indignation, the French minister forgets his Spanish. Something must be done, he says to Carlos, about the disgraceful disturbance outside the palace grounds. The mob has stoned two of a party of *gabachos*—the local epithet for French citizens living in Madrid—in retaliation for their chanting a discourteous rhyme about Carlos's teeth. The Spaniards tore the *gaba-chos'* clothes off and threw them in the bonfires. The two naked corpses now hang from the gatepost. French and Spanish alike keep calling out the queen's name, *Ma–ría! Lu–isa!* And their howls do not subside but grow louder as the crowds increase.

The Spanish troops are having no success in quieting the mob. Fires rage; fed by trash, papers and whatever can be snatched and thrown, they burn high around the walls. Rioters have broken into unguarded homes along the Calle de Arenal, they have dragged out tables and chairs, rugs and draperies. They throw everything into the fires, sometimes before the very eyes of the owners of the pillaged homes—for all of Madrid, it seems, is waiting outside the palace grounds, screaming the queen's name.

Ma–ría! Lu–isa!

"*Cabrónes!* Bastards!" cries a man as he sees his bed, linens and all, fly through the air and onto the top of the biggest fire. The stench of feathers from the pillows reaches him just as he himself is picked up and hurled after his furnishings. "Burn in your blankets then, *Gillipolas! Coño! Hijo de puta!*" the rioters call after him. "You asshole! You idiot pig! You son of a whoring bitch!" The man's screams are lost in the chanting.

The queen's name has become an invocation, a taunt, a spell. Its syllables both express and excite the anger of the masses. At times the shouting grows so loud that down here, in our prison, the walls shake until it seems they will fall, crushing us. Releasing us.

"*Si votre seigneur ne—*" sputters Rébenac, and then corrects himself. He speaks in Spanish, uttering each syllable with enraged precision. "Unless Your Highness summons the armed forces to squelch this rabble, I shall have no choice but to send an envoy to France! Then Louis himself will take care of the situation."

Carlos squints as though he does not understand. He will go upstairs where it is peaceful, he will go up to Estrellita.

Outside, the mob has begun to dismantle the wall around the palace grounds. The guards have locked themselves in the gatehouse. They have stuffed their ears with scraps of wool felt torn out of their uniforms. They are frightened of these people, the citizens of Madrid, who, just last week, were peaceable. They do not want to hear any more of the shouting.

"*María Marrana!*" the crowds scream now, having replaced the queen's second name with a slur, unnaming her, taking away what her mother had given her, the name Maman chose over those picked by the queen's father, "No, not Thérèse! Not Colette! It is Louise, Louise! Yes, Marie Louise."

"*María Marrana!*" come the cries. María the Slut. They penetrate locked casements. They rattle the panes.

The palace shudders. What a sorrowful place it is. Each lamp and doorstop and chair is groaning. Plates ooze tears of misery, candles sputter in dismay and each hinge moans. The very halls tremble and heave with weeping. By tomorrow, even the smallest corner will be saturated with unhappiness, as if sorrow were a kind of liquid that could leak over every garment and drapery, staining them, leaving rings upon the carpet, marks of tidal wretchedness upon the walls. The rooms will have a mildewed smell of melancholy, the floorboards will be warped with weeping.

But that is tomorrow. Now is the hour for grand gestures, and Severo is making himself ready to flay the white goat in the queen's apartments. It is as good as an admission that he has failed, that all of his expensive training and equipment cannot save a life. With my mother they used the pigeons, dipping her cold feet into their opened breasts, the little hearts beating yet under toes as good as dead. One last chance to live: to stand in the breasts of creatures so recently flying.

They summon the little saint who, with such concentration that her head shakes on the rigid stalk of her neck, can slow the palace clocks, all of them, and all the clocks in the city of Madrid, and once, even those as far away as Toledo. Carlos accompanies Estrellita as she is carried down the stairs by two nuns who make a seat for her with their strong hands and arms. She will buy for the queen an hour, a few minutes, however much she can.

The goat is a pretty creature. Not knowing her doom, nevertheless she suspects it, and her hooves slip and scramble on the floor as the two pages drag her into María's chamber. A hand on either side of her red bridle ensures her captivity until Dr. Severo's assistant comes and takes her from them.

From a wheeled chest filled with knives, Dr. Severo selects one with a short, bright blade. His assistant holds the goat tight, he locks her head between his knees, and Severo makes a quick, expert cut from her chin down her breast and then a long slice along her belly. His knife is so sharp that it requires no force to move it. It almost eludes the doctor's fingers, so quickly does it rush ahead to part the animal's flesh. It must be this sharp, because if the cure is to work, the goat has to be skinned so fast that she remains alive. Stands, living, without her hide, which is to be laid over the queen.

If Severo has any true skills, they are taxidermic: he has the hide off the goat in two minutes, less time than one turn of the sandglass, and he leaves her standing absolutely still, amazed by her fatal nakedness. Her long beast's eyelashes quiver under absent lids, and her naked knees knock as her pretty white coat, spattered with red, is carried steaming to the queen.

Without her hide, the goat's life expands and fills María's chamber. It presses up to the ceiling and sets the chandelier swaying. The lights shiver. For a moment, it overpowers the growing smell of death's arrival, the smell that the doctor carries away in his clothes, that the maids try to shake from their aprons when they walk for a moment outside in the cold, flapping their skirts. It does not smell bad, that's the surprising aspect. Illness and excrement smell noxious, but death smells sweet, mysterious and forbidden. No matter that the secret will in time be divulged to all, the smell makes fingers itch with curiosity. Outside María's maids flap and shake even their underclothes.

The little creature's hide is surprisingly heavy. It takes two, Dr. Severo and his assistant, to bear it, slick and hot and dripping, to María's bed, and to drape it over her. She herself has been stripped for the occasion and lies completely unclothed beneath a sheet of linen, which at the last is whisked away by Obdulia before the hide is dropped down, whisked away when only an inch remains between the two skins: the queen's and the

goat's. The blood drips on the floor in oily, shining, perfect circles, which dry quickly, first congealing so that the light disappears from their surface, then turning black and sullen like
plague spots.

As she sees it approach, María grimaces slightly, but then she
relaxes under its warmth. It is distasteful, but she is helpless to
resist its comfort. There is nothing that feels like this wearing of
two living skins. A second skin, an extra skin, feels as good as
one imagines it might. She will have an hour or two of warm
comfort before it cools and dries, sticking to her.

My health must be deemed a little frail, for I was spared the fire
today. Of course, they cannot burn us every time, and while the
blisters are healing, the *garrucha* is useful. One White Hood
made my arms fast behind my back while another set the pulley.
Then a rope was bound around my wrists held behind my back
and I was hoisted and dropped, hoisted and dropped.

I have become like those holy acrobats who pass from town
to town around the Feast of Saint John, leaping through bonfires, their features hidden behind grotesque masks that make
their heads as big as pumpkins, their tricky joints bending impossibly backward. Dolores and I would scream when we saw
them in their black hose, their painted Devil's grimaces howling
at the lick of holy fire. Do I look like that now, I wonder, my
mouth set in an endless scream?

While I sit here in the dark, head on knees, arms clasped
around ankles, joints swollen stiff, I helplessly recall the little
vessel I was to be at my first holy communion: a cup to be filled
with the Holy Spirit. *Spiritus Sancti.*

Try as I may, I no longer know whether I am empty or full.

This morning the Purple Hood told me that I am descended
from a family that counts a very famous heretic among its members. My mother's mother's mother's mother's mother was
Jeanne. She wasn't a virgin at all, he told me.

Jeanne d'Arc.

They say that when Jeanne d'Arc was burned at the stake her
heart would not be consumed by the flames. Though they
burned it for a month without cease, tending the fire high—the

wood was oak and it burned hot—her heart would not be consumed, so they cast it into the Seine. From there it tumbled along the riverbed. It floated past stones and fish and eelgrass. It passed under the bridges of Rouen, under oars and through nets. That most courageous heart, that stubborn, undefeated heart, traveled on to the ocean through tides of algae and rubbish, and its only reverence came from blind snails, from an old frog diving for his den in the mud.

Did my mother inherit such a heart? Did I?

Will nothing destroy our hearts?

ATEO. MATEO. NAMED FOR THE AUTHOR OF the first book of the New Covenant, the new order, the rebuilding of the world. The same book that begins with so many begats that the queen used to yawn and swoon with boredom before bed, but nonetheless, Mateo: a name of surpassing hope.

From the beginning, I loved him so that I covered him with kisses each minute that he was awake, I held him the whole day, and would only put him down in fear that, as Dolores said, I would love him to death. Later, when he could creep along the floor and then walk, when he was a big boy whom I could gather up and hold tightly to myself, when he woke to the world and began to see where he was, then I loved him all the more. "Alvaro is in you," I would whisper when I lay on the bed with him. I wanted to make his life good, I wanted to keep him safe. This was all I thought of.

Francisca, I told myself, you tempt fate. Do not be such a fool! For I knew it was a danger to so love any mortal creature, and what I felt for my child I cannot call wrong, but it was too much. I was crazy with it, I wanted to eat him. I danced with him, kissed his lips when his mouth was still wet with my milk. I worried that what the grandmothers said was true. *Rein in your heart, Francisca. Keep it back,* the old women at the well told me. *Don't love him so much until he is older.* Half of the children—oh, at least that many—end up in the ground before their first or second saint's day. Only fools give their hearts to babies. But there was no teaching me.

As Mateo suckled I would take his fingers into my mouth and taste with my tongue's tip the sweetness of him, bite between my teeth the little papery nails so that he could not scratch himself. My hair was caught fast in his hand; his fingers held so tight that it hurt, he took a writhing pleasure as he suckled. I can yet feel his hand on my side as he drank from me, fingers squeezing, digging in, but they felt so good. With Mateo in my arms, eating me up, I had a glimpse of holiness. I understood finally what my mother's life had been and what it had meant.

The sweetness of his exhalation: I smelled myself, the best of myself, the sweet whole pure of myself, on his breath as he lay sleeping. I would bend over him in his basket, smelling the air around his face for any sour or stale scent, but it was sweet, uncorrupted. How could I stop myself from loving him so?

I would roll with him in the bedclothes when Dolores was out and when no one else was there to see. We would turn over and over, and I would tickle and kiss him, and he would laugh and I would laugh, and then suddenly my laughter would turn to tears and I would be holding him too tightly in my arms, and he would struggle to escape and begin to cry. I wanted time to cease passing. Oh, God, just long enough that I could drink him up before the inexorable, unkind march of days tore my child away from me. There had never been time for anything I had wanted. Never time to lie in my mama's lap. No time for Alvaro's mouth to linger on mine. And no time for me to hold my son to myself. Of course, he was not his mother's. No child is.

I was slow to wean Mateo. He was hungry, and I did not have enough for him. I was not like my mama, full to bursting, and what I did have began to dry up. I grew thin and then thinner, as if it had taken what small portion of flesh I had to feed him for as long as I did. We would sit at the hearth of an evening, Mateo at my breast for two hours, longer, trying to get what he needed. He was so hungry, he could not stop; if I took my tit away he cried.

"Give him food!" Dolores would say. "It is time you weaned him."

But I could not stand the idea that my child would be anything other than all mine. Whenever I looked upon him I thought to myself, *He is purely me. Mine.*

One day I came home from a chore to find Dolores sitting before Mateo, a spoon in her hand. She startled at my footfalls. I stood at the open door, looking at the little bowl of porridge in her hand, and at him reaching for the spoon. She was doing no harm, but I slapped her, and the bowl fell on the floor.

She stood up. "You're starving the child," she said. "An hour after you left, he was crying and pulling at my skirts." She held her hand to her face, her fingers met the red marks mine had left. "You've seen him as we eat," she said. "His eyes follow our spoons to our mouths. How can you let him be hungry? You are no mother. You are a beast. He snatches at crusts, he—"

I covered my ears. I knew what it was: She wanted him. She wanted to take my son from me. Even though she had been fearful before his birth, afraid he would be a monster, Dolores now separated my child from the evil I had done. My sister loved Mateo as I did, as a gift of God, but one she felt she deserved more than I did.

I could have killed her in that moment, pushed her into the fire and then smashed the lamp and burned the house down, too. But I did nothing, I surprised myself by falling onto my knees weeping. Perhaps she had been feeding him all the while, whenever I left him with her. Perhaps he was not mine at all. Mateo was screaming, and I tried to force my tit into his mouth, but he turned his head away. He shoved his hands at my chest, pushing me, for I stank of despair and he would have none of it.

Dolores held him as I sat in the furthest corner of the house, my knees drawn up. *Francisca,* I said my name to myself over and over, as if to call myself back, but my teeth were chattering, and Mateo went on crying.

"Take him, *Santa María,* take him, Francisca," Dolores begged me. "He's crying for you," she said. She tried to pull his fingers off her dress.

"No!" I could not stand hearing it, the crying. *Leave me, leave me,* I thought. Only one thing I had for him and he refused it. Me.

My love for him was not exalted, it brought out nothing but the basest in me. In him I felt I had a prize, and someone— Dolores!—would take it. I felt I could have stood sharing my son with any woman besides my sister.

When Mateo passed through my legs, it was as if I were given back my innocence, I felt myself a virgin again, not only a virgin, but the Francisca who sat at her mama's feet as she tended babies by the fire: a child. I gave birth to myself. While suckling Mateo I had no monthly flow, and I felt a purity that separated me from Dolores and her little cloths stained with blood, her smell of a woman. It was wrong, I know it was, but at the time I felt I had transcended the flesh, the material that imprisoned her, that I had stepped into a cleaner world.

There were many locusts that season, small and brown, and they jumped up into my face as I walked toward the mulberry grove the next day. Their legs caught in my hair when I tried to brush them away. Mateo bounced on my hip, his fingers holding tight to my dress.

Truly, I thought, I was not my mother. I did not have this endless river of milk. And when I looked down at my body, my breasts shrunk flat against my ribs, I felt like an old woman, felt weak as I carried him, riding on my hip with his legs kicking and those little black eyes bright. I was walking through the trees, the even rows of them. They made what seemed like an aisle in a cathedral; the light came through the green leaves as if through colored glass. I sat down with him upon the ground, and held him close. The noise of the wind wailing past did not trouble me, and neither did the mournful cries of birds and far-off children.

The sun was shining brightly. It revealed a fine tracing of gold hairs all over his body, his back, his arms and legs. The hairs were almost too fine to see individually, but gave to his whole form a shimmer, a luster, as if he were a celestial creature: something revealed by a trick of the light, something that would disappear if I blinked. I uncurled his fist under the bright spring sky, turned it up to the sun, tasted it with my tongue, looked at it.

I knew then that I did not care for books so much as before. In the fine and complex lines there on Mateo's palm, the history of the world was written. Each planet's turning, the great celestial dance: an eternal logging of spring rains, birds' flight, lovers' kisses, leaves falling—it was all there, I saw it written on his hand. I held him tightly to me and buried my face in his flesh.

Here is heresy for you, you in your robes and your hoods,

featureless, cowardly. I will not tell you this next time, if you ask. I will not give this away. But, here, listen: Every mother is the mother of God. She knows it when she holds her child and sees that the world is not reflected but *contained* in his eyes. He puts his hands on her face, and she feels it, *this is* the love of God. Not some dim, imperfect copy, but love itself. And for that instant—And why is it not the truest and most real of all moments?—a woman knows that she has given birth to God, and God loves her for the life she gave, and God returns it to her.

That is the center. All else spins off it. Like Francisca dancing in the grove, her skirts twirling out from her belly big with child, she is the center of the universe.

I began that evening with goat's milk in the same little cup that Dolores and then I, as babies, had used. Mateo liked it and drank with it spilling down his neck and wetting his clothes. He liked it enough that we had to mix it with water to make it last.

It was the year that people got sick from the water. Far above our heads the past winter's snows melted and ran down through the high pastures carrying some evil spirit into the aqueduct, and the spirit got into the bowels and brains of children and some grown persons, too, and they all got the flux; before a month passed they went into fits and died.

I know all mothers say the same, but my child was an angel. He had gold ringlets and a red mouth, his cheeks were round, his eyes were black. I have never seen any living thing like him, he looked like the paintings in the cathedral.

We thought at first that it was one of the common diarrheas that children get from time to time. We gave him the bayberry drink, but it was bitter, and he swallowed little of it. After a week of the sickness, Mateo was suffering so that he called for me even when I was just an arm's length away. He would call out over and over, *Mam Mam Mam Mam Mam,* repeating the syllable almost to himself. Like some prayer of grief, it strikes me now. As if he expected nothing, but could not help himself from crying.

The following week, he was not calling out with vigor as before, but moaning and talking at once. And the sobs came out jumbled with my name, *MamMamMam,* or just *MM MM MM,* his lips together and the sound broken by hiccoughing, his cheeks wet with tears.

When I could sleep, I dreamed over and over of my mother. I was able to do this purposely. Indeed, the only way I could find my way out of my troubled waking life was to meditate on my mama and her skirts. I pictured myself running home to our hearth, as a little child. I saw her so tall that my face reached only to her thighs. Mama stood by the fire, so real to me that I had to keep from calling out from my bed. I saw myself run to her and hide my face in her skirts, my cold hands reaching into the warm folds of cloth.

re they wrapping me in my shroud? the queen wonders. Obdulia at her head, Jeanette at her feet: they lift the linen upon which the queen lies, and the chambermaids quickly strip the bed beneath her, pulling away layers of soiled bedclothes. They are gentle, they could not be more gentle, but even so, this brief ascension hurts María. She feels her bones are out of joint.

The slight sway of the makeshift sling nauseates her. The sense of nothing solid beneath her frightens her. Is this what it is like to be dead and disembodied? Awful, endless suspension? Even were it painless, this swaying and hanging—eternal limbo—could it be bearable?

Perhaps there is no purgatory. Perhaps it is as the gardener told her long before. The princess Marie was in the greenhouse admiring the violets. She was so young that her head came up only as far as the gardener's shoulder. Monsieur Clément reached forward and plucked a snail shell from the lip of a pot. He peered inside it, then showed her the small orifice: a body with but one hole, both entry and exit. The shell was empty and dry, and when Clément crushed it between his thumb and forefinger, there was nothing left inside, only a brown crust. He grunted.

"You do not like the snails?" she asked.

"They eat the flowers," he replied.

He brushed his hands together and held them before her eyes. "See? Nothing left." He wiped his hands against his black breeches. "So it is for every living thing," he said. "This is how it ends."

The queen's bed stinks, but it is not the familiar stench of illness that the maids are trying to banish. It is that other smell, the dizzy, sickly sweetish one. "What is it like up there?" the cook asks Obdulia in the kitchen.

What *is* the smell like, other than itself? Obdulia shrugs, tries to think of it in terms the cook will appreciate. "A rotting pumpkin," she says. A pumpkin overripe and pungent and left upon the coals until the skin is brown and blistered. Then, stick a knife into its side: would that first hot, wet, vegetable exhalation approach it? Obdulia shakes her head. "No," she says. "That's not it. It is something you have to smell for yourself."

No matter how often they scrub the floor and sprinkle lime into the corners; no matter how many times they swab her arms and legs, back and belly with spirits of alcohol; no matter if they exchange her pillow for another, tear down the draperies, take away her hairbrush and coifs—and all of this was required after the goat's blood sprayed everything the night before, after they removed its skin, gelid and sticky and vile, from the queen's—no matter what they do, the smell of death remains.

This is the end, now, the evening that María will die, and the smell is so intense that it affects the queen's visitors. Either they cannot sit still, or they fall asleep. The fidgeters pace and tap and twiddle. They adjust the draperies, move the chairs about. They pick up their needlework, break threads and miscount stitches. They stay no longer than a quarter of an hour before they find an errand that will not wait. As for the sleepers, they say they have come to read, either silently to themselves or out loud to María. But they mumble, the words jumble, and even as they try to sit up in their chairs, they slump over, cheek to page.

The maids lay the queen on her clean bed. Obdulia takes her right arm and holds it firmly just below the shoulder. Her Highness's skin has grown slack. The bone slips in its loose envelope of flesh, and only by an effort of will does the maid not shudder as she pulls her mistress toward her. Obdulia tugs the queen's shoulder as Jeanette pulls her hip, and in this way the two of them roll María gently onto one side and then back onto the other, so that the chambermaids can quickly gather up the soiled sheet that served as her sling. When at last they are all through, María is left neatly in the middle of a layer of clean linens.

Obdulia brings a fresh white nightdress and lays it facedown on the queen, its unbuttoned neck pointing toward her feet. They pull her limp arms from the sleeves of the soiled nightdress and then thread them through the sleeves of the clean one, and when Obdulia lifts María's head, Jeanette draws the soiled garment over it and pulls the clean one down at so nearly the same instant that no one can look on the queen's nakedness. It is a complicated process, and one at which they have grown more adept, having had in the past days twenty-three opportunities to practice it.

When they are done at last, when María has no strength left with which even to moan, the queen mother comes for a last visit. Marianna is one of the fidgeters, her page carries her needlework in a basket. "What did Dr. Severo say?" she asks Obdulia.

The maid curtsies nervously. "He came as we were just beginning to change Her Majesty's linens," she says. "He said he would return in the next hour to bleed Her Highness." She curtsies again. Marianna nods.

"Well," says Marianna, and says no more. She sits and gathers up her sewing—she is making undervests for the twins, expected next month—then lets it fall into her lap. She begins to speak to the queen, who lies silent and still. "I know it has not been easy for you here," she says. "I imagine you must have been lonely these years. That is why, despite her frightful reputation and the vulgar rumors about your friend the comtesse, we were indulgent when she came to visit." Marianna sighs.

Though María makes no answers, her mother-in-law pauses between remarks, as if the queen utters words that only she can hear.

"*La Jolie Araignée.*" Marianna's accent is flawless, and acid. "I fear now we did you a grave disservice." She makes a stitch in the tiny white vest, drawing a strand of thread too tight. The fabric puckers, and she drops the needle to loosen the stitch with her fingernails. She is not yet accustomed to the new glycerin preparation she is using on her thread. It makes the usually sticky linen so slippery that she does not have to tug at the needle.

María is too weak to turn her head, to look at Marianna as she speaks. Is this soliloquy for the benefit of the listening maid, she wonders, so that Obdulia may convey its content to the gossiping servants?

Outside, the rioting mob has scaled the wall. Eleven persons have been trampled to death, five crushed against the gate by those who used their heads as stepping-stones. Now their faces are caught between the bars of the great entrance, they peer blindly over the frozen lawns. People gather under the queen's window, calling to her. The soldiery has armed all entrances, every window and door on the first two stories. The corridor of living saints has a triple guard. Carlos is quaking under Estrellita's skirts.

María! María! María Marrana!

In the dark, before my eyes, a huge, luminous insect hovers. It holds still, as if to allow me to admire how it shines. Its wings beat so fast that they are visible only as a tremor in the air. A beautiful creature, a beetle with a shell the green-blue iridescence of a peacock's neck.

A blister beetle. Dolores and I would see them clustered on the elder trees. Sometimes, one would find its way among the insects we collected for Papa's experiments with colored silk.

Once, in the early morning, my sister and I went with our baskets through the fields, stepping high over the neighbor's furrows, over stiles and past sheep chewing, past the stream and past the bleaching greens where long swaths of linen were laid out so the sun could whiten them. We climbed a hill to the place where the oak trees grew, and before we got there, we saw a party of veiled women bearing folded sheets into an elder grove. Their faces, their hands, their necks—all were obscured by a drapery of heavy white fabric.

"Look at the brides," said Dolores.

"Nuns," I answered.

The women spread their sheets under the elders and began to shake the trees' boughs. Around them rained glittering, green fruit: thousands of beetles clumped together, too sluggish in the early chill to fly off. The women bound them tightly in the sheet and carried them away, making a strange, silent procession.

Later, as we walked back through the elder trees with our baskets filled, as I walked dreaming of what my work might earn for me—a toy, a handful of sweets, a velvet ribbon—one of the pretty beetles lit on Dolores's skirt. It folded its trembling glassy wings under its shell. She brushed it off. "Oh!" she said. Her fingertip burned where she had touched it, burned and burned until a blister appeared, its fragile skin lifting over a clear fluid. Dolores held the finger out stiffly as we walked. When we came home, Mama looked at the finger and put a salve on Dolores's hand and bound it up with a bit of cloth.

"Do not handle blister beetles," she said. "Never touch them." She gave Dolores a tea of thistle and horehound and put her to bed, her hand wrapped and stinging. A few days later the skin on my sister's finger peeled off and left it raw.

It is said that in the heat of the day, blister beetles will fly at your eyes and blind you. They are gathered only at first sunrise, when there is enough light to see them but they will not fly from the branches. The women who collect the beetles shake them loose without touching them. When they have enough of them in the winding-sheets they carry, they roll the fabric tight and carry it rolled back to their homes. They leave the insects bound up in the sheet for a week, and when they undo it, the beetles are dead. They dry them in an oven, still without handling them and crush their dried bodies to powder. They use pestles to do it, the beetle harvesters: they grind the legs and shells and heads and wings together until all that is left is a black, acrid dust.

Cantharidian powder. Sticky, stinging, darkly iridescent, it is sold at the apothecary market. Buyers pay a good deal for it—as much as a ducado for an ounce—and they dissolve it in spirits of wine. The resulting tincture is bottled in vials so small they hold no more than a spoonful. People in Madrid call it passion fly. In Paris they ask for Spanish fly. When Papa took us to market we saw the little bottles lined up at the perfumer's, between aloes and clove oil at the spice trader's and at the barber's counter, among the soaps and salves.

A gentleman comes in, he buys one—nine times out of ten it is a man who makes the purchase. Later, at his lodgings, he makes up a wash: a toilet water for his lady love's nether parts. So diluted, one drop dispersed through the contents of a hundred-dram bottle, it causes no blister, no burning, just a pleasant warming of the flesh, a little inflammation easily confused with that of desire.

One drop, one drop diluted in a wash and dribbled over a woman's secret parts: an aphrodisiac. Two drops taken by mouth, in a glass of wine or in any medium that would mask its bite—a dose of laudanum would do—a deadly poison.

The queen mother stands so near María's bed that the queen can smell the glycerin Marianna uses as she sews, the pungent, slippery jelly into which she dips her middle finger and anoints her thread. The smell, at once sweet and acrid, is familiar to the queen—she smelled it for the first time just recently, but it takes her a moment to remember when.

Eduardo's hands had smelled of glycerin. They smelled of it the night the queen went to the theater with Olympe, the night she was taken ill. The queen and her dwarf met as María was getting into her carriage.

"I hear it is a remarkably tedious production," Eduardo said, and discreetly he showed her a new vial of laudanum in his palm. Accepting it, María gave his hand a quick kiss.

"Is that a new pomade?" she said, making a face at the scent: sharp, sweet. "You need a better perfumer," she teased. But Eduardo did not respond, and she thought no more about it until now.

For Eduardo's hand to bear the smell of glycerin, it would have had to touch Marianna's. Not merely touched but grasped and wrung it. Taken something from her pungent fingers.

The queen's heart, weak as it is, beats faster. She manages to turn her head and look at Marianna.

You made me kill myself! she thinks. *Made me administer the dose. Made my friend your envoy. I would never hesitate to empty the little blue vial directly onto my tongue. I would think little of it, were it more bitter than usual. You knew that, and you knew I would sooner blame any illness on what I had eaten at dinner than blame it on a kind gesture from a friend.*

It was easy. It required no finesse. Of course you allowed Olympe to visit. The comtesse's reputation was all the security you needed. And now Olympe is in a coach, traveling quickly north from Madrid. The road will give out, she will be forced to switch to a litter, she will be bounced and jounced over rocks. But, God willing, she will be over the border and into France before she can be arrested.

Marianna hands her needlework to her little page. She replaces the lid on the little tin of glycerin. It works so well, it makes sewing effortless. How is it she had never heard of it before? How lucky that she found it at the druggist's. She looks at the queen for one long moment, meets her open-eyed gaze, and then she leaves.

María closes her eyes. *One thousand orange trees,* she says inside her head, and she pictures them in circles, one inside another, her mother in the center of all the white blossoms.

Should she tell someone it was Marianna? Who would believe her? She has no proof, and the surmises of a woman addicted to laudanum are likely to be dismissed.

What María does not think, what she cannot bear to think, is this: The dwarf himself conspired against her. Her friend went to the queen mother after his apprehension on the stair. He confessed to her, apologized, kissed the hem of her gown and the soles of her shoes.

Eduardo offered to kill María. He said he wanted revenge as well. He wanted it as much as she. "The queen set a spell on me," he told Marianna. He claimed she had bewitched him and had made him love her. When the pig's blood dripped down the stairs and accused him, the dwarf recovered from the enchantment.

Eduardo did not lie to the queen mother. He had loved María, loved her enough to lose his head for a time. But, ultimately, he loved his life more, and he knew the workings of the palace. From the time the French queen arrived, he had guessed her fate.

When María remained childless, he warned her of what would come to pass. He knew she would be sacrificed, and he told her so. He confessed the murder years before committing it.

Marianna folded her arms. She nodded at the dwarf on his knees before her. "Get up," she said. She would test him. She needed Eduardo: after all, a willing murderer is hard to come by. He could be discarded after he made himself useful. "We must wait for the arrival of the comtesse de Soissons," she said to him. In the meantime, Marianna herself would obtain the poison. Something common, something she could get from any city shop.

Eduardo knew María was afraid of her mother-in-law, so afraid after the discovery of the false miscarriages that she would take no drug from Marianna's stores—she was afraid that Marianna might try to do Eduardo some harm. So the dwarf told the queen that he had some laudanum put away, that he had saved some from those years before the queen began using it, enough to tide her over until he could discover another source.

When Marianna summoned Eduardo to her apartments, when she handed him the poison and said its name, the dwarf started. Cantharide! Had the queen mother chosen passion fly for its ironical value? Was this her message: that as María Luisa had aroused her son insufficiently to produce an heir, she would die by an overdose of aphrodisiac? He did not ask Marianna these questions, of course. He accepted the packet of black powder and returned to his apartments to mix the poison.

The final bleeding is not in the least successful. Severo gets no more than a thimbleful—María has no life left to give—and he sends a message to the king and queen mother as they sit down to dinner.

"Come!" Severo's assistant says. "Come immediately!"

The queen of Spain is hot. She wants the window opened. She wants the cold air to pass over her body, for winter to breathe upon her and make her skin cool, to make it sparkle with frost as if new, to make it feel the way it did when she was riding: the ride when autumn is just ceding to winter, leaves blowing dry upon the ground, blowing, scattering, rustling. When Lucie's hooves stirred them, they seemed to whisper. Rocinante's came down harder, drove them into the mud.

The trees are bare, the light comes through the boughs. The woods are so filled with light that the frost on the trees and bits of ice here and there catch the sun's rays. Everything is turned to silver.

Open the window! she calls. *Please, I beg of you, open it!* But no one pays her any heed. Even were her requests audible, the windows would not be opened, for they do not open.

Open the window! There is an errand she must accomplish, there is a place she must get to.

You open it, I tell her. *Concentrate yourself. Focus your will.*

The bedchamber is silent. The maids, Eduardo, Carlos, Marianna: no one says anything. The queen mother's industrious fingers have abandoned their rosary beads. María is motionless, yet she seems poised as if for some action. What if she should speak? thinks Marianna. What if she should accuse her? The queen mother will not be safe until the queen is buried.

The wind blows outside, calling to María, lowing under the eaves, rattling the panes. The glass creaks and shivers.

Open it, I say to her. *Do not be afraid. You can go now. You can go now to your mother.*

When I was a child, I told Dolores that the dead could feel the cold, and that they came to the hearth as we slept and blew on the embers until the fire burned bright. They took logs and threw them on the coals, but logs would not be consumed or even scorched by the fires made by the dead. When we woke to find new wood on the grate, I would say, "Look! Mama has been here trying to get warm."

How she hated to hear that and to think of Mama cold and wandering and coming to warm her hands at our hearth. In those days my father walked in his sleep, and *"It was Papa, you idiot, Papa!"* Dolores told me. "He put the logs on!" she would yell.

I would answer calmly, saying, "No, Mama comes back here." Dolores believed that I knew something she did not. She believed that Mama visited and spoke with me and not her.

"And, you know, they are busy, the dead," I used to tell my sister.

"Doing what?" she would say.

"Oh, making pilgrimages."

Everyone dies with some stain of sin left unrepented, some love left undeclared. There is always much to be done, even after death. Most people die young, so there are not so many old souls, and I told Dolores that in the next life the old people are so light that the breath of God or of the Devil blows them hither and yon, their feet never touch the ground. If you get to be old enough before you die, it does not matter whether you had sinned or were pure, since all that was left was a bit of skin buffeted by the winds of the afterlife. "We must pray," I would say. "Pray and pray that Mama can rest and not scurry about purgatory forever." When our mother was all finished and atoned, then she could come back in a new body.

But to myself I thought, What wrong could Mama have done? When Saint Michael came and stood at the head of her deathbed and read from the book of her deeds, he must have found it filled with far more good than evil. And any sin that she committed, would it not have been erased by her regrets?

The first cracks in the window opposite the queen's bed are silent, but as Eduardo looks the glass turns to lace, and with a sudden burst the window gives way. At the sound of the explosion overhead, there is a gasp from the rioters standing below. Slivers of glass fall like rain on their heads.

The bells begin to toll, and the mob falls silent. They stop their terrible song.

The dead do make pilgrimages, but they are different from those I described to my sister. I no longer believe that people travel about to undo their sins. No, they go one last time to touch the people they love best.

 TOOK MY CHILD TO ALL THE HOLY PLACES I could get to, to any place I heard of, there was always a miracle of which I was told. In that time of pilgrimages, I became part of a company of miracle seekers.

It was not belief that bound us one to another, not faith but fear. We were desperate and deluded persons who kept moving, trying to outrun our fate. We recognized one another at various shrines, we spread word of cures and successes, of news like that of a certain Xavier's son who had been crushed by a plow and regained the use of his legs after a visit to the weeping statue of Our Lady at Campo. She took pity on him, so they said, and we all rushed there so that she might feel sorry for us, too.

I stood in lines so long that I lay down and slept in line, waiting my turn to scrape a bit of earth from the ground where a saint had trod, to hold Mateo under a trickle of some holy stream, to add my own votive offering to the piles left at the feet of wooden and plaster holies.

Libera nos, Domine. Libera nos, libera nos. Deliver us, O Lord. The eternal prayer of mankind, all of us so weary of our lives.

Anima Christi, sanctifica me. Corpus Christi, salva me. Sanguis Christi, inebria me. Soul of Christ, body of Christ, blood of Christ. Sanctify me, heal me, drench me.

Sometimes it was only the press of other bodies around mine that kept me standing with my baby in my arms. I was so tired that even his small weight was like a stone. When I slept I had a nightmare, the same dream each time, of a red ocean, like a vast bleeding of color. There was a staircase in the ocean of red, stairs like those that lead down from the pulpit in the cathedral, and some of them were under the red sea. The sky was white. Not blue, but white like a shroud. Every time I dreamed this dream, more of the stairs were submerged. Even if I were not brave enough to go down the stairs, as I knew I was meant to do, the water would rise inexorably. In my arms, instead of Mateo, I would be holding a child my mother had suckled long ago, the one I had started to smother. I would drop her into the red waves, and then wake up in a fearful state, clutching my son.

His hair lost its shine, his eyes went blank. They stopped reflecting the sun, the light went into them and disappeared. They died first, his eyes, and then I saw that Mateo was nothing but a bag of wrinkled skin, with a little skeleton inside. I was so filled with remorse that it was like an obstruction in my throat, and when I opened my mouth to speak I was surprised by sobs instead of words.

The roads to the holy places were filled with men and women hawking whatever they took into their heads might sell. Trinkets or remembrances of the particular place—beads, prayer books and relics for those credulous enough to suppose that the dog legs and rabbit leather displayed had once borne the spirit of a saint. Desperation bred ugliness in the pilgrims. People were fearful that the holiness would dry up before even half of the long line of hopeful had a chance to see or touch—as if the miracle was *not* miraculous but limited and would run out, like bread from the baker on the day before a feast. Fights broke out, and bandits took advantage of the confusion to steal what little they could.

A much renowned *santiguardo,* or what is sometimes called a faith healer, the seventh son of a daughterless union, lived in the foothills below Avila. He was very old, and as he no longer left his pallet to greet the pilgrims, they came to touch him. People had to be restrained from crushing him, so many hands plucking at his ragged clothes, trying to pull one thread to save their lives. I saw him, and I thought of the little cakes of soap Mama made. When we used one long enough, the figure on it would be almost gone, no more than a raised spot on the soap; and just so, the touching of so many hands seemed to have worn the features off the old man's face. But I had made my way to his pallet after many hours, and I raked at his sheets as well, I pressed Mateo's hot hands to his lips, withdrawing them with white flecks of spittle on the palms.

I learned to visit places at odd hours, to travel by night while most people slept. I walked under a clouded, starless sky, and I listened to the night, to sheep coughing in a distant pasture, to the wind and, once, to a dog licking himself somewhere nearby. The loud slopping noise of his tongue filled the dark, and the sound of the animal grew until I could see his teeth and his wet gullet before me, and it seemed like *time* itself, always ready to swallow us all. No matter how tired I was, I could not bear to remain still and do nothing for Mateo. Not even for an hour could I rest before I was up again, relieved to hear the noise of twigs breaking under my shoes.

The shrine at Tordeso was no more than a cross set up over a hole in the earth. Pilgrims had scraped away all the dirt they could carry, the ground upon which it was said our Holy Mother had wept. Years before, the Virgin had appeared no higher than my knee and sitting upon a snow-white ass no bigger than a cat. The peasant girl who witnessed the apparition saw Her for fifteen consecutive nights; on the last night, the Virgin caused a lily to sprout from the earth. The peasant girl was taken away by White Hoods. She stood before the tribunal in the auto-da-fé of 1616, and onlookers stoned her to death. Since that day people have come to the town to take earth from that spot where the lily grew.

I arrived at Tordeso before daybreak. An old man was filling the hole with spadefuls of earth he took from his wheeled barrow.

"Who are you?" I asked. "What are you doing?" I began to laugh, I could not stop. "Is *this* the holy ground, then? Dirt from your spade!" I had traveled so far that several times in the night I had had to lie down on the ground with Mateo until I could walk with him once more.

The old man looked up from his occupation. "Señora," he said, and the voice that scolded me was my grandfather's. "How do you think, with so many coming each day, that there would be any ground left? The forest would be uprooted."

"So it is a lie?" I said. "Holy dirt! I have walked all night to get to this place!"

"Not a lie." He threw his spade back into the empty barrow and it made a hollow ringing sound, like a bell.

The sun was coming from the east, fingers of light through the trees. One fell upon his face, and I saw the lines etched deep around his mouth: my grandfather's mouth, twisting down on one side as it used to do when he argued with my father. Gusts of wind hissed through the leaves like serpents.

"All that matters is faith," my grandfather said. He reached forward and touched my shawl just where my heart was, the place where my sick child slept. He withdrew his hand and rubbed his fingers together, as if the material of my clothing, or my soul, were still between them, as if to test what I was made of.

He gestured toward the empty cup he saw in my hand. I looked at it before holding it out to him. He bent and dug the cup into the soil he had thrown into the hole, and offered it to me like a drink. "Your child is dying," he said. "There will be no more Luarcas." I looked down at Mateo, his face white, asleep in the shawl. That morning I had licked the crust from his eyes. I had sucked the snot from his nostrils so he could breathe. In the early light, Mateo's face looked ancient, bones emerging as if in the past weeks he had hurried forward through the years to arrive early at his death: a tiny old man.

"Have you made all the usual promises?" my grandfather asked me. "What you will do, and how fervently you will believe, if only he lives?"

I paused, I looked at him. He wore a gray apron with a pocket, the same one he had worn in the silk house. The pocket held the tiny pair of calipers he had used to measure the cocoons, to see, when the worms were finished, if they had spun the largest grade of cocoon. "Francisca?" he said.

I nodded. "Yes, I have promised," I whispered.

He knocked the cup from my hand.

"You are right," he said. "You have traveled all night to be tricked." I opened my mouth, said nothing. The dirt fell onto our shoes.

There was no holy place left, no road unwalked, and I returned home. It was the week after Eastertide, the risen Lord's promises bursting into flower on every branch. Dolores and Papa did not seem surprised to see me, nor did they question me about my absence. It was as if my travels were in truth the strange dream they had seemed.

At night I lay with Mateo on top of me, his head tucked under my chin. I could smell the mulberry blossoms, the sweet scent of them sliding down the hillside, through door and windows, through the cracks and under the eaves, down the chimney.

I tried to take his sickness into my body, as healers say they can do. I concentrated and I called to him, not aloud, just my flesh desiring it. My flesh addressing the fever itself, *Come in. Come in. Pass from him to me.* Sometimes I felt it working. Mateo would relax, his breathing would ease, and I would feel a sick shiver in my bowels. But I could not do it completely, I did not have the concentration. His head moved back and forth fitfully on my chest until my bodice came undone. His fretting left smears of mucus, which dried and drew my skin tight like a scab.

At the end the fever grew high and confused him. One night, in the light of the candle as I was trying to wrap him more comfortably, he looked at me and his eyes showed that he did not know me. They opened wide in fear. Every noise, an ember falling to the hearth, made his legs twitch with terror, and I would weep, it seemed to me so unfair. What nightmares could he have already?

Mateo could not talk—not more than a few words—and yet his babblings had the quality of a language that I could not understand, one only he knew. The wasted hours of my tutelage! All that I had learned and none of it of any use to me. My child's was the only speech I must understand, and I could not.

I considered, for a moment, that I should smother him, that it would be the most merciful thing. I kept trying to pray, saying to myself over and over, *Francisca, Francisca, just breathe, you must breathe, you must hold him.* In the dark I would have a vision of my heart, red and gushing and terrible inside me.

I had seen the hearts of beasts, pigs or sheep slaughtered. As a child I used to watch my papa skin and gut the squirrels he trapped. He made a tidy pile of the skins, another of meat and one of entrails. His hand cut the smooth muscle that separates the lungs from the belly, and he reached a finger up into the cage of the ribs, feeling for the little heart. Often the tiny heart would still be beating, the foolish little engine of life ignorant of its plight.

My bodice undone, I felt the hot, dry skin of his cheek against me, and I no longer called to the sickness but to my child himself, saying to him, *Come back. Come back into me, Mateo. Come back in and I will make you over again. I will give you another, better house of flesh.* His breathing was so faint it was almost silent, motionless. I got up, I lit a candle and gently separated Mateo's flesh from mine. I held him just far enough from me that I might look at him, and as I did, it happened, life left him.

What I had dreaded passed without moment, it was nothing, almost. The departure of Mateo looked like nothing, sounded like nothing, smelled and tasted like nothing. There was only one difference: he was suddenly heavier in my arms. I blew out the candle, and I got back into bed with him, and I slept. Slept holding tight to him for I do not know how long.

Dolores said that Papa took Mateo out of my arms, and that I was with them when we buried Alvaro's son in the mulberry grove, not far from my mother's dead children, my little dead brothers all in a row by the silk house. There was no one else there, no priest. A little way beyond our small party I saw two laborers dragging a plow through the grass. They were making their way to the hops field, and I watched their slow progress and saw how the big blade opened up the earth and separated the grass like a part drawn by a comb through a woman's hair. Like the two smooth wings of my mama's hair swooping away from the white parting. I felt that if only my mother were with me, I could bear losing my son.

Perhaps I was a child myself, for I still so loved my mother that the world around me was a series of reflections of that person I loved best—as if my grief over Alvaro and over Mateo were echoes of my first unhappiness, that of losing her. As if she stood between mirrors, as if all of reality offered endless likenesses of Concepción de Luarca. The earth opened under the blade, and I watched until the workers disappeared from view. My father's spade hit stones as he dug, they made a rasping ringing sound against its blade.

Birds filled the mulberry grove. Owls and every other bird. The useless grove of trees, left to grow as it would, never stripped of its leaves, never pruned, was beautiful. Animals ate the fruit off the trees, and their leaves made a yellow fire on the hills in autumn. The grove was now a place where lovers met, where laborers from the nearby flax fields brought their noonday meal, a place where I myself wandered, and one where now I dream I wander.

Mateo was buried on the highest ground of the mulberry grove, under the branches of the tree that was planted first. I would go and sit there and know that my child was in the ground under me, and out of the earth came an ache that got into my bones on even the hottest day. The body of my son would dissolve, it would go back into the earth and into the first tree of all those trees I loved. That tree would have my bone, my flesh in it. I lay under its leaves, my cheek to the earth.

It had been weeks since last I had suckled Mateo, and my breasts had shrunken to nothing. But after we buried him the milk came back like a curse, burning me. I felt it under my skin, hot, like retribution, it pained me from my neck all the way to my groin. I beat my body saying *Why! Why!* Why should it come back now, and too late?

For a week my milk flowed like tears. My bodice, and even my skirts as far as my knees, stiffened and smelled of dried milk. But I would not change my clothes, I would not suffer them to be washed. I chose to wear my misery.

On the second day after my mother died and before I had begun to cry, I listed for my papa every wrong she had ever done me. I reminded him of how bad-tempered she had always been at the worms' fourth molt. How she had cut off my hair when I complained of her combing it. I said that she had required too many chores from us each day and that she had put the babies before me and my sister. I said that she had gone off happily to live in a palace and get sick there. A whole litany I had, and one that I rehearsed to myself, silently counting up the slights and wrongs as I sat by her empty bed.

My papa looked at me, and he said, "But, Francisca, child, these amount to no more than an instant measured against years of affection." I looked into my papa's kind eyes then, and I saw how it was with me, that I had soothed myself with the memory of little hurts, saying to myself, Well, she is gone, so much the better. Grief lay in remembering how happy I had been in her arms, how loved I had felt then. Grief is the memory of happiness.

All I saw for months after Mateo died was decay. It rained often the rest of that spring, and even where the roads were paved with cobbles, worms writhed in the puddles and I would walk over them and taste death as I watched them pink and blind and squirming. I hated my flesh and begrudged its health. I wished that it would sympathize with my soul, which was so sick and weary.

I slept and slept. I fell asleep at table, on the hearth, outside. I could sleep in any posture and under any circumstance. When it appeared to others that I was awake, when my eyes were open, even then I was asleep.

Then, one night, I awoke. My papa's small house was awash with the sounds of sleep: his snoring and Dolores's sighing breaths, as if even in dreams she regretted her life with us. I woke and dressed quickly and slipped out the door. The moon was not full, but the night was sufficiently clear that I had enough light to find my way, a way I knew so well: the road to Alvaro's old lodgings. My feet could have gone to that place without eyes to guide them.

When I arrived I stood for a moment beneath his window, in the very place where I had stood so many nights, waiting to hear the sounds of his studying there alone. The night was filled with noises I had never heard when I was so intent on him: the great birds of night, the rustlings of weasels and badgers, of porcupines, all those creatures, who, like myself, pursued their desires while the rest of creation slumbered. The shutter was broken, and I easily climbed and wriggled through the window.

After Alvaro was taken away, his books and papers, his every quill and inkwell and blotter were gathered into sacks and crates and borne away in a black carriage to Madrid, where the officers of God began their lengthy deliberations. As for the people of Quintanapalla, they knew it would be many months, even years, before the satisfaction of a sentence. And as there would never be any burning they would witness, they had undertaken their own haphazard exorcism. They had desecrated the little rooms where Alvaro once read and made his notes. Boys had thrown rocks in the windows and had torn down whatever they could reach. After they were done, little animals came to make their homes inside.

I stood in the room where once we had studied, and where we had taken our pleasure together, its walls barely delineated by the night's faint light. I ran my hands over the table where we had sat, I lay on the floor where we had lain, I reached out into the shadows, but so thoroughly was he banished that not even a ghost remained.

Alvaro was nowhere. I tried, alone and curled on my side in his study, to remember those three days we had spent in the silk house, the storm of ice, my face between his warm flesh and the fur of his cape. But I could no more conjure his arms around me than I could my mother's or my son's. Why am I not crying? I wondered.

Awake, having slept enough, I was entering a new and more dangerous chapter of my life, the one that brought me to my final home.

HESE," SAID A PROFESSOR AT LEYDEN, DIS-
cussing the work of the great Fallopio and
holding forth on his white palm what looked
like two little burst and tattered blossoms,
"these are the source of your life, every one of
you."

Severo had leaned forward in his seat around the stage of Leyden's famous anatomical theater. He could hardly see what his
teacher held out, but in his lap was an expensive medical text,
whose lavish illustrations included a series of drawings of female parts. The ovaries grew inside a woman, two little flowers
borne on stems named for the great physician. Severo made a
note in his text. *Source of life,* he wrote, and he drew an arrow
to the spot.

The queen's body is not yet cool when the medical inquest
begins. The king, queen mother, confessor, dwarf and minister,
all take their leave of María; they kiss her one last time. Then,
following Dr. Severo, chirurgeons file in from the crowded corridor where, for the last hours of the queen's life, they have been
waiting with their saws and their basins, their glass-stoppered
demijohns, their linens and bright knives.

The queen's maids undress her corpse, and the doctors cut her
open. From her breastbone down to the hair covering her
shameful parts, they make one long, deep incision. They retrieve
her heart and her liver. Onto a spool they wind the long loops of
her bowels. Her spongy lungs, sighs still bubbling through the
blood of severed windpipes, are dropped into a dish. Her gall-
bladder, swollen green and distended with bile—that little purse
where María safeguarded her hatreds and her disappointments—is stolen, drawstrings intact, and taken away in a bottle.
Her kidneys, wizened and hanging on their stalks, are picked
and laid in a bowl.

All her viscera are borne down the stone stairs to Dr. Severo's laboratory, and there this physician, trained by the century's greatest minds, cuts into each part of the queen. He lays open the secret chambers of her heart; he examines under his microscope sections of her intestines. In the six basins of María's cooling and coagulating innards, Severo looks for little flowers the same as those that his teacher had long ago harvested from the cadaver on the stage. He searches for some time without finding the queen's ovaries, but the doctor is not deterred by their minuteness, and the little flowers give themselves up at last, clinging to her bladder.

"She did have them," he reports to Marianna.

"Well, perhaps they were diseased," says the queen mother.

The doctor nods. "Yes," he says.

María is far from her body in Severo's laboratory. Once she was up—once she gathered herself, sprang from the bed, shattered the window—it took but an instant for her to find her way home. The passage many years before from her mother's side to Carlos's may have taken long enough that the princess thought it would never end, but this backward journey is so fast that María does not so much arrive back at the château as find herself suddenly there among all that she so loved and missed. She sobs with relief, and the halls are filled with the sound. A maid bearing a coal scuttle starts and looks outside the window for an explanation. Perhaps a sudden wind is blowing.

María—no, call her Marie again, call her Marie now that she is home at last—Marie is in the east wing, where her mother's apartments are. The floors shine under the light cast from the wall sconces, and the shadows of chairs and of pedestals, of vases and of flowers, leap and dance under the soft light of candles.

Her mother cannot be far. Henrietta's scent, the smell Marie has never forgotten, is strong and definite. She must have been writing letters tonight, for along with the woman, along with *her*, Marie smells sealing wax, the little square red tablet Henrietta keeps locked in her writing desk.

Long ago her mother would sometimes allow her to play with the wax, and Marie dripped a red pool onto the blotter and pressed in the seal. Or she used her finger, leaving its print on the surface of the soft, cooling wax, and then held it under the lamp to examine the tiny whorl, a downward draining spiral. Maman would sit next to Marie. Her voluminous skirts rose around them as she perched on the edge of her chair, a sudden rush of perfume gusting out through the seams. She took the wax from Marie's hand. "*Regarde*," she said. "Now, watch," and she withdrew a sheet of writing paper and an envelope from the small drawer that held them. She wrote on the page, *Chère Marie, Maman t'aime,* and below she made a little drawing of a woman holding a flower stiffly out from her side. She folded the page and put it in the envelope, whose flap she held down as she melted the wax over the lamp's wick.

Marie's mother dripped sealing wax until a little pool of it held the envelope closed. She pulled out one hair from her temple, one brown hair just where it peeped out from under her powdered white wig. She put the hair into the hot wax and pressed her seal into it, drowning the hair. Marie looked at the two ends of her mother's hair protruding from the wax. Henrietta waved the envelope for a moment to set the seal, and then she handed it to Marie.

"That is what you shall do one day when you find a gentleman to love," Henrietta said. "You shall send him a note and put your hair into its seal."

Marie had never done that, locked up a love letter with a hair from her head. She had saved the sentimental gesture for the man she would marry, but, as it turned out, she never felt so inclined. She kept the *billet doux* from her mother, though. She did not open it, nor did she disrupt the hair. It was in Spain, in her apartments, hidden among her belongings.

Searching among his dead wife's things, opening chests, picking locks with a wire when he can find no key, Carlos has come across the old letter from her mother. He weighs it in his hand a moment, then breaks the long sealed seal and reads the note. *Dear Marie, Maman loves you.* He understands that much French, anyway. He places the letter on a pile of things to be burned, and then goes on sorting, his secretary making notes and binding up packets for this person and that. But, after a moment, Carlos retrieves the page and its envelope with the cracked red wax, the broken hair. "Send that back to France," he says. "Put it in the box with her braid and her prayer book and her hair combs."

After retiring for the night—after hot milk, a few minutes with Estrellita, a prayer with his confessor—Carlos finds himself thinking of the letter and of the love sealed under the wax. He cannot sleep, he calls for a candle. With his valet he makes his way back to his dead bride's apartments, where he retrieves the small box meant for Henrietta. He takes it back to his own chamber and tucks it under his bed where other relics lie. A small box of mementos of a departed princess, of vanished happiness: he will keep these with his other holy things.

The scent of wax draws Marie along the second-floor gallery and into a small sitting room, where Henrietta is seated at her hearth. As she reads, a screen protects her face from the fire's heat, her wig is off, and her hair is not yet brushed but still stuck against her scalp like so many little gray leaves.

Oh! Marie thinks. *She is so old! Why, her hair is thin, and her hand is not steady as she holds her book! How can it be that my Maman has grown old?* And even as she thinks this, Marie is in her mother's lap, she puts herself between the red leather-bound pages and the woman.

Henrietta shifts in her chair, she lays down her book, a novel by Scarron, his last, published posthumously. She slips her paper knife into its chamois case for safekeeping. If it were to fall on the floor, a child or one of her cats might tread on it and hurt themselves. The two fat felines look up at Marie and, hissing, slink under the chaise.

"Why, what is it, Minou?" Marie's mother calls, "Félicité!" Silly creatures.

Indigestion, Henrietta thinks, such a strange heaviness on her chest. It must be from the pheasant, the rich sauce. She is too old to eat sauces, but she cannot resist them. Where are her charcoal pills? Oh, in the morning room, such a distance! But the heaviness is too intense to ignore, she will have to ring for the maid to fetch them. Nothing the matter with her heart, she hopes, but, Mother of God, she can hardly breathe.

Henrietta hates to be old. She thought she would have been tamed by the passage of years, content with comfort and with the memory of passion. Like all women, Henrietta had expected that as she grew to be old, inside her would beat a heart as gray and thin and flattened as her hair. She feels betrayed by a life that leaves a girl's heart clamoring inside a ruined body.

Perhaps she is not suffering from indigestion but grief. Marie's mother received word today of the death of a man she once loved, someone who lived on in her mind as a boy, in the same way that she herself was years younger in her daughter's memory. Why, the marquis de Brinvilliers *was* a boy, a boy with golden hair, strong legs and arms. The news had brought a quick wrench of grief, sudden and brutal, like wringing the neck of a kitten. It instantly killed the joy in her.

Henrietta rings a bell, and at the entrance of the servant, Marie startles and withdraws from her mother's lap.

"My pills," her mother says to the maid. "Please fetch them."

Marie lingers at the transom, she watches her mother reach again for her knife case and take her book in her hand. Henrietta cuts the next page, but she does not read it. Instead she leans back in her chair, she leaves her book in her lap and closes her eyes. She cannot keep from worrying about Marie. Certainly there had been news of ill health before the previous day's communication, but her daughter had always recovered. And this latest report sounded no more grave than earlier such tidings. The tone, as usual, was businesslike; the missive gave few details. *María Luisa, Regina, etc., was taken ill at the theater on the evening of the 17th day of the 12th month, at which time the court physician determined cholera morbus.*

The dispatch was read to the king, he betrayed no emotion, and other news was read as well. But then, at dinner, Louis quit the table before the last course was served. He stopped behind Henrietta's chair. "Madame?" he asked. "There was a spray of asphodel in your daughter's wedding bouquet, was there not?"

"Yes," Henrietta answered.

"And jonquils and lilies?"

"Yes," she said again. "Several varieties of lily."

He nodded. "I thought there were," he said, and then he left the room.

Marie Louise's wedding day in Paris, the proxy, the first of the weddings between the princess from France and the king of Spain: her father gave her away to a foreign minister bearing a cushion on which was a miniature portrait of the king of Spain. It was a sweltering August day, impossible to breathe inside the château and out. The wedding guests assembled under a great tent in the garden. Feet blistered in open-toed slippers, wigs grew as heavy as helmets. Lilies dropped their petals. They rubbed their naked, sticky stamens into the folds of passing skirts, brown pollen staining the material forever. Perspiration gathered over women's lips, and sour runnels of sweat disappeared into their bodices, bosoms rising and falling as they panted. Sweat rendered wig powder into a paste that trickled slowly down from ear to throat, dulling the stones of earrings.

By the end of the ceremony each lady-in-waiting was carrying all of her mistress's jewels and anything else that might decently be removed: wigs and ribbons and corsets and chokers, camisoles, farthingales, sashes and fans and fichus, everything collected into hampers and carried behind the lady, in case a breeze stirred and she felt sufficiently cool to be refurbished. But the air was so still that not one leaf moved, and each maid trailed uselessly after her stripped mistress, who looked as odd as a plucked peahen.

The next day, a great wind had blown over Paris. It chased the breathless heat away and blew so extravagantly that it tore the roof tiles off the château and sent them spinning over the parks and fountains, decapitating flowers and chipping the noses of marble nymphs. Henrietta stood with Marie and watched the windstorm from the gallery above the croquet lawns. She put her hand under her daughter's hair to touch the sweet, moist nape of her neck.

Somehow, though she knows it is foolish, Henrietta continued over the years to think of her daughter making her home not with a man but with a little picture in a jeweled frame. She saw Marie sitting at table with it, conversing with it and retiring of an evening with her head resting on a pillow next to a little painting whose frame glinted as the light was snuffed. Silly. But then, it was no more ridiculous, and a good deal more reassuring, than much of what was rumored about Carlos.

"Marie!" Henrietta calls suddenly, and she opens her eyes.

Marie Louise: her favorite child, her pet, her prize. With Marie, Henrietta had lying-in fever. She was very ill, her belly as great after the birth as before. Her fever climbed, and with it her mood. She was taken by that wild elation that some mothers get with milk fever. And the intoxication of it never wore off, it had made her love Marie all the more.

Henrietta stands and moves toward her letter case on her desk. She sits down. *Chère Marie,* she writes, *I think of you every minute. I am deeply worried, and in truth—*

Marie draws close behind her mother's chair and reads the letter as it is written, a letter she will never receive. Henrietta writes her daughter passionately, several times each month. Her letters are all tied in a ribbon; they are hidden in a chest in the queen mother's dressing room. When Marianna dies, someone will find them, perhaps.

We are all thinking of you and praying for your recovery, Henrietta writes. *Your uncle, the king, asked at dinner last evening what flowers were in your wedding bouquet. Our separation—can it be ten years? It is still difficult to walk in the garden, to enjoy the allées and the little bridge and footpath without missing you. It seems—*

Marie falls upon her mother's neck, and Henrietta drops her quill, caught up in an impossible embrace. When the daughter releases the mother, Henrietta slumps over her desk.

Tomorrow the doctor will call her swoon an indisposition provoked by overly larded meats, and Henrietta will be put on a restricted diet. She will argue with her doctor, a famous man from the famous medical school at Montpellier, saying that she does not know why a rich sauce should make her neck feel broken, her head pound and her throat constrict. "This kind of *crise*," she will sputter and weep, "it was not like any attack of indigestion I have ever suffered! It was not!"

But for now, Marie leaves her mother with a burning kiss on her temple, another on her forehead, nape and shoulder. One last kiss on her palm, upturned and empty, her quill on the floor.

F ONLY I HAD HAD SOME SENSE, SOME PLAN, some reason. If only I had made my way to Madrid—for what was there to keep me in Quintanapalla?—or to Paris. Yes, if only I had left Spain and disappeared into a northern city.

Sometimes, now, I imagine myself leaving everything behind me: my *sanbenito,* that shameful smock, empty and folded on the bench before our hearth. I leave the small chest containing my mother's things, Mateo's cup and spoon, and the little gold curl I cut from his head and laid in the ancestor box. I leave Papa and Dolores and travel north, find my way through the Cantabrian Mountains and then the Pyrenees.

In my mind I take the journey that I had once imagined for a strand of silk seeking a needle in Paris, a needle to lash it to a button made by Alvaro. Like his brother Tomás, I lose myself in Paris, where my wantonness might earn me a living.

As it was, I did not go. At the time when I might have escaped, I lacked the power to make any plan, large or small. My minutes, hours and days were all without purpose, my weeks and months as well.

I had no monthly flow, no blood to spare perhaps, and I never got with child again. But not because I was chaste. It was as if I wore a different sign upon my robe than the warning I knew to be stitched there. An invitation. Suddenly it seemed that every swain and his father knew I was there for the taking, that they need not even ask: I would join in carnal embrace with anyone.

They knew where to find me, in the old silk house that Papa had abandoned. No one bought my father's little toys anymore, his hair ornaments, his cups and rattles. He spent his days checking his squirrel traps and tending our meager garden, leaving the silk house to me. I built a fire on one of the four hearths, and I huddled near to its light and warmth.

I expected that the mute touch of flesh to flesh would be some sort of solace. But the men would not be silent. They talked and talked. They told me that the price of wool was falling, that their sons had consumption or their sisters were too ugly to find husbands. I put my hands on their lips or covered my own ears to keep out their sick sheep and sick mothers, their crops of beans and the price of lard, and how it was that they worried over lying with me and telling lies to their wives. For they told me their sins, too. They made me into the confessor Alvaro had been.

Above our heads, louder than they, I would hear my grandfather's voice. "In this world there are the givers and the takers," he said once. "Which are you?"

"I don't know, Grandfather," I answered.

They talked to me, I talked to him.

I did other things that frightened the men. Not purposely. Nothing sinister or magical. It takes so little to frighten people. Do you know what they were afraid of? The dark. I had only to snuff a light and they would scramble for their clothes, they would stammer and gasp and hiccough with fear.

The seasons revolved. It was spring. It was summer. It was fall again. Stones under my shoes, a vast scattering of yellow leaves that stirred with any slight wind. The ground beneath my feet looked alive, swarming. The sun was so bright I had trouble opening my eyes. Wind hissed through what leaves remained on the trees, hissed so that I heard whispering all around me.

Untended, the mulberry trees thrived, but still I struggled under the yoke and buckets, water spilling cold onto my skirts. I liked to care for them. It made them that much lovelier to me that they were unnecessary. Like jewels, like the silk they never became, they were wealth in and of themselves.

Grief was not what I expected. When I knew Mateo was gravely sick I contemplated my sorrow from a distance. I looked ahead to what I thought grief would hold, and I counted the leaves of anguish on each tree. But as it turned out, grief was not a dark, tangled wood but a flat, brown wasteland. As if worms had consumed every last twig of feeling. As if my father had passed a flame over the trees with his torch and reduced them to ash. All dead, all brown, all dry, no single leaf of pain or of pleasure.

Two mirrors with nothing in between, a blank cold winter of feeling.

I had not sufficient shame, perhaps. I did not hide myself under a magic cloak of composure, as women ought to do. My unhappiness should have been veiled.

In the marketplace, a peddler sold perfume and bracelets and little mirrors with pictures of Saint Lucy on their backs. Saint Lucy without her eyes. Saint Lucy who saw not this world but another. This peddler had been coming through town for many years, and one day my mama had bought me a looking glass with some of the money she earned from the orphans' asylum.

I kept that mirror in my skirt now. I looked at my face when no one could observe me, but not out of vanity. I was looking to see who was there. Who was this Francisca who had taken carnal pleasure with a priest, who had been given an angel and failed to protect him? In my mind's eye I had grown to be a monster, and each time that I looked at my reflection I was surprised to see the pale, dark-eyed face of a girl shining back from the little mirror. A *moza*, as we call them, a girl just past her innocence.

It became a bad habit with me, looking in the little glass. It got so that I went nowhere without it in my palm. Sometimes I bounced a pretty little circle of light before me on the ground, or I let it play along the walls of houses. "She is casting spells with that," I heard a boy whisper. "Do not let the shining circle touch you, it will burn you." I flashed it on his thigh and he screamed.

Mad Francisca. Francisca the witch.

I heard Mateo's cry everywhere, in the wind, in the yowling of hungry cats, in the babble of the marketplace. I would turn suddenly, having heard him. But there was no one, not even a cat or a crow, behind me. Walking through the marketplace, mirror in my palm, I did not lift up my head, I did not look before me, I did not meet any eye. I saw the ground under my feet, and I avoided accidents with the aid of my mirror.

I saw lips move in the palm of my hand, the black holes of nostrils. Good day, Francisca. How goes it with you this morning? When they laughed, their mouths stretched wet and open, teeth in my palm. I could feel that even the people who spoke to me were afraid and testing their fear.

I walked and walked. Sometimes I would see the looks exchanged by people as I passed. They stared after me and shook their heads. They said my mother's name to one another, I heard it almost like a sigh on the wind, following me, *Concepción, Concepción.* They wondered how the Luarcas had come to this. How sad Concepción would be to see her daughter now.

I revisited all the shrines, not traveling purposefully as I had then, but helplessly. I walked some days until I was faint, until I lost the feeling of the ground under my feet and came back to the grove, to the wind blowing spinning clouds of yellow leaves. Each so bright, circles of light falling, falling, spinning, sailing. Courageous, hopeful, burning bright with color. Spinning down, one last flight upon the wind, and then sunk in black November mud. I trod on them. With my toe I smeared the gold with mud.

I spoke to no one. All the words I had—the Latin and the Spanish ones—a vast sea of language now rose up to rebuke me. I had believed in their power; now I saw that they offered no salvation. Language mocked me, it made me that much more aware of my damnation, just a greater means of expressing my own wretchedness.

In Quintanapalla, thirteen houses were burned that autumn, not by churchmen, not by the civilized Church, but by suspicious neighbors. Some of the people who lived in those burning houses had no time to flee their masked persecutors. Manuel Xavier, the hop farmer, was caught at the gate. The next morning I saw his hat and boots there. In the mud, signs of a struggle gave way to a set of footprints and two long tracks that had unfurled from Manuel's unshod, unconscious feet. Well, frostbite would not trouble him. His body was found at the end of those tracks, at the mill, crushed between the stones. That must have forced all heretical thoughts from his head. Ilena Xavier's tongue was cut out for bearing false witness when she named the man who she thought had killed her husband.

From the time of Alvaro's arrest, I had been allowed to remain in Quintanapalla, free, as long as I always had upon me, even as I slept, my *sanbenito* proclaiming heresies and other wanton deeds. In this way, a person not familiar with my sins, a stranger to the town, perhaps, might know of the infection I represented and would keep apart from me.

Only an Inquisitor could afford a horse. A cold evening, light snow, the smell of wood smoke, a drip of pork fat sizzled on the hearth. A bird called out, a log fell into coals, trees creaked in the wind. Was that the noise of hooves over cobbles, muffled by rags? The wind picked up, a distant bough snapped. To me everything sounded like the approach of a horse.

White Hoods came through town on a regular basis, on their way to Burgos with its great cathedral, stronghold of the Church. One afternoon, as they passed through the plaza, one of them motioned to his deputy, and I was collected and thrown into the cart with two other condemned: Ilena Xavier, whose confiscated tongue only whetted the Holy Office's appetite for the rest of her, I guess, and an old man known as Caballo, who had claimed certain visions of having been escorted by an angel to a bullring in the sky where he saw Jesus dressed as a matador.

Arrested on suspicion of witchcraft, I joined those hungry women who said they attended midnight banquets, those earth-bound women who so longed to rise above their cares that they claimed they could fly, those lonely women who said they lay down with a dark horned man. I joined other women unfortunate enough to lose their babies.

Once in the custody of the Inquisition, there was the possibility of release if fines were paid, but Papa had no money. There was little money in Quintanapalla, and the fine for a witch was expensive, ten ducados, an amount impossible to imagine paying, even were we all to labor from dawn to dusk for a year. We paid one ducado, the last that was left from my grandfather's savings, the last of the silkworms' earnings, and I was remanded to my father's care until eight Sabbaths should have passed. Then the other nine were due.

Papa set about in earnest to earn the money, stealing more and more minutes from each night's sleep so he could make more traps, trap more squirrels, skin more squirrels and sell more skins each month to the trader who came to town: fifty little hides for one ducado. But before he worked himself into his grave, Cristina García came forward, the daughter of one of the local merchants, and she settled the issue. She finished what my sister had begun long before.

If ever there was a God in heaven, He knew that Cristina was a girl whose blood ran too hot and fevered her thinking. She was one of the few who colored her lips and her cheeks, she always found some bit of money for a ribbon or a charm to wear about her neck. She went about with her head uncovered. Secretly I liked to watch her, for she was bright and lively, and as soon as she was out of the grandmothers' sight she was tugging at her clothes, rearranging her bodice to show more of her skin. That year she had bought little bells from the peddler who sold such trinkets, the same who sold the mirrors, and she tied these little bells to her shoes so that you could hear her run from the boys that she teased.

Blood must have its due. Cristina fell in love with a boy named Alonso, a boy who had no time for her. His brothers were dead and he worked hard to care for his father and mother, who were old. He did not even hear the merry noise of Cristina's boots, which she polished with grease until they shone, the little silver bells ringing against them. She decided that he was bewitched.

Francisca, she thought to herself, *Francisca has bounced her witch glass on his head. She has shined it in his eyes and beamed it over his heart.* She went to the wheelwright. Francisca has an enchanted glass, she told him, and she holds it out to steal the soul of whomever it touches. With it she peeled the soul right off Alonso Manteña, she sucked the marrow from his bones.

Fate conspired with Cristina García. Not a week after the time of her accusation Alonso grew gravely sick, and then I was as good as sentenced. It did not matter that he had fallen ill with

the same sickness that plagued his father's servant. No one
stopped to say, Look, this boy has been sleeping in the same
place with his father's cow and pigs and the plowboy who has
been coughing and spitting blood all winter.

I was at our own hearth when Dolores came in. "Alonso is
very ill," she said. "They do not expect that he will live." Nothing in her face, in her manner or her voice, betrayed how my
sister felt delivering such news.

I put down the trap I had been helping my father to make.
With the imminent death of Alonso, there was no reason to
work so hard. We could give up, at last. I went to Papa and I
untangled the length of gut from his fingers, stopped them from
tying and setting yet another little trap.

"How relieved the squirrels will be," I said. And I kissed my
father's forehead.

As it happened, Alonso tarried, he took his time dying, and
Papa's life was over first. My father announced his death a week
before its arrival. Not long after we heard of Alonso's sickness,
Papa had a fall outside our door. He grew dizzy, stumbled, and
when we took him into the house, we found that of his two
hands, only one had strength. Of two legs, only one could walk.
His spirit left one side of his body first, and when he drank
water, it escaped from the slack half of his mouth.

He told us he would die. He knew it, he said, for he had been
dreaming each night of his own father and mother, of Ernesto,
who had fallen with his ass and his plague coins into the ravine.
"There *is* a coach made all of pearl," he told Dolores and me
excitedly. "Just as Concepción said there was."

He saw Mama in his dreams, of course. It became so that he
spent each night in her arms. With his one leg, he danced with
her under the sheet, and he was happy. At last he was no longer
alone. Mama was visiting him, and soon he would be crossing
over to her, he would see once more his reflection in the shiny
tips of her black shoes. He told us that now Mama was always
dressed in her finest clothes. "As she was for her wedding day,"
he said.

Dolores sat by Papa's bed with her hand on his head. She
leaned forward and looked closely at his face as he rested. When

he slept, she placed her thumb on his eyelid and pushed it up. The dreaming eye moved crazily over the room, it passed over her face without recognition. Over walls and ceiling, past the fire, past the window and around again, lighting on nothing. She let the lid fall closed and settled back in her chair. *"Papa!"* she would yell, and she would shake his shoulder. She could not stand it, to be so dutiful and to have him escape into the next world and leave only his ungrateful body behind.

My sister never wanted to do any kindness that wasn't noted and tallied. She misered up lists of good deeds, never missed a holy day, never skipped a bead on her rosary. She trusted that all the arithmetic would come out right and she would earn her place in heaven.

I was with my father the night he died. Dolores had set a lighted candle by his bed. We were waiting for the last breath, the vapor on the looking glass, when suddenly he reached his arms out.

"Francisca!" Papa cried. His eyes opened and he saw me.

"Daughter!" he said, and by my dress he pulled me close to him. The slack side of his mouth was white with spittle and his voice was hoarse in its insistence. "Do not neglect the worms!" he said, and then he stopped talking, stopped breathing.

We let him lie dead in his bed for the rest of that night. We left a lamp burning, wasted oil until dawn, waiting until the next day to wash his body. When the sun rose, Dolores brought a basin of water, she brought two clean linens. "Here," she said to me. "You do it."

What happened, finally, with my sister was this: she never did have a child. She married on Ascension Day, as I said she would when we were young. But she did not marry Luis Robredo, and she did not move to a warm southern place. She stayed near to Quintanapalla, she went no farther than the neighboring town of Rubena. Her husband is a flax farmer. I know this much. I was not there when she married, but I know it nonetheless.

In the spring, at Eastertide, when we used to hatch out our worms, Dolores helps her husband in the planting of flax seeds. They sow them very thickly, so thickly that the plants, each trying to reach past its neighbors to the sun, grow straight and tall. In the summer, they pull the plants up by the roots. They remove the seeds and put them aside for the following spring, and they set the stalks to soak in the pond. It is Dolores who beats the soaked and dried stalks, who separates out the chaff from the stems, and who hackles the flax—using a comb fashioned from twelve iron teeth set in a jaw of wood.

She gets together all the long, sticky fibers, and Dolores and her neighbors spin and gossip together until the women have wound up all the work of the fields onto bobbins. It takes many weeks. Worms are quick at their work, but spinning flax is a slow occupation, and in Rubena they have no time for Saint John's bonfires, no time for harvest feasts. No matters other than spinning flax can claim their attention, for in the late fall the weaver arrives.

A taciturn man, he sets up his loom in Dolores's barn. The cow and the goat must survive out of doors until he is through with her thread. The weaver says nothing to Dolores, he is well suited to his solitary occupation. When she sets his evening meal before him, he does not look up. It is as though he still sees cloth under his nose, and he passes his spoon from hand to hand as he does the loom's shuttle. In a week he is finished weaving, taking the best cloth and leaving behind what Dolores will bleach and piece together into bed and table linens for her husband to sell at market.

They are not poor. My sister is one of the few in Rubena who have an oven in the house, and it is to her hearth that others come to bake and to gossip. Apart from her childlessness, she considers herself happy. Dolores has spent these first years of her marriage in consultation with healers, who try to defeat whatever evil eye has dried up her womb, a curse blamed on me, the pollution of my sins. She sits herself on baskets upturned over boiling pots of wild rue and fenugreek. She swallows bitter medicines.

She gives herself airs, trying to get with child. She tells her husband that her constitution is more delicate than most, that washing his clothes in the winter and chilling herself with cold water might steal heat from her body and keep her from conceiving. She says she cannot wade into the pond to collect the bundles of flax soaking there, and that too much beating and hackling might further shrivel her womb. He loves her enough that he has bought her a servant; he takes her to every shrine to the Virgin within a hundred leagues. He is a thin man with a mustache, which he pulls when he is worried. He has pulled almost all of it out because of Dolores.

My sister's dreams are of proving herself a woman, that is what she wants. Even if the cures render only one miscarried child, then Dolores will be satisfied. For a miscarriage is a grief she can share with her gossiping friends; they will mourn and keen with her, they will help her forget. But barrenness is a burden that a woman bears alone.

When she is not spinning Dolores spends evenings making soap, as our mother and grandmother used to do. Making soap. Mending. Scouring. The Devil loves idle hands, so my sister keeps herself busy. Her fingers are raw and red. In the evenings, as she stirs the soap kettle, she must think of Mama, for the dead are always with us, we cannot escape them.

Just last night Alvaro came to me, and I wept in my sleep, wept and laughed at once. I cried out and stood from the floor where I lay. In my sleep I shook the bars of my cell.

Yes, it is true, Alvaro. You came to me. You fucked me all night in my dreams. Your tongue was so hot and you held me so tightly, your embrace broke my spine, your lips burned my forehead. Your tongue fucked my ears and my eyes, your mouth on my neck was so wet and so wide that I felt the whole of myself slip into your throat. You bit me all over, my nipples were bleeding.

I heard you cry out as you parted my legs. Were you surprised that my desire was so evident, that I made myself no more than a cup for you to spill? But you drank me up, I was gone and then restored to you, and so you tore me open, you fucked my heart.

You came to me and I was glad, for I am not so proud that I would rebuff you merely on the grounds that you are impossible. I am impossible, too. Impossible that you are dead, impossible that I still live.

 HAT WAS LEFT OF THE QUEEN EVAPORATED like a sweet fragrance from the palms of those hands she longed for. One moment her mother felt her—a weight on her neck, a pain in her chest—and the next, nothing.

In Madrid the poison worked its final magic. Death has returned the queen, as it does all of us, to her true, first self. Once again her waist is the narrow span of Marie Louise de Bourbon, the prettiest princess on the Continent. Once again, the one hundred buttons of her wedding gown fasten easily, each tiny, silk-covered sphere slipping through the embrace of a waiting buttonhole. The people at last can see Her Highness in her nuptial finery, in the French gown she wore when married in secret. Spain could not afford such a gown—not then, not now—no more than she could have procured the mountains of flowers upon which the dead queen lies.

In all of our country there are not such flowers as the Sun King has sent. A convoy of flowers was dispatched with military speed, the same expeditiousness that propels French armies into battle before enemies even know they are besieged. King Louis sent them as soon as he heard María was ill. After all, flowers would be good for either outcome, convalescence or death. But this many flowers in winter! Even from a monarch whose every gesture is grand, they are a ridiculous extravagance. Did the king at last regret his harshness in marrying his niece to Carlos? His relentless insistence on politics before romance, when anyone else but himself was involved?

Perhaps when her uncle learned of her sudden illness, he recalled the letters María had sent over the years, recalled her begging him to do something, anything to save her. Because Louis had received those letters. Spies, enemies, mothers-in-law might dare to empty a queen's envelopes, but no one tampers with the Sun King's correspondence.

Perhaps on the morning after the envoys brought news of María's illness, the Sun King rose from his mistress's embrace and remarked to himself that she was the four hundred and sixty-seventh woman to whom he had made love, and that under his wig dyed so black, his own hair had thinned and turned a color that only four hundred and sixty-seven vain, demanding mistresses might have made it. Perhaps his surgeries of late, those notorious attempts to stitch up a royal asshole which also had suffered grand gestures—and which have made it fashionable this year in Paris to claim piles, fissures and fistulas among one's trials—perhaps all of these reminded the most splendid monarch that as life is short, so is suffering long.

For whatever reason, Louis did remember his prettiest niece, and he summoned the gardener—the same who gladly provided nosegays for hangings—to his chamber. Monsieur Clément arrived and stepped delicately over the current favorite's camisole, which the previous evening, after an embrace disruptive to undergarments, had slipped to the floor from the chaise longue.

"Your Highness?" Clément asked.

"You remember Marie?" said the king.

"I do, of course," said Clément.

"And those flowers that particularly pleased her?"

"Yes."

"What were they?" asked Louis.

"Lavender. Lilac. Stock. Narcissus. Peony—"

"Yes, you need not list them all." Louis looked out the frost-blurred windows to his hothouses, which perspired pinkly on the snow-covered lawns. "Gather together a good lot of them," he said to Clément. "And a few of the orange trees, as well."

"As you wish," said Clément. He stepped backward as if to leave the room, entirely avoiding the corset strings.

"And ready yourself for travel," said the king, and then dismissed him.

Tuberoses. Jasmine. Jonquils and violets. Asphodel. Tulips. Narcissus. Lavender, lilac and stock. Twelve miniature orange trees in constant bloom, bearing never fruit but only white blossoms. Flowers of all different climates, yet blooming simultaneously in the delicious seasonless limbo of the royal hothouses.

In the glass-paned buildings, Clément's staff gathered the flowers together, still potted, and they packed them into nine huge glass caskets. Thus protected from winter snows and bitter winds, they were carried by livery boys to the great cobbled courtyard enclosed behind Versailles's east gate, and there they were loaded into three black coaches, whose side panels bore golden suns and whose seats had been torn out so that three long boxes might fit in a stack inside each, a deerskin spread between one's glass lid and the glass bottom of another.

As they were loaded, a page holding the end of the ninth casket lost his footing and slipped from the running board to the cobbles. Everyone in attendance, the whole staff and every occupant of Versailles—an audience of nearly four hundred—held his or her breath as the glass box filled with living flowers slid to the ground. Marie's mother, leaning heavily on the arm of her maid, closed her eyes.

The angry cry of Monsieur Clément obscured the sound of glass hitting stones. It must have. Or maybe there was no noise, for the casket did not shatter, or even chip. Perhaps this was the first evidence of the miraculous luck, the seemingly holy protection, that the romantic undertaking was to enjoy. For the journey of the flowers, through winter snows whose bitterness stilled commerce and stopped battles, proceeded as if enchanted.

Nothing could stop the three enormous black coaches. Though roads were either dangerous or impassable, though the stars were invisible and the moon on the wane, though all the rest of the world was stopped and sleeping, the flowers made their way.

The roads were indeed so deep in frozen mud that the flowers went by river wherever possible. After the initial day's journey to Bonneval—the three teams of black horses whipped white into lather and lamed beyond recovery, Clément standing the whole way in the box of the first coach and yelling at the driver to go faster, "*Plus vite! Cochon!* You lout!" into his red ear—

the carriages were taken off their axles and set on barques on the Loire. Inside the first lowered coach, on a makeshift seat, an armless ballroom chair nailed to the floor, sat Clément, looking over his charges in their glass boxes and drinking brandy from a flask as he wrapped and rewrapped his knees in a fur-lined lap robe. Outside, unprotected by anything other than stable blankets and straw, and miserably sick from the pitching currents that knocked the boats about like sticks, the drivers, footmen and all the rest of the flowers' retinue shivered and huddled together for warmth.

When ice floes made passage impossible rather than merely foolhardy, the barques docked, the carriages were set back upon their wheels, and teams of horses were procured instantly with bags of louis d'or. When the stable masters saw the gold glint under the lantern's flame, grooms were roused and doors opened despite the late hour, and the little image of the king on each coin seemed actually to wink in conspiracy. Stable boys wondered the next day what could have happened when horses found their way home with legs bloodied and shaking, tails wet, tongues swollen, their hooves scorched and their bits turned to gold.

The flowers sped over frozen, rutted roads to the nearest spot where water flowed freely and where again the coaches were plucked off their axles and set on fresh barques. White foam leaped from the rivers' currents into the black sky and blended with the snow falling onto the carriage roofs. Icicles froze ever longer from their darkened side lamps; one carriage body had to be hacked off the deck of its barque.

But at least a river runs a decided course, for the skies were so overcast that sidereal navigation was impossible. During the days of that voyage, winds lashed the oceans into a vortex such that a hundred ships were lost, masts snapped, useless sextants sinking quickly under the waves. But a river runs a course that even a maelstrom cannot alter, and the barques shot on without guidance. From the Loire to the Vienne to the Vézère to the Dordogne, to the foaming Garonne, which flowed into the Baise, a river whose name spells kiss.

To storm the fortress of the Pyrenees, the carriages' wheels alone were stripped off, making handles of axles, and the flowers were thus transported through mountain passes in fantastically huge and unwieldy litters. The carriage bodies were so heavy that it required sixteen men to lift and carry each. Then on to the Spanish rivers Gallego and Jalón, and into the Duero looping around Soria, whose silk mills were silenced in the terrible freeze. And finally to the Henares, frozen solid into a road of ice so that carriages had to be set on runners and pulled by horses galloping on the banks: carriages became sledges.

Two days before Christmas, in the year of our Lord 1689, the gates of the city of Madrid swung wide to admit the gardener of the Sun King riding on the first of three black coaches, their panels emblazoned with golden-rayed suns. As custom demands that all vehicles pull to the side of the road to allow the passage of any royal conveyance, a path opened for the carriages of flowers from Paris.

Crowds greeted the procession. Despite the cold, people thronged the streets, and no guards could keep them back. They scrambled for a hold on the carriages' sides, they tore off hardware as they tried to climb and peer inside and see the faces of the flowers, the dark-eyed violets and sweet-throated tuberoses nodding in their glass caskets. The horses reared in panic and Clément was forced to climb to the safety of the driver's box.

In the days since the queen's death those unruly subjects who had ceaselessly called María's name, who had broken down royal gates and trampled royal spirits, had remained silent. They had not returned to their homes, though, and it seemed that every citizen of Madrid had forsaken his hearth to camp on the royal grounds, the palace besieged by its own subjects.

And what were they waiting for? Marianna wanted to know. It was to be hoped that the catharsis and pomp of a really grand funeral would satisfy them, would lay dissension to rest along with the dead queen.

Through the throngs, the flowers proceeded slowly to the royal residence, so slowly that it seemed to Clément that the last miles took longer than all the rest of the journey. The carriages creaked past the smoldering bonfires to the heavily guarded palace. Inside the great audience chamber, María lay in state, her arms empty, awaiting her bouquet.

Spain may not trouble to grow flowers in the dead of winter, but her funerary arts are without peer. After they removed the last of the queen's blood, Severo and a team of physicians filled her empty veins with a sweet philter—a recipe of civet and myrrh and other secret ingredients, all steeped in spirits of alcohol, which they poured into her neck. Now perfume rises from her every pore, a fragrance sweet and holy, her hollowed body transformed to some fantastic mortal incense vessel. The smell of her is such that even eyes that would refuse to weep do so. The sour courtiers who paced with impatience outside the queen's chamber, so eager for her death were they, now weep helplessly over María's body, they beat their breasts, they tear their hair. All those grandees and duques who manage to secure permission to view the dead queen press forward with their families, and they, too, lament loudly.

Clément and his staff arrange the flowers themselves, unpack and heap them all around, orange trees and peonies and a thousand tulips in bloom. They lay a huge bouquet in her arms, one with sprays and cascades of every white blossom: roses and narcissus and asphodel, muguet and chrysanthemum, white lilies and even whiter gladioli.

María's body goes to its rest with hair unbound and washed with rose water, dressed with pearls. Pearls were made to adorn hair such as hers, its waves black like the waves of the dark and distant ocean that yielded them. The queen's face is lovely in death, for what died was grief and bitterness and boredom. What was stripped away was the flesh of unhappy consolations. Her eyes look as though they might at any moment open, her lips are parted slightly, and their beauty remains intact through the long days of services, through vespers and vigils and prayers of absolution, through lauds sung by one hundred eunuchs and through high Masses chanted by a holy army of priests.

The secret corridor of saints is opened for the final day of funeral Masses. Under heavy guard, its occupants leave the royal residence for the cathedral, where Sister Tomita hovers, the weepers weep, the twins pay homage and Estrellita's couch is carried through the nave and up to the chancel rail. When María and her flowers are at last ready for the procession from altar to tomb, she seems to smile a secret smile, as if at last she is satisfied. Indeed, something comes to pass that might have pleased her.

Is it some property of the flowers, perhaps, the intense perfume released as they are strewn before the catafalque and crushed under its wheels? Or is it the smell and sight of the queen, at last released to her public, her strangely blazing beauty, long anticipated, that works an enchantment? Does the look and smell of her make the mob, which had been calm, begin to rage once more? The long procession through the streets commences with shouts and howls and keening cries of what sounds like grief.

Can it be that they are *missing* her? thinks Marianna, as she walks beside Carlos. Why, just last week they were calling for her death, they were intoxicated by her torment.

Even Rébenac, who busies himself during the interminable services by mentally packing and repacking his trunks, thinking such thoughts as I must not forget that doublet I left with the seamstress, and calculating just how many weeks will pass before he is once again settled in his apartments in Paris; yes, even the bitter French minister takes note of the cries, and how bereft the people sound.

They have forgotten the rhyme and the taunts. They call her by her name only. *"María Luisa!"* they scream, and they do not stop, but call ever more loudly.

The nine virgins whose job it is to prepare the path for the catafalque, spreading the queen's flowers before her, cringe at the noise. Hands occupied, they cannot cover their ears. And the horse, the one horse allowed by custom in a state funeral, the one pulling the queen, shies.

It is a peculiar accident. Afterward, no one can recall exactly how it happened. The horse drawing the catafalque suddenly rears and plunges to the side. He is a black horse, over twenty-two hands high. His head is dressed with black plumes, his back is draped in black silk, and when he goes up on his hindquarters, only his rolling eyes and his teeth flash white. The rest is a thrashing darkness, a storm of black silk.

"But was not Marianna walking a good distance behind the body?" people ask the next day.

Crowds are thick, and few see clearly. The ash from braziers and burning cedar boughs, from bonfires and from torches, blows into bystanders' eyes. The smoke overpowers.

"It was my belief that she was standing beside Carlos," Rébenac will write to King Louis. To his wife's funeral Carlos wore breeches of tight black velvet and a short doublet with long full sleeves lined with purple. Though one might have judged him too frail to bear the weight of stiletto and sword and walking stick, yet he carried these implements of murder and locomotion as he walked beside the dead queen's body. His mourning collar was so high that he could not turn his head, and when the horse's hooves came down on his mother, he did not see them.

"Oddly," Eduardo will write to the comtesse de Soissons, safe at last in a castle in Antwerp, "the beast who killed Marianna was brother to the very one María used to ride, the one called Rocinante. The horse trod upon Marianna's train, it was a heavy one of black brocade, and the train did not tear but pulled the queen mother under the animal's hooves."

Olympe will pause in her reading of the dwarf's letter. Outside her window the sun will be sparkling on the river. "And here is the best of all possible postscripts," Eduardo's message will conclude. "The groom did not kill the animal, but this time disobeyed the king's orders. He escaped from Madrid on its back."

The comtesse will tear the letter into four pieces, she will burn it. Now what, my friend? she will think. What is to become of you now that your powerful protector is dead? Olympe will not honor Eduardo's letter with any reply.

The funeral procession was, of course, delayed by the accident, delayed for whole hours. There was talk of holding the queen's body in Madrid, and then taking the two of them, María and Marianna, together through the hills to the Escorial. But no one wanted to risk inciting the mob again, which, though it fell quiet after the queen mother's death, continued to call for

María's body, temporarily removed to the safety of the guard-house at the city's west gate.

In the end, Carlos retired to the palace with Estrellita and his mother's corpse, and María continued on her bier before her mourners. She was bound for her white marble tomb in the hills, a tomb for a childless bride, a child bride.

Ever a child and ever a bride, María Luisa is blanketed in the white reserved for barren queens, the blinding white of innocence restored. Having died without issue, it is as if María has died a virgin, some little recompense for cruelty, this posthumous reinstatement to virtue. From being the most generally and vociferously reviled of women, she is made a saint. It happens this way:

People begin by praying for the dead queen's soul. They petition the saints that María not have to remain in limbo too long. She suffered enough on earth, they say, the very people who had marched from the theater to the palace, who had called her a whore and demanded she be whipped. They spend their money on Masses to shorten the queen's stay in purgatory.

For that is where she is now, in purgatory. With my mama and my papa, with Alvaro. But not Mateo. Children do not tarry in the netherworld. The old men, the messengers of souls, promise that there are no children under the age of seven in purgatory. Dying so young, they say, you go straight to your rest, you need not tarry in a place that is gray and cold and sorrowful.

I try to comfort myself thinking of this. I repeat this promise over and over to myself.

What do I believe? In nothing, and in everything. When Mateo died, whatever faith I had in life's goodness evaporated. Like the faint moisture of the last breath that clouds the mirror, when my child died that thin mist of my faith evaporated.

Still, I pray. We all do. We cannot help ourselves.

There is another city under Madrid, another country under Spain. And its citizens know all of what comes to pass in the streets above. They know the world which is revealed by a sun they never see.

The citizens of Spain, below and above, who began by praying for María, soon find themselves praying to her. It is because of the dead queen's name, perhaps. Because her mother called her Marie, because we call her María, popular memory, so short and undiscerning, soon confuses her with the Virgin.

People mumbling their Ave Marias unwittingly repeat their prayers with the extra name added. They exchange the immortal Queen of Heaven with the late queen of Spain. *Ave María Luisa,* they pray.

And someone, some visitor to Queranna, where my papa poured out a libation of good oil to ensure his worms' success, to Queranna, where Natalia was buried and where I carried my dying child, some pilgrim has painted a new face upon the effigy of the Virgin there. Like the faces of the Virgins in one and then another shrine all over Spain, its features are those of Queen María Luisa's.

Left at the Virgin's ivory feet are tuberoses, jasmine and those sweet little white flowers that grow nowhere but in the woods outside Versailles. Impossible, but there they are. María has her flowers, the pilgrims keep bringing them to her.

The Virgin at Queranna wears a dress of silk—as do all the Virgins from here to San Sebastián—she wears a white silk underskirt and a blue silk overdress that is faded now from the strong sun that slants into the chapel each morning. The silk has begun to rot and fray, it splits where the bodice joins the skirt. Stitches unravel, but its luster is not lost. Silk will shine until it falls into dust.

The robe on the Virgin at Queranna is old. It was made years ago, a lifetime ago, when my papa was a silk farmer. When Francisca de Luarca imagined that her father's worms made in one extraordinary season a hundred thousand dresses for the queen of Spain, or for the Queen of Heaven. If I had looked then at the Virgin's dress—if I had seen that dress as a child—I would have proclaimed it the work of Luarca worms.

Of worms who lived and spun and died so long ago. Spun silk, and dreams, as well.

The author wishes to thank Jack Hitt, Professor Karl Krober, Christine Pevitt, Diane Sabbarese and Thomas Spaccarelli, PhD, as well as the following institutions for guidance in the research for this novel: the Brooklyn Public Library, the Columbia University Libraries, The Hispanic Society of America, the Metropolitan Museum of Art, the National Health Museum, the Prado Museum and the Textile Museum Library, in Washington, D.C.

I am grateful to Janet Gibbs and to Joan Gould, for their support of me and of my writing in general. And I consider myself fortunate to have Elauriana Hunter care for our young children while I work.

I am both indebted and devoted to my agent, Amanda Urban, and to my editor, Kate Medina.

And, of course, I thank Colin, always the first champion of my work.

Much of what inspired *A Thousand Orange Trees* is borrowed from history, but I took enough license with whatever truths remain after three centuries that it seems to me if I were to cite individually the works I consulted, my doing so would implicate rather than honor the scholarship that yielded them.

For the record, Marie Louise de Bourbon was the niece of Louis XIV. Her father was the king's brother, the famously dissipated Monsieur, the duke of Orléans; and her mother was Henrietta of England. Henrietta died in Paris in 1670, poisoned, some say, by two of Monsieur's more dashing diversions, the Chevalier de Lorraine and the Marquis d'Effiat. As history is more sordid than the general audience of the novel would permit, and as tragedy becomes burlesque in heaping doses, I allowed Henrietta to live years longer than she did in actuality; I let her live beyond the death of her unfortunate daughter. This was the first intentional distortion of what I had painstakingly taught myself, and it was that first lie which encouraged many more untruths.

Like Francisca, I had a grandfather given to aphorisms. "Lies have no legs" was a favorite of his, which I understand to mean that one fib will not carry itself and always has to be pushed along by another, and so forth. "Oh what a tangled web . . ." he would go on, and I confess that at this point I cannot untangle fact from fancy, at least not in the seventeenth century of Spain.

Historians, however, concur that Marie Louise de Bourbon married Carlos II, the last of the Spanish Hapsburgs, in Quintanapalla in 1679. Bride and groom were both eighteen, and both were descended from Juana la Loca, the brilliant, mad daughter of Ferdinand of Aragon and Isabella of Castile. María Luisa, as she was called in Spain, remained childless from the time of her marriage to that of her death in 1689, at the age of twenty-eight.

The circumstances surrounding the death of the queen of Spain remain mysterious. The fullest account I have found appears in John Nada's *Carlos the Bewitched*, which is also the source of the unkind rhyme appearing on page 40. On Tuesday afternoon, February 8, María had a riding accident and chose to have dinner in bed that evening: "puff paste," Chinese oranges and cold milk. On Wednesday, February 9, she ate a dish of broth, as well as oysters with lemon, cold milk, French olives and Chinese oranges. At five o'clock on the morning of February 10, she awoke feeling suffocated and suffering a severe gastrointestinal upset. Her condition deteriorated rapidly throughout that day and the next, and she died on the morning of February 12. While it was never proved that the queen was poisoned, most historians assume that she was. Their theories usually implicate the notorious Olympe de Soissons (ever seeking revenge against Louis XIV for spurning her, Olympe is suspected of trying to undo the alliance of Spain and France) and suggest that the fatal drug was administered in a cup of hot chocolate. None point to the culpability of María's mother-in-law, Marianna of Austria. No one has ventured that cantharides might have killed María Luisa, as it did some of the victims of a dangerous gentleman who lived a century after her, in Paris. That poisoner was the marquis de Sade.

María Luisa de Borbón was succeeded by the Austrian princess Maria Ana of Neuburg, who also never bore a child by the king of Spain.

Carlos II died on All Souls' Day, 1700, without any blood heirs. His will, made one month before his death, gave all the Spanish dominions to Philip, the duke of Anjou, and grandson of Louis XIV. Of his possible successors, Carlos chose the duke of Anjou because he believed he would prove a strong ruler who would keep the empire intact, and because Philip had assured the dying king that he would make his home in Spain.

All Fourth Estate books are available at your local bookshop or newsagent, or can be ordered direct from the publisher.

Indicate the number of copies required and quote the author and title.

Send cheque/eurocheque/postal order (Sterling only), made payable to Book Service by Post, to:

Fourth Estate Books
Book Service By Post
PO Box 29, Douglas
I-O-M, IM99 1BQ.

Or phone: 01624 675137

Or fax: 01624 670923

Alternatively pay by Access, Visa or Mastercard

Card number:

Expiry date

Signature

Please allow 75 pence per book for post and packing in the UK. Overseas customers please allow £1.00 per book for post and packing.

Name

Address

Please allow 28 days for delivery. Please tick the box if you do not wish to receive any additional information.

Prices and availability subject to change without notice.